Babbithole

Nights of Alice #1

Melissa Rea

I dedicate this book to you, my precious friends, for your inspiration and support.

Chapter One

WANNA BE A ROCKSTAR

Alice Hightower's childhood ended one scorching summer morning on the parking lot of an Oklahoma truck stop. She held her breath and watched the heat rise in ripples off the blacktop. The car was gone. Mama, Daddy and her big brother Sean had disappeared down the turnpike and left her behind.

She didn't really blame them. She tried hard, but she was not a very good girl. Her corner of the bedroom did look like a tornado hit it. She never went to bed when it was time but hid where no one could find her.

Mama always said she took too long in the bathroom. This time she'd just been trying to make her white-blonde hair lay flat in the wavy gas station restroom mirror. Tears gathered on her pale lashes. She blinked in the bright sunshine, and the tears ran down her sun-pink cheeks. She stood in the middle of a black ocean of sticky asphalt holding her teddy bear in one hand and her story book in the other. The sound of the blood rushing in her ears couldn't drown out the cicadas screaming from every tree. She was alone.

Alice dropped the teddy bear and clutched her *Alice's Adventures in Wonderland* picture-book with both hands. At that moment, it was as if the little tumblers in her head that held the combination to childhood began to spin. When they stopped, a new combination locked into place forever. She would not trust anyone to love or take care of her again.

Alice was six years old.

❧

Grown-up Alice at forty-nine, didn't believe in fairytales and had no time for fantasy. Hers was a sensible world of profit and loss statements, production schedules and sales projections. There was only one explanation for what happened to her last night. She had completely lost her mind.

Right this minute her impending insanity didn't matter. Six impossible things had to be done before this breakfast meeting ended. Her adulteration of Mr. Carrol's words nearly made her laugh, but she stopped herself. The other five people around the conference table might wonder why Excellcardia's CEO, their boss, laughed at nothing. Dr. Elliott had a psychiatric explanation, but this wasn't the time to worry about that.

Alice continued addressing the assembled members of her team. "Item number four on this morning's agenda, Kirasaki. What the hell, Brad? I thought this was a done deal. Now they're backing out of a two-million-dollar commitment?" Alice looked over her laptop at her Vice President of Sales. Though he was the object of her current ire, she couldn't help but admire Bradley James, all cool, blue-eyed handsome like Paul Newman in *The Color of Money*. Alice knew Mr. Newman from her mother's old movies and the salad dressing bottle. *Stop it, she told herself. Concentrate.*

"Under control," Bradley said. "They're surprisingly cheap bastards and if we give them our rock bottom quote, they'll come crawling back. Just a little dance we have to do."

His obvious command of the situation let Alice breathe easier for an entire second. "I want something signed on my desk by day's end and I know very well what time it is in Osaka." Alice looked at her laptop screen for the next item on her agenda. The man sitting on Alice's right at the long black marble conference table, had opened his mouth to speak, but now just nodded at her. Jonathan Salter, Alice's administrative assistant, typed furiously on the silver laptop in front of him. She knew he wouldn't miss a single pertinent detail and a perfect summary of this meeting's discussions would be in her inbox thirty minutes after the meeting ended.

"Okay then, on to number five, the revised Mark IV schedule for BJC. Louise?"

Louise O'Neil raised two perfectly plucked and shaped dark eyebrows and said, "No way Alice. We can't get the raw materials all on this continent in time let alone produce enough for BJC's monster order. Maybe if we push it back two weeks."

"I have checked on all the materials personally," Alice said. "Everything can be here in time, and if we just add a single shift for 3 days to production, it won't wreck the P & L. BJC needs them by the second of the month and we can do that. The sooner we get them to the patients, the better their lives will be."

Louise narrowed her eyes. "If you say so, Alice." Alice caught the doubt in Louise's voice. "The Mark IV is the best pacemaker on the market. Nobody can touch its reliability and ease of implantation for the price point. You should be proud of your baby, Louise." Alice served up a wide and appreciative smile to go with the compliment. *Engineers can be such children,* she thought. Louise was one of the best on the planet, so Alice could take a little extra time to pat her on the back. She glanced down at her laptop's screen and cleared her throat. "Okay, now on to the Biocardia project. I've increased the security in the lab. There's a retinal scanner on the door now and two more cameras. Please stop by security to have your eyeballs registered soonest. We can't have any of our ground-breaking technology stolen by a competitor. Dr. Petrus is here to update everyone for the board presentation. Proceed please."

Petrus sat staring for one minute too long, as if to focus the group's attention on him. Then he said, "The animal trials are proceeding on schedule by some miracle. What trials I can afford on this puny budget. Barney will be ready to show off to the rich old geezers on the Board. They'd be completely nuts not to approve more funds. The Biocardia device will revolutionize bypass surgery." The man in the rumpled lab coat nodded to emphasize his words, shaking the long silver hair that always reminded Alice of the mad scientist in *Back to the Future*. She knew the good doctor was only fifty-two years old. Perhaps genius stripped the color from his hair.

It was brilliant work Alice knew full well. When approved and in production the device would make Excellcardia one of the top medical device companies in the world. Hopefully, the world would never find out such a company was run by a complete lunatic. She wasn't going to tell.

The last order of business was a report by Arthur, head of the patent and clearance department. Alice had nearly forgotten he was there at all. She would have preferred to merely read his departmental reports, but Arthur Thomas insisted on being at the Friday morning meetings. His squeaky voice and rat-like eyes suggested a long hairless pink tail might be tucked into the back of the trousers in his baggy brown suit. She reminded herself that his expertise, not his appearance, made him vital to the company. Without clearance, no new device could be brought to the market. Arthur's inarguable value didn't prevent his reports from being torturous. She stared at her favorite baby pink pumps under the table and tried not to think about the strange goings-on in her apartment last night.

Jonathan nudged her foot gently under the desk, a reminder to look up so no one would think she hadn't been listening. Some assistants, she thought, were worth their weight in gold.

"Alright people, thank you and let's end this week with a bang rather than a whimper." Alice nodded, scooped up her laptop, and headed to her office one floor up. When the elevator doors opened onto the twenty-third floor, she paused to survey the cool black and white scene.

Onyx marble floor tiles and white leather furniture gave the reception area the proper weight. One of her first executive actions three years ago, had been to claim the entire floor for her office and decorate to her particular taste. A company the size of Excellcardia needed a whole floor for its CEO, Alice had reasoned. It wasn't vanity but necessity. The twenty-third floor wasn't just her office, but the center of the company's communications. The huge-framed photographs of scarlet flowers were the only hint at the passion of Excellcardia's CEO. She straightened a picture, unacceptably crooked by two millimeters, and double-checked the others as she walked by.

The black marble slab of Jonathan's desk sat shining and empty. He never went home with anything left undone. A handsome male administrative assistant had always been Alice's secret dream, and Jonathan Salter was certainly that. He wore a suit as well as any man she'd ever seen. Something about men in business attire got Alice all moist and tingly. If he wasn't quite so good at what he did, she wouldn't have cared—much.

Alice liked to start the coffee, read emails, and watch the parking lot fill up twenty-three floors below. She knew who arrived early and who was perpetually late.

This morning, she forgot the password to open her emails. Panic! She used the same one every day, but today she couldn't remember it. *What would Dr. Elliot say? Is memory loss a new symptom?* Heart racing, she searched her mental files. "Slythy-Toves49, that's it," she said out loud and exhaled with relief. This morning, at least, the men in the white coats could pass her by.

Louise O Neil appeared in the doorway. Brow furrowed and lips a tight red-lip sticked line, she slammed the door to Alice's office. "I'm glad to go along with the revised schedule but I do not appreciate being blindsided at the Friday meeting."

"Coffee, Louise?"

"Damn it, Alice, I would appreciate a little more respect than that, and thank you."

People in the company called her Jackie O. The same meticulously coiffed dark hair, lean arrow-straight frame, and perfect sense of style had something to do with the nickname; but Louise also carried herself like a Bouvier. Louise's African-American heritage did not lessen her resemblance to one of America's best loved first ladies one little bit. Alice doubted the late former first lady would have let her feathers be ruffled by a simple change in a manufacturing schedule. Alice needed to smooth the feathers right back down on this important peahen.

"We deliver what our clients need when they need it on my watch. Sit down and have coffee with me. It's been a while since we talked about anything but business." Louise poured herself a half cup of coffee from the pot on the credenza and dropped gracefully into the white leather chair in front of Alice's black desk.

"I would appreciate a little warning next time." Louise's eyes were still narrowed but her lips relaxed a bit. Least you could do for a friend who didn't even hate you when you got the top job, even though she had ten years more experience. A friend who made sure you ate something healthy once in a while after you and Robert split. A friend who—"

"I get it, Louise, and I do really appreciate all you've done for me. I'll have Jonathan email you any and all changes to the production schedules immediately in the future."

"Thank you. Now tell me about the exciting life of a single CEO."

"Nothing exciting about my life. I go home alone every night. I'm certainly not looking for love. That crap doesn't exist outside of romance novels and Hallmark Original movies."

"Such a cynic," Louise said. "I can help change your mind, you know. Say the word. Older or younger, Bill and I know lots of people. How much weight have you lost? You look great. You know cool-laser-liposuction really works for those stubborn areas. Not that you need it of course."

Of course she's talking about my ass.

"Do you want some of my breakfast smoothie? Organic kale, wheatgrass, and mango? I have plenty left in my office."

"No thank you, Lou. No more of your health goo for me. Not enough preservatives. There could be God knows what flesh-eating bacteria on that kale without serious chemicals to kill it. I'm way too busy for any kind of romance and no laser's touching this fine derriere, hot or cool. It's only been a year since—"

"Since that man-dog cheated on you and left you for a twenty-five-year-old child?" said Louise. "It's actually nearly two years. No one deserves a good time more than you. Who said anything about romance? Just some dinner and maybe a little dancing in the sheets with some nice guy. You can't live and breathe this place. You need a hobby. Some kind of distraction."

Alice burst out laughing. Could Louise somehow know about the completely insane thing that happened to her last night? Louise's irritation was replaced by concern, even a little speck of fear.

Inappropriate affect, Alice thought. Common in people with her diagnosis, according to Dr. Elliot.

"Sorry. I do appreciate your concern." Alice looked down to compose herself. The first edition of Lewis Carroll's most famous work, *Alice's Adventures in Wonderland*, sitting on her desk always brought her comfort. She ran her hand over the lovely brown leather-bound book, her favorite since childhood.

As a child, she was positive it had been written just for her. When she learned the book was published over a hundred years before her birth, she'd cried for hours. Alice had finally decided Mr. Carroll must have been a special kind of magician, to write a story that would come to mean so much to her.

"Now," Alice said, "tell me what's going on with you." She tried hard to look interested as Louise launched into an account of her adult children's activities and the upcoming holiday parties, hoping the occasional nod and '*hmm*' sufficed. How could such a brilliant woman be so good at prattling on about such trivial matters?

Jonathan opened Alice's office door and placed the doorstop in its usual place, after a reassuring look and head nod from his boss. He made sure Alice's door always remained open.

"It's important," he'd said when she first hired him. "Gives the impression you are approachable and are always ready to listen to anyone's ideas. Adds to the team mentality, don't you think?" His thick mahogany hair moussed straight back and black-framed glasses gave him a definite Clark Kent appeal. The suit that hung so nicely on his six-foot-two-inch frame today was moss green, Alice noted.

"Brad James is on his way up," he said. "He says he absolutely has to talk to you before your ten o'clock. Shall I have him wait?" Jonathan shot Louise a quick glance and focused his dark eyes on Alice.

"No. I need to talk to him about his trip to Sweden. Give us two minutes."

Louise watched him walk out. She gave Alice a sly smile and spoke softly. "Of course you don't need me to set you up. That hotness could put a smile on any girl's face."

"You know damn well I would never—"

"Uh huh," Louise lowered her voice. "He looks at you like a sick puppy. Everyone thinks he's in love with you."

Seriously? My co-workers need to get to work and not waste time speculating about me. How ridiculous. He's far too young, gorgeous or not. That little hint of an English accent has to keep his bed full of hot young babes. Not that she cared. What he did on his own time didn't matter as long as he continued to give Excellcardia his best during his workday.

Alice had to admit, occasionally she would call Jonathan into her office and ask him some trivial question she didn't really need the answer to just to listen to the music of his voice. His formal phrasing seemed a little odd for someone so young, but it added a certain richness to his armamentarium of interesting traits, including a droll sense of humor that could defuse the most intense situation.

Great male administrative assistants were rare—especially one who could type, handle all forms of office software, speak six languages fluently, and decorate the outer office so exquisitely. He didn't come cheap, but he kept Alice's days running smoothly, which was worth a good deal.

Louise headed to the door. "If I were you," she said, "I would watch that James. There is something about him. He's a little too slick."

"Thanks, Mother Louise. All salesmen are slick, and he's one of the best. He's doubled our international sales with his considerable charm." Alice swallowed hard and composed herself for her second meeting of the new day and hoping the sudden color in her cheeks went unnoticed.

Eight meetings, four international conference calls, and too many hours later, Alice unlocked the door to her apartment. She owned half of the top floor of a lovely, old, refurbished building in the newly trendy Benton Park neighborhood of St. Louis. The bright red-orange bricks of her home's interior walls were original. Looking up at the rough-hewn beams in her combination living room/kitchen, made Alice feel is if she lived in a castle. Her watch said six-fifteen. It would be dark in less than an hour. Alice always knew what time it was. This little talent had served her well, but she preferred to wear a watch, even though it was mostly out of fashion. It gave her an odd pleasure when the watch was off by minute or two. Today it was two minutes fast.

She fed her cat, Otis, and scanned her mail. Throwing everything needing attention into her briefcase, Alice enjoyed the leftover Chinese food from lunch. Jonathan knew the very best takeout places in St. Louis, and this was his favorite. Even cold, the almond chicken still tasted crisp and delicious. Alice couldn't be bothered to use the microwave tonight.

Her days as Excellcardia's chief executive officer were always challenging. That was a good thing, no simple job could satisfy Alice. A shameless accomplishment junkie, she continually chased the next challenge. Still, none of her accomplishments ever made her feel quite good enough.

Long before she finished medical school, Alice knew in her heart that a career in medicine wasn't for her. For one thing, it didn't help that she couldn't stand the sight of bodily fluids, and for another, sick people gave her the creeping willies. Medical school had been one hell of an amazing trip, but the profession was far too messy. Besides the fluids, there were way too many untidy emotions to be dealt with. "Chasing the next challenge," was what she called quitting so it didn't feel so much like failure.

An MBA from Northwestern gave her the credentials she needed in business. Her ambition, hard work, and teeny bit of luck helped her succeed. She loved the tidy world of phone conferences, meetings, and endless emails. In this world, nobody barfed, bled, or crapped on you. Most importantly, no one died because you couldn't respond to their email in a timely manner. Alice's current career filled her days with the pure, clean black and white of the business world. It wasn't always clear cut, but it smelled much better than medicine.

A meow from the cat on the floor demanded her attention and she had to deal with what happened last night. She turned to walk down the hall. She could go left to her bedroom and pretend nothing odd had ever happened. But as she turned right into the guest room, her heart began to pound. Even if she was losing her mind, she had to deal with it. Losing her mind was the reason she went to Dr. Elliot in the first place, wasn't it? She had hoped a good shrink could help her avoid the fate now consuming her mother. Who could blame her for finally coming unglued? Alice's family history was riddled with straightjackets, institutions, and Electro-Convulsive Therapy treatments.

The face she saw reflected in the mirrored door of the guest room closet appeared ten years older than the face she'd seen just that morning. Last evening, she'd come to the guest room to find an old, ragged robe of her mother's. Fuzzy and pink, this robe always gave her comfort after an especially hard day. The robe still smelled faintly like her mother's Chantilly perfume. She closed her eyes and remembered what she found the previous evening when she slid open the door.

She'd been searching among her work suits, all neatly zipped into their matching black garment bags, when her hand felt naked fabric. She used both hands to make an opening in the wall of black bagged work suits. "What the—?"

On a single gold colored hanger hung a foreign suit, naked of any bag. There was a short olive-drab jacket with military insignia and a matching strait skirt that she imagined would have fallen just past her knees. She could see a white blouse under the jacket. On the floor lay a pair of black shoes with heels her grandmother would have called 'sensible'. A pair of old-style stockings were neatly folded on top of an odd-looking belted contraption with garters. Underneath the stockings and garters Alice saw a pointy bra and a pair of white granny panties.

Reaching down to the clothes on the floor, Alice felt the

stockings. "Silk, and I bet that seam goes down the back. Cool." The name plate on the jacket read 'Hightower'. Susan must have stashed next year's Halloween costume in here. Her best friend was always trying to get Alice to go to one of her crazy parties. Seemed like a hell of an effort to go to, though.

A cute little green hat had been clipped on to the hanger beneath the jacket. This unexpected gift in her closet had given Alice a little boost in energy and she decided to try the outfit on. It fit perfectly.

"Damn, Susan," whispered Alice. It was as if some unknown tailor had secretly fit her while she slept. The skirt hugged her butt cheeks like it had known them all her life. Tugging on the stockings, struggling not to snag the silk, she still managed to stick her thumb through the filmy things twice. Hopefully, the long skirt would hide the holes. Alice remembered seeing a picture of a girl with seamed stockings from sometime long ago. As she slid them up her legs, she'd wondered how in the world a girl got the seams straight? The black tie shoes, though serviceable with a square chunky heal, were cute in a cool retro way.

"How smart." Alice addressed her image in the mirror as she sat the cute little hat on her head. "Private Hightower reporting for duty." She saluted her reflection. She thought she looked like Patricia Neal in her favorite black and white World War II movie, *In Harm's Way*.

On her way to the hall closet to get a garment bag for this cute little number, she'd heard the strangest sounds which seemed to come from beyond her guest room's balcony door. Impossible, she'd told herself. There couldn't really be voices and music coming from a balcony far above the street.

She unlatched the door and slid it open. Alice gasped. Where her balcony should have been was a room full of people, mostly men in uniforms. She smelled cigarette smoke and heard music coming from a badly tuned piano. Some-where a chorus of voices sang, "Over there, over there."

Alice couldn't move. The hallucination, which it sure as hell had to be, held her transfixed. A line of men with military short hair wearing green uniforms stood at a bar not twenty feet from her. The tall one nearest her with a dashing bit of silver at his temples, set down his drink. He turned to her and yelled over the other voices.

"Hey Doll, trade you a drink for a dance?" Alice jumped back and slammed the balcony door. When the door was shut tight, she saw only the St. Louis skyline through the glass. She sat on the bed, her eyes wide and her heart pounding.

"Well, Alice, you have gone and done it now. An honest to goodness hallucination," she'd said out loud. Somehow, she'd managed to skip over most of the more minor neurotic symptoms of losing one's mind and move straight to a big bad psychotic break with reality.

She had taken off the costume, hung it neatly back on the hanger in the closet, and planned to call her psychiatrist in the morning. Should she also call building security, she'd wondered? What if someone had broken in and left the clothes? The thought of trying to explain what she had found on her balcony changed her mind.

She lay awake for hours thinking of the man's offer and wondering what would have happened if she had stepped into that room and said yes to that man and the drink.

This evening, her hand shaking slightly, she slowly slid open the mirrored door to the closet once more. Alice inhaled sharply. When she pushed aside the garment bags, the golden hanger she knew she hadn't purchased now held a worn and faded pair of blue jeans and a buff-colored suede leather vest. There were no shoes and no underwear.

"Commando jeans and a fringed vest. If you're going to go crazy, go all the way." Alice began to remove her own clothes and put on the clothes her craziness has somehow provided. What did she have to lose?

The enormous belled-bottomed legs of the jeans were

perfectly frayed from dragging the ground. Of course they fit her, hanging low on her hips. The vest barely covered her breasts when she tied the front, and the fringe around the bottom fell to her knees. In the pocket of the vest, she found a pair of round, green-tinted sunglasses with wire-rimmed frames. She took the clip out of her hair and put on the glasses. Her reflection in the mirror looked like the cover of one of her mother's vinyl albums from the seventies.

Alice walked to the sliding door to her balcony. Tonight when she slid it open, would there be a completely different scene? She closed her eyes, unlatched the door and opened it slowly.

This evening, warm humid air, fragrant with night-blooming flowers and a hint of diesel, enveloped her as she stepped through the door. Though fall held Missouri firmly in its grip, the soft summer voices of chirping crickets assured her this was no longer St. Louis. "Down the rabbit-hole, here I go." Alice opened her eyes.

Taking a few steps, Alice reveled in the soft night air and warm pavement beneath her bare feet. A long black bus rose out of the dark ten feet in front of her. Huge yellow, orange, and red letters made of graphic flames and read "Nickel Bag," below a row of black-out glassed windows." *A tour bus?* As if to answer her question, a man—young, not much older than thirty—stood on the stairs of the bus. He looked at her with an exuberance that even the fake sophistication of his age couldn't hide. He stood shirtless, a pair of white pony leather pants hung low on his hips, a handsome smiling angel silhouetted against the interior bus lights. This angel came complete with a halo framing his shoulder-length brown hair. It didn't matter that the halo was produced by the plastic lenses in the glasses Alice wore. She swallowed hard.

He stroked his long mustache slowly with his index finger. "We're late for a very important date. You comin', love? We've got a spot of room for one more." His voice deep, warm, and rich made Alice shiver even on this warm night. He shifted his weight, and Alice watched the muscles of his stomach ripple, not from hours of crunches and steroids, but just youth. The dark hairs on his chest swirled around his nipples and knitted into a line Alice's eyes followed until it disappeared into the white leather at his waist. How delicious would it be to follow that trail with her fingers or her tongue? After all, if she'd lost her mind, she might as well enjoy it.

He took her hand and led her up the stairs to the bus. Here, wherever this *here* was, it didn't seem to matter Alice might be old enough to be his mother. In Crazy Town, there's no cradle robbing.

"Hey, what you got there, Sir William?" A young man sat in the front seat tuning a guitar. He looked up as Alice climbed the steps. "A bit o'lovely stuff for the long, bleeding ride to Bumfuck, USA?" This one had curly black hair with a red bandana tied around it. The round glasses perched on the end of his nose were the twin of Alice's own.

"I'm not opposed to sharing, Jon me boy, but me bein' the lead singer, I'll be getting first rights for a while, if you catch my meanin'." William turned to Alice, wrapped his arms around her, and kissed her deeply. She could hardly breathe for the feel of the long hard length of him against her body.

He tasted of cigarettes and Binaca. He teased her tongue with the tip of his. Now that is a tongue I can work with, she thought. His right hand slid under the leather of her vest and caressed her erect left nipple. She moaned and leaned into him.

"Oh, this is going to be a bit of fun." William's voice and his touch made Alice exceedingly wet. He led her by the hand, down the short aisle of the bus past two girls sitting in the same seat, arms entwined. They looked like twins, but when Alice looked a bit closer, it was just the similarity in style typical of girls that age. Same long brown hair, short, flowered dresses and bare feet. The girls stared out the window with eyes wide and blank, and paid no attention to her.

A doorway led to an enormous bed that stretched from one wall to the other. On the bed lay a white fur cover and at least ten pillows covered in shiny black imitation satin. On the left side of the bed lay a completely naked young man with blond hair tied back in a ponytail. His eyes were squeezed tight with pleasure. A very naked and very thin girl rode the blond. By the sound of it, she was about to climax.

William sat on the bed and pulled her astride him, untying her vest. "Yummy, love," he said taking one nipple in his mouth and rolling the other between his thumb and forefinger.

Alice inhaled deeply and buried her hands in his wavy hair, soft as a baby's. She could feel the motion of the blond and the skinny girl. "A waterbed," she said. Her uncle Jim had one when she was a little girl and jumping on it had seemed the most fun possible. Alice felt pretty certain she was about to discover the real reason some genius invented the waterbed.

She could see the outline of William's erection straining at the white leather of his pants. Sliding down the zipper of the pony pants, she gasped. Alice thought few things in this universe more beautiful than an erect penis. She'd always thought penis was a stupid flaccid word to describe something so incredible. She preferred a far more powerful one. Some people might think the word cock crude, but to Alice it seemed perfect. She had married her college boyfriend because his was the most beautiful thing she'd seen in all her nineteen years. She hadn't really been in love. Yet even now, thinking of him made her heart quicken.

This cock in front of her was long, deep lavender-pink, and seemed hard enough to cut glass. "Oh my God," was all she could say.

"Thank you, love, but you can call me Will." His voice now husky, he looked at her with lovely large gray eyes fringed with dark lashes, half closed. Alice felt certain those eyes and that voice attracted countless groupies. Right this minute, she didn't mind at all being one of them. He leaned back on the bed, but his eyes never left hers. Alice reached down and wrapped her fingers around the long, luscious length of him. The feel of the warm silky flesh covering solid steel made her even wetter, like that was possible.

She unzipped her jeans and kicked free of them as quickly as she could. Wrapping her fingers once again around him, she slid her tongue along the underside of his honey-sweet and lovely cock. Her tongue slipped lovingly over each ridge and velvet-covered vein. She loved the musky-earth-and-sweat smell of the curly hair around that work of art. Alice knew from Cosmo that many men today shaved their privates bare. Too bad, she thought.

"Bloody God! I think you've done this before." Will's rich voice went up a little.

"You can call me Alice." Her fingers continued to slide up and down the length of him. Needing to taste of him, she sucked the delicious head of his erection into her mouth and slid her tongue up and down against its delicious underside. Alice savored the taste and the essence of Will.

The movement of his hips caused waves that bounced the bed and brushed the fur cover against her nipples with each thrust. Each little bounce sent waves of pleasure through her nipples to the wet between her legs.

"Stop! Now!" Will said. Alice complied, looking up at him. "I've got a little something for you too." He sat up, extended his tongue, and made an unbelievably hot licking motion with it.

"You want some of that, little Alice?"

"Oh, yes, please."

"Well, then, get up here." He leaned back and Alice scrambled up rather ungracefully to straddle his face. He extended his tongue, and after stroking her slippery clitoris for a few hot liquid strokes, plunged it into the core of her. Alice found it hard to breathe, the pleasure too intense.

She moved her hips against him as he again stroked her. Alice heard someone screaming as she came. Only when she collapsed back onto the fur did she realize it was her voice that threatened to scream the paint off the walls and break the bus windows.

"Damn, Will, that bird is loud," said a voice next to her, muffled by the fur.

"And wetter than the mother Atlantic Ocean," Will said. His breath hot against Alice's ear as his large, callused fingers caressed her. "Come on, Alice my girl, ride me to Wonderland."

She obliged, lowering herself slowly onto him, still slick with her saliva. Caressing him with her inner-most folds, she slid slowly all the way up and down the length of his cock. In no time, he stiffened and came with a soft moan. Alice sat up, savoring another delicious sensation as the warm semen ran down her thighs.

Will reached up and cupped her breasts. "You, Alice, know how to fuck a bloke."

"Thank you. And what a bloke you are, William."

"Give me a spot of rest and I'll fuck you again for Queen and country." He settled his head back into the pillows and closed his eyes.

Alice laughed. From her right, a voice said, "That is some limey bullshit, Babe. I'm ready now." The blond man got to his knees, displaying his own weapon, completely ready to do battle. His cock was not as large as Will's but was hard and handy. The skinny chick had long since come or passed out or both, and now lay in a silent heap facing the wall. Alice stared briefly and marveled, she could count the vertebrae in the girls back. Her partner, it seemed, was not quite finished.

Alice ran her fingers through his long surfer-blond hair and looked into his bright blue eyes. "I'm Alice, and you are?"

A lady had certain standards after all even in one totally crazy hallucination.

"Randy." He reached out and took her left breast in his hand.

"I can see that." Alice lay down beside him.

"These are some righteous tits." He rolled on top of her. Alice gasped, surprised at her own reaction to his hard young body against hers. Reaching for her breasts, he rubbed the palms of his hands against each one slowly as he kissed her. His kisses were no gentle little teasings. He rammed his tongue into her mouth and flicked his thumbs flicked against her nipples. He came up for air briefly. "How can such great big juicy tits have such tiny nipples?"

"Just lucky, I guess." Alice writhed at his touch and hungered for him inside her. Breathless, she spread her legs and wrapped them around Randy.

"Damn that juicy slit of yours is too hot." He slammed into her fast and hard. The long nails he must have used to play his guitar dug into the flesh of her ass.

"Oh, God, Randy," she cried, "fuck me hard, fuck me hard, right now!"

Holding her breasts, his eyes shut tight, he bucked his hips hard and shot into her, filling her once again with liquid passion.

He lay on top of her and said, warm breath against her ear, "Want some grass, Alice? The night ain't over."

It had been over twenty-five years since she'd smoked marijuana in college, but she'd never had sex while stoned, or baked, or whatever they called it on this bus. "Okay," she said.

From a cabinet above the bed, Randy produced a long glass tube attached to a glass bowl full of water. He held a match to the bowl. A smaller bowl suspended above the water held more weed than Alice had ever seen in one place. He inhaled, the device made a bubbling sound and he passed it to Alice. She inhaled deeply. The water cooled the smoke and enabled her to hold it in her lungs for a good long minute. She sat cross-legged facing Randy as Will snored softly next to them.

"You into chicks at all?" He stared at her crotch with his head cocked to one side. "Cuz there are a couple of girls up front who will eat that pretty pussy of yours six ways to Sunday. They're English. I think all those English chicks are lesbians or at least bi. They're always ready to go down on each other."

"Nope," Alice said. She exhaled slowly. "I only like the hard stuff. Nothing soft." She figured the silly weed smoke grin on her face probably mirrored Randy's own.

"Too bad. I love watching two girls balling."

"You and every other man I've ever known." Alice smiled at him sweetly as she took another long deep drag. The THC tickled her neurons. She wondered if the drug would affect sex. Seemed a shame not to find out. "Will the Large" still slept. His cock, now flaccid, looked equally lovely lying there against his thigh, all shiny with her lust and his satisfaction.

She realized, as she stared at him, he had opened his eyes and was watching her. He grew hard under her gaze, and she could feel her own humid response. She had to have Will's gorgeous cock in her mouth once more and acted quickly on the thought.

"I'll give you exactly two days to stop that," he said.

While she enjoyed the very best of Will on her hands and knees, other hands reached around her from behind and caressed her breasts. Someone's head leaned on her shoulder, and curly hair tickled her ear. Alice moaned as the hands gently pinched her nipples and lips kissed her neck nipping the flesh tenderly. A wave of electric desire shot through the length of Alice, and already on her knees, she spread her legs widely. The tongue slid slowly along the cheeks of her ass.

"Ummm," she moaned long and low. Immediately, something wonderfully hard and definitely male filled the empty place she much preferred full. Her mouth full of Will, she moved her hips against the cock filling her from behind. He thrust into her at an ever-increasing pace. *This is the stuff of dreams.*

She stopped the motions of her lips, tongue, and hands just long enough for another impossibly long climax. This was not the usual sweet, exciting climb up and then quickly down of most orgasms. This time she hung at the peak. This time it seemed to last for minutes not mere seconds. There was no other world but the one in her mouth and between her legs. The pleasure went on washing over her in exquisite waves for what had to be at least a week.

Marijuana made her orgasms last so much longer—who knew? Certainly not the serious, conservative CEO that was Alice in the daylight. *This stuff has to be legalized, if for nothing else but glaucoma, chemotherapy, and sex,* thought nighttime Alice. Will came again hot and hard against her tongue's eager ministrations.

Alice found herself in a warm cuddly pile of Nickel Bag, arms around waists, heads on shoulders, sticky legs entwined. Drowsy and satisfied, she fell asleep.

❧

Clinical Notes on Client Hightower, Alice B.

Strong family history and onset of recent symptoms suggest diagnosis of Bipolar II. Client presents with recent weight loss, lapses in judgement, and reports bouts of hyper-sexuality in vivid fantasies related in pressured speech. Past history of running from stressful situations. However, client is extremely high-functioning. Though she came seeking treatment, completely denies the need for medication.

Chapter Two

SUITE MADAM BLUE

Otis's meow roused Alice as usual. Wild, impossible, delicious memories lingered that felt much more real than any dream. She sat up and put her feet on the thick rose and blue Persian rug of her bedroom. It had cost a fortune but made her happy every time her feet touched the tightly woven wool flowers. "Besides, they wear like iron and last a lifetime," the salesman had said in response to her gasp of horror at the price.

"Damn Otis, who knew insanity could feel this good? Alice had always enjoyed sex, but since her disastrous mistake a year ago resulting in the best sex of her life, she thought of it far too often. That kind of mistake couldn't be repeated. But maybe the closet crazy had solved that problem.

Saturday. Damn. How can it be Saturday again? Her silly satisfied feeling turned to sick cold dread. She'd visited her mother at the Mary Center every Saturday for two years. Would it ever get easier?

She spent fifty minutes on the elliptical, instead of her usual thirty, and dressed as slowly as possible. She did this without any conscious attempt to delay the inevitable; her sloth was an involuntary reaction. Her movements seemed to slow almost against her will, and the minutes seemed endless. Did the clock on her kitchen wall move in slow motion, or did she?

Normally, Alice loved breakfast and would have two eggs, two strips of bacon, and maybe a large cup of Earl Grey. But on visiting days she couldn't even swallow water and would have to take her vitamins when she got home.

The route to the Mary Center was short and scenic. Alice drove along the streets of an old and lovely part of St. Louis near Forest Park. Thirty-room mansions with turrets, pillared balconies, and huge ancient trees lined both side of the streets. Instead of admiring the stately neighborhood, Alice clenched her teeth and fought the urge to vomit.

The Mary Center, once the sprawling country home of a St. Louis beer baron, was now a private care facility. They called it a memory care unit, but Alice's mother, who knew perfectly well where she was, refused to call it anything but "the nuthouse."

Alice sat in her car in the center's parking lot, staring at her watch. Visiting hours started at ten. The minute hand of her watch seemed stuck on nine fifty-eight. She breathed in and out slowly for a long time and listened to her pulse pound in her ears. *Beep* went the little hourly alarm on her watch, as if she could ever forget. The watch came with that feature and she couldn't find the instructions to turn it off. Today the chime sounded like Big Ben echoing inside her car.

Walking up the winter-gray stone steps, Alice tried to stay positive by remembering the feel of the beautiful young man kissing her last night, the passionate thrusts of the man inside of her, and the taste of him as he came hot and hard in her mouth. Nothing helped. No pleasant fantasy memories could lessen her horror, or assuage her greatest fear—that someday, she would call the Mary Center home.

In the hall leading to her mother's room, Alice passed fragile, wheelchair bound creatures who were once vital human beings. Teachers, policemen, and poets now sat in soft restraints "for their own good." White padded Velcro straps kept the prisoners fastened safely to the chairs.

Most had given up and accepted their fate. They were frail or demented and seemed to belong here. Restraining them kept them from hurting themselves or others. This wing of the Mary Center was dedicated mostly to Alzheimer's patients, their amylin-choked brain cells dying off by the millions while their bodies sat safely restrained.

The usual quiet of the hallway was broken by the rhythmic moaning of one poor soul, a man in a blue robe who refused to be restrained and silent. He reached out a boney hand and grabbed at Alice's sweater as she walked past. She turned to give him her most benevolent smile; but when she looked into his eyes, she saw no light, no animation, nothing to show he was anything but a bent and moaning shadow, Velcroed to a wheelchair.

For the rest of the way to her mother's room at the end of the hall, Alice kept her eyes on the lovely oak-inlaid parquet floor. She unlocked the heavy steel door by entering the code, 3/12/49, her mother's birthday, and tried to look happy. "Good morning, Mother."

"Is it? Is it? Is it, Alice? Good or morning or both. Is it, Alice?" The tall woman in a long floral robe did not sit restrained. Beverly Hightower paced back and forth in the small room, looking only at the floor. The bones of her shoulders stood out against the soft silk of the robe Alice had given her for Christmas. She ran her fingers rhythmically through her silver laced white-blonde hair. "Tell me, Alice, which is it?"

"Well, Mother, it is morning, and it is good to see you." Manic was what they used to call her mother's present state. Now they called it hyper-something or other. It didn't really matter. Beverly stopped pacing and sat on the bed, smoothing the spread rhythmically with both hands and tapping her foot in time. Alice wasn't sure which state she preferred. At least in this state, her mother talked. Other times, she lay curled up in bed or sat in a chair in soft restraints, staring at the floor in silence.

Beverly always knew her daughter when she came to visit. Alice thought those whose loved ones didn't recognize them were lucky. They could stop coming, secure in knowing they wouldn't be missed. It wasn't her mother's memories that were lost, but the balance of her once-sharp mind. Her life had become only the violent peaks and silent valleys of her turbulent emotions. There were rarely pleasant, peaceful, or completely lucid times anymore. This morning words erupted from her mother, as if she would burst if she held them one second longer.

"Tell me, Alice, my pretty girl, have you seen Sean? Do you think he will visit today? Stand up straight. You won't hide those great big tits by slouching, you know. It won't help hide that butt of yours either. You didn't get that from my side of the family. We have always been trim and slim of hip. You'll never get any boys to fuck you if you slouch. That color of blue doesn't suit you. You, all in blue. Such an odd child you always were. A whole tribe of imaginary Indians for childhood friends. Always whispering in the dark. Do you still whisper to yourself, Alice, dreaming up stories nobody wants to hear?"

She tried not to wince at her mother's words. Inappropriate sexuality, Alice knew was a symptom of her mother's disease. It still disturbed her deeply each time she heard her very proper mother say such things. Today the deep blue of the sweater she wore suited Alice's mood. She stiffened betraying her feelings of discomfort.

Beverly sensed it and started to laugh not because she thought it funny, Alice knew, but at this stage of her illness it was one of the few emotions she could command. Alice sat down on the bed and hugged her mother tight.

"Fantasy boys don't seem to care much about my posture," was what she wanted to say. But this was her mother, so she held her as she laughed, and they rocked together on the pink chenille-covered hospital bed. She squeezed her eyes tight trying in vain to hold in her tears. She never wanted anyone see her cry, not ever. Her mother saw a single tear as it escaped and rolled down her cheek.

"Poor little Alice. Her mother is mad as a hatter, did you know? You were always such an odd child, whispering and whispering and whispering." Her mother laughed.

"I'm not sure about Sean. He might be busy," Alice lied. She knew he would not be visiting. It had been just the three of them after her father deserted them, first by leaving, then by dying when Alice was eight. Her memory of her father was limited to the yelling and spanking. Sean had been the best big brother he could be for as long as he could after Daddy left. She would always love him for that, although loving Sean was rarely easy.

Her father's abandonment had left a small, barely noticeable hole in Alice's world, but his replacements terrified her. After her father's death, the parade of her mother's boyfriends began. Beverly then was a rare and exquisite beauty with platinum hair and pale gray eyes. There were always boyfriends. These strange men sometimes winked or leered in Alice's direction, saying things she didn't understand. It got decidedly worse once the boob fairy paid Alice her miraculous visit.

That memory made Alice shudder. One day she was flat as an ironing board and then, overnight, there were bumps under her clothes on her chest. They weren't the little half lemons of the other girls in her grade, but large, round woman's breasts, impossible to hide or fit into any of her clothes.

Sean, two years older, had been their mother's favorite. He'd told Alice two years ago that he couldn't take seeing their mother this way, and then he, too, disappeared.

"I'll need to get my hair done if he is coming," her mother said. "The nuthouse hairdresser isn't worth a damn. Will you take me to Woody? He's such a genius, he could make a mop head look pretty." Alice felt grateful for even a little morsel of her mother's once brilliant wit.

"Sure," she said, another lie. The stress and stimulation of leaving the Center for a short trip had sent Beverly into an acute psychotic episode a year ago. Her doctor would never allow it. Truthfully, Alice felt relieved at the doctor's orders. Remembering the lovely poetry her mother once wrote, and how she had impressed the professors at Washington University where she worked with her paintings. It broke Alice's heart. She had to stay strong; but the fear and pity in people's eyes, when they saw what brilliant, vivacious Beverly had become, was more than Alice could bear.

Finally Beverly fell silent and began to stare intensely at nothing, Alice sighed deeply, kissed her mother goodbye, let herself out and locked her mother in. As she hurried past the door to her mother's shrink's office, a voice called to her. "I need to speak to you. Ms. Hightower."

Damn, she thought, nearly got away.

Alice sighed, walked into the office and dropped into the visitor's chair in front of the metal desk.

"Your mother is extremely agitated right now," Dr. Langer said, "and has been for days." She was a small woman with light eyes sitting behind a desk containing nothing but a computer monitor and keyboard. Pushing her tortoiseshell reading glasses up on her nose, she peered at Alice. As many times as Alice had sat opposite this woman, she'd never gotten used to the intensity of that gaze,...or her. The good doctor's hair was a deep burgundy color rarely found in nature. It stuck out from her head like she styled it daily with an angry brush. She reminded Alice of Ozzie Osbourne's wife Sharon. Sharon Osbourne would never look over her glasses at Alice as if she wanted to rip Alice's head off.

"Yesterday she refused to speak anything but Italian. At first we took it for word-salad, but then, Maria, one of the housekeepers, understood what she was saying. She was speaking in some old dialect of Italian. Your mother has become quite a problem. Because she can't tolerate lithium, our options are somewhat limited. Everything we tried of late seems to flip her to a hallucinatory state. I've never seen anything like it." Dr. Langer stopped speaking but didn't remove her little blue eyes from Alice's.

"She still recognizes me. I had no idea she spoke any language but English." Alice raised her eyes and searched the doctor's face trying to find some magic answer to help her mother in the doctor's silent stare.

"Yes. Well. She doesn't have dementia. Her memory is mostly intact, but her personality is unraveling due to the progression and severity of her bipolar depression. We're keeping her room locked, not so much for her, but for the other patients. There was an incident." The doctor paused as if to emphasize the weight of what she was about to say. "She got into bed with Mr. Roth the other night completely naked. The poor old gentleman nearly suffered a stroke. We cannot tolerate such behavior here."

Laughter burst out of Alice. The look of horror on Dr. Langer's face only made her laugh harder. She couldn't decide which she found more hilarious: the mental picture of her mother molesting some horrified old geezer, or the look on the doctor's face at her laughter.

As the doctor's visible surprise turned to irritation, Alice straightened up and composed herself. "Sorry, Dr. Langer. I just can't imagine my prim and proper mother accosting some-one. It's just…"

"Well, I am glad you find this funny, but some decisions have to be made. I want to try ECT."

Alice shuddered. When she was eighteen, she'd witnessed her Aunt Evelyn receiving electroconvulsive therapy, permis-sion granted because she was about to start an accelerated medical school program. The treatment came in response to

Evelyn doing nothing for months but pacing, looking at the floor, and saying only, "Okay."

Looking now at the almost identical green tile floor, Alice remembered. Evelyn had lain restrained on a gurney with electrodes stuck to her temples. A nurse, in a white starched uniform complete with immaculate white stockings and nurse-white, lace-up shoes, put a tongue depressor wrapped in medical tape in Evelyn's mouth. The actual convulsions were not as violent as Alice expected but upsetting anyway. There lay sweet, funny, batty Evelyn, who'd tickled her as a little girl and always had something amusing to say, twitching as electricity surged through her brain. The sound of dripping had drawn Alice's gaze to the floor, where a small puddle of urine formed under the gurney, and Alice headed for the trash can.

An orderly stood by watching in a stained white shirt and matching pants. "Hell of a doctor you'll make, little girl, if the sight of some pee sets you to puking," said the huge bald man who waited leaning against the green tile wall.

Alice shuddered a little at the Addams Family's Uncle Fester look alike who waited to take Evelyn back to her room. After the ECT, it took Evelyn years to be her funny and original self.

Dr. Langer cleared her throat in an effort to bring Alice's focus off the floor and back to her mother's treatment. "It's your decision. As an alternative, I will double up on her antipsychotics and add a potentiater, but the ECT would be the most expedient."

Alice stood, hands on hips. "Absolutely not! I have power of attorney as well as a full medical directive, and I will not allow it. I will not let you shock what's left of my mother's personality out of existence. Do whatever you have to with the meds, but I'll never agree to ECT." She turned and headed out the door, satisfied she'd done her duty as a daughter for this week.

Saturdays, Alice ran errands and handled the mundane paper-work it took to live in this world. Checkbook in hand, she tackled bills, taxes, and the odd charitable gift. She could never resist a sad kitty plea of any kind. The doorbell rang and saved her from sending all her money to Alley Cats Anonymous.

Susan had come to rescue her from herself, as she had done countless times since they met in college.

"Hey, Girlie. I made some zucchini bread, and you know how I hate to bake. Not sure what got into me. Need some validation. Some kinda attagirl for all my effort. You wanna?" Holding up a platter in front of her face, Susan Anderson lowered it just enough to reveal her bright green eyes with one eyebrow raised.

"Sure. I don't believe you really hate baking. You're too good at it." Alice opened the door. They walked to the solid block of black granite separating her main living area into kitchen and living room. Susan sat the plate on the bar.

"Well," she said "you'd better have some coffee for me, with maybe a little Bailey's. Carrying this bread all the way up two floors and across this hall kinda pooped me out. The air is awfully thin up here on the rich people's floor."

"Yeah, yeah, Your place is bigger and probably cost more too." Alice hugged her friend. "Sorry, no coffee. I could get you some tea." She sat down and looked at the toasty-brown bread. "Smells great."

"My place ain't the penthouse, though. That's yours and yours alone, Ms. Hightower. Okay, you and old lady Goldstein across the hall. No tea for me." Susan opened a drawer and took out a knife. She grabbed the butter off the top shelf of the refrigerator without looking, pulled out an unpainted maple stool and sat next to Alice. The bar was big enough to seat eight people, but Alice had only two stools. She didn't do much entertaining.

"Damn, girl! How much weight have you lost? I don't see you for a few weeks and you get skinny." Susan pulled out a stool and sat next to Alice.

"Thanks. I haven't weighed myself in a while. Maybe five pounds?"

"Hell no. More than that. Now I know something is wrong. You used to weigh at least three times a day in college. First thing every morning, I'd hear you getting on the scale next to your bed."

"Sorry if it bothered you. You were brave enough to room with the weird girl. I should have been more considerate."

"Of course it didn't bother me. I never thought you odd. You were best roommate ever. You never ate my food, always lent me your perfect papers, and even a castoff boyfriend once. Remember that guy? What the hell was his name?"

"Mike, maybe? I didn't do you any favors there. He always liked you better anyway. Legs man, I remember. You have the best legs." Alice smiled at her friend.

"Yeah, well, it's the rack most men adore, and few can hold a candle to you in the boob department. 36DD, is that still your size? The fact that your butt will always be a little too big for the rest of you can totally be overlooked." Susan cut a piece of bread, buttered it and handed it to Alice.

"Thanks. Without your reminder, I might have thought I was perfect." Alice had always been a little jealous of her friend's compact gymnast's figure. Even after two children, Susan's sleek build complemented her killer legs so well, she wore shorts even in late November.

Alice took a bite of the still warm bread. The softened butter dripped onto her shirt front. Susan laughed. "A large chest does have its disadvantages," said Alice. She didn't join her friend's good-hearted laughter but grew silent.

Susan pushed her short wavy brown hair out of her eyes and sighed. Sitting at the bar with her head propped on her elbows, she said, "Please tell me what's wrong? Don't say 'nothing,' cuz I will have to throw the bullshit card on you for that." Susan pantomimed the throwing of an imaginary card, which always made Alice laugh.

Alice did not laugh.

"Oh, God, honey, I'm sorry. How could I forget what happens every Saturday?" Susan wrapped her arms around her friend. "Is she much worse?"

"Not really. It's just that she will never get better, and someday that will probably be me."

"You don't know that. Your mother had already been hospitalized a time or two for breakdowns by your age. You run a whole company, for God's sake. You're the sanest person I know."

This made Alice laugh a little too long.

"Hey." Susan turned to her friend. "David and I have tickets to a cool charity thing tonight. He can stay home, and you can go with me. It'll be a boring bunch of dentists, but we can dress all formal and start rumors you're my hot new lesbian lover."

"No, thanks. I—"

"I know—except for me, dentists are boring. Come on. It'll be fun. I know how you love to dress up. You can wear a pair of those gorgeous shoes that aren't even dirty on the bottom. I'll even let you lean on me so you don't fall off." Susan giggled.

Alice closed her eyes. Sunset would occur in three hours. The thought made her shiver a little. What might wait behind her closet door? "Can't. I have a huge report to give to the board, and it's taking all my time."

"Don't you have staff to do that? If I didn't know better, I'd think you were avoiding me. This is the third time you've turned me down for some kind of fun thing. If I were a more sensitive sort, I'd get a complex."

"I always do my own reports." Alice stopped eating and set her piece of bread on the black stone.

"Really well, as I remember. Well then, I'll have to settle for David. He looks so hot in a tux." Susan hugged her friend once more, left the platter on the kitchen counter, and headed out the door.

Otis sat looking up from the kitchen floor where he conveniently sat by his empty food bowl. She scraped the bread into the trash and rinsed the platter under hot water in her huge, black, farm-style sink. It tasted great, and it was sweet of Susan to bring it, but it was way too many carbs. Maintaining her weight at a healthy level had always been a struggle, one way or another.

Starving half to death at twelve didn't keep puberty away. Alice could still remember her mother's compliments on how nice and thin was. Mother found it so hard to believe the doctor when he said Alice's newly svelte figure was a disease. Even when Alice's hair had begun to fall out and her periods stopped, her mother questioned the diagnosis.

"Anorexia: stuff and nonsense," Beverly Hightower had said, although she'd finally agreed to pay for a stay at camp for kids with eating disorders. Alice quickly plumped back up to see herself as merely chubby. Looking back, she realized she had been a fairly normal sized child.

Alice figured she must have been descended from the last member of a caveman tribe that didn't starve to death after all the mastodon meat ran out. Her body normally held on to fat for dear life. The recent bipolar thing seemed to help with her struggle against fat. Eating just didn't seem a priority.

Alice hardly ever took naps, but Saturdays sapped her energy, and she just needed to shut her eyes for a few minutes. Her bedroom on the east side of the building, was invitingly shady in the afternoons. The cool, powder-blue sheets on her bed called her name, and she answered.

Her eyes flew open, and she sat up. How long had she been asleep? No time to work on the report or eat, barely time to shower before sunset, when the clothes might appear. She decided to take a shower. Maybe tonight there would be more clothes and another amazing adventure.

Knowing when the sun would set came as naturally as losing her mind evidently. Wrapped in a towel, Alice slid the door to the closet open. It was one minute after sunset. She gasped. There were three hangers, a small pile of what appeared to be under garments, and a red wooden box. Folded in the pile were a dimity whale-boned corset, three petticoats, and a strange contraption that maybe went under the skirt.

Opening the red box, Alice found a faceless wooden head topped by a tall, powdered wig. It looked like a Christmas tree made of powdered curls. "Women actually wore these?" she said to the wig, which fortunately didn't answer.

One hanger held a straight shift made of crimson silk, one a long black velvet skirt, and on the third hung a jacket with laces and enormous belled sleeves. The velvet of the jacket was covered in intricately embroidered scarlet roses.

This is awfully elaborate for a costume party, thought Alice. There were no labels in any of the clothes, and the tiny stitches appeared to be made by hand. The night before might have seemed a few of decades in the past, the first one could have been during WWII; but this stuff looked eighteenth-century. A chill ran through her. This would be a night to remember—not that she could forget the other two.

Dressing took some time. First she put on the shift, then the corset. Next the skirt, slit down the front to expose a panel of red silk ruffles. The hoop thingy had so many straps and ties it wasn't easy to put on without help or fit under the skirt. Finally Alice put on the lovely rose-covered jacket. It took forever to lace up the front. She wondered when and by whom it might be unlaced.

She rolled on the red silk stockings she found in the shoes

and attached garters made of black ribbon with red ribbon roses on either side of gold buckles. She could find no elastic of any kind in those garters and Alice doubted they would hold the stockings up with just buckles. She pulled the ribbons tight through the buckles and marveled at how well they worked. Finally, she wadded her dark blonde hair up on her head and tugged on the wig. While it fit her head well, it felt stiff and itchy and smelled like lilacs and old kitchen grease.

One last glimpse in the mirror. "Marie Antoinette, here I come." Kirsten Dunst as the ill-fated monarch in the movie, may have worn it better, but Alice thought she rocked it.

Alice's heart raced as she grabbed the handle of the balcony door and slid it open to reveal a dimly lit room. Just inside the door a free-standing candelabra taller than she was, lit the room with the light of least thirty candles. Alice stepped into the room.

A sour-faced woman in a long black dress, white apron, and white lace cap came bustling up to Alice, her arms crossed. "You are late. He expected you half an hour ago." The wisps of hair that escaped her cap were curly and bright carrot-orange. A chambermaid maybe? Alice surveyed her new, or very old surroundings.

Mahogany wainscoting reached three quarters of the way up the wall toward a ceiling at least twelve feet above her. Faded gold and white flowers were splashed across the wallpaper above the dark wood. A plain, square raw-wood table stood on the left side of the door. The carpet covering the rough floor resembled the lovely one in Alice's own bedroom. The salesman must have been right about it being a classic pattern. This one had obviously seen a lot more foot traffic.

Alice saw a large window and couldn't help taking a quick peek. A buildup of black grime coated the window. Her attempt to clean it with the sleeve of her jacket revealed the black stuff to be on the outside. She peered out a small clear spot near the edge of the thick glass. The scene on the other side of the window reminded Alice of a set for a movie. "Les Miz" perhaps or "A Christmas Carol?" The buildings were half-timber and stucco. She could see down a long street to a wharf where wooden ships with tall mast loomed out of the gathering darkness of evening. This was certainly no longer 2018.

The door to wherever and whoever was a huge affair, carved with oak leaves and acorns from top to bottom. Not, thought Alice, something you'd find at Home Depot.

The maid walked around Alice, looking her up and down. After a thorough inspection, she put her hands on her hips, threw back her head, and laughed. "I'd like to know if you think wearing your mantua backwards is some kind of new style from Paris. But, by the manner you be wearin' that wig, I think 'tis quite by accident." The woman still chuckled.

Alice's cheeks colored. The maid began unlacing the jacket she'd called a mantua, and Alice pulled the wig off her head. "This outfit is terribly complicated. I'd really appreciate your help."

"Well, why he wants a girl who don't even know how to dress is beyond me. It's clear you ain't no girl, neither. No business of mine who he wants, I am quite sure. But I can't have some chippie that wears her dress backwards and her wig on willy-nilly getting' past me, I'll have you know." She finished unlacing the jacket, turned it around, and deftly laced it up the back. She then reached down the front and arranged Alice's breasts for maximum visibility. "A good bit better. He should see what he'll be getting, I'd say."

Alice chuckled. Last night's men hadn't seemed to notice the jiggly bits or imperfections of her figure which might have complicated dating real men. The porn-addicted modern guy's possible reaction to her forty-nine-year-old physique was one reason she'd stayed home evenings, that and her history of choosing partners wholly inappropriate and even dangerous to her career. But maybe by creating the magic closet, her crazy-hood had given her an excellent reason not to venture out.

"There's no accounting for my master's tastes, but you have a cheeky look about you. He does like the smart ones, and sometimes they got a little age on 'em like you. He seems to enjoy 'em a bit broad in the hips, I've noticed. I ain't no hairdresser neither, but I'll give the wig a go." Carefully setting the wig back on Alice's head, the maid pulled at the curls and straightened until she stood back and looked satisfied.

"I guess that'll do. Ain't none of that'll be on very long, anyways. He don't have girls in for supper to play chess. Nip along smartly, now. He's waited long enough, and you sure ain't getting no younger as I stand here flappin' my jaw. Go on now." She slapped Alice on her hooped ass and opened the door.

This inner room had the same mahogany wainscoting, running at least six feet up the walls. Above the wood, dark green watered silk highlighted paintings of landscapes and sea battles. Across the back wall, an enormous stone fireplace ran the entire width of the room. A man poked the blazing wood with an iron. Sparks flew from his efforts.

He faced the fire, and Alice could see only his back. She drew in her breath sharply at the sight. He seemed just a bit taller than she. His wide shoulders strained the cloth of his rose velvet jacket as he attacked the fireplace logs with the poker. Rose brocade pants hugged his legs, and the muscles in his calves strained the white silk of his stockings. Alice felt slightly disappointed in his jacket that fell nearly to his knees. The ass that went with those legs was bound to be impressive. A little giggle escaped her involuntarily, and she clapped her hand over her mouth.

The man turned and smiled at her. His large dark eyes cut through the distance between them. He had night-black hair pulled back into a ponytail with a black ribbon. His white ruffled shirt, unbuttoned to his waist, displayed a trail of black curls that thickened and disappeared into the waist of his pants. Alice reluctantly raised her eyes from the trail of dark curls when he spoke.

"Ah, at last you have arrived. Welcome, Madame—" His musical voice was rich with an unusual accent that sounded French but had an overlay of something else—Italian?

"It's Mademoiselle Alice Hightower. Señore?" She took a chance. His prominent nose and dark Botticelli angel eyes made her choose Italian rather than French, though his voice definitely held notes of both.

"Seingalt, my dear. But you may call me Jacques. Please come and warm yourself by the fire. I have taken the liberty of ordering supper for us both. I hope you don't mind." He walked across the room to her and took her hand. Looking into her eyes, he kissed her hand softly, then led her to a small burgundy velvet settee near the fire. He sat next to her.

"Though we have not met previously, I would very much like to know you better, my dear." Jacques took her hand again and covered it with kisses. He dragged his tongue slowly across her palm, and the look in his dark eyes raised her temperature at least two degrees. Alice let out a little moan and a shudder. Her host answered with a deep and seductive laugh.

A knock on the door made her jump. Jacques rose to answer. A young waiter in a long white apron and a ratty blond wig far too small for his head, rolled in a cart loaded with covered silver chafing dishes. Each dish sat on its own silver box of steaming water. The boy set the table in the middle of the room with white napkins and gleaming silver. He then carefully unloaded his cart as Alice watched. Jacques stood by, watching only her, as if she were the most delicious dish on the menu.

Where and when exactly she was didn't matter to her. Here stood a hot man from some other time, and she would be happy to let him eat her. She always loved the hairdos on the pictures of George Washington and Thomas Jefferson. This guy definitely had style. Guessing his age was difficult. His eyes held the sort of wisdom learned over at least four decades of life, but he moved with the athletic grace of a much younger man.

"You need not stay to serve, boy. I will do the honors, if Mademoiselle will allow?" He pulled out a lovely gilt Queen Anne chair from the table and indicated she sit.

"Of course, Señore Seingalt." Alice flashed a smile at him as he tucked in her chair. He poured her a glass of dark red wine in a crystal goblet etched with leaves that encircled the rim and trailed down the slender stem. He served her a slice of fowl in a mushroom sauce on a snow-white china plate. After filling his own plate and glass, he waited patiently for her to take the first bite.

The fowl turned out to be roast duck, Alice's favorite. The exquisite sauce was made with truffles rather than plain old mushrooms. She tried to eat like a lady, but missing her dinner, she was starving, and quickly cleaned her plate.

"I like nothing better than a lady with a healthy appetite." His dark eyes glittered by the light of the candelabra on the table.

She could have eaten another plateful but thought better of it. Though fantasy food couldn't possibly make you fat, with any luck, this scrumptious man would have another activity in mind for dessert. "It is really wonderful. I guess I was hungrier than I thought." Alice took a sip of her wine. It was the best she'd ever had. Certainly no wine expert, her one evening course had taught her little beyond the difference between good wine and cheap box wine.

"I am afraid, Alice, your beauty has aroused in me a hunger that cannot be satisfied merely with food." He rose from his chair and extended his hand. When she stood, he kissed her on either side of her face and then brushed her lips with his. He tasted of wine, duck and truffles.

Taking her hand once more, he led her to a dark alcove hidden by an intricately painted wooden screen. The scene on the screen showed a satyr chasing a nymph. *This nymph didn't intend to run anywhere.*

Putting his hands on her waist, he guided her in the dim light to sit on a narrow bed. *Oh goody,* she thought. He then disappeared behind the screen and reappeared carrying the candelabra from the dining table, which he set on a little table next to the bed. Smiling down at her, he removed his jacket and unbuttoned his pants. With deep anticipation, Alice again followed the dark trail of curls with her eyes.

Jacques knelt in front of her. His fingers undid her lacings without looking as if he'd done it a hundred times. After removing her little jacket, he stopped to admire the meal he meant to make of Alice's breasts peeking over the red silk of the shift. He caressed her left nipple with his remarkably smooth fingers as he circled the right one with his tongue. Alice moaned softly and wrapped her legs around his waist.

"Patience, my lovely angel, the whole night is ours." His breath against her nipple made her moan again.

"Please, Jacques. I want you inside me, please."

"Ah, I cannot let you want in vain." In one lightning move, he untied and removed the hoop and petticoat, raised her skirt, and plunged deep into her.

The candlelight was reflected in his eyes now locked on hers. She took in a deep breath. He slid in and out of her slowly, never taking his eyes from hers. As she got closer to coming with each stroke, he tightened his grip on her nipple. The pleasure was almost unbearable. *How could he know?* The eye contact and the little touch of tender sweet pain so perfectly close to her climax increased her pleasure beyond her imagination. His talented attentions made Alice come hard.

As she clung to him breathless, he whispered into her ear, "Now, my eager Alice, we will take our time." She felt him move off of her as she lay still, too stunned to move at all.

He tugged off her shift, and she again felt the weight of him. Alice always loved the feel of a man's weight. She was, as her grandmother once said, "a tall sturdy girl," and could take a good deal of man on top of her. She could feel the lean power of him against the length of her body, and she felt whole. She raised her legs again to allow him easier entry, but he just laughed.

"Soon enough, Alice. You are so well prepared to love me, I fear I cannot control myself." Now spreading her legs and kneeling between them, Jacques slipped his fingers into her liquid core. First one long smooth finger entered, then two and three. With his other hand, he stroked her clitoris. The fingers inside her spread slowly apart, stretching her as they slid in and out. One knuckle pressed the button of deep pleasure hidden there.

She came again quickly with a long loud cry. When she opened her eyes, his were only inches from hers. She felt his weight again as he slowly withdrew his fingers, and a smile spread slowly across his face—not a proud "look how hard I made you come" smile, but a hot and hungry smile that made her wet all over again.

This time as she raised her legs, he said only, "Yes, my angel."

Alice felt him enter, but not hard, as she expected. He eased into her slippery folds slowly and tenderly. She could feel the muscles of his thighs and stomach contract against her with each thrust, his eyes still locked on hers. Jacque gently kissed each of her eyelids. His expression was not one she'd ever seen on a man's face during sex. Jacque's eyes worshiped her. He celebrated sex with her like a sacrament, each thrust and resulting moan, a sacred holy act.

Alice closed her eyes to remember. Opening them, she saw only the side of his face tight against hers as he lay still on top of her. His wavy dark hair had escaped its binding and a stray strand lay across her eyes. She couldn't move, but just breathe and savor the masculine weight of him. She felt his heart beat against her breasts.

Alice lay content, wondering at this man. Clearly, she'd had more experience of late with men, mostly in her head of course, but Jacques imaginary or not was no ordinary fantasy. He said softly against her ear, "Shall we have some more wine, Alice? It is a good vintage, yes?"

He could have suggested setting her on fire right this minute and she probably would have agreed. "Of course, Jacques."

They drank wine and ate more duck with truffles. When his hunger for her grew impossible to ignore, he took her back to the bed and they continued their previous activities. She finally fell asleep with Jacques wrapped around her.

❧

Clinical Notes on Client Hightower, Alice B.

Client continues to describe vivid sexual fantasies in an agitated manner. When asked directly if she believed them to have actually happened, client responded, "Of course not, that would be insane." Some symptoms less present this day and her ability to function still remains remarkable. Issues with feelings of failure and unworthiness were discussed; the roots of same seem to stem from childhood. Client's hyper-sexuality will make possibility of transference a serious concern. Medication was recommended and refused.

Chapter Three

HELPLESSLY HOPING

This morning Alice woke and just lay in her bed, remembering. Last night's offering was not just any man, this Jacques Seingalt. She treasured the memory of how it felt when he touched her face, her breasts, her... She wondered if he could have been a real historical person. Of course not; none of these fantasies were real and Dr. Elliot had made sure she admitted it. They were merely the products of her hyper-sexual bipolar delusions. At least her current hallucinations were unbelievably entertaining. That she felt no fear during these fantastic occurrences was further proof of her insanity. These were strange men in strange times, and yet she'd savored every second.

Alice rarely used an alarm clock. Her days would not start with some screaming little box ripping her from her sleep and dragging her into the day. Her nights had become too precious to end that way. At Otis's meow, she opened her eyes.

"Chill, fuzzbucket. You are the prettiest kitty in the world," she said to the cat. Alice needed to wash away all the imaginary evidence of her delusions. Did she see, as she soaped, a few scratches and a faint bite mark on her left breast? Of course not. Reaching up to the showerhead, she felt the water run through her fingers. No matter how tightly she squeezed, she couldn't hold the water in her hands. Like happiness, it always dripped through her fingers. But she felt happy right this minute, in this shower, and that would have to be enough.

As she arranged her dark blonde hair into a casual French twist and clipped it into place, she thought she could see redness on her chin. "Who knew an imaginary man's stubble would leave so much evidence?" she said to her reflection.

"Well worth it," the smiling pink face in the mirror answered.

Alice never wore much makeup, only a little mascara, to play up her best feature—her blue-green eyes. The mirror reflected nothing else remarkable. Her cheekbones were nice and high, but her nose was too long and her chin a little too prominent. Alice considered herself neither plain nor beautiful, but "pretty" might apply when she felt happy. When she smiled, her eyes turned up at the corners and the planes of her face softened someone once told her.

She dusted on a little extra powdered concealer as if anyone else could see the beard-burn of her night's passionate pursuit. Still, better safe than snickered about. She couldn't have any of Excellcardia's three hundred and eighty-four employees snickering about the boss's personal life. At forty-nine, it was difficult enough to play the "Iron Lady" without them snickering. She preferred they continue to think of her as not quite human. As long as no one could see the secrets she kept locked away, she would be golden.

A hot pink power suit fit her mood today perfectly. The little peplum on the jacket flattered her figure, she thought, although hiding her ass with a long blazer was like a snake hiding a deer by swallowing it. Black pumps with dangerously high heels completed her look.

She grabbed a backup pair in case of a broken heel. Somehow this happened about twice a month, and she'd learned to accept it. Who'd mind an opportunity to buy new shoes? A last once-over in the mirror revealed a presentably professional picture of a CEO. As for the body she saw in the mirror, it had never been perfect, and age had certainly enhanced its lack of perfection, but the opposite sex still to seemed to find her tasty enough—at least in her nightly imaginings.

Otis jumped on the sink as she dropped in some eye drops. "I'm sorry, big fella. I know you miss our nights together." Alice couldn't help but wonder if she were really here all night, why did Otis seem to miss her in the morning? Did her wild imaginary sleep-sex thrashing keep him from sleeping curled up next to her? "Silly cat. Cat love can't compare to man love, little buddy, even imaginary men. Maybe I should get you a brother. Mine has never done me any good. Cat brothers are bound to be better."

She rubbed his huge black head, and he made the appropriate cat-bliss rumble. Otis was a large cat. At twenty-two pounds, he approached the size of a small dog. His purr was not the little pop-pop of some kitties, but a chainsaw-deep rumble, the perfect reward for a loving head rub.

This morning, she hummed as she took the elevator to the garage where her baby slept—a torch-red 2001 Porsche Carrera. It had always been her favorite model of car and she had paid dearly to have it meticulously restored. The sports car, though a foolish splurge, always made her smile when she saw it. She'd earned a good deal of money in the last two decades, which made little difference to her. Alice saved a nickel of every dime she made. The years and dollars spent to achieve her business goals had taught her that much. It had been no smooth climb. One never knew when a company would restructure, with unemployment the terrifying result. Alice had been restructured out of a job twice in her career. Being CEO offered little protection. Replacing the CEO seemed to be the cure for many a company's financial ills these days. It was a risk Alice was willing to take.

Highway 270 was truly the "Highway to Hell" and usually slowed to a crawl by now. Humming to herself happily, she wondered a little at the absence of cars in the parking lot. It wasn't until she approached the automatic door, and it didn't open that she realized something was wrong. Today was Sunday.

Alice felt as if someone had just let the air out of her sanity balloon. *Dr. Elliot was right, getting worse is inevitable.* She turned to walk back to her car.

Only then did she notice Jonathan's Miata in its space next to hers.

Pulling out her cell phone, she called his desk.

"Hello," he said. "Ms. Hightower's office," would have been his weekday response.

"Jonathan, what are you doing here on Sunday? Can you come down and let me in?"

"Certainly, Alice, but what are you doing here yourself?" He sounded much less serious than usual. When she did not answer, he said, "I'll be right down."

She'd forbidden him to call her "ma'am" or even "Ms. Hightower" long ago. They worked too closely together for formalities. She knew he respected her, and Alice was her name. Sometimes he called her "Boss." That somewhat sarcastic address was reserved for those rare occasions when she had done something completely un-boss-like, such as ordering him to go home after ten-hour days.

He stood waiting at the door by the time she got there. How did he get there so fast? Maybe he really was Clark Kent in more than his looks. Alice gave a tiny sigh of disappointment that he wasn't wearing his usual lovely business suit this Sunday morning. Today he wore jeans and an off-white fisherman's sweater that hugged his chest and shoulders wonderfully. *Well, that will do. It is Sunday.*

He smiled at her through the glass as he punched in the codes to open the door.

"I figured I would drop by and pick up some files I forgot. Thank goodness you were here." She hoped her story sounded even slightly believable.

"You can work the codes from the outside of the door, too. The little gray covered box has a keypad." Jonathan gave her an amused look through the glass.

"Oh. To tell you the truth, I can never remember them."

"Alice, the code is your birthday 1, 19, 68.

She shrugged and walked through the open glass door. They rode the elevator to the twenty-third floor, and he pushed the door to her inner sanctum all the way open for her. He then put the doorstop in place and followed close behind her. She always assumed he wanted the door open because he didn't want to miss anything that went on inside her office. It seemed a little odd today with no one but the two of them in the building.

"Just can't stay away?" Jonathan shot her a sidewise glance.

"Of course not. I—uh."

"No matter. I'm glad for the company. I've made some coffee, strong and nasty as you like it. Six packets of sweetener and it's your perfect poison." He looked at her with amusement. Not waiting for an answer, he poured her a cup from the credenza near the window. Ripping open and dumping in the yellow sweetener packets, Jonathan stirred the coffee and walked around her desk to hand it to her.

Alice sat staring at her desk until she got the courage to speak.

"Jonathan, I have to tell you something." She looked at the floor and swallowed hard. Her heartbeat roared in her ears and her cheeks felt hot. *How can I tell him something I've never said out loud even to myself? Maybe it's time I told us both.* "I'm sure you've noticed I've been having some trouble lately with things I normally shouldn't have trouble with."

"You're under a good deal of extra stress of late. The BioCardia line alone is a tremendous risk. I'm sure it will pay off brilliantly, but the initial R & D outlay right now is massive. I need to make sure—"

She set the coffee cup on the desk and stood to put her index finger on his lips for a second, then took a step back. "No, that's just making excuses. I am beyond that. I'm sure you've seen the mood swings, difficulty concentrating, forgetting things I shouldn't. I—uh—have been seeing someone and —well, I've been evaluated. I'm seeing a doctor for bipolar disorder. I think I may be losing my mind." She looked up into his eyes and saw compassion, not fear or doubt or disbelief. Then pain, as if he'd heard something terrible about someone important to him. She quickly looked away, clearing her throat. "Well. Do you still want to work for a crazy woman?"

"Bipolar disorder is a manageable condition. You are far from crazy, Alice. I think the BioCardia line is quite possibly genius, and it's your baby." Jonathan took a step closer to her and put his hands on her shoulders. "I'll work for you as long as you'll have me."

Still no pity on his face, only concern, reassurance, and affection. Alice knew he wasn't in love with her no matter what Louise said. He was simply an excellent, caring, and loyal employee.

"What are you really doing here?" Alice backed away, sat down in a chair, and pretended great interest in the bottom of her coffee cup.

"The handout for the meeting with the board tomorrow. I wanted to make a few corrections." His voice trailed off. Something of what she felt must have shown in her face.

"You were here fixing my report," she said softly. "You were covering for me. Weren't you?"

"It's not covering. Editing is part of my job, and like it or not, your comma use is random at best." Jonathan shuffled the papers in his hands.

"Look, I appreciate your help. We do make a good team. Just know that there may come a time when you can't cover for me sufficiently. There may come a time when—"

He put his finger to her lips this time. He didn't remove it as quickly as she had, but held it there, brushing her lower lip tenderly. "That will never happen."

She rolled her chair back a foot to escape the gravity of him, and he looked embarrassed. "It may, Jonathan. I know exactly what can happen. My mother is in an institution, remember. Someday I may have trouble telling what's real and what isn't." Alice felt tempted to tell him about her adventures, but then he would know she was already crazy. This made her laugh a little. His surprise at her unexpected laughter reassured her she'd made the right decision.

"Well," he said, "anytime you doubt your sanity, just ask me."

"It's a deal, Jonathan. Now let's go over that report once more. I'm the one who'll look like an idiot tomorrow if it's not perfect. I just pray the board agrees BioCardia's genius deserves a budget increase and isn't just a huge waste of millions of dollars."

"It's brilliant, Alice. It's what the industry needs right now. Stem cell technology will soon dominate every market in the health care field. As long as you don't use embryonic cells, nobody cares. The research was a bit pricey, but once it comes online and docs will use nothing else."

"First we have to get the patents and clearances. I've heard a rumor that Patterson Tech has something similar in development."

"Oh, I seriously doubt it." Jonathan took a sip of his coffee and sat on the edge of her desk. "The process is all Dr. Petrus. He's odd, but nobody does cell growth better. He could get human cells to grow on this marble." Jonathan tapped the top of her desk, and she noticed his long, slender, perfectly manicured fingers. *I wonder if he plays the violin or—stop it, Alice, now!*

Looking out the window, Alice noticed another familiar car in the parking lot. "Hey, isn't that Brad James's car?"

He joined her at the window. "I believe so. Why would he be here today?" Jonathan said. Alice felt her heart race the way is always did at the mention of her Vice President of sales.

"Louise doesn't trust him. What do you think?"

"He's certainly good at what he does. He doesn't strike me as quite genuine, I'm afraid."

"Well, I appreciate anyone dedicated enough to show up on Sunday." She shot him a teasing look and headed to the elevator. "I think we should ask him," she called to Jonathan who hurried to catch up.

She had intended to go to Brad's office, but the elevator light showed someone had stopped on the tenth floor.

"What would he be doing in the research lab on Sunday?" Jonathan's dark brows knitted into a fierce line.

Alice's heart rate doubled, and her mouth went desert dry. This felt terribly wrong. Brad has no business in the lab even on a weekday, much less on Sunday when the place was deserted. *Please don't let anything jeopardize BioCardia. Please, please, please!*

When they reached the tenth floor, both Jonathan and Alice broke into a little trot to the door at the end of the hall, dedicated for the last year to BioCardia. The largest of all the research labs, this one now required a retinal scan to open the door. Alice's heart pounded in her chest as she looked into the red light of the retinal scanner. Her thoughts raced. Did Brad know enough about the project to indulge in industrial espionage? The scientific information in BioCardia would be worth a fortune to a competitor. Alice's thoughts raced. "Retina identified," the emotionless computer voice said.

The door slid open to reveal a silver-haired man in nylon

athletic pants and a black sweater that emphasized his lean build. He held the leash of an ancient basset hound who wagged his tail enthusiastically at the sight of Alice.

"Barney," Alice dropped to her knees and rubbed the dog's head and gray muzzle. He wasn't just an old dog; he was critical to the success of her presentation.

"I live close, and sometimes I come by to take our star outside for a little walk." Brad smiled at Alice.

The lines of his face were smooth and relaxed, with a smile. The look he most often wore could have been loosely called a smile, with every muscle tensed and his brows scrunched into a half-scowl. No matter how good he looked today, if she found out he'd done anything to endanger this project, she would strangle him herself with Barney's leash.

"Barney doesn't need to go outside to relieve himself. The exercise area has a self-cleaning turf for that purpose."

Brad crouched down beside the dog, now eye to eye with Alice. Suddenly she found it hard to breathe, let alone think. Dread saved her. This dog and this presentation meant her job and her job was her life.

"He doesn't need any additional stress. You have no authority to take him anywhere. You're putting an important part of tomorrow's presentation at risk. This is reckless, Brad."

"Sure enough, Boss Lady. But he's a dog. He needs to see the sun and pee on the grass once in a while. I don't let him chase squirrels. Dr. P. okayed it." Brad stood up but continued to smile down at her.

The basset rolled over to his side as Alice rubbed his belly. She gently ran her fingers over the long pink scar on his chest. Then she stood, "I appreciate your sentiment, but that dog does not leave this floor today. Am I clear, Brad?"

"Aye, aye, skipper." Brad saluted but gave her a wholly inappropriate and extremely smoldering look. He turned and headed back down the hall to the dog cages, slowly trailing the old dog.

"He seems genuinely concerned about the dog," Jonathan said. "Anybody who'd give up some of his weekend to walk a lonely old dog has some good points."

"People can use kindness as a cover, Jonathan. I want Chuck from security notified. There will be no unauthorized dog walking. No animals will leave the lab without my okay. Until the processes are approved, and the device cleared, security must be air-tight. Alice took a deep reassuring breath and still tried hard not to think of those eyes.

❧

On Sundays, Alice usually prepared for the week ahead. She had to pick up and put away laundry, buy food, and organize things unorganized. Everything that had somehow moved from its proper place had to be returned to it. Anything crooked had to be straightened. Every speck of foreign matter must be removed from the snowy whiteness of her pristine couch. Her shoes had to be placed in a completely straight line around the floor of her closet, toes pointing out, of course. Having things out of place made Alice uneasy. The universe needed order, and she needed to impose it. It might make up for the disorder gathering in her head.

Once these important tasks were completed, there might be time for lunch with Susan or a walk in Forest Park, but today's little weekend trip to the office had used up all this Sunday's discretionary time. The rest of her afternoon would be needed to review the BioCardia presentation yet again.

She paced and read the BioCardia script for tomorrow's presentation to the board. Alice managed to shove her fear of industrial espionage down some, but every once in a while, a twinge of fear would speed up her heart. A company's fortunes could be made by stealing the right process or device and saving all the research and development funds. She was afraid these days, theft was much more common than actual research and hard work. This was her first major project as CEO, the first project she'd been a part of from the beginning. She'd been promoted mostly on the promise of this project. It required a metric-crap-ton of cash and energy, but it was revolutionary and could make or end her career. She took a deep relaxing breath and hoped with every fiber of her body for the former to be true. She would call Security Chuck herself, first thing in the morning.

Alice felt a little dizzy and couldn't remember if she had eaten today. "Hmmm, what will it be, Otis? Spaghetti-Os or ravioli?" Canned or frozen delights were all she ever bought. Alice found grocery shopping incredibly difficult. She had four degrees, but the overwhelming number of trivial choices in the store undid her. To handle the stress of it, Alice had resorted to picking up staples once per month. She got the same three kinds of frozen dinners, three kinds of canned pasta, and precooked bacon that as far as she could tell never expired. It never expired because it probably wasn't actually food, but a delicious combination of grease and chemicals with a little pig waved over it. Once a week she would stop at the local Quik-Trip, fuel her car, and grab some eggs and butter. Eggs were the one fresh food she couldn't do without. Alice ate two every morning, when she remembered, because brains needed B vitamins to function. *Even a messed-up bipolar brain.*

"Okay, Otis, spaghetti with mini-meatballs it is." Alice sighed, remembering the wonderful duck she'd dreamed of the night before and the amazing man she'd shared it with in her dream. Alice stuck the container in the microwave for sixty seconds. She preferred food that came in microwavable plastic containers because you could eat right out of them. Washing dishes was an activity to be avoided. To do dishes, you had to buy soap and towels and all kinds of things Alice had no idea about. Her fancy black dishwasher had been used exactly twice in four years, and Susan ran it both times. Alice thoroughly rinsed the spoon she used and put it back in the drawer.

There was just enough time for the elliptical and a shower before sunset.

❧

Her hand shook a little with anticipation as she opened the closet door. Tonight's hangers were in the closet as expected. There were two. One held a floor length formal gown made of rich green silk. A black fur wrap hung on the second hanger. A pair of black kitten heeled pumps lay on the floor next to a pair of lacy black panties and a black satin mask. The dress's high-waisted style seemed reminiscent of a few hundred years past, but the modern workmanship and label that read, "Custom Costume Couture," told her otherwise. The panties were completely modern, and the wrap looked like one hanging in her other closet.

When Alice checked the look in the mirror she felt ready for whatever party this gorgeous gown would get her into." The gown hung sensuously off her shoulders with large, puffed sleeves gathered at her wrist in black lace cuffs. It revealed much more cleavage than Alice would have been comfortable with in the real world. The dress barely covered her nipples in a daring plunge southward nearly to her navel. *No wonder there was no bra.*

She slipped on the mask and opened her balcony door. The crisp air and fading light of sunset showed her a familiar scene. She knew where she was immediately. These were the concrete stairs leading to the Sheldon Concert Hall in her own home-town. The air smelled of humidity and car exhaust. She and her ex-husband had been there several times for various perfor-mances. Above the entrance a large banner proclaimed, "A Night in Venice."

"Coolest," Alice said. She carried no purse, as the closet hadn't given her one, and she hoped no invitation was required to get in. *I make up the rules, so probably not.* Two men in tuxedos stood behind a table. One man's suit hung on him as if he had rented it, then lost half his body weight.

"Your name, please," said the man whose tux wore him.

"Alice Hightower." She saw no reason to be anybody else.

"Of course, Ms., Hightower. Thank you so much for your extremely generous donation. There are so many homeless kitties who will lead better lives for your generosity."

The other man said, "Please enjoy the many delights of our Venetian Carnival. We're so pleased to host an amazing evening for our most generous patrons." This man looked a bit familiar, though she couldn't think from where. His tuxedo squeezed just a tad too tight. She thought better of asking the two men to switch clothes and flashed what she hoped looked like a benevolent, kitty-loving smile. This was her favorite charity even in the daylight. After all, she had found Otis at "Open Door."

In fact, Alice thought the whole affair seemed familiar. She'd given a rather large amount to "Open Door" sanctuary a couple of months ago, and she thought she remembered getting a pretty post card saying an invitation to a formal event would follow. Who knew how her brain made up these escapades? She hadn't decided whether or not to go, but maybe her brain provided a what-the-hell-if situation. She read once that dreams often are our unconscious attempt to answer questions or solve problems. Dr. Elliot would probably be glad to hear this extremely logical explanation of this adventure.

Somewhere off to her right, Alice heard the stains of a baroque string quartet. The large foyer was full of scores of people in elegant costumes. The women wore long gowns of rich velvets and satins in an array of rich blues, reds and purples. The men wore black pants, white full sleeved shirts with long cloaks over the outfits. Everyone wore a mask. Some were simple black satin like Alice's own. Others wore elaborate masks of various designs complete with black, silver or gold feathers.

Waiters dressed like clowns circulated with trays of golden bubbly liquid in elegant flutes. These were not ordinary modern clowns with grease-paint faces. Each server wore a harlequin half-red half-black satin costume, with a huge neck ruff and puffed sleeves and pant legs. White masks covered their faces. The waiter's masks were strange glossy white things. Half of each mask wore a frown and the other half an exaggerated smile.

"I wonder how much you had to give to get the gold feathers," Alice said to no one in particular. Grabbing a flute off the tray of a passing clown, she surveyed the room. A few feet away, Alice noticed an interesting figure. The man's chest stretched the material of his puffy white shirt attractively. He wore some sort of black hood connected to a more elaborate version of the waiter's harlequin mask and looked well over six feet tall. It was half silver and half gold and exposed only his eyes and the lower half of his face. He smiled at her almost like he knew her. She smiled back. The handsome drink of water extended his hand.

Alice closed the space between them with a single step and took that hand. She smiled again as she noticed his eyes were the exact color of a Dove milk chocolate. The man put two fingers to his lips. She chugged her champagne and set the glass on the nearest clown's tray. He led her between masked folk to the concert hall proper. A soprano stood on stage singing an aria accompanied by a string quartet. The dark concert hall, lite by a single spot on the singer, had an eerie quality. The room must have been full of people, but it was far too dark to see them.

The man led her smoothly and quietly along a side wall of the hall to a curtain. The hand holding hers felt smooth and strong. He moved the curtain aside, led her behind it and pulled her to him. She felt him remove his mask before his lips found hers in the darkness. He tasted like champagne and good caviar and kissed like an expert.

He brushed her lips softly at first with his own. Alice let out a little moan. Again the fingers to her lips as he whispered against her ear. "Silence, or audience will hear us."

He reached down her bodice, caressed her breasts with one hand, and covered her mouth with the other. It was all she could do to remain silent as he gently, slowly, torturously caressed her. He pulled up her gown's long shirt and skillfully maneuvered his finger beneath the black panties into her liquid center. His fingers stroked her clit, and it took everything she had not to join the singer in a loud exclamation of appreciation. Next he slid the panties down her legs, and she stepped out of them. His tongue was on her lips and in her mouth again teasing and tasting her.

He dropped silently to his knees. Alice pulled the long skirt up to her waist as his tongue explored her. She couldn't have him smothering to death under that skirt before he finished the important task at hand. Alice leaned against the wall to keep from collapsing as he stroked her slippery flesh with his tongue.

Just when she didn't care if anyone heard her, he stopped and pulled away. Again he took her hand and led her through the complete darkness up three steps onto the dimly lit stage. A heavy curtain across the back of the stage separated them from the performers and the audience. Faint blue light from the spot on the singer came through a small opening in the curtain. The space between this curtain and a wall was several feet wide. *What delicious performance does maestro have in mind?*

The man again knelt and, placing his hands on her waist, guided her to kneel beside him. He pulled her close enough to kiss her, unzipped her gown to free her breasts and raised her skirt again. Alice wondered how much it would cost to clean the gown, but that was the fantasy fairy's problem, not hers. The clothes were always gone from the closet in the morning. His pants were open, and he was inside her in an instant.

Alice reached up to remove his mask and stopped her with his hands soft but insistent.

"Not yet," he whispered. His long slow strokes erased any concern about this unknown man who seemed to have reason to stay unknown. There was only the pleasure from his lips, his hands, his cock.

Alice gasped. The man pulled out of her and put his fingers to her lips.

"Come," he murmured.

"I was just about to." She saw him smile in the faint light. He has a great smile, and he was well equipped to satisfy. Who the hell cared who he is?

The man tucked in his shirt, zipped his pants slowly and silently, and replaced his mask just as she got close enough to the light to see him clearly. He pulled Alice close, kissing her neck as he slowly zipped up her gown. Silent again, he turned and led her along the wall to a door he opened just enough to squeeze through. He held the door open, and Alice wiggled through the opening, squishing her chest flat to fit. They stood in a hallway flooded with light and full of people.

Alice felt quite sure the people standing at a nearby buffet table could tell by the silly look on her face and her pink cheeks, exactly what they had been doing. Not that she cared. She looked down at the man's hand holding hers. Beautiful, tapered fingers held her hand like a treasure he couldn't bear to part with. He led her down the hall away from the crowd and opened a door. There were no lights on, and Mr. Do-It-In-The-Dark-Silently made no effort to find any.

He weaved between large dark shapes in the room as if he knew it well. As her eyes adjusted to the darkness, Alice could make out a harp, a tuba and some shapes that might be drums. He stopped near a piano. Taking off his cloak, he spread it on the floor. *Oh goody. Maybe now this maestro can finish this piece.*

The mysterious man unzipped his pants and kissed her

again. Unzipping her gown, this time he slid the dress down over her shoulders. She stepped out of it.

"I think I left my panties backstage, Maestro," she said. The man said nothing. He took a step back and from the rustling of cloth she hoped he'd removed his clothes. Now Alice felt a little irritated she couldn't see well enough to enjoy the vision undoubtedly hidden beneath those clothes.

The man removed the hood but left his mask in place. In an instant she was on the floor, her legs wrapped around him, enjoying the wondrous weight of him on her. He entered her slowly, as if savoring a long-anticipated moment.

"My lovely, precious, Alice." He spoke in a course whisper.

"You know my name. Can't I know yours?" she said.

His strokes stopped. "How often you have screamed it in passion's throws," whispered the man. Alice reached up and ran her fingers through his thick hair. He quickened his stokes. She wrapped her legs tighter to pull him deeper inside. He stopped just as she was about to climax. Kissing her, he began again slowly. She could feel the power in his muscles as they contracted against her. He increased his pace again and as she was about to come, he stopped.

"You are going to kill me," she said.

"La petit mort." Again the whisper. He seemed to be taking pains not to let her hear his voice. She quickly let any concerns go as his long slow strokes sped up. This time Alice stopped. The man collapsed against her. She'd learned the game. Get as close to climax as possible and stop. Each time they began again the pleasure increased exponentially.

They continued for ten more cycles of fucktus interruptus until the cataclysmic orgasm struck Alice dumb. She had neither the will nor the energy to make a sound. They lay silently panting. Alice felt hungry and meant to suggest that they try some of the buffet she'd spied earlier. She closed her eyes for a moment.

❦

Clinical notes on Client Hightower, Alice B.

This session concentrated on client's past history with men. Last relationship lasted seven years. Client related never feeling any passion between them. The relationship ended when husband left her for a much younger woman. A deep-seated sense of self-loathing and body image issues may stem from this. Ms. Hightower offered her own preoccupation with her career as an explanation for the disintegration of her marriage. She alluded to the fact she felt ill equipped to choose an appropriate partner. He had pursued her, and she reported it was "Just easier to give in and marry him." It was then suggested this difficulty choosing the right partner was perhaps the source of the fantasies.

Chapter Four

BOOGIE SHOES

A lice paced. Even memories of last night couldn't calm this morning's jitters. Today she would attempt to impress the Excellcardia board of directors and get approval for a much larger budget than originally been proposed. The Biocardia Project had far exceeded its original cost estimate and could not proceed without a juicy cash infusion. It wouldn't be easy to talk the board out of another cent, let alone fifty million dollars.

Alice looked at her reflection in the glass window of her office as she paced. She had chosen her clothes carefully this morning. She couldn't decide whether to play up to the sleepy old geezers on the board by working her femininity, or choose something ultra-conservative, but in the end she'd opted for the conservative choice. A navy suit with a bit of crimson trim for pizzazz.

She looked at her shoes as she proceeded to wear a rut in the short pile of her office's white carpet. This terribly important morning, Alice picked a pair of scarlet satin peep-toe platform stilettos. Who cared if they were summer shoes? These magnificent beauties cost two hundred dollars and would make her six foot two inches tall. *Now these are the shoes of a*

CEO. By walking a little more slowly and carefully than normal, she could manage them. Concentrating on trivial things chased away the flop-sweat fear of failure for a couple of heartbeats. She continued to distract herself and examined her reflection in her office window once again.

Alice had taken extra time with her hair this morning. Her nice shade of dark blonde needed some highlights, she noticed. Last night's concert seemed to have left her cheeks and chin with a slight pink beard burn. Of course that couldn't really be the cause. She needed to check into some sheets with a higher thread count. The Hightower skin could be terribly sensitive. Alice remembered as a teenager how the pillowcase would have spots of blood on it when she woke, the result of whatever new acne treatment her mother was experimenting with at the moment.

"No one in history has ever had such skin," said Beverly Hightower to teenage Alice. She had always laughed when mother said things like that. How could she have known about all of history? Alice was grateful her acne had not left scars and had served a useful purpose. Acne and loose-fitting shirts had kept mother's boyfriends from paying much attention to her. She certainly couldn't have escaped to a friend's house back then. Making friends was one of the social skills that eluded her until her sophomore year in college.

Time to concentrate. Alice looked down at the script one more time and paced in a different direction. BioCardia would be a brilliant advancement in medical devices. Once more money was approved by the board. The FDA would clear the device for human trials. With the patents approved, the device could be cleared, and fame and fortune would follow hopefully. Alice prayed the success of the dog trials couldn't help but impress.

The Excellcardia board had an unfortunate history of conservatism. This time they had to be reasonable. This project would revolutionize the bypass device market. Patients would no longer have to endure two surgical procedures and suffer the healing of two surgical sites. The harvesting of leg vessels would be unnecessary. The BioCardia vessels were better and even more cost-effective than the old, harvested vessels. Less surgical time, less recovery, and the use of a 3-D printer to print the matrix would keep the manufacturing costs down. Now she just had to convince them.

§

"Well, Alice, this is the day, three years in the making. Today our incredible advancement can't help but impress the board." Jonathan's voice over her shoulder made her jump a few inches. She was thankful she didn't fall off her shoes. His suit this morning was a sophisticated black and his tie lavender. *Does he know that's my favorite of all his ties?*

Alice looked up at him hoping she didn't look like a fool. His eyes swept over her and rested on her shoes. She couldn't read his face. Shock or disapproval? "Too much?" Her voice shook slightly. "I have some plain black pumps in my desk. I just thought bold might be…"

"Perfect." The reassuring look he returned went a long way to calming her nerves.

Usually she had a sixth sense about what was right or not right in her wardrobe and almost every aspect of her life—except men, of course. Her judgment in that direction had never been good.

Lately she wasn't so sure about other aspects. Was her previously excellent judgment failing her? She knew poor judgment could be a cardinal symptom of bipolar disorder. Jonathan's reassurance calmed her nerves. If he lied, he deserved a raise for it.

§

"Thank you. I shouldn't be nervous. I've dealt with this board for three years and they trust me." Alice realized she was pacing again. Remembering her mother's pacing, she stopped, sat in her chair and tried desperately to keep her hands still.

"They know the genius of it. You remember how enthusiastic they were when the project was suggested. These new salient details of Biocardia, our star subject, and some potential profit projections will do the trick. We have come this far and without more funds it can't go forward. I am not sure the board cares about saving lives. Most of them look like they could use a few new cardiac vessels. But I am certain they care about profits."

In the last couple of years so much had fallen away in Alice's life, and taken some confidence with it. She hadn't been hopelessly in love with Robert, but when he left her for a woman twenty years younger, insecurity about her looks crept up on her. Even her recent incendiary and completely inappropriate affair only made her feel worse about herself, with good reason. *How could I have been so stupid?*

A brief knock and the door opened wider. Brad James walked in, beaming and holding Barney's leash.

"He's ready for his close-up. He's been walked, fed, bathed, and here is his EKG." Brad handed Alice a folder. "His injection fraction is amazing, and he smells like a spring meadow with a hint of dog breath."

Today Brad wore a lovely blue suit cut like he had a tailor on retainer. The sky-blue shirt and deep blue tie made his eyes seem even bluer than usual. Alice forced herself to look only at the dog.

Louise stuck her head in. Though she smiled, her deeply furrowed brows betrayed her concern. "Okay, kids, this is it. They're all in the main conference room. Let's get this show on the road."

They all agreed that Alice and Barney should make a dramatic entrance. Louise, Brad, and Jonathan walked into the large conference room first. Alice knew the layout of the conference room and waited for her instructions to be followed. Around the long onyx table were thirteen chrome and white leather chairs, six on each side and one at the head. All the chairs would be occupied save the one at the head of the table. Along one wall there were four other chairs, and Alice's supporting trinity would take those seats. The eight men and four women of the board would need time to make useless small talk, Alice knew.

Five minutes later, Alice walked in with Barney, and the room fell silent. *I will not trip, I will not trip, I will not.* She took a deep breath and led the gray-muzzled basset in like he was Westminster's Best in Show.

"This is Barney Clark. Barney is fifteen, which, for a basset, is ancient." She let go of his leash and wagging his tail, he ran to the closest board member. *Mrs. Carlisle. Good choice, Barney.* The stern white-haired woman reached down to pet him and grinned like a six-year-old girl. He gave a little bounce and put his paws on her chair, revealing the long pink scar on his chest.

"As you can see by the freshly healed scar on his chest, Barney's had revolutionary bypass surgery. His ancient cardiac vessels have been replaced by BioCardia vessels. These vessels were produced in our lab and were implanted a month ago." Alice pushed a button and a screen dropped down from the ceiling to cover the entire wall behind her. She stepped to the side and continued.

"His old, tired vessels were removed and, unlike in humans who now have to undergo a second surgery to harvest leg vessels, the BioCardia vessels were implanted in a surgery lasting less than an hour. Because the vessels were exact copies of his originals in size, the surgical time is minimized. His original vessels were scanned."

Alice pushed a button on a wireless device and the picture on the screen changed. "After the scan of his vessels and repair of any and all defects and narrowing, a matrix was printed out on a 3-D printer. As you know, this matrix is a framework of a revolutionary material. The microscopically porous matrix material is then coated with cells from Barney, and within days the vessels resemble his own when he was just a puppy. After implantation, the matrix is absorbed by his body and, within three months the vessels are virtually indistinguishable from those he was born with. As you all undoubtedly know, ejection fraction is a percentage that describes how well his heart pumps. Barney's ejection fraction has improved by ninety percent. An improvement of this magnitude is remarkable."

Alice knelt down and Barney ran to her with the energy of a much younger dog. She rubbed his belly and looked up at the board members. She couldn't read the board members faces at all. No one made a sound. Had she dumbed it down enough? Didn't they see how important this could be for medicine and for Excellcardia?

It started slowly from the left side of the table, the clapping. In a minute, every board joined in the salute. Alice breathed again. Now for the pitch.

"Nothing like this has ever been attempted, and Excellcardia is on the verge of making it a reality. I'm sure you will all agree the additional funds required, found on the last page of your hand-out, are well worth it to give the world this medical miracle." Alice heard the sound of the board members' pages turning and then silence. She was certain she could hear Barney pant. *Carry on Alice, let it soak in.*

"Barney's had quite a morning, and I'm sure he has doggie business to do." Alice headed toward the door, pausing to face the board again. "Louise O'Neil is here to answer the manufacturing questions and discuss a possible timetable for production. Brad James will share a little about his plans for marketing and projected profitability. Of course, there will be the FDA to deal with. This road we travel will lead to the most bio-compatible and least invasive bypass surgery imaginable. With these additional funds, we can make this possible. Thank you, ladies and gentlemen."

Alice paced in her office. An hour later, Jonathan's face gave away nothing as he crossed the threshold to her office.

"Mostly good news, Alice." Jonathan produced a bottle of Dom Pérignon and two glasses from behind his back. She stood up from her seat at her desk and put her hands on her hips.

"Details, now!"

"They approved more funds but not the full fifty million we requested. They'll give us twenty now and they'll revisit the request after the patents and clearances come in. I think we still have grounds for celebration." Jonathan held up the glasses.

"I expected them to come in short of fifty million. So yes, I guess a small celebration is appropriate." Alice accepted the glass of champagne Jonathan poured for her.

Brad arrived. He strode across the room and wrapped his arms around Alice. She stiffened.

"I think I deserve some of that," he said releasing her but keeping his hand on the small of her back a little too long. Jonathan shot him a fiercely disapproving look. Brad returned the look in full measure. Alice ignored them both and drank her glass of champagne.

The rest of the day's business passed as usual after the short and muted celebration. There were meetings and more meetings. When Alice finally closed the door to her apartment, she thought briefly of falling into bed. But sunset was coming.

What adventure might wait on the other side of her balcony door?

It had been one bitch of a day, yet miraculously, at sunset Alice felt energized and eager. Had moved all her work suits to the hall closet so not to interfere with the magic, however it happened. In the closet hung a single piece of something silky. The off-white garment fell barely past the cheeks of her butt. It didn't quite cover the weird wiggly skin at the top of her thighs, but what the hell; cellulite didn't matter in Wonderland. A golden cord that must have been a sash lay on the floor beneath the hanger.

Her image in the mirrored door brought Alice no closer to guessing exactly what this outfit was. "An odd ancient tennis outfit?" she said out loud. There were no shoes and no underwear. A circle of leaves and flowers lay next to the sash. Too big for her wrist and too small for her waist; it had to go on her head.

"What kind of leaves are those?" Alice asked the mirror. It didn't answer, thank God. She tied the cord around her waist and set the leaves on her head. Pulling the tiny skirt down to cover as much of her as possible, she opened the sliding glass door.

Sunshine streamed in through a stone opening.

"Whoa!" she said, reaching up to shade her eyes. A long line of slender pine trees outside the glassless stone window led to what looked like the ancient Coliseum of Rome—except it wasn't a ruin. It stood gleaming in the distance, whole and new. There were no cars, paved city streets or souvenir vendors surrounding it.

Someone grabbed her roughly by the arm and spun her around. A young man dressed exactly like Alice glared at her. He said something that sounded like Latin, but she had no idea what his words meant. Too bad she only knew Latin from long ago medical school jargon. If he had asked her to take one tablet by mouth three times per day, she'd have been good.

The young man threw up his arms, rolled his brown eyes and motioned for her to follow him.

She followed him down a long narrow hall. The bleached white stones of the floor felt smooth and cool under her feet. On each side of the hall, brightly painted murals depicted scenes of a battle, men in chariots and on horseback hacking each other with short swords. She heard the murmur of voices, pierced by shouts and laughter, as they neared a large arched doorway draped in burgundy cloth.

The young man disappeared through the curtains and Alice followed into a huge circular room. A circle of marble columns inscribed a smaller circle in the room's center. The torches in sconces on the walls must have burned some scented oil, the huge room was not smoky but fragrant with lavender and sage. Beyond the circle, Alice glimpsed richly upholstered benches made for reclining, a low round table sat beside each couch. There must have been thirty or more evenly spaced around the perimeter of the room. Most benches were occupied by one or more reclining figures. People in short tennis outfits like Alice were sprinkled here and there between the couches. Her blond guide took her by the hand along the wall. Pointing to a line of three women and three men in shorty-short skirts, he gave her some orders she didn't understand and

Alice joined the line. What were the shorty toga wearers here to do? She'd watch and see.

Delicate blue wisps from the torches formed a pale blue veil shrouding the figures. She squinted to see through the haze. Some of the figures on the couches moved with the unmistakable rhythm of sexual pleasure and she heard moans of ecstasy.

"Oh my God," she said. "It's a Roman orgy. Good job, freaky brain. This is gonna be mega maximus fun!" Everyone else seemed too busy to notice she spoke a language that wouldn't exist in its current form for over a thousand years.

There were no couches along the wall where she stood, but

tables piled high with delicious-smelling food and tall earthen-ware jars of libations; wine, no doubt, and maybe mead. Huge platters held sliced meat. The delicious scent made her mouth water. An entire roasted peacock with the bright head and tail intact lay next to a whole piglet covered with figs. Large bowls were filled with bread that looked like pita pockets. Piles of figs dripped with honey, and grapes and pomegranates decorated silver platters.

Alice eyed the rest of her group standing against the wall. Though all were dressed like her, they were a mixed bag. Two of the three men looked to be under twenty. The third one seemed ancient, with short white hair and bowed legs that, though they made him look like a cartoon cowboy, didn't seem to hinder him at all. He was obviously in charge of carving. He wielded a huge knife that looked more like a sword and smiled as he filled plates.

All of the women were at least as old as Alice. She guessed they might have been chosen for something other than their gams. Hers were the best legs of the trio. Were the servants chosen for faithful service, or perhaps discretion?

"Hey, I guess this is the on-deck circle, right? How do you know what to bring and where to take it?" The woman next to Alice smiled at her without comprehension.

The woman farthest from Alice's end of the line watched the center of the room intently. Responding to a signal some-where in the room, she filled two gold-colored goblets with a red liquid. The servant skinny as a broomstick, had a shock of silver-streaked black hair and a spine bent at a nearly ninety-degree angle. The woman's posture affected her serving ability very little. She ran off toward a couch spilling not a single drop.

It must have been near dusk; the room grew steadily darker. There were no windows in the chamber, but smaller pillars supported a raised dome in the ceiling. The day's last sunbeams streamed in through openings between the pillars, focusing the light into the middle of the room.

A slightly raised stage was inscribed within a circle of light. A checkerboard pattern of red and black decorated the floor. Two pretty young women danced as another played a flute in the circle of light. There must have been torches outside the dome in the ceiling. As the daylight faded, from somewhere light continued to flood the center of the room through the pillars near the top of the dome.

As Alice watched, the three young women vanished into the room. Nine young men seemed to appear out of nowhere, wearing nothing but blindfolds and small black or red pieces of cloth around their waists. Each stood in a square on the checkerboard. Someone in the room shouted, and a gigantic man grabbed one of the young men, removed his scrap of clothing, and left it in the square on the floor. Another shout, and the giant hauled the young man off to the darker recesses of the room on his shoulders. This action repeated several times as Alice watched, fascinated. Only two servants stood near her now. "Tic-tac-toe," she said. "They're playing with clothes as markers." The woman she spoke to shot Alice a look she thought that said, "Stupid foreigner."

Finally, when there were three red loincloths in a line, clapping erupted and the remaining two young men were carried off and presumably delivered to someone.

The game was played a second time, this time with bare-breasted young women who squealed with delight as they were carried off to who-knows-where to do who-knows-what. Alice squinted into the gloom around the perimeter of the room. She could see few details, but the occasional squeal or series of moans left little doubt as to what activities were being enjoyed on those fancy couches.

It struck Alice at that moment that it was no accident that every one of these fantasies offered an opportunity for fantastic sex. As inappropriate as these nocturnal excursions would seem to some, they helped her scratch a persistent itch that had begun with a terrible mistake. The last time she'd tried to satisfy her yearning in the real world, her choice endangered her career and her company.

"So all we do is get people wine?" Alice turned to the woman next to her, who picked up two glasses of wine, took a sip from each, and ran off. Now, as Alice stood alone against the wall, she noticed two sentries a few feet away on either side of her.

"Oh goody, legionnaires," she said. It seemed okay to talk to oneself in fantastic locations. She had managed to break herself of delivering these audible monologues sophomore year at St. Louis University. Now that she had a cat, talking to him was even better, but probably just as nutty. Surely no one would think her odd in this fantastic situation of her own creation.

These ancient soldiers would have been totally at home in old Caesars Palace in Las Vegas. Short red tunics, strong muscular legs wrapped in the braided leather strands attached to sandals, and helmets decorated with horsehair brushes, confirmed her first impression. She marveled at the leather breastplate with sculpted abs and pecs each soldier wore and wondered if the man beneath the leather was as impressive as the costume. Alice swallowed hard and focused her attention on new action in the middle of the room.

Two gigantic men stood in the center circle of light, back to back, naked. One was tall, pale, and blond; the other just as tall, but as dark as his counterpart was pale. Both looked as if carved of stone. Muscles like those, she reflected, didn't come from serving wine. The crowd grew silent. Two women stepped forward from somewhere in the room. From their rich dress, they were no servants. Their gowns were long and decorated with gold and silver ribbons. One woman had a tower of dark hair woven with ropes of pearls. The other's light hair hung long and loose. Each woman seemed to make a choice and then knelt in front of the ebony or the ivory colossus.

"Oh, this is gonna be good, don't you think, Marcus Whoeverus?" Alice turned to the nearer of the two Roman soldiers. He nodded at her, but kept his eyes fixed on the stage. Did she imagine it or was he standing closer than before?

The women shed their clothes. One knelt, slowly rubbing the nipples of her large breasts with her thumbs. The other lay on her back with her fingers disappearing inside of her. It seemed they were trying to excite the huge men without touching them.

The blond man's cock rose to the occasion first, and the crowd clapped and cheered. When the black man's impressive erection manifested, the crowd began to chant. Shouts from around the room sounded to Alice like bidding. The shouts eventually stopped, and each man was led off into the darkness by his fluffer.

"Even if all I get to do is watch, it's one hell of a show." Alice leaned back against the smooth stone wall. As a naked man and woman appeared in the circle of light, one of the soldiers approached her with his helmet in his hand. His eyes were half closed, his chin lowered as if to charge her. He smiled at her with perfect white teeth and raised his eyebrows in an unspoken question.

"It's making me beyond horny too, Marcus, but…"

He took her hand and led her along the wall to a little alcove cut into the stone. It was certainly no private room, but it just might do. From her vantage, she could see two couches. On the one nearest to them, a middle-aged naked man rode a younger man. On the other she saw the blond giant's considerable endowment disappearing alternately into the vaginas of two women on their hands and knees side by side. He stood at the end of the couch and went from one to the other so quickly they seemed to climax at almost the same moment.

Alice's soldier turned her to him and kissed her roughly;

she kissed back. He smelled like pine branches and tasted a little of salty fish and olives. He put one hand on her breast and, reaching between her legs with the other, plunged two fingers into her. Conveniently, he stood a few inches taller than Alice. She leaned back against the wall and welcomed his exploration. His fingers were large, rough, and talented. He laughed low and said something she thought must be, "Damn, you are a wet little serving slut."

"Oh, yes, I am. Let's see what's under that dress, soldier." She reached out to take a very lovely erection in her hand, and gasped. "Hey! It's wearing a turtleneck."

She dropped to her knees. He was uncircumcised, something she had to see up close. As so recent a connoisseur of cocks, she couldn't help but marvel at the sheath of skin covering one of her favorite things in the entire world. She took it in her mouth, and her tongue circled the foreskin, gently tasting. She spent some time caressing his testicles and entwining her fingers in the thick curls she found there. Salty, masculine, and decidedly delicious.

"Ummmhh. I like that." Alice stood up and leaned back against the stone this time spreading her legs and arching her back in an obvious invitation. He slid his cock deep into her. Alice moaned. The angle of his attack drove his cock into her in the most perfect trajectory. *This must be why people fuck standing up.* He buried his face in her hair and continued to thrust into her until she let out another low moan as she came. He followed shortly with a loud moan and a grunt.

The soldier held her long after their climax nuzzling and kissing her neck. Who would guess ancient Roman soldiers liked to cuddle? Men could be so surprising. Maybe that's why she loved them so much—in her dreams, at least. She'd never realized how much she loved them before the adventures began. Men were so pretty, and they tasted so good. Just when you thought you knew them, they completely surprised you. And then they ripped out your heart or left you for someone half your age. Or you found out what a terrible liar they actually were, again leaving your heart in shreds.

Alice enjoyed the sensations as the warm product of their passion ran down her legs. Finally he let her go and stood close, looking into her eyes. His eyes were a light golden brown. Although his face bore an old, deep scar across his left cheek, from a battle she assumed, he was handsome. High cheekbones and a strong square jaw complemented his long classical Roman nose. The short cut she had seen on statues of ancient Romans, made the most of his curly black hair. He looked at her through his dark lashes. It didn't matter that she couldn't understand a word he said. They spoke the universal language of lust.

He kissed her again and led her by the hand along the wall. His kisses were hard and hungry. His mouth devoured hers. They stopped at another alcove in the stone wall. He backed into the recess, wrapped his arms around her and turned her to face the couches. He rested his chin on her shoulder. The sword-hardened arms held her gently.

"Well, I like to watch too, Marcus. You don't mind if I call you Marcus, do you? Of course you have no idea what I'm saying. It gives me quite an appetite too." Again they could see two couches clearly. On the one to the right, two men sat kissing. One looked to be in his forties at least and wore a rich robe and gold laurel leaves on his bald head. The man he was passionately kissing was about the same age; wore short dark curls and nothing else. Each held the other's erect cock and stroked gently. The only thing Alice liked more than one hard cock was two. Neither of those looked to be interested in pleasing her, evidently, but she didn't mind watching.

Tearing her eyes from the two men, she looked to the other couch. From this vantage she could see a woman, or at least the ass end of a woman who evidently had the upper half of her body on the floor. Only her enormous white posterior and gaping vagina were in clear view. The owner of the cavern evidently won the earlier bidding. Alice watched as the mountain of Nubian muscle rewarded his benefactor by plunging his impressive weapon into her. As she watched, Alice felt her soldier rise to the occasion against her.

"Doggie style it is, Marcus." She knelt down and spread her legs. They imitated the couple on the couch, climaxing just a little behind their entertainment.

Alice followed him from one alcove to another, finding something interesting to watch or imitate for the rest of this fantastic evening.

Exhausted by pleasure of historic proportions, Alice fell asleep sitting on the stone floor with her head on her legionnaire's shoulder.

Clinical Notes on Client Hightower, Alice B.

Continued discussion of relationships in an attempt to uncover need for nightly fantasies. Client avoided relationships during adolescence and college. Inappropriate attention from mother's partners offered as an explanation and dismissed. Continued to express dissatisfaction with her looks wholly inappropriate to reality. First husband was first sexual relationship and ended after twelve years. "We changed in different directions," the client reported. The end of marriage resulted in client's first related bout of clinical depression, lasting four weeks. "I felt like a failure at something women are not supposed to fail at," the client related. Six-year period of celibacy and second marriage after a brief courtship. Two failed marriages with limited previous sexual experimentation offered as an answer to client's need for fantasies. Sleeping medication was suggested and refused.

Chapter Five

I WANT A NEW DRUG

S he opened her eyes to bright sunshine streaming in. *Too much sunshine, she thought*, leaping out of bed. Her watch wasn't in its usual place on the nightstand. The clock in the kitchen said seven-fifty. Alice had never been late for work in her life. She was horrified. Damn Dr. Eliot, did he have to be right? Maybe she did need meds.

She called Jonathan. "I don't feel well, but I'll be in as soon as I can." So now she was lying to cover her symptoms?

"Don't worry. I pushed your eight o'clock meeting to tomorrow. The Dallas Presbyterian rep cancelled, so—"

"What? Why did they cancel? What did they say? Get Brad on it. They can't pull this crap again. If they won't come here, someone needs to go there. Get me a meeting with him as soon as possible." Her voice grew louder with each word.

"Alice, it will be fine. Come in when you feel better. I can take care of everything here. You—"

"No! I'll be there in an hour." Trusting others to handle her problems was not something Alice did. Trusting people period was not her strong suit. She slammed down the phone and ran to the shower. Scrubbing the night's imagined Roman romp off of her as quickly as possible, she threw on a suit and hastily arranged her hair. She grabbed some shoes and ran out the door.

Two blocks from home, she remembered she'd forgotten to feed Otis. He wouldn't starve, but that was inexcusable. His little life and happiness depended solely on her. Spending all day without any food would not make him happy. She turned her car around, ran through the garage, and stood punching the button frantically. Was she getting too crazy to take care of her own cat? The elevator took forever. Dumping the canned food into his dish, Alice said, "Sorry, little fur buddy. No time for a proper head rub this morning. Make sure none of your toys get into my shoes."

She arrived at Excellcardia at fifteen minutes past nine. She ran past Andy the door guard without her usual greeting. When she finally got to her office, she walked right past Jonathan, sat down in the white leather chair behind her desk and burst into tears.

Jonathan stood beside her desk in an instant.

"Alice, I really think you should have—"

"I—I—just—just—couldn't wake up. I've never been late to anything in my life. I always know the time."

Jonathan put one hand on her shoulder and lifted her chin with his other hand until her eyes met his. "Maybe you should be late once in a while. You put yourself under more stress than anyone should have to endure."

"It's what I do. It's who I am. It is the only way I matter." She looked at the floor. No matter where she looked, she would not meet his big brown eyes again. She couldn't. Squeezing her eyes tight, she took a deep breath. "Where is Brad? I need him in here now." Concentrating on work issues would take her mind off the mess she was making of her life. It always did.

Jonathan shot her a slightly scolding look and returned to his desk.

Alice dabbed her eyes and dropped Visine into each one. Bradley James stood in front of her desk five minutes later.

"I'm ready to go wherever you say, Alice, as soon as you say." He looked at her earnestly with those eyes. Today he wore a pale gray suit, white shirt, and red tie. His body in that suit made Alice take in a deep breath and let it out slowly.

"Brad, honestly, I'm not sure what to do about Presby. Why can't they just commit? You've dealt with them before on other projects, and I really need your input."

"I'll give them the old, 'Maybe this is too big for you, and I understand if you're not ready'. I know Tom Renkin their head of purchasing. His ego will never let him pass up the deal we're offering. They couldn't get a line half as good as ours at the price and he knows it. They have to realize they've gotta commit to our minimum order and none of this small sample crap. I can fly down there next week. Give him a little time to stew." Brad's gaze and the passion in his voice made her shiver.

Alice nodded. This was just what she needed at this moment. Brad had been one of her best hires right after she became CEO. She knew leaders have to delegate, but that never came easy to her. Brad made it feel almost comfortable delegating. She looked down at his hands on her desk.

He leaned in close to her. "Anything I can do to help, Boss Lady." The words sounded comforting, but the tone and the intense look were not. A warmth spread slowly down her body and made her want to do him right now on her desk. Nothing wrong with imagining. Thank goodness she had more self-control in the daylight.

"Thank you, Brad," she said just a little breathless.

She watched him walk out the door and her pulse returned to normal.

This morning passed slowly. The odd, disoriented feeling lifted a bit as she sat eating the tuna sandwich Jonathan brought her from the cafeteria. Alice knew what she had to do. She could not lose track of time again. Maybe she needed to stop spending her nights having imaginary, albeit amazing, sex fantasies. The ordered fabric of her daytime life could not further unravel. She had to call Dr. Elliot.

Alice felt defeated as she put down the phone. Wrapping most of the sandwich in a napkin, she dropped it in the trash can next to her desk. Sleeping medication. She was going to be one of those women now. The ones who took pills to sleep.

"Bipolar disorder one: Alice zero." She sat in her car, holding the bag from the pharmacy. She opened the bag and took out the bottle. "I wonder if these will make me bigger or smaller. I'm hoping for smaller." This time she spoke to the bottle— certainly not to herself.

Tonight, no matter who she was, Alice didn't want to eat alone. She knocked on Susan's door. Her friend's surprised and happy expression as she opened the door, warmed Alice's heart.

"What a nice surprise. I was beginning to think you were like some kind of reverse vampire, coming out only in the light of day and retreating to your coffin at sunset."

"Good one. It's been way too long since we had dinner. Sorry not to give you any notice. I just felt kinda lonely and thought I would take a chance you were home."

Susan and David's home always gave Alice a cozy feeling, and something smelled delicious. Their apartment was as warm and inviting as Alice's was clean and austere. Susan's furniture consisted of impossibly overstuffed pieces in pastel colors. Too many chairs and loveseats made it feel like company would always be welcome. Somehow, it looked homey rather than cluttered. The beautiful quilts Susan had lovingly made hung on the walls and completed the picture. It was the best decision Alice had ever made, buying an apartment in the same building as her best friend.

"Well, you won the jackpot. I'm home, David is traveling, and I put a big hunk of brisket in the crock-pot this morning."

Susan smiled and opened the door wide. "Smells good doesn't it?"

"Sure does. I didn't eat much lunch."

"Doesn't look like you ever eat. That suit is hanging off you."

"Don't be ridiculous, I'm still fat." Alice grabbed some skin on her stomach to demonstrate.

"I have a great Cab to go with the beef."

"No wine for me." Alice dropped into her favorite seat, the baby pink and white striped chair with the triple ruffle around the bottom. It felt like sitting in a cotton–candy cloud.

"What? You on the wagon? Isn't that the last sign of the impending apocalypse, Alice Hightower not drinking at least one glass of my wine? Okay, but you owe me an explanation. I'm pretty sure you're not an alcoholic. You're not pregnant—you get those shots. I give up. Explain!"

"I'm taking sleep meds, and you're not supposed to mix them with alcohol. It's that simple." Alice looked down.

"Well, you never were a good sleeper, but you also hate the idea any kind of psych meds. So what gives?"

Alice hated to abandon her chair but followed. Susan perched on a black stool at a large, ruby-red quartz kitchen island. Alice stood beside her. "I was late for work." A tear rolled down Alice's cheek.

"Oh my God! Stop the world, Alice Hightower was late to work." Susan clapped her hands to the sides of her face, imitating Edvard Munch's "The Scream."

Alice couldn't help but laugh. "Can you ever remember me being late to anything?"

"Well, no. Maybe it's about damn time."

"Susan, it's who I am. I'm never late. I'm—unraveling." Another tear joined the first and her lip quivered. She wiped her eye. Was this crying in front of people thing getting to be a habit?

Susan ignored the tears. "I thought I saw the story on

CNN, but then I said, 'No, can't be, more fake news. Alice Hightower is never late.' Cut yourself some slack! It happens."

"Not to me. I haven't really been sleeping well. The shrink thinks this will help."

Susan looked skeptical but said nothing as she moved to the stove. "Okay, here's my specialty. Beef in Italian salad dressing au crock-pot. Even you could make it. I gave you a crock-pot for your birthday a couple of years ago." She dipped into the crock and spooned a large serving on a plate and handed it to Alice.

"It is wonderful." Alice said with her mouth full.

"Yep, and takes ten minutes to prepare, no kidding. You haven't said what you think of my new paint." Susan pointed to her bright lavender kitchen walls.

"I love it. Only you could make lavender, red, and black a color scheme for a kitchen."

"I stole it from an HGTV show. Some cute gay guys were horrifying their neighbors by painting their house while they were gone. It looked cool to me."

"I really love it. The purple is set off by the black cabinets and stools. The red accent wall and countertop makes it pop. I wish I had the courage with color you do." Alice sniffed back a tear.

"Well, you could change, Miss White-on-White-with-Black-Accents. Honestly. Even your freaky three-legged, one-eared cat is black."

"Don't call him freaky. He's a treasure. They were going to euthanize him just because he lost an ear and a leg. He was only a year old. He's the sweetest cat in the world. Anyway, white and black are orderly, and everything matches them. I'm sure if I were to pick colors, they'd be the wrong ones."

"Why are you so hard on yourself? You're hot, smart, and successful. When will it be enough?"

Never, thought Alice. She finished every bite on her plate and looked out the window in Susan's kitchen. The sun had gone down ten minutes ago. Tonight she wasn't going anywhere.

"Want to stay for a movie? I have *Magic Mike* in my Netflix streaming queue. Not much of a story, but the boys are pretty."

"Sure," Alice said. The tears started again, and this time Susan couldn't pretend not to notice.

She got up from her stool and put her arm around Alice's shoulder. "Honey, what's the matter?"

"Dr. Elliot says I'm bipolar just like Mother. Oh, Susan, I'm going to lose my mind."

Susan took a step back and put her hands on her hips. "Oh please! I've seen you do your roller coaster thing for almost three decades. Frankly, I kinda like it. It's like having a couple of best friends instead of just one. I'm not sure which one I like best—the hyper-talky one who stays up all night with me, or the one who sleeps too much and eats everything in sight. You've got one of the best minds I've ever known, and I can't see you losing it anytime soon."

"But..." Alice sniffed and blew her nose on the paper towels Susan always used as napkins.

"You are ten kinds of successful and I love you just the way you are. Who the hell is this doctor to slap a label on you and make you feel defective? There are too many people who use a diagnosis as an excuse. Even some related to you."

"You mean my brother?"

"Hell yeah, I mean Sean! Does he still use coke to get up and alcohol to come down? He jumped on the bipolar band-wagon to get sympathy back when they called it manic-depressive."

"Last time I saw him he was clean."

"Really Alice, it's a mood disorder. You can handle that, and I think you do it beautifully. If you need sleeping pills once in a while, what the hell? Do it."

"Thank you. You said something about a movie?" Her friend's words helped a little and Alice felt lighter.

"All right, all right, all right! You'll think that's funny after you watch this. There is a little surprise for you too."

"What?"

"I'm not telling. Just watch the movie. There might be something a little familiar in it. Let's nuke this bag of fake butter popcorn and go crazy."

When the whole apartment smelled like a movie theatre, Susan pulled up the movie from her Netflix queue.

Two minutes into the first scene, Alice looked at Susan and both women burst out laughing.

"He does, doesn't he?" Susan turned to her friend.

"Look just like my first husband? Yes, I've admired Channing Tatum for that very reason more than once."

"God he was gorgeous. Couldn't you have stuck it out so I could look at him once in a while?"

"He wasn't really such a bad guy. But you know me. When the going gets tough, Alice gets going."

"Not so much lately. You have been at Excellcardia for years now. Seems like you've found a good fit there."

"I'm the CEO. No place else to go. Roll that scene back. I want to see the part where he takes off his shirt again." Both women leaned toward the screen.

When the movie ended and the last bites of the popcorn were gone, Alice hugged her friend and took the elevator home.

Otis waited at the door and rubbed against her legs, purring like a chainsaw.

"Yep, I'm all yours tonight, my beautiful boy." She knelt down and rubbed the little stump where his left ear used to be. "Shame on Susan, you are my gorgeous boy." The portly black feline rubbed his head against her in ecstasy.

Clinical Notes on Client Hightower, Alice B.

Client called today to request sleep meds. Wrote script for Ambien #30, one tab at bedtime, three refills. Will be interested to see the impact on existence of sexual fantasies.

Chapter Six

AFTERNOON DELIGHT

B y the time she arrived at the Excellcardia building, Alice had reached about three quarters of her regular speed. Although groggy from the sleeping pill, she managed to walk through the door at her regular time by using an alarm and getting up an hour early. She saluted Andy and walked to the elevators. Usually she hurried, but not today. Her watch agreed that it was seven-twenty-five, perfect.

The elevator doors closed, then opened again immediately. There stood Brad James, beaming at her, in a double-breasted navy sport coat had bright gold buttons that emphasized his body.

"Good morning, Boss Lady."

"Morning, Mr. James."

"Mr. James, is it now? I think we know each other better than that, Alice." He stepped into the elevator and stood far too close. Her heartbeat went crazy.

He turned to Alice as the elevator started its journey. "Sleep well last night, Alice?"

"Yes, thank you." She looked straight ahead. The question should have been innocent, but she knew there was nothing innocent about Bradley James. Why were her ears ringing and her cheeks getting hot?

"Good. I'm glad. If there is ever anything I can do to make sure you get your beauty sleep, let me know." He winked at her and got off the elevator at his floor. Perhaps it had been a dangerous mistake to keep him on, no matter how well he did his job.

Coffee made and one sip downed, she checked her email inbox. One hundred eighty-nine emails this morning. Well, they could wait. She felt like doing a little bit of Internet exploring. She typed *Jacques Seingalt* into Google. *Wouldn't it be fun if—oh my God!*

"Jacques de Seingalt: a pseudonym frequently used by Giacomo Casanova."

No wonder he was so—But the man in her fantasy wasn't real. How could she have known that name? She must have read that somewhere.

She typed in *Nickel Bag.*

"A rock group from Manchester, England, touring the US in the mid-1970s."

"Wow! They're real too," Alice said to herself. "How could —" She looked up as someone came in the door.

"Good morning. How could what?" said Jonathan. He adjusted the door to the same perfect openness like every morning and walked to the credenza that held the coffee. He wore a taupe suit with a peach-colored shirt and a tie a shade darker. She was sure the models in GQ couldn't look any better in a suit.

Shut up, she told herself. "Oh, just looking up some silly stuff before I dive into the ocean of emails."

"Silly stuff can be fun." He smiled as he poured his coffee. It was a warm, friendly smile with a hint of something else: mischief, maybe? That was not a look she remembered ever seeing before.

What the hell? Was everyone getting some invisible, "I

missed my nightly escapade and am in dire need of a man" signal from her? Or did the Ambien fog in her head make her imagine things even in the daylight? This needed to stop. She shook her head hard.

"I'm feeling a little foggy this morning, Jonathan. Would you run through my emails and sort by priority. I will get to them shortly."

As Alice sat down to her desk and opened her laptop, she heard an unmistakable gruff voice. Dr. Henry Petrus barged right past Jonathan.

"Alice, this can't go on! You can't expect me to get decent results using those goddamn old dogs." Dressed in blue scrubs and a rumpled lab coat, Dr. Petrus stood drumming his fingers on Alice's desk.

"Good morning to you, Henry. We've had this conversation before. You know how I feel about it. The dogs we use have to be rescues. I'd prefer if you're going to cut them open, they deserve the benefit of a happy home afterward. Young dogs get adopted. The older ones are more often slated to be euthanized, using them most likely saves their lives."

"Horseshit!" He pounded his fist on the desk, dropped into the chair, and ran his hands through white hair that couldn't have seen a barber in months. Dr. Henry Petrus had pioneered the cell growth processes that made BioCardia possible. Alice knew he personally held eleven patents on processes and even several cell lines. Why did he choose this moment to bring up a long-standing dispute between them?

❧

Six years ago they had both worked for a small medical research company. Alice had been in charge of Henry's department, and she'd recognized his singular talent. He'd never accepted her as his equal, let alone his boss. His attitude hadn't changed one bit here at Excellcardia. Never mind she had managed to secure him a huge increase in pay in his new position. Of course she had gained too. Though it pained her, a little to admit, part of her meteoric rise to CEO had been due to her recruiting Henry Petrus.

"If we don't get some younger dogs," he said, "I can't get the numbers up on implantations, and if I can't do that, we'll never get the FDA to approve human trials. I mean it, Alice. The subject dogs need to be younger. Keeping those old mutts healthy enough for surgery takes up too much of my time and effort. I've gone along with your damn bleeding-heart crap so far, but to save human lives we have to sacrifice some dogs. I need to start doing surgery in greater numbers. If I have to get along with this damn tight budget, I at least need this. Be glad we aren't doing neuro research. Chimps cost a fortune and are meaner than—"

She scowled. "All right. Do what you have to."

"I'm going to need more funds, too." Dr. Petrus's grey eyes went from angry and menacing to almost kindly.

"The board has agreed to a whole new budget to keep the ball rolling with the FDA. Jonathan will see to the funds you need released."

"James wants to adopt our star Barney. We don't need him anymore, and it would save cage space." Dr. Petrus headed out the door without another word.

Lucky Barney, thought Alice.

She spent the rest of her day in various meetings, attending to the myriad details that kept her going. At work, Alice rarely thought about the state of her mind or her emotions. She devoted one hundred percent of her attention to her job and that was enough. Still, today, she felt strange and dull, the effect of the sleeping meds, no doubt. She wondered if the veil of brain fog would lift before it was time to take another pill. *This pill definitely made me smaller, and not in a good way, Mr. Carroll.* Alice stopped herself from making this proclamation out loud.

❦

The traffic was worse than usual and by the time Alice arrived home, she could have sworn Otis's meow sounded scolding.

"That's okay, pretty boy. I feel too groggy still to open the guest room closet door, let alone go anywhere there might be hot men. It did seem oddly convenient that her hallucinations always included delicious and willing men." She had definitely changed in the sexual appetite department since that afternoon eighteen months ago.

Alice could barely manage thirty minutes on her elliptical. After swallowing something microwaved nearly whole, she put on her lavender print pajamas and got into bed. Otis jumped up beside her.

"You want to hear a really tawdry story, Otis?" She reached over to pet the kitty. "It's pretty bad."

"Mama did a bad thing and maybe the guilt of it contributed to her going crazy." The cat curled at her feet as an answer. She decided against telling the cat. The thought of him judging her more harshly than she did herself was too much. Alice propped herself up on all four of her pillows and gave herself over to remembering, vividly and in perfect detail, an afternoon it would have been better to forget.

❦

It had been a bright early spring day when the chairman of the St. Louis Cardiologists Association had introduced her to a crowd of medical conventioneers as Dr. Hightower. Though it was true she'd earned an MD, Alice had never practiced one day, so the introduction felt a like a fraud. Still she gave an informative hour-long dissertation on new advances in implantable cardiac devices to a group of cardiologists. She'd looked out over the crowd in the Airport Marriott ballroom and wondered: *could I ever have been one of them?* They all looked so serious and so unbearably dull. When she called for questions at the end of her talk, no one raised a hand. Did they know all the answers, or did they just not care enough to ask? But these doctors performed a vital service; so what if they were not very interesting.

Brad James was working the Excellcardia booth in the exhibit hall at the conference. Someone needed to charm the docs into demanding the superior quality of Excellcardia's life-saving merchandise, and Brad was their designated charmer. The product booth with its dazzling video screen showed how safe and simple her company's devices were. There played wide-screen videos of her company's devices being surgically implanted, complete with digitally enhanced rivers of human blood. Alice preferred to keep her back to the screen.

Bradley James had come to Excellcardia with glowing recommendations from his former employer, oozing charm from every seam in his well-tailored suit. He worked the room like the pro he was. In the first three weeks Brad had been on board, he'd closed two huge deals with hospital systems Alice had been after for months. Making the best product didn't matter if nobody bought it. This guy could sell.

Alice peeked into the exhibit hall. Brad stood facing the video screen and talking to a small brown man with demeanor and posture of a surgeon. Three young women stood by, admiring Mr. James's style.

He seemed to be earning his keep. Alice had no intention of attending the conference's cocktail reception. She had given her talk, Brad was moving the merchandise, and she could go home after finishing a few last tasks.

But by the time she answered forty emails and checked today's sales numbers on her laptop, it was almost five. The witching hour for hellacious traffic on 270 would last until at least six-thirty. Leaving now, would mean an extra hour or more in traffic. With time to kill, Alice wondered if the Marriott bartender could shake a good martini. It might be fun to watch the Friday night pick-up dance. Did people still go to bars to hook up in the age of Tinder? She decided to find out and headed to the lobby bar.

The door to the lobby slid open silently to reveal a sea of white marble and glass. A leather-upholstered glass-topped bar covered the whole back wall of the lobby.

She planned to slowly savor a martini, people watch, and relax until the traffic died down.

There were several possible targets for flirty but harmless eye contact sitting on various stools along the fifty-foot bar. Could she muster any interest at all? She eyed a spot between the loveliest two suits: a dark-haired man in black and a silver-haired one in a dark gray. They sat near the end of the bar with one stool conveniently between them. Alice took the stool and looked to her right.

This man in the black suit looked about forty. His curly black hair was tousled in a way that must have required a lot of hair product, but his face was handsome enough. He gave Alice a speculative smile, as if this hot cougar was on the menu. He took a sip of something pink. Do real men drink pink? She wondered and answered herself: Of course they do.

She turned to check out the man to her left and inhaled sharply. Brad James smiled back at her. How hadn't she recognized him from earlier? Maybe she had and deep down she didn't care exactly who this silver fox was seated next to her?

He held a martini glass in his hand. It might have been vodka instead of the gin Alice preferred, but at least it was clear. He took a sip and chewed an olive slowly, never taking his extraordinary blue eyes from hers. It wasn't the color of his eyes that made her heart race. It was the hungry heat in them. The look that said without her, he would starve to death.

The bartender came over and she ordered a Tanqueray martini up with three olives. Brad signaled to the bartender to put it on his tab. Alice smiled and said nothing. What could it hurt, one drink with a new employee?

As Alice sat sipping her pine-flavored delight, she felt no desire to discuss business. She merely smiled at him and waited for him to speak first.

"You come here often, Miss?" Brad asked. *So he wanted to play that game.*

"Smith, Jane Smith, at your service, Mr...?"

"Jones, John Jones. Equally interested in servicing you." He flashed her a bright white smile, and his face lit up with genuine warmth. "I'm staying here until I have time to house hunt. I like a drink and some interesting conversation before retiring. Sort of shake off the day."

"I've felt a little thirsty and hungry for some conversation myself." Alice laughed, leaned closer, and touched the sleeve of his jacket lightly. She'd thought him hot when she first hired him, but tonight, with gin tickling her brain cells, he was irresistible. The warning bells that rang in her head should have deafened her. Fraternizing with an employee was not wise. But it had been entirely too long since Alice felt this strongly drawn to a man, and the suddenly active hungry little slut between her legs plugged her ears to all warnings.

Setting down her glass, she ran her fingers slowly up and down its stem as she smiled at him. He shook his head again, laughing. He too seemed to be enjoying the game. The ball now deeply in his court, Alice took another long, delicious sip, and kept her eyes on his.

"Do you like white wines, Miss Smith? I know a little place that has a wonderful J. Lohr chardonnay, if you're interested?"

She leaned back on her stool, legs crossed, back straight, and chest out. "I love chardonnay. Where might this place be, Mr. Smith?"

"Jones, I'm Jones you're Smith," he said, and they laughed like naughty children.

He reached into the inside pocket of his lovely gray suit and pulled out a black plastic card. "Room 716." He lowered his chin and focused those dangerous eyes on hers, waiting for her response.

Alice downed her last sip of martini and slid off the white leather bar stool to stand beside him. Her voice barely a whisper, close to his ear, she said, "I'd absolutely love to, Bra —John."

He'd paid for their drinks and motioned toward the elevator. She walked close beside him. Once the elevator door closed, Alice wanted to kiss those smiling lips. She wanted him to unbutton her jacket and touch her breasts. She wouldn't have minded if he'd unzipped his pants right there, but he merely stood there, smiling at her and saying nothing. Something animal she hadn't felt in a while took control of her.

The elevator stopped at the seventh floor, and without a word he took her hand and led her down the hall to room 716.

Once inside, Alice spied an ice bucket cooling the promised bottle of wine. Brad took a wine opener from his pocket, opened the bottle, and filled the two wine glasses. Who had he been expecting? She remembered thinking he probably had his eye on one of the cute little nurses who seemed to be everywhere in the exhibit hall.

Though there was a couch, Alice chose to sit on the bed. She crossed her legs and leaned back a bit, appraising her prey. Or was she the prey?

He handed her a glass, took a sip from his own, and with the same warm smile she'd seen before. She melted.

"Shall we get on with the interview, Miss Smith?"

So now it's my turn to be interviewed. Gladly for a taste of what's under that pretty suit. Setting her glass carefully on the floor, she removed her jacket. "What makes you think you have what it takes for this position, Miss Smith?" He gave a little chuckle and took another sip of his wine.

Alice unbuttoned her blouse, reached up, and unhooked the lacy black bra's oh-so-convenient front hooks. She tossed the bra toward him and leaned back a little. He did a combination laugh and spit-take and set down his wine glass.

"Will these do, sir?" Alice looked up at him, no longer smiling, eyebrows raised.

"Uh, yes. That's what I've dreamed they'd look like since the first minute we met." Brad loosened the knot of his tie, silver with a pretty geometric pattern, so much like the one on the front of *Fifty Shades*. Alice had never had time to read the book, but she'd certainly seen the cover often enough as it seemed to be on sale everywhere a few years ago. He slipped it off and dropped it on the credenza. Then unbuttoning each of his French cuffs, he removed the onyx and silver cufflinks and dropped each one with a clunk next to his tie.

That sound made Alice nearly as hot as those eyes, now looking at her with obvious intent. They swept from the top of her head to the tip of her toes, slowly appraising every inch. She uncrossed her legs and spread her knees slightly. The knee-length navy skirt she wore that day was short enough to undoubtedly give him a little peek at her lacy black panties.

"God, I want to eat your pussy," he said, his voice now husky.

"Please."

He dropped to his knees in front of her, and she leaned back on the bed. She knew he would take it from there. She was so right. He quickly pulled off the panties and spread her knees with his hands. His hot wet tongue on her made her gasp: she made a little animal noise deep in her throat. He increased the pace, running the length of her clitoris in firm liquid strokes.

She felt two fingers slip inside her as she climbed the hill of pleasure toward her climax, moaning loudly.

"Oh, you like that, do you, Alice?" he said.

"Yes, please." Alice ran her fingers through his silver hair, and he increased the pressure and the speed of his lingual strokes until her moans reached their crescendo. She laughed out loud, a self-conscious little laugh. It always surprised her just how much noise she made.

"Well, Miss Smith, I trust you will find the work satisfying," he said, laughing too. He got off his knees, removed his pale blue shirt and placed it neatly over the end of the couch. Alice watched him as he unzipped and removed his gray trousers. She appraised the lovely round cheeks of his ass as he stood with his back to her, wearing only black boxer briefs. She did appreciate a man's nice muscular behind. Alice had noticed his backside before at work but never dared to imagine what it would look like without the suit. *Okay rarely.* Mr. Jones did not disappoint.

Sitting up, Alice slipped off her skirt and blouse and threw them somewhere. She picked up her wine glass and took a slow sip. Brad brought his glass and sat next to her, sipping his wine and looking at her with his amazing eyes. "Tell me, Alice, what you want."

She swallowed another sip of her wine and, leaning toward him, whispered her answer. "You, inside me."

His lips on hers, she parted her lips and welcomed his tongue with hers. Alice ran the tip of her tongue along the underside of his upper lip and traced the outline of the smile she'd just discovered. His kisses were soft and skillful.

When her breaths were again ragged and she began to make wet little moans, he stood up and removed the black briefs.

"Oh, my, Mr. James." His was a large and lovely erection, a nice length and exceptionally thick.

"Whatever you want, Alice."

She lay back on the bed and he took the perfect position on top of her. She wrapped her legs around him and pulled him deep inside her. "I've wanted to fuck you since we first met," he said.

"But Mr. Jones." Alice couldn't help but giggle. "We just met a few minutes ago."

"This is my fantasy, Alice. Just go with it." He laughed with his face buried in her hair. "See what you've done to me, Alice? Feel how hard you've made me?"

"I do the best I can, sir."

He stopped his thrusts and they both laughed. "You certainly do. You are one wet little applicant." He lifted his upper body, leaning his weight on his arms and looked deep into her soul. The intensity of his gaze increased the pleasure of each stroke as he slid slowly in and out of her. "Fuck me, Alice, like I've always wanted."

"Oh God, Brad, yes." No more Mr. Jones and Miss Smith. They were Brad and Alice. He continued his long slow strokes. His lovely thick cock hit the sides of her just right to make her pant and moan.

He stopped his movements and pulled out of her. Holding his cock so slippery with her desire, he said, "It's your cock, Alice. Put it where you want it."

She gasped. Wrapping her fingers around him, she rubbed the head of his glorious thick cock against her clitoris never breaking eye contact for a second.

"Ummmh." This time it was Brad who moaned. He reached up and rolled her left nipple gently between his thumb and index finger as she rubbed his cock against her. The faster she stroked, the faster he flicked and pulled on her nipple. She lunged against him and cried out loud enough to wake the residents of the cemetery half a mile away.

"I'm sorry. I'm really loud when—"

"Don't ever apologize for enjoying yourself. That's why I'm here." Now he thrust deeper and harder as she caressed the hard round muscles of the ass that powered those thrusts.

He came, and she again embarrassed herself with her loud passionate cries. Brad turned Alice on her side and, without a word, spooned her and kissed her neck. She was happy lying against him. He snored softly for a few minutes, then woke, let out at little gasp and kissed her neck again. Alice wiggled her hips, pressing her ass against him. He reached around her and rubbed his palms against her nipples and kissed her neck. Taking her hand, he placed it on his cock.

"Now, see what you've done, Alice. What are you going to do about it?"

"Whatever you want me to do, Brad. He rolled her over and pulled her in deeply with his gaze.

They pleased each other one more time. He then lay snoring softly, his arms around her, her head on his chest.

Her mind raced as they lay together. *This was by far the best sex of my life.* She'd never dreamt eye contact could increase her pleasure as it had with Brad. The connection between them was white hot and undeniable. Excellcardia had no official prohibition against fraternization. They just needed to keep their work and personal life separate, she had thought. Piece of cake.

❧

Clinical Notes on Client Hightower, Alice B.

Client reports taking Ambien one night. She states that that night she had no fantasy and slept eight uninterrupted hours. However, client discontinued use, as the resultant residual drowsiness was unacceptable to her. Next session will suggest hypnotic regression to explore the possible source of the fantasies based in childhood.

Chapter Seven

LADY IN RED

She fell asleep to the memory of her afternoon with Brad and woke feeling cheery. She had forgotten to take her sleeping pill and was glad of it. She stretched and reached over to rub Otis's furry black head. "Ah, I'm glad you enjoyed the good night sleep as much as I did, beautiful boy. Who needs a pill that makes you feel like a zombie?"

If she closed her eyes she could still see Brad's hot blue eyes looking into hers. She could taste him on her lips, feel the weight of him. It couldn't hurt to remember, could it? The fear and self-doubt that often accompanied her day's beginning could wait a bit longer this morning.

❦

It made Alice happy each morning to see Andy Sanchez at his post by the lobby door. His stocky build and imposing presence made her feel safe as he guarded the building. He was a Hispanic version of Mr. Clean, all muscles, shiny head, and blinding white smile. His hand smartly next to his brow, he grinned at her. She returned the salute—their shared morning joke. He began saluting her three years ago after she recommended changing his utilitarian blue cotton uniform to a black wool number with gold buttons and braid on the epaulets. She felt it gave the place an added air of class. Andy never laughed when she tripped on the doormat, which happened at least twice a week. Alice never thought of herself as clumsy. "Preoccupied with important thoughts," was her preferred description of the occasional difficulty walking.

Better tone it down, Alice. Someone might guess she wasn't playing with an entirely full deck. She gave Andy a little extra head nod and a wink along with the usual salute. Alice Hightower felt like an entirely capable CEO this morning even on the inside.

Her excellent mood continued throughout her day. The most annoying little tasks seemed more fun than usual. Eight hours later, Jonathan stood in front of her desk looking eager to receive the day's last instruction.

"Shall I pick you up tonight, same time as last year?" he said.

"What?"

"For the holiday party. Tonight, seven-thirty?"

How could she have forgotten? The year before last, she had so recently split with Robert, she couldn't bear walking in alone to all those pitying looks. Jonathan had graciously offered to escort her, and a tradition was born. This year, he volunteered again without being asked.

"Absolutely. We make a gorgeous pair." *Let them all think I am a cradle robber.* She laughed as she walked out the door.

❧

"Black, white, or red," she asked her large closet. Alice assessed the three formal dresses she owned: the black sequined one, the almost virginal white one in shiny satin, or—oh, definitely the red off-the-shoulder number. The subtle beading on the bodice and skirt looked lovely, and she didn't think it revealed too much cleavage. A little tight in the derriere, but she hoped the elegant beads provided enough camouflage for her ass to look shapely, rather than too large. How perfect for the Red Queen to preside over her court.

Did she want to look hot for Brad, who would undoubtedly be there? Alice put on her highest red slippers.

"Can I dance in these?" she asked Otis. Who cares? They look amazing." She flat-ironed her hair within an inch of its life and parted it on the side, Veronica Lake style. Did she look great, or was she just doing a bad Jessica Rabbit imitation? She took a last look in the mirror on the way to answer the door when the bell rang. She only stumbled once; definitely a good sign.

As she opened the door for Jonathan, the look on his face and the accompanying wolf-whistle answered her question.

"I'm not sure it's legal in this state to look that hot," he said. "Good thing you have a suitable escort." His cream-colored tuxedo perfectly complemented her dress, and his cummerbund and bowtie were, of course, red.

&

When the doors to the twenty-second floor opened, revealing Alice and Jonathan, a hush fell over the hundred or so people gathered.

"Oh, come on, people, Alice said. "You couldn't all been talking about me at once." From the back of the room, someone started applause, and the rest of the room followed. Alice gave a small bow, and everyone resumed their conversations.

The twenty-second floor, usually the employee cafeteria, sparkled with red and gold and blue and white decorations. This holiday party boasted both Christmas trees and a menorah. Alice had implemented this policy at her first party as CEO, three years ago.

This year's Alice was a very different creature than the defeated shade who'd entered the party on the arm of her assistant two years ago. She could still feel a tiny stab of pain at the memory of catching Robert with his twenty-five-year-old admin in her bed that terrible day. Such was her penance for leaving work early.

"What did you expect?" Robert had said when she opened her bedroom door on the couple. "We never have sex anymore. A man has needs." As he stood up, Alice noticed his Viagra-powered erection had yet to get the word that this particular episode of "screwing the admin" was cancelled. Alice remembered hearing herself laugh, though she'd felt nothing but pain. Although she had never really loved Robert, the end of her second marriage still felt like failure.

She'd known for a while their relationship was in trouble. Robert traveled more and more and almost never touched her, probably because she cringed when he did. Her reaction came naturally after her gynecologist informed her she had chlamydia. She'd slept with no one but Robert for seven years. He, obviously, had no such concept of fidelity. The thought of another divorce pushed the hurt from her mind, but not the memory. She grew numb inside and said nothing, until the day of the "fucking the admin" incident. No one could be numb enough to ignore that and divorce ensued.

Robert hadn't seemed to care she wasn't wild in bed when they first met. Because he was sweet and gentle with her, she'd assumed he thought the sex was good. She knew now because of her nightly fantasies that she had probably not been a particularly good lay. Before Brad, that is.

❦

Brad appeared out of the crowd as if her thoughts had somehow summoned him.

"I would love a dance with our queen in red, who has never looked hotter." Brad bowed low and grinned up at Alice.

"Thanks, Brad. Later? I need to circulate. I promise not to say, 'Off with your head.'" She let go of Jonathan's arm, but he stayed glued to her side.

"Make sure that doesn't happen," Alice whispered to Jonathan. "If you see him dancing with me, cut in. Until then, go circulate. I don't really need a babysitter this year. Have some fun. That pretty HR admin is looking at you with lust in her eyes. Go." Alice made shooing motions with her hands. Jonathan obeyed.

Brad, too, was walking away. His lovely black tux fit him, as did everything he wore, perfectly. It hugged his broad shoulders and made Alice swallow hard. *Eyes off his ass!*

She headed to the buffet. Louise joined her, her eyes sweeping the crowd. "That dress is killer," Louise said. "Thanks for the vegetarian selections this year. I appreciate you flesh-eaters making allowances for little old me." Louise had opted for a less formal look, but Alice was sure her white sheath dress had a designer label in it. The color of the dress complemented her lovely chocolate complexion. The fact that Louise had not an ounce of extra fat made the plain dress beyond elegant.

The party was "as formal as you like," officially. Anyone owning a formal and itching to wear it could do so, while those who felt comfortable in a nice church dress or sport coat would feel welcome, too. Alice spotted Dr. Petrus approaching dressed in tuxedo pants, a black bow tie and cummerbund, with his usual rumpled lab coat over them. Genius had its own style.

"I like your jacket, Henry," she said.

"I have to check on Barney later, and I don't want to get dog hair or blood on my jacket."

"Barney? Didn't Brad adopt him?"

"The new Barney. Barney 234." He picked up a plate and stabbed some steamed vegetables with his fork. It bothered

Alice there were so many dogs. Except for the star of her presentation, who kept his name, each new test subject got the name and a number after the death of its predecessor. For her, lives were lives, each one precious. She would never accept the dogs as merely research material. It had broken her heart to sacrifice even the rats in college physiology class. Opening the eggs before the chicks were finished in embryology had been difficult for her. Still, those chick embryos, stained, sectioned and examined under a microscope, had taught her things she could have learned no other way. That was the cruel reality of scientific research—difficult but necessary.

Alice turned to examine the enticing array of food that covered the buffet table along one entire wall. Signs separated the goodies into kosher, vegan, and omnivore. The party committee had done an incredible job. Alice was proud to see how relaxed and happy her employees looked. The men shone in lovely tuxes and dark suits. The women sparkled like tree ornaments in holiday hues.

"Aren't you eating, my queen?" Brad's voice came from behind her. Alice turned and he handed her a glass of gold-colored liquid.

"Chardonnay. I seem to remember you like it?"

"Yes. Thank you." Alice took a sip and said, "Where is the lovely Mrs. James this evening? I can't wait to see what she's wearing."

"She's not here." His expression didn't change. No explanation or reaction at all, only those incendiary eyes focused on her. His beautiful wife was with him at last year's party: a tiny vivacious brunette, everything Alice was not and never could be. Next to her, Alice had felt huge and clumsy. Olivia James had used her dazzling dark eyes to wrap the whole room around her teeny-tiny size zero finger. Zero! That wasn't a size, it wasn't even a number. It was a placeholder.

He is a married man. It was over. Her memories would

have to be enough. She turned to find Jonathan standing at her side.

"May I have this dance?" he asked.

"You know I'm a terrible dancer, but I'm game if you are." Alice set down the glass of wine and raised her hand for him to take. He pulled her tight against him and looked over his shoulder at the leader of the Motown Hits group hired for the evening. The singer nodded and the band broke into Eric Clapton's "Lady in Red."

His hand caressed her back as they moved across the floor. He even smelled sexy.

"You are, you know," he whispered into her ear.

His breath against her ear sent a wave of desire that travelled the length of her body. "I am what?" The wine and very little food gave his voice a dreamy quality.

"Beautiful." He was echoing the lyric of the song. Alice stiffened. Was this another fantasy? It was after sunset; but this was definitely the company holiday party, not the product of her ever-increasing insanity.

She pulled away a little and looked up at him. Jonathan looked amused. Alice relaxed. *He's not in love with me. I really do look amazing tonight.*

Alice let the rhythm of the song carry her, trusting it and Jonathan's excellent dancing ability. He did feel wonderful, pressed against the length of her. She could enjoy dancing with him, couldn't she? No law against that. When the song ended, she sent him on his way to circulate once more. Brad cut through the crowd to stand beside her again. *Is he stalking me? Do I hope so?*

"You promised me a dance," he said, grabbing her hand. The group played "Unchained Melody." Brad wrapped his arms around her waist and pulled her far too close. She stood still, not moving an inch. She knew where a dance could lead.

"Just because your wife isn't here," she said softly, "doesn't mean I've forgotten. I am not an adulteress."

"Aren't you though?" Brad laughed at her.

"I didn't know you were married when we...."

"Oh come on, Alice. It's in my personnel file. I never tried to hide it."

She turned and walked away, not caring what anyone thought. She would circulate and keep away from Brad.

To keep away from the dangerous Mr. Bradley James, she flitted from table to table greeting everyone. She spent a good deal of time sitting with some folks from the manufacturing unit. Her three foremen and their wives, had all indulged in enough alcohol to feel comfortable with the CEO at their table and made her feel particularly welcome.

When she felt she'd visited enough, she looked toward the dance floor. Last year Jonathan had never left her side and danced with her for several dances. This year, an adorable little redhead was keeping him occupied. It made her happy to see him enjoying himself. Jonathan always seemed an old soul and far too serious for his years. Maybe he spent too much time dealing with her issues.

She felt a tap on her shoulder and turned to find Chuck, Excellcardia's head of security standing beside her. Why couldn't she ever remember his last name? He wore his blue uniform and did not look in a festive mood.

"I need to speak to you, Ms. Hightower. Privately." He had a soft, southeast Missouri accent, but his round, usually pleasant face held not a single remnant of holiday cheer this evening. He led the way down the hall and Alice hurried after him.

He stopped outside the elevator door and turned to her. "Sorry to bother you tonight, but I noticed something a few minutes ago and I thought you should know as soon as possible. There could have been some security issues in the dog labs."

"When?" Alice's head was suddenly clear as crystal. Her heart pounded.

"Over several nights in the last two weeks. I'll show you if you wanna come to my office." Chuck turned and hurried down the hall to the elevator. He wore his long dark hair pulled back in a ponytail. She'd always thought of him as the most serious of old hippies. *Concentrate, Alice.*

She had to hurry to keep up. Not easy in her Christmas shoes. She stopped for a second to pull up her dress so she wouldn't tear off the beads on the scalloped hem as she hurried.

The security office contained a single desk and a wall of twenty television screens. Cameras watched all the most sensitive areas of Excellcardia. Chuck walked up to one screen and hit a button. The screen flickered and showed the security door to the labs on the tenth floor.

"I review the tapes every morning, and in the past two weeks, I've noticed some damned strange things. I found this one tonight and decided you had to know. You asked me to pay special attention, so I've been lookin' almost frame by frame and…"

The picture seemed to flicker for a second, but Alice couldn't see anything particularly odd. "What am I supposed to be looking at?" She sat on the desk, squinting at the screen.

"The time stamp in the corner." He reached over to point to a tiny blue number in the corner of the screen. She walked closer to the screen.

"See how it jumps from eleven-fifteen p.m. last night to eleven-nineteen? It's like those minutes are just gone. The machines record every second of everyone who comes and goes. I can't explain how or who coulda done it."

"Is this room ever left unattended?" she asked.

"Well, a man's gotta answer the call of nature once in a while, but it's just a short time. I make everybody log their comings and goings and limit the amount of time it's unattended. The door is always locked, and retinal scanner protected, empty or not. Nobody can get in here without the right pattern on the back of their eyeballs, you know."

"Couldn't it be a glitch in the recording device?" Alice bit her lip and tried to slow her breathing.

"Sure, it could be. It's never happened before, though, so I thought you oughta know, is all."

"Thank you, Chuck. I appreciate your diligence. If any of the Biocardia information leaks out, it could jeopardize the whole project. The BioCardia process would be a high-value target for someone with no scruples and industrial espionage on their mind." Her hands were balled into nervous fists at her sides, but her voice remained calm. Inside her head, the fear increased exponentially.

"I've seen the machine mess up, but it's never lost minutes. There are three more incidents on three previous nights with losses of a minute or two. Can't figure why anybody'd want to do this on purpose." Chuck looked only at the screen as he replayed the skipped sections.

"Why would anyone erase a few minutes?" *Oh, please just let it be nothing. Please, please, please.* But she knew it wasn't nothing. The fear roared in her ears like a train, fierce and unstoppable. She drew in a deep breath and let it out slowly. "What do you really think, Chuck?"

He looked shocked she would ask his opinion, and his hands shook a little as he turned to hit the buttons on the monitor. "I—I—think it's just a glitch. It hasta be. Nothing odd showed up on the retinal scanners—I checked. The fact it happened more than once makes it that even more likely. Maybe the damn machine is wearing out. No machine is perfect. I'll order a new one first thing tomorrow morning."

Alice watched as Chuck ran the section of tape once more. It looked neither terribly ominous nor exactly innocent. Why would anyone remove a few random minutes from the security tapes unless they were covering an unauthorized entrance or exit? But wouldn't those be logged on the Labs retinal scanners? Why would the only machine with a glitch be the one watching the most sensitive of areas? Was she being paranoid? A recording glitch sounded plausible. Could paranoia be another symptom of bipolar disorder? She'd have to remember to ask Dr. Elliot.

"Is there any way to restore the missing minutes?"

"Not that I know of Ms. Hightower."

"Double check the retinal scanners against the time stamps on the entry doors for those nights. See if anyone came in or out at those times and let me know if you find anything. I want every bit of this old equipment replaced as soon as possible. There can be no more glitches, and under no circumstance is this room to be left unguarded. Hire more help if you need to. You know what a sensitive time this is." Alice patted him on the shoulder in appreciation. He looked up at her, black eyes unreadable behind his seventies style wire-rimmed glasses.

Chuck opened the secure door for her by pushing a button on his desk, but never looked up to meet her eyes again. Alice found it amusing some people seemed intimidated by their CEO, even in a red beaded dress.

Fear cut through the residual effect of the holiday wine. There seemed to be no way to know if it was a glitch or a disaster. Freaking out would change nothing. She would make sure her orders were followed and made a mental note to check back with Chuck. For now, she stuffed this fear down with all the others in a deep dark pit in her stomach. Alice took in a long cleansing breath and suddenly felt exhausted. Her favorite bedmate surely waited at home, eager and happy to curl up behind her knees.

&.

"Yep, my little furry friend, Mama's sleeping with you again tonight." Alice stoked his black head in response to the cat's meow. She undressed quickly, made her nightly ablutions, and got into bed.

She lay there for hours going over in her head who, how and why someone would steal BioCardia's world-changing secrets. Odd thoughts popped into her restless head. She couldn't forget the feel of Jonathan's hand caressing her back or the look in his gorgeous chocolate brown eyes. *Oh my God,* now she lusted after her administrative assistant. Something had to be done. She would call Dr. Elliot in the morning.

❧

Clinical Notes on Client Hightower, Alice B.

Patient called in requesting to increase her sessions from one to two per week. Extremely agitated at having inappropriate feelings for one of her co-workers. She agreed verbally to hypnotic regression. Will attempt same at next session.

Chapter Eight

NINETEENTH NERVOUS BREAKDOWN

Which mother would she find this morning? Alice wondered as she pulled into the Mary Center's parking lot.

The bright periwinkle-blue winter sky usually made her feel cheerful, but not on Saturdays. This sky was rare and beautiful in a city so often under a haze of humidity. But today Alice barely noticed it. The fist of dread gripped her too tight.

Alice waited with her head down as the automatic door to the Mary Center slid open. The smells of Lysol and urine made her stomach clench. She nearly walked into a rumpled figure in a wheelchair just inside the door. Startled, Alice hurried down the hall without the courage to look back.

Surprised that her mother's door wasn't latched, Alice pushed the door open cautiously. Beverly Hightower lay curled on her side facing the window. As Alice moved closer, she saw her mother's large gray eyes were open, staring far into the distance.

"Good morning, Mother." Alice walked to the window without waiting for a reply she knew wouldn't be coming. She pulled the white Windsor-backed chair close to her mother's bed. This chair used to be in her mother's room when she was a little girl. The paint worn off the edges made it feel like an old friend.

"I'll just sit here and catch you up on my life, okay?" No answer came from the woman in the bed.

"Well, the Board approved BioCardia's budget increase and it's moving forward toward human trials and hopefully clearance. Someone might have broken into the lab. There is no way to know so let's keep our fingers crossed, shall we." Alice imitated her mother's falsely cheerful tone: the one used when Beverly shared bad news.

"There's a man at work I can't stop thinking about. Only he's married, and I ended it a while ago, so now I think I would like to jump my hot admin's bones. Aren't you proud? I spent some time in ancient Rome and eighteenth-century London, I think. In my head at least. Both involved gobs of glorious sex."

Still no reaction from her mother. The door opened without a sound and an attendant entered. Judging by the look on his acne-scarred face, the young man had heard her final words. His cheeks were nearly as red as his uniform's clip-on tie. Alice covered her mouth with her hand and to hide her laughter.

The boy looked at the floor. "I've come to turn Mrs. Hightower. She gets turned every two hours. No bedsores here at the Mary Center." He nodded and came around to the opposite side of the bed.

"Merry Christmas, Mother. Now you behave." She stood to walk to the door but stopped and turned back around. The young man gently turned Beverly and plumped her pillows. These were her mother's favorite lavender-striped sheets. Alice had bought them on her birthday. Beverly's eyes were now aimed at Alice, but they looked right through her. Alice thought she should kiss her mother on her cheek or display some kind of affection for the shell that was her mother today, but she couldn't stand there one more second. She couldn't breathe; it felt as if someone had sucked all the oxygen out of the room.

As she hurried toward the door, head down to hide her tears, she nearly ran into Dr. Langer.

"How long do you intend to let her remain in this state, Ms. Hightower?" the doctor demanded. "The ECT can be effective in breaking these unresponsive bouts of depression."

"Like I said last time, no shock treatments." Alice continued down the hall at a full run, narrowly avoiding the wheelchairs and their ancient occupants.

꿏

When Alice reached her apartment, she walked directly to her bedroom. She took off her black jeans and the lavender cashmere sweater she'd worn because it was a gift from her mother and left them crumpled on the floor.

She pulled back the covers and got into the bed in her bra and panties. Lying on her side, she felt Otis curl up behind her knees. "Just a little nap, Sir Otis, and I'll get you your Christmas Eve dinner. Mama needs to sleep."

Alice stayed in bed for twenty-four hours. She felt too tired to do anything else, and she could think of no better way to pass a holiday meant for fun, families, and feasting.

Her mind didn't race as usual, handling a thousand details at once. Her brain cells felt wrapped with lead. The lead insulated her brain, keeping the neurons from firing, and she just lay there, not exactly asleep, but not completely awake. The time passed with no delineation of day from night. She listened only to the cat's meow when he reminded her he needed food, and her bladder when it reminded her it was full. Once she gave these actions the very minimum of effort, Alice returned to the sanctuary of her bed.

Monday morning, her phone rang. It kept ringing till she answered it.

"Alice, you okay?" It was Jonathan.

"Sure, I'm just coming in late today. I have a hair appointment this morning. But I'll be in this afternoon. Thanks for checking. See you soon."

"I can handle it, take care of yourself." His voice sounded so steady and sure. She was certain he could probably handle anything.

She had tried to sound chipper, but seriously doubted she pulled it off. Jonathan probably knew her hair appointments were not really hair appointments. She'd told him she was seeing a shrink, and her hair never looked any different after the appointment. He knew she went to the psychiatrist once per week. Now it would be twice.

Clinical Notes on Client Hightower, Alice B.

Client appeared to be suffering acute bout of depression. Affect appeared flattened and the client spoke only when asked direct questions, to which she answered with one-word replies. The episode may have been precipitated by a visit to her mother, who was withdrawn and unresponsive. The hypnotic regression was postponed at the client's request.

Chapter Nine

LOVE UNDERGROUND

Alice didn't go to the office after Dr. Elliot. She just couldn't. She went home, where the sight of her bed reminded her how tired she felt, and she got back in.

An hour later the doorbell rang. She heard Susan's muffled voice through the door as she rolled over and covered her head with her pillow. Susan rang again and yelled louder. "What the hell, Alice? Your car has been in the same spot for days. What is going on?"

Finally Alice gave up and opened the door. "I'm really tired. I need to go back to bed. Maybe I'm coming down with a bug."

She pushed the door closed, but Susan stuck her foot in. "Oh, no, you are not. I know the deal. Let me in. This is my late day, so you're not getting rid of me."

Alice sighed and let go of the door.

"Christmas is over, and there is plenty of awful shit in this world, but we can't let it send us to bed," Susan said. "None of that bipolar crap either."

"It isn't crap, it's a diagnosis."

"Yes, and a diagnosis is an excuse a lot of people use. Hell, I think people make up diseases to explain their bad behavior.

Put on some clothes and do thirty minutes on that torture device you love so much, and I'll be back with the medicine."

Susan would be back. Alice pulled on her black leggings and a pink T-shirt and climbed onto the elliptical. Her limbs felt heavy and stiff. As she took step after step, she could feel her blood flowing and flushing away the lead in her brain. This was exactly what she needed.

Susan rang the doorbell thirty minutes later. "Here it is, the best frozen custard on the planet. This is the cure for everything that could ever ail anyone, except maybe diabetes."

"I didn't think they were even open yet," Alice said.

"They weren't. They don't open for an hour, but I have connections. People can be very grateful when you fix their broken front tooth the day before graduation. Here, vanilla, your favorite."

Alice reached out to take the container of Ted Drewe's frozen custard from Susan's hand. This St. Louis specialty was probably the world's most perfect food. The texture was unbelievably smooth. The actual recipe for the stuff was a secret but was rumored to include honey, incredibly therapeutic.

Alice ate slowly, taking small bites. She couldn't remember when she'd eaten last, but this stuff had to be savored. Wolfing it down was wrong on so many levels.

"When did we first have this together?" Alice sat on a stool in her kitchen. Her brain cells were firing now. She savored the exquisite cold confection and looked at Susan almost wistfully.

"I think after P Chem. Someone suggested Ted Drewe's instead of drowning our study sorrows in beer at Dr. Redbird's and we all piled in Crystal's car.

"Yeah. Where's Crystal now?" Alice said.

"She went over to the dark side and went to dental school too. Practices way out in western Kansas."

"Yeah. I think medicine may be the real dark side." Alice scraped the bottom of the paper container with the plastic spoon.

Susan stopped eating and looked at Alice. "Psychiatry for sure. That's some screwed-up shit. Telling people what's normal and how they should think and feel. We all have some messed-up can of worms in our head. As long as we don't start chopping people up, and can do our jobs, what does it matter?"

Alice burst out laughing.

"Another one of my favorite things about you, Alice. You're such a great audience." Susan sat down on the couch eating her frozen custard. "I hope my butt is clean enough for this couch." Alice shot her a look. Chocolate on her white couch? *Oh what the hell.*

"Probably not." Alice threw her empty container in the kitchen trash and walked back to sit next to her friend. "I need your help. I've been sleepwalking at night, I think. I have the wildest dreams, and I go out on the balcony, maybe. I know it makes no sense, but I need someone to come over, maybe about midnight, and see exactly what I do."

"Sure, glad to help," Susan answered with her mouth full of custard. "Does it matter when? David and I are going to visit Bailey for a few days, but I'll be glad to when we get home. I'll curl up on this snow-on-a-polar-bear's-ass-white couch. Should I wake you? No, they say that's dangerous."

"No, just watch and tell me what happens. I can't stay here all day eating ice cream. I have work to go to. Thank you, Susan." Alice smiled at her friend with the love and gratitude born of decades of friendship.

Susan left, and Alice showered and dressed for work. Susan had made an excellent point. There was nothing worth taking to her bed. Not even her mother's taking to her own bed. Enough was enough.

Alice's abbreviated day went smoothly. Her story of a forty-eight-hour stomach bug got her some sympathy and seemed to be genuinely believed. Even Jonathan accepted her story as she described the symptoms of her imaginary illness. Lying wasn't her strong suit but she could remember the last time she had a bug, and she was not ready to explain that she just couldn't get out of bed.

The evening's heavy traffic had Alice checking her watch and fretting. *Don't these idiots have fabulous fantasies of their own to get home to?*

Her dinner eaten, Alice paced. *Just like mother.* At home, she wore the ever-present fear of failure and inadequacy like a ragged gray scarf around her neck. At work, the challenges kept those fears at bay.

She wondered if the clothes would still be in her closet. It had been days and she'd not opened the closet door once. Was the spell broken somehow? Why didn't that feel like a good thing? If there were no clothes, wouldn't that mean she was better? Did she want to be better if it meant the fantasies ended? Her cracked bipolar brain gave her what she needed without endangering any important working relationships or risking any messy emotional attachments. It was a total win-win. It seemed far too late now to end the adventures. She loved the crazy too much.

With the days so short this time of year, she knew she had only ten minutes to sunset.

The minutes crawled by. Finally, at one minute after sunset, Alice slid open the door just enough to peek inside.

When she saw the long dark cloak hanging on the golden hanger, she let out a relieved sigh. She couldn't resist running her fingers along the enormous hood. The blue-black long-napped velvet caressed her fingertips. She slid her hand into the lining to find cool, smooth satin.

"How yummy would that feel against my skin?" She could think of one or two things that might feel better.

Nothing but the cloak hung in the closet; no underwear, no shoes, or anything else at all. She slipped off her clothes, and instead of hanging them neatly as usual, left them in a pile. Throwing clothes on the floor was getting to be a habit of late. It felt a tiny bit good, further proof she was losing it.

Her hands actually trembled as she opened the balcony door. Alice peered into the gloom. Ahead of her she saw only darkness with a small circle of light far down some kind of tunnel. Beneath her feet, cold rough stones added to her trepidation. It smelled of mold and damp. "This isn't real. It can't hurt me. This isn't real," she chanted.

Cold liquid puddles on the stones made Alice chant faster with each step. She reached out to touch the walls of the tunnel and found it no wider than the tips of her outstretched fingers. The walls felt as clammy as Alice felt. She quickened her pace toward the light. *Surely there was something fun at the end of this tunnel?*

Alice could see the light flickering as if produced by candles or torches. Her heart beat faster.

"I wonder when this is? Never mind where." Her voice echoed off the walls.

She stepped into a wider stone chamber lit by torches in rusted metal sconces fixed to the walls. It looked more like a cave than a room; the walls curved into the ceiling and the floor looked to be carved of solid black rock. A narrow path of what looked like dried corn husks led around a bend. At least she'd left the slimy puddles behind as the husks crunched beneath her feet.

Chanting echoed off the cavern walls. She'd once heard an album of monks' chants like this; rhythmically soft, deep, and eerie. The words sounded like Latin, part of some ancient religious ritual, perhaps? The echo wrapped her in deep male voices. Alice smelled something like the spicy incense used in the Christmas high masses her mother took her to as a small child. She coughed, just as she had when she was a little girl.

Alice followed the now wider and brighter chamber a little way until it opened into an even larger chamber. As soon as she stepped into the light, her feet felt soft carpet, and someone wrapped strong arms around her from behind. That someone held her tightly with one arm and pulled the hood of her cloak over her face with the other.

He moved her forward. She could see only about a foot off the floor below the hood. Bright red carpet with a border of gold leaves now caressed her feet, removing the tunnel's filth with each step. Alice was glad she wasn't the one who would have to scrub her nasty footprints off this carpet. None of her fantasies had included tidying up. She was pulled toward the chanting, figuratively and literally.

"Hey! Not so rough," she said.

"Sur mujer tranquila!" said the man, holding her a little too tightly.

Spanish. He just told me to shut up. Alice hadn't spoken Spanish since high school, but she was pretty sure that was what he'd said. She thought of resisting but, he wasn't really hurting her, and it seemed smarter to cooperate than to mess with a man big enough to carry her. She reminded herself again that these evening romps had never been violent and always pleasurable, and let the strong arms guide her.

They stopped suddenly. Below the hood Alice saw the hems of a line of black robes. All looked to be of the same rich velvet as hers. In the middle of the line of ten or so, she saw a red velvet skirt that looked more constructed than her loose cloak. The scarlet velvet hung in folds, forming definite pleats. On a chain hung an upside down crucifix. As she tried to raise her head for a better view, the man holding her pulled the hood back down, completely blocking her sight.

"Prepara el sacrificio." The loud deep voice boomed from the direction of the figure in red.

"Sacrifice! What the hell!" For the first time in all her nocturnal adventures, Alice was afraid. She bent over and tried a backward kick to break the man's hold.

"No te resistas. Me haran dano," her handler said. His soft

voice, muffled by the cloak, sounded almost kind, but he was threatening to hurt her. Alice froze.

As suddenly as he'd grabbed her, he let her go. Someone pulled off her cloak, and, in a single quick motion, tied a smooth piece of cloth around her head, completely blocking her view again. She had been facing the stone wall, so her fleeting glimpse showed her nothing of the undoubtedly weird scene.

"Stop this! now!" she said. "I'm no virgin. Won't that mess up your ceremony?"

"Silencio!" came the same booming voice from the line of cloaked figures. It sounded like James Earl Jones. Was he in her nightly fantasies now?

Alice stood shivering, naked, and terrified in a damp cavern. She wasn't supposed to be frightened. Her mind made up these fantasies to fill her idle time and to entertain, perhaps. Wasn't that what Dr. Elliot said? This didn't feel like entertainment.

Soft hands began to caress her shoulders, breasts, belly, and legs. Alice couldn't tell how many, but the hands soothed her. Then, soft wet lips began to caress her as the hands had done. Lips and tongues kissed and licked. On each nipple greedy lips sucked and teased. From her neck, a pair of lips kissed their way down to the small of her back. Soft warm hands took her hands and led her a few steps until her knees touched a smooth cold surface. The gentle and magical hands, dozens of pairs, helped her to climb up on a flat structure. The silent caresses somehow made her feel it would be okay. As she lay down, again guided by the hands, she felt calm. After all, she told herself, as real as this felt, it was all in her mind.

The hands spread her legs with soft caresses and gentle guidance. Fingers slid into her and incredibly, despite her fear, she was wet and ready. Sucking on her nipples always did the trick. The owner of those fingers laughed: it was a deep laugh, unmistakably female.

Alice tried to rise, but even in their softness, the hands were too many. She felt her own hands separated and fixed to the cold smooth stone with silken cords. Her legs, spread wide, were fixed at the ankles by the same soft cord holding her hands. It didn't hurt. *This isn't real, this isn't real, dreams can't hurt me.* She stopped struggling and gave in.

Suddenly the hands were gone. Lips touched hers, not the soft lips she'd kissed earlier. These lips, rough and demanding, belonged to a man. As he kissed her, someone else's tongue licked slowly down her belly. Facial hair tickled her, and she squirmed. She could feel breath on the wet between her legs and then a strong, slick tongue on her clitoris. The strokes long and slow, as if he was savoring the taste of her with every stroke.

Rough fingers entered her, stroking her inner recesses as the tongue licked. Two mouths sucked at her breasts, now tenderly, now nipping. Alice moaned. In both of her hands she could feel the length of a hard cock. There was just enough play in her restraints for her to close her fingers around and stroke each invisible appendage. She slid her fingers up and down, enjoying the sensation. The lips stopped their kissing, and the tip of an erection brushed against her lips. She opened her mouth to take it. The tongue licking her clit increased the pace until Alice could do nothing but let the climax wash over her. But her unseen lovers were far from finished.

She slid her tongue along the length of the cock in her mouth. She heard the owner of the cock sigh, and he suddenly pulled out of her mouth. Something warm and wet fell on her breasts as the man moaned with satisfaction.

The chanting stopped, and with it, the disturbing and delicious sensations stopped. Alice heard the rustling of cloth. Warm liquid was poured over her slowly, from her neck to her toes. Then the hands were back, gently drying her with soft cloths, soothing her with tender caresses.

"Purificar el sacrificio," said the booming voice. Purify the

sacrifice. Involuntary shivers began at the top of her head and ran the length of her. It was not cold in the chamber, but the hands were gone, and the fear crept back. Her heart pounded in her ears and she stifled the urge to scream. Why couldn't she just wake up?

Little drops of sweet-scented liquid splashed her, and fingers drew an X pattern on her forehead, her belly, and her pubis. Again the rustle of cloth, and Alice, legs still splayed, felt velvet against the length of her body. A smooth hard object slid into her gently. Large, hard and cold, it felt like stone or glass.

"Oh, God," she cried. "Please don't hurt me!" Her voice echoed off the walls.

"*Tranquilo a mi hijo. Vas a ser honrado grandemente,*" said the familiar deep voice close to her ear. She would not be quiet, and this did not feel like any honor. Someone removed the hard, cold object as slowly as it had been inserted. Flesh took its place, a man's cock sliding reverently into her. It filled her completely, and she relaxed, sighing with relief. The man's rich velvet clothing brushed the length of her body with every stroke, but he made no move to kiss or caress her. It didn't feel like rape, but neither was this unseen man making love to her. She thought she could pull her hands free. If she screamed, she could surely wake herself from this particular dream, but to her surprise, she didn't want to. This mysterious ceremony seemed both holy and forbidden. If one had to be sacrificed, this was certainly not the worst way.

Sex for Alice in the past had been largely visual. Now she couldn't believe how much she wanted this unseen partner to continue. It amazed her how fast this strange, velvet-clad man made her climax, her body was completely out of her control. He seemed to take no notice, merely continued the delicious work of sliding in and out of her as the universe unfolded and exploded between her legs. She could not make a sound, so profound and intense was this orgasmic cataclysm.

His pace quickened. She could hear his breathing now. He gave her a few more hard thrusts and Alice felt his leg muscles stiffen beneath the velvet as he came and filled her. There was a moment of stillness, and with the rustle of velvet, he was gone.

The soft hands again. This time they wiped as they caressed. She felt a tongue lapping at the semen dripping out of her. Moist cloths performed ablutions that surely felt sacred. The hands untied her and helped her to sit up. In an instant her blindfold was gone.

Soft candlelight lit the chamber. Alice stood beside a black stone table. This was the altar upon which she had sacrificed to the pleasure of letting go. She shivered even in the warmth of the chamber. A dozen women, whose long, dark hair hung loose, stood in a circle smiling at Alice. Each woman wore the same simple outfit, white garments tied with red sashes. Here were the hands both sacred and profane.

There were tables set up near the wall, and Alice smelled food. One woman brought her a golden plate covered with roasted meat and a large piece of coarse bread. Another stood by with a cup. The cupbearer dropped to her knees and offered the cup to Alice. A third woman wrapped Alice in a long cloak of white fur, as soft as angel wings. Alice took the cup and drank deep of a rich, sweet wine, flavored with fruit and spices.

No one offered utensils. She took a few bites of meat using her fingers and realized how exhausted she felt. Still, no one uttered a word. Bearded men in long garments exactly like the women's, but black, stood against the wall. It seemed so strange to be in a room full of people where no one spoke. Where were the velvet cloaks and the man in red velvet?

"Where is this place?" Alice asked in crappy high school Spanish. The pretty young woman who had given her the plate pointed to her own mouth and shook her head. *Are they mutes or just forbidden to talk?*

Alice leaned back into the cushion of the chair. Two women stood by as if awaiting her to command. Other women moved toward the men, who threw off the black garments, as naked under them as she had been. This caught Alice's attention—nobody loved a good orgy better than Alice Hightower in her fantasies—but the fear and tension of this evening took its toll. She snuggled into the soft fur and closed her eyes for just a minute.

❦

Clinical Notes on Client Hightower, Alice B.

Client has cancelled last three sessions.

Chapter Ten

THESE BOOTS ARE MADE FOR WALKING

S trange thoughts swirled around in Alice's brain as she drove to work. The macabre scenes from last night played over and over in her head. She could still feel the hands all over her, the velvet between her thighs. She'd felt happy and relaxed when she remembered her earlier fantasies, but this morning, Alice was anxious and uneasy. Why had she been so willing to let go and participate in a dark and dangerous game. Even the thought of this fantasy made her shiver with her car's heat set on high.

Maybe it really was time for the regression Dr. Elliot thought would help her get to the reason for the fantasies and even some of her unhappiness. Hypnosis could help her remember things she'd repressed. She'd felt before that some things should stay repressed. Would rehashing her past really explain how she got the way she was? If she knew the answer could she change?

The uneasy hangover from last night's romp dogged Alice throughout her work day. At lunchtime, she wanted nothing but to sit quietly alone in her office. Usually Jonathan brought her something whether she asked or not, but today he didn't trouble her. She sat behind her desk, her hands folded in her lap, eyes closed. She opened them to the sound of Louise's voice.

"Sorry to interrupt your nap, girl, but you missed a lot of excitement in the cafeteria. Can I get you some herbal tea?" Her dark hair was pulled into such a tight bun today that Alice couldn't tell if she was smiling or grimacing in pain.

"No, thanks. "Why, what happened?"

"Jonathan and Brad James went at each other." Louise waited for the news to sink in, then continued. "Jonathan threw the first punch, which glanced off. Then Brad flattened him, but Jonathan wouldn't stay down. He got up off the floor and threw another punch. Brad ducked, and Jonathan's fist hit the wall. It looked like he hurt his hand, but he managed to get off one more punch. He hit Brad square in the face." Louise put her hands in the pockets of her expensive-looking black and white herringbone suit.

"Oh, my God." Alice was on her feet. "Where are they?"

"Chuck from security drove them to the urgent care clinic on Washington."

"Together?"

"Yeah. By then, Brad seemed more concerned with keeping the blood from his nose off his Italian suit, and Jonathan went along quiet as a lamb."

"What the hell? Does anyone know why they were fighting?"

"Oh, yeah. Several people overheard them. They started this melee in the salad line. Rosemary for accounting heard Brad mention your name, though she couldn't hear exactly what he said. Must have been something, though, because Jonathan just hauled off and smacked him." Louise leaned on the door jamb, waiting on Alice's reaction.

Alice said nothing for an entire minute. *This is my fault. All my fault. Two perfectly sane grown men fighting each other. Maybe my crazy's become contagious.* That strange thought nearly made Alice smile, until she realized how inappropriate her reaction would seem to Louise.

She grabbed her coat and purse. "Get someone to cover Jonathan's desk, will you?"

Traffic was epic. It took forty minutes to get to the clinic. Did medical facilities always smell the same, like isopropanol and germs, she thought as the automatic doors opened. Chuck sat in one of the waiting room's orange plastic chairs, reading People magazine. Jonathan sat a few chairs away, holding an ice pack on his left hand. The flesh below his left eye was purple, his eye nearly swollen shut. He grinned at her.

"What the hell, Jonathan?" she said. "Louise said you started this ridiculous thing."

"Brad James defamed your honor. I was compelled to defend it."

Alice dropped into the chair next to him. She didn't know whether to slug him in his good eye or hug him. No one had ever felt the need to defend her honor, yet the act was inexcusable. She looked at his swollen eye and the goofy-proud look on his face for a long minute. "My 'honor' is nothing to throw punches for. There's no excuse for violence in the workplace."

"I happen to think your honor is very much worth defending." Jonathan said defiantly. Then he lowered his voice. "He had the unmitigated gall to ask me if I had—well if we had ever—had sexual relations. When I, of course, told him we had not, he implied you and he had."

The look on Jonathan's face was priceless. Alice burst out laughing. As soon as she could catch her breath, she said. "That's just trash talk. Kind of like saying he slept with your mother, just to piss you off. You completely overreacted. You'd better hope Brad doesn't press assault charges."

Now he looked crushed. Alice curtailed her rant and asked, "Is your hand broken?"

"No, just bruised. I can go back to work as soon as some papers are signed."

"Chuck can drive you back to your car, but I want you to take the afternoon off. Get some ice on that eye." She reached out and touched his uninjured hand, hoping the look in her eyes told him she appreciated his effort, even though she had to officially condemn it. "I'll expect you at work tomorrow."

"Of course. James got the worst of it, anyway." Jonathan said.

The receptionist waved him over. Alice watched as he signed some forms, and disappeared out the automatic doors, followed by silent, dependable Chuck.

Her hopeful feeling about this disaster faded when she thought of Brad James. *Please, please, please let his injuries be minor.* If he pressed charges, the resultant shitstorm would be hard to weather. He was so good at what he did. Any restriction in his ability to do his job would hurt Excellcardia, but his value to the company could not excuse behavior that undermined her authority.

She walked to the desk to ask about Brad and felt a tap her on the shoulder. Alice turned. Brad looked like he'd definitely lost the fight. Large blue bruises under both his eyes, seemed to grow as she watched. His nose was covered with gauze and tape, but still he smiled. "What's up, Boss Lady? Don't tell me you came all the way down here to check on yours truly?"

"Are you all right?"

"Yep. Nose is broken, but it's not the first time. Your lapdog got lucky. I walked into his fist, or he wouldn't have left a mark on me."

"His behavior was inexcusable. Violence is never the answer. As for your behavior, What the hell were you thinking?"

"Alice, relax. I'm okay. I'm not calling my lawyer. I know junior has the hots for you, and I couldn't resist yanking his chain. It was irresponsible on my part, and I apologize." He put his hand on her shoulder. "Private matters should stay private. But really, you should have seen the look on his face."

Brad chuckled and looked at her with those ridiculous blue eyes.

Alice let out a long slow breath. She stood with and her hands on her hips. "'Junior' is a valuable member of the Excell-cardia team. How he feels about me has no bearing on how he performs his job. And he certainly does not 'have the hots' for me. Any relationship you and I shared in the past is over. Your little trash talk was beyond inappropriate and had better not be repeated."

Brad moved closer to her and lowered his voice. "You can tell yourself whatever you want, Alice, but I know lust when I see it. Don't you want to know exactly what I said?"

"No." She felt a surge of anger that surprised her. Why did she let him affect her like this? Heart pounding, she took a step back.

Once again he closed the distance between them. "I get it and I'm sorry. It was juvenile of me. Are you afraid of me, Alice?"

"No." Could she sound less believable? Why did he insist on standing so close? "I want you to take a cab home, take whatever pain meds they gave you, and just chill," Alice said. "Maybe you should take a couple of days off."

"No can do. I'm flying to Dallas tonight to get to that meeting. But I can change my plans if you want to take me to your place, tuck me in your bed, wrap those long legs around me, and fuck me better."

Even with his nose covered with gauze and two black eyes, that suggestion made the blood rush in her ears. She ignored it and said, "How will you explain your injuries to the client?"

"I won't. They'll think what they want no matter what I say, so why bother?"

"At least have you Uber to and from the airport. Don't rent a car. I don't want to lose you in a hydrocodone-fueled car wreck."

"I knew you still cared," Brad said.

❦

Alice gasped to see Jonathan sitting at his desk when she returned to the twenty-third floor.

"Jonathan: my office, now." He followed her inside and she closed the door and took a deep calming breath. This had to be addressed. He was the best assistant of all possible assistants, but insubordination could not be tolerated. She'd learned long ago as a woman in business to allow no one to mistake orders for suggestions.

"Alice, we've talked about the door, and I really—"

"Leave it closed for now."

He obeyed and stood in front of her desk. "I couldn't go home," he said. "I have plenty of ice for my hand and my eye. The Compton contracts have to be sent to legal for review today. There are some inquiries from the FDA that must be addressed as soon as possible. This company does not come to a halt because I broke Brad James's smug and incredibly rude nose." He wore a rather smug look on his own face.

"Jonathan, why did you start this crap with Brad, really?"

"Because he implied you and he'd had intimate relations. I couldn't let—"

"What would that matter? Don't you see? He just said something he thought would anger you, and it worked. You know how much I value you. You and I work so well together, but it is a working relationship. You are hardly responsible for my honor."

"Understood," Jonathan said. The hurt Alice saw in his eyes surprised her. The hurt she felt in causing him pain, surprised her even more.

Maybe her colleagues were right. Maybe Jonathan did have a crush on her. If so, it was more important than ever to set him straight. The cute little HR redhead would be happy to have his babies, and that was a much more appropriate object for his affections. Too bad Brad had to sacrifice his nose for her to learn this very important bit of information. She would have to be very careful with Jonathan's feelings in the future. The only thing worse than having an affair with her VP of sales would be having one with her invaluable assistant, no matter how tempting.

🦋

In her car on the way home, the possibility of the night's fantasy began to wipe away the tension on Alice's weary face. With the day's insanity, she'd forgotten to go to her appointment with Dr. Elliot. She felt just fine, knowing what she really needed waited at home for her, one slide of her balcony door away. She swallowed hard as she remembered how strange and dark last night's offering had been. Why would her mind make up such a thing? She'd experienced pleasure, but she'd also felt she was in real danger and had no control at all. She wasn't harmed; but she felt like she could have been at any moment. It didn't turn out to be dangerous, still. She shivered inside her heavy winter coat. All her other trips had been good, clean, naughty fun. What if they continued to get scarier and scarier? What if this was the progression of her disease? Maybe she would take a peek at the golden hanger before deciding.

She fed Otis, gulped down some ravioli, and had enough time for twenty minutes on the elliptical before sunset. Then, with her heart pounding, she opened her closet door.

"Groovy," said Alice to herself. The pink shift dress with huge orange polka dots looked like something she'd seen her mother wearing in pictures from the late sixties. What could possibly be frightening about that? After the trials of this day she needed a little fun, not scary dungeon sex. She could only hope that Crazy Central, deep in her head, would understand and comply.

Next to a small pile of underclothes stood a pair of knee-high white patent boots. Did she hear Nancy Sinatra on her mother's old scratchy record player? She couldn't wait to see where these fun boots would take her, because they were certainly made for walking.

The shift dress barely reached past the hot pink silky panties with *Wednesday* printed across the front. It was Thursday in Alice's daytime reality.

Sliding open the door, she smiled as the warm sunshine fell on her face. Alice found herself on the sidewalk in front of a two-story frame house surrounded by an actual picket fence. The click of her white boots on the concrete and the smell of fresh-cut grass made her shiver with anticipation. *What else to do but ring the doorbell?*

"Hi," said the blonde woman who opened the door. "You are…?"

"Alice."

"Right. I'm Cindy. Marsha said she sent a couple of her girlfriends. Are you the nurse or the secretary?"

"I'm a nurse," Alice said. That just seemed the right thing to say.

"Far out. Come on in. You're a little early, but I could use some help getting the refreshments ready. Everyone works up quite an appetite if you know what I mean." The woman's pale hair was swept up on her head in a hairdo Alice knew was called a beehive. She had watched her mother torture her platinum hair into the same do as a little girl. Her dress made Alice's own look positively puritanical in its length, and the lime green stripes matched her high-heeled pumps perfectly.

"Last time I ran out of everything, so I bought extra this time. Marsha said you were a lot of fun and have been to these kinds of parties before." Cindy raised her eyebrows.

"Sure," Alice said. She gave Cindy a reassuring smile and followed her to the kitchen, reminded her of her grandmother's. The orange plaid wallpaper sprinkled with bright yellow teapots was so cheerful.

"Your dress is groovy, and those boots are so mod! We

always need extra girls. Some of the girls get all squeamish when the rubber hits the road, so to speak. Last time Linda Vogel left before the martinis were even served and walked all the way home. Her husband stayed, though. She knew what goes on, she just chickened out." Cindy handed Alice a glass bowl, a box of soup mix, and a container of sour cream. "You make the dip and I'll get the chips. I got those new wavy ones. Made the sandwiches already. Just need to cut off the crusts and cut them into quarters. Hope we have enough glasses. Martinis don't taste right in paper cups."

Cindy pulled out a chrome and yellow vinyl chair from the yellow Formica-topped dinette and waited for Alice to sit down. "I think tonight will be a gas."

Alice poured the dry soup mix into the bowl and stirred in the sour cream.

"I usually do that the other way around, but that works too, I guess. My Bruce will really love you. He's a real bust man, and my A cups don't get him going anymore."

"Thank you." Alice decided to just let Cindy blather on and soak in as much information as she could.

"Won't be long now," Cindy said. "Where are your keys? Might as well be the first to throw them in." She held out a large crystal bowl to Alice.

"Uh, I don't have any. Someone dropped me off."

"Not a problem. You can use these I found them in Bruce's pocket. He won't tell me where they came from or who they belong to. Kind of sweet he thinks I'd even care." Cindy dropped three keys on a ring with a pink rabbit's foot into the crystal bowl. "Easy to remember. Pink rabbit's foot is yours." The doorbell rang.

"Here we go!" Cindy giggled and ran to the door as fast as her little green pumps would take her. She returned to the kitchen to introduce Ray and Tabatha Weber. He was a hand-some man with a crewcut, dark brown eyes and a large infectious smile. She was a tiny shy brown-haired mouse of a girl who looked only at the floor. The doorbell rang again.

"Alice, please grab the chips and dip and bring them to the living room." With that, Cindy disappeared.

In the living room, there were two, long, brown-striped couches facing each other, a coffee table of glass and chrome, and six chairs scattered around the room in groupings of two. Alice set the bowls of dip and chips, on the coffee table. She sat down in the middle of one of the couches tugging the hem of her little dotted dress.

The doorbell rang several more times, and in less than half an hour, eight people sat with Alice in the living room. A short balding man and his fat wife were on one side of her and two delicious twin brothers on the other.

"Dan," said one of the brothers, extending his hand to Alice. "I'm the handsome one. The ugly one is Don." They appeared identical, except one wore a tweed jacket and tie, while the other wore a red turtleneck under tweed jacket. *Tweedle Don and Tweedle Dan. Too perfect.* Both brothers had black hair that was combed back and held in place with some kind of grease. Each twin looked at her with the same dark eyes and gave her a nice warm smile, although Dan evidently did the talking for both.

The other guests all seemed to know each other, and Cindy didn't bother to introduce Alice. A man in a black suit and tie carried a huge silver tray covered with martini glasses, a crystal pitcher full of clear liquid, and a small glass bowl of toothpick-skewered olives. He stood over six feet with curly mahogany hair and the kind of wide-shouldered build that always got Alice's notice.

"Okay, kids, here is tonight's lubrication. No offense, ladies," he said. He looked around the room and then walked straight to Alice. "Bruce Turner. And who, pray tell, are you?" He set down the tray on the coffee table, poured the clear liquid from the pitcher, and handed it to Alice without ever taking his eyes off her chest or spilling a drop.

"Alice—uh—Carroll."

"Well, aren't you easy on the eyes?" He reached over to drop a skewer of three olives into her drink and leaned close. This evening comes complete with my favorite libation, she thought. Well done, Crazy Central!

"I can't wait to see what's under those spots," he said in a whisper. "Didn't Cindy tell you? I'm the master of this house and I always get first choice."

Alice returned a look that said fine with her. Bruce's lovely dark green eyes appraised Alice. He smelled like salt air and leather she noticed as he leaned close. The skinny lapels of his suit and even skinnier black tie reminded her of Don Draper on *Mad Men*. Before the fantasies started, when she had time for TV, it had been her favorite show. She might have to binge stream the old episodes soon to relive this evening. Who knew vintage business attire was even hotter than the modern suit?

She took a sip of her martini and focused her eyes on him over her glass. He smiled back and began serving the rest of the guests. Cindy placed a crystal bowl and a tray of sandwiches next to the other snacks. The bowl, Alice noticed, was now full of keys.

"You a friend of Cindy's?" Tweedle Dan asked as he put his arm around her.

"No, dullard, can't you tell she's a friend of Bruce's?" said his twin.

"No, Marsha sent me," Alice said.

"Oh," said the twins in unison.

Dan ran his index finger slowly up Alice's leg. "Well, then, I'm sure you wouldn't mind a little challenge. Don and I like to share everything."

"Like the Doublemint Twins. Double your pleasure," Don said.

It made her hot just to think of those pretty twins all over her, on her, and inside her. "That would be—"

Ladies and gentleman! Bruce interrupted. He held up the bowl full of keys, closed his eyes, and fished around until he found the pink rabbit's foot from which dangled three keys. "I wonder to whom these belong?" He made a circle around the room, smiling at each of the other women. Some smiled back boldly, and one or two other women looked away, or at the floor. The little, short woman, whose name was evidently Joan, gave him a hopeful grin and bounced a little on the couch. He returned her smile but moved on. Finally, he stopped at Alice.

"They're mine," Alice said. Behind him, the bowl of keys passed from man to man. With the touch of his hand, Bruce erased any thought of the other pairings.

Pulling her to her feet, he put his hand on her waist and led her down to the end of the hall. Bruce opened the door to a bedroom. She closed the door behind them and leaned against him. His body felt hard and strong beneath his suit. He made a move to remove his coat.

"Don't. I love a man in a suit." His kiss felt as hot and wet as the contents of her pink Wednesday panties. She took the tip of her tongue and teased the inside of his upper lip, her favorite move. He moaned. She laughed and pulled away.

"Don't move." Alice knelt in front of him. Looking up at his face, she slowly unzipped the zipper of his black trousers. The cock that greeted her was not at all disappointing. It was not huge, but a good size and extremely erect.

"Oh, yes." She slipped the brownish pink head of it between her lips.

"God damn, Marsha was right about you." Bruce's voice was a coarse whisper as she slid her tongue along the underside of his luscious erection. He leaned back against the wall with his legs apart and his eyes closed. Neither of them heard the door open.

"Excuse me," said a voice, tearing Alice from the pleasure

of Bruce. Cindy peeked in through the small crack in the door. "So sorry, honey," she said to Bruce. "Marsha's other friend never showed. There's no one for the twins. I'd have been glad to help out, but…"

"What the hell, Cin?" Bruce said. He opened the door wide, not bothering to put away his cock.

"They want her." Cindy smiled down at Alice, still on her knees. "Just because their dad owns half of Detroit, they think they can make demands."

"And right they are." Bruce tucked in and zipped up.

"The Webers will switch with us. She likes you, but she's kind of shy. She's sitting in the living room kissing her own husband, if you can imagine." Cindy laughed and turned to Alice with a wide, perfect hostess smile, complete with dimples. "Is this okay with you, Alice?"

"Sure." Alice thought those scrumptious twins would do quite nicely.

"Oh, I will have to thank Marsha for sending you. I'm going to take her a lemon ice-box pie as soon as she gets home from the hospital. Sally told me she had a girl." Cindy turned to leave, leading her husband by the hand. Bruce gave Alice one last, longing look before closing the door.

Alice sat on the end of the bed. She ran her hand nervously over the little ridges of baby-blue chenille bedspread. The door opened and in walked Dan and Don.

"I hope you don't mind, Alice, Dan said. "It's just that Don here, well, he really loves big boobs. Me, I don't care, big or small. I'm a snatch man, and I assume you have one of those." He had shed his coat and tie somewhere and now knelt on the powder-blue carpet. Don took off all his clothes in record time and sat next to her on the bed.

As Dan pulled off her panties, Don kissed her. His tongue sliding in and out of her mouth exactly matched his brother's long wet strokes on her clitoris. Fingers teased her nipples and she climaxed quickly.

"Now that's how I like 'em. All tight and wet." Dan slid his fingers in and out of her. "You can't imagine what giving birth does to them. I see the ruined wrecks of them every day and it makes me sad."

He's a gynecologist," said the lips against hers.

"And you?"

Dan answered for him. "Oh, he's a plastic surgeon. Specializing in breast augmentation." Dan pulled off her dress and unhooked her bra. He stopped further questions by exploring her mouth with his tongue. His brother said, "He fills funbags with silicone all day long and wants nothing more than to touch real ones. It'd be sad if it wasn't so goddamn funny."

Don lay back on the bed, pulling Alice with him. As she lay on her side, he sucked her left nipple and squeezed and caressed her right one. Alice felt lips on her neck and the hard length of Dan against her. His steel-hard cock pressed against the small of her back. She lifted her leg and he slipped into her. Again his brother matched him stroke for stroke, one inside her and the other licking her nipple in the same rhythm.

"How in God's name do you do that? Telepathy of some kind?" She barely had breath to talk but had to know.

"Umm. Shut up and fuck us," said the lips kissing her neck. The cock and tongue duo again brought her to another speedy crescendo.

She lay still, catching her breath. Neither twin moved at all for several minutes.

"Now that you're all hot and juicy, it's time for our specialty." Dan slowly planted moist kisses down her back. He stopped and she felt him spreading the cheeks of her ass, his tongue caressing her. This was something Alice had never felt before, and it surprised her. She moaned softly, "Oh, God."

She felt a finger slide into her rear entrance, and she stiffened. "I'm not sure I—"

"Oh yes you are. Relax." Don stopped sucking her nipple and now lay face to face with her, looking deeply into her eyes.

He slid his tongue into her mouth just as she felt the pressure of Dan's cock against her back door. There was a sharpness. She wanted to cry out, and then she understood why people did this. As he slid slowly and gently in and out of her, she felt Don slide into her vagina. It felt like her clitoris was being stimulated from both inside and out, simultaneously.

They slid in and out of her in perfect unison. Alice told herself she was not going to come. She didn't want this to end, ever. But the brothers increased their pace, and she came hard enough to nearly lose consciousness, just before the twins climaxed together.

For several minutes, no one moved. The only sound was breathing: Alice's ragged pants and the brothers' deep slow breaths. Alice realized with amazement their breathing was perfectly synchronized, one sound coming from two directions.

As if he read her mind, said Dan, "Our heartbeats are synched, too. It used to freak out our physiology professor. We were forever demonstrating this amazing fact in some class or another."

"But now we only use it for pleasure, Alice. Ours and yours." Don stopped talking and again sucked each of her nipples. She could feel Dan get off the bed and heard water running in the bathroom. "My brother is so thoughtful, washing his cock so he can stick it in that hungry little mouth of yours. Or maybe in this pussy he so admired." Don's breath against her nipple, his fingers caressing her slippery clit. Alice gasped.

Dan returned, and with his hand under her buttocks, he rolled her on her back. Spreading her knees with his, he entered her. "Even slick with my brother's come, you are so nice and tight."

Don now knelt on the bed beside her. His cock in his hand, he slid his hand up and down, stroking the length of it and rubbing its head against her left nipple. "He can fuck your pussy. I want to fuck these tits. So soft and so real. Watch me, Alice. Watch me come on your gorgeous real tits." Alice couldn't take her eyes from the hard cock head rubbing against her, sending waves of pleasure rocketing to where his brother fucked her properly. She couldn't take her eyes off of him as he stopped pumping his cock and the lovely white semen shot all over her breasts. She closed her eyes to came once again.

Some hours later, Alice fell asleep, the satisfied meat in a delicious brother sandwich.

&.

Clinical Notes on Client Hightower, Alice B.

Client DNAed her scheduled appointment and failed to reschedule.

Chapter Eleven

GOODBYE YELLOW BRICK ROAD

D r. Henry Petrus stood outside Alice's office door as she hung up her coat, whistling and tapping his foot impatiently. His hair looked like squirrels had nested in it, and his lab coat had surely been slept in more than once.

"Good morning, Dr. P., Alice said. "You're in awfully early this morning."

"Who the hell says I ever went home? We have ten dogs with fresh bypasses, and we can't afford to lose a single one. The FDA will want to see numbers. I'll give them the damn numbers. I want you to see the new expansion. I did the best I can with the chump change of a budget you gave me. It is ridiculous to waste money keeping our research subjects happy, if you ask me, but you wanted it, so you should see it."

"I'll be glad to. How did you get it done so quickly? And why are you watching the dogs. Don't we have lab assistants to do that? You really don't have to—"

"Don't tell me how to do my job. I'm not losing dogs because Heckle and Jeckle are off boning each other instead of watching my subjects. They're okay during the day, but at night when nobody's around, they do whatever the hell they please. I've come in late and found nobody at all watching the store. Damn kids left, both of them, when they're scheduled to be here all night. There's two new ones, but I sure as hell won't trust them."

"I'll have Jonathan check into it. Can you wait till I have my coffee? Would you like a cup?" Alice trained her sweetest smile at the irascible doctor.

"Hell, no. I can't sit around drinking coffee. The first twenty-four hours are critical. You know that."

"Okay. I'll join you there as soon as my schedule allows." She couldn't let him just come and fetch her. She would not be summoned.

Jonathan stuck his head in the door. "Alice, the call you were expecting is on line one."

"Thank you," she said to Jonathan. "I'll see you soon, Henry." Alice picked up the phone, and it was Jonathan's voice she heard.

"I could tell you needed to be saved from our resident mad scientist," he said quietly. Dr. Petrus huffed to the elevator.

"You are a lifesaver, even if you still look like you lost the fight." Alice smiled at him through the glass wall of her office. He did look awfully cute, all proud of the black eye earned fighting for her honor. If only he just weren't much younger and her assistant. *Oh, now there is a dangerous thought.* She would need to tell Dr. Elliot—*oh my God.* She couldn't remember her last visit.

Alice picked up the phone and dialed the number she knew by heart. There should be no hard feelings as long as she paid for the missed sessions. Wasting money on missed appointment fees would hurt, but at least she would still have a shrink. She made an appointment for tomorrow and began wading through the sea of emails. Only 143—a light load today. She'd learned a long time ago, one had to answer correspondence no matter how long it took.

By eleven o'clock, she'd answered all her emails and held two meetings. It was time to visit Dr. Petrus and his doggies.

She'd loved the lab when it was only Barney. Now she had to see for herself the new $250,000 expansion.

"Good morning, Ms. Hightower," said the retinal scanner. When had it been reprogrammed to be friendly? The smoky female voice almost sounded sexy. *Who approved the budget for that ridiculousness?*

The stainless steel door whooshed open, and there stood a bright and shiny young brunette in blue scrubs. The girl dropped the folders she held and scrambled to pick up the papers that flew out.

"Oh, hello, Ms. Hightower. Dr. P. didn't tell us when exactly you were coming."

"You are Emily?" Alice searched her brain for the girl's last name but could not pull it up. She tried not to look annoyed.

"House, Emily House, yes." Flustered, the girl frantically shoved the papers into the folder, then pushed her red-framed glasses up on her pert little nose. "Dr. Petrus is in his office."

"Thank you, Emily. I don't bite you, you know. We're all important members of the Excellcardia team. Welcome aboard." Alice extended her hand to the girl, whose sweaty palm betrayed her nerves at meeting the CEO.

Alice hadn't been much past the white air lock doors in ages. The little anteroom still contained the lockers where anyone wishing to enter the treatment room had to put on a yellow isolation gown, head cover, and paper booties. The surgical area had to be protected. Outside germs were not welcome at the heart of the BioCardia project.

All decked out in isolation yellow, Alice pushed the button to open the airlock. She waited while the doors closed behind her and the doors in front of her whooshed open.

Along the hall were six swinging silver doors. Two of them led to surgical suites. The last door in the line was the one she was looking for: Henry Petrus's office.

As she walked to the end of the hall, the scents of the lab assaulted her nose. Disinfectant of course, a little whiff of dog pee understandably, but the one really bothered her was the sickly sweet smell of formalin. Everything needed to be preserved. It always caused a flashback to medical school and human anatomy. The first time she saw the bodies they were to dissect, Alice nearly lost it. *These were people's grandmothers and dads*, she'd thought all those years ago.

"So happy you found time to stop by." Henry Petrus looked up from the papers on his desk, piled high with folders, scientific journals, and books. Most were opened and stacked precariously. The stack reached halfway to the ceiling. *Has he never heard of bookmarks?*

"I will always make time for you, Henry," she said.

Alice surveyed his office. Besides his desk, the clutter of which made Alice's skin crawl, there was nothing else except a laptop and the Wall of Blondes. It always surprised her that a man like Henry Petrus would take the time to cut out magazine pictures and stick them up on his wall. The pictures made a floor-to-ceiling collage. There were pictures of Grace Kelly, Jean Harlow, Cameron Diaz, Pamela Anderson, and January Jones, but the majority, were of Marilyn Monroe.

"They are my muses," he'd once told her with an embarrassed grin. There was no such vulnerability on his face today. His lips were tight, and his wooly-worm thick brows were tightly knitted together.

"I lost one this morning," he said.

"There are always losses. The numbers are still good, aren't they?" She hoped her words sounded confident and reassuring. "Well, then, show me where the money went, please." He led her to the door closest to his, the surgical suite.

"We have some great new stuff in here. New lights like those in hospital surgical suites. We need all the advantages of the big boys. That is a machine that more accurately delivers the anesthetic." He pointed with pride to a stainless box four feet tall and covered with LED readouts. "These dogs weigh less than forty pounds and it's really easy to overdose them.

Killing the damn dogs before we even cut them makes the numbers really suck."

"Impressive." Alice followed along, letting Henry show off his new toys.

"Most of the money, went for the two new 3-D printers and the new dog pens. *Somebody insisted they be overly humane.*"

"Wouldn't one printer have been enough?"

"Hell no! I'm not wasting money here, Alice. This is my shot at a Nobel Prize in medicine, and I am not going to lose it because your cranky richer-than-Croesus board members won't let go and give approval to spend some of the company's precious money."

"Okay. Henry, I'll have to take your word for it." Finally, she saw his face relax a little.

"Let's go see where all good dogs would love to go when they die." He gave her his stripped-down version of a smile.

The bright sunlight in the Dog Containment Area made Alice wish she had her sunglasses. *Great, that's just what they deserve.* If they're giving their little doggie lives for science and profit, they deserve the best in comfort.

"Replacing the back wall with glass cost a shit pot of money," Henry said.

"They deserve to see the sun." Alice walked to the little fence surrounding a grassy area. She knew it couldn't be live grass because the mostly indoor light wouldn't sustain it, but she had been assured it was as close to the real thing as possible. Two brown and white beagles ran the forty-foot length of the "grass" toward Alice. She opened the gate in the three-foot-high chain-link fence and stepped in. It certainly felt like real grass beneath her feet. She knelt down to pet the dogs. Both wagged their tails vigorously in response.

The dogs slept in comfortable crates surrounding the grassy playground. Each crate contained a soft fleece blanket and a chew toy chosen by the dog, from a pile of the best. Doggie doors allowed the dogs to come and go as they pleased.

"These two are the liveliest, Marilyn and Grace. The rest of the princesses are too lazy to leave their little castles." The look on Henry's face betrayed his pleasure at their subjects' new surroundings.

"I thought they were all named Barney? Those are girls' names." Alice stopped mid-stride and turned toward him.

"They're only numbered Barneys while they're still subjects. Once their surgical incisions heal and they're counted as a successful statistic, they get names." *So Professor Grumpy-Pants has a heart after all.*

"They can come and go when they want no matter what their names. That's the point." She counted the crates: twenty. "I thought there were fifty dogs?"

"Forty-nine. These thirty in the rehab, and nineteen in recovery. We send them off-site to foster homes after they have served their purpose, as my bleeding heart of a CEO insists. They're all put up for adoption like you wanted, so don't give me that look, Alice."

"I want to see recovery," she said.

"Okay, but remember, this new group were all cut recently. Won't be any tail wagging, and don't even think about touching them." Dr. Petrus opened the door reverently, as if it were the door to a chapel.

The Recovery Ward's green tile walls and floor matched the surgical suites. Along the back wall stood twenty pediatric hospital cribs, and in each bed lay a dog attached to an octopus of tubes and electrical monitoring leads. Peter Cottontail looked down on each patient from the headboard of each little bed. Alice wondered who had chosen this theme for the beds. Whoever it was should get a raise. Maybe they would all dream of chasing bunnies who wore little blue coats.

"Why are they so still?" asked Alice.

"We have to sedate them for a short while to simulate how

humans act. These were all pretty young, and we can't risk them blowing out the implants by being too frisky too soon. We learned that with the first couple of younger Barneys. The surgery really doesn't slow them down much, so we have to keep them sedated for a while."

Alice noticed a little lump under a green surgical drape on a stainless cart. She pulled back the drape to see a black, white, and brown basset. This must have been the one who didn't make it. The large brown eyes were open and still glistened, but there was no life in them.

"Yeah. That was Barney 290. Once she's autopsied to try and figure out what killed her, we'll cremate her and put her with the others. They all died to save human lives, Alice. Small price to pay."

"Yeah," was all she could say.

"You did notice they're all female now. We found they seem to do better without males around. We will have to run some all-male trials and mixed trials, too, so we no one can allege sex bias. That will come later."

"Makes sense." Alice suddenly felt profoundly sad. Her history with males of her own species was filled with dismal failures. Maybe she, like the dogs, was better off without males. Maybe it was best if she met them only in her dreams.

Her visit colored the rest of Alice's day. She knew they had to do animal testing. She just didn't have to like it. *Time to act like a grownup and let it go.* She was not the ten-year-old blonde girl in the pinafore on the front of Mr. Carroll's book. She was the chief executive officer of a company whose new product would soon change the nature of bypass surgery forever. The little girl inside would have to stay there; and today, she did.

Alice was putting on her coat to go home when Jonathan popped in his head. "There's a group of us going out for happy hour. Why don't you join us? It will be good for company morale."

"Will that cute little redhead from HR be going?" she teased.

"No. She's really much too young for me. She's not even thirty."

"Jonathan, sometimes you act like a stodgy old man. What are you, thirty-two?"

"My next birthday will be my forty-fifth."

Alice looked closely at him. He did have some tiny lines around his eyes, but he had the posture of a younger man, and not a single gray hair on his head.

"My mother was Chinese, we have good skin, it's said." He smiled at Alice. She admired his tender smile she'd seen a thousand times. She'd always thought him simply an old soul. Alice had no idea so few years separated them. But she saw something else in his face this evening: something dangerous to her heart. It would be dangerous only if she allowed it to be dangerous. *Sometimes you just need to live on the edge.*

"You know, Jonathan, I think that's exactly what I need tonight. Where can I meet you?"

"Oh, I would be happy to drive you." He looked far too hopeful.

"I'll take my own car. If Brad James were to hear we left together, it might give him fuel to goad you into another fight. His nose couldn't take it." She managed to make him laugh and kept him at an appropriate arms-length. One day her weaknesses would likely take her down, but today was not the day.

❧

Harry's was the upscale downtown bar and restaurant the group had chosen for this evening's happy hour. She had been there once for a client dinner with Robert and found it pretentious, the kind of place young professionals went to meet and greet, and with any luck, find someone to bone. Since people met on the internet now, the place would be half empty. Back in the day, girls would stroll in on barrowed Louboutins, carrying a bag they couldn't afford, and sit at the bar next to boys in J. C. Penney's suits with the sleeves pushed up to expose a brand-new used Rolex. She supposed the whole Happy Hour scene was mostly over now in the texting age. It didn't matter, it still made her feel old. Tonight was about nothing but a casual drink with her valued coworkers. Alice decided she would spend time with Jonathan in a group and enjoy his company, while reinforcing the professional nature of their relationship. *Would that sound as much like bullshit if she said it out loud?*

She planned to arrive last, after the speculation about her appearance died down. It also seemed wise to let everyone else have a drink before she joined them. It would give her the advantage of a clear head and relax the others. Alice couldn't resist having an advantage however small, in any situation, one character flaw that had served her well.

The sound of familiar laughter hit her the second she opened the front door to Harry's. Evidently, her employees had downed more than one drink by the time she arrived. She followed the sounds of laughter and the occasional raised voice. Jonathan peered over the group, spying her long before the others. There were four young women, not much past thirty, and three men looked no older. Somehow Jonathan fit right in.

His cheeks were a little flushed and his eyes glassy. Of course this just made him look even more handsome. Alice walked up to the table.

"Welly, well, well, well! Here she is. Pay up, everybody. I

told you she would come." Grinning, he stuck out his hand. Twenty-dollar bills were soon piled high in his palm.

Alice climbed upon the empty stool next to his. There sat a martini with three olives waiting for her. "You were that sure of me?" Alice leaned toward him and raised her voice over the sounds of alcohol-fueled frivolity. This happy hour at Harry's was happy indeed. Alice greeted everyone at the table by name. Sometimes she couldn't remember her own password, but she had a talent for names, at least first names. Jonathan put his arm around her. Alice went stiff and he quickly dropped his arm, looking embarrassed.

The table's conversation was about who had just broken up with whom and various other social trivialities. Alice pretended to be interested. Jonathan listened to the conversation, but every time she looked his way, he gave her a look she thought far too earnest and hungry. That would be hard to ignore for much longer. She sipped her drink, carefully looking anywhere but at Jonathan. Finally, her martini finished, she said good night and excused herself. She would leave the young people to their silliness and head home to Otis. Before leaving, though, she stopped in the ladies room.

Two young women came in right after Alice. Even through the stall door, she recognized their voices: they were Ashley and Madison from the happy hour group.

"Can you believe she had the nerve to actually show up?" Ashley said.

"Oh she's got balls, our Cunt Executive Officer." Madison replied.

"Did you see her freeze him? I'd be happy to screw Mr. Gorgeous half to death. Seems all he wants is her."

"Ew. Can you imagine what those great big things look like without a bra? And that huge ass is probably all old-lady veins and cellulite. Why would a hot guy want to do anyone that old?"

"Oh, burn!"

"He danced with Heather from HR all night at the Holiday party, then totally ghosted. She tried to give him a hummer and he actually said, 'No thank you.'" The two broke into the kind of spontaneous laughter that happens only after three drinks and goes on far too long.

It was too late to pretend she hadn't heard all this. Alice was trapped in the bathroom stall.

"Maybe he's gay," Madison said, "and she's like his Lady Gaga." Again the peals of inebriated laughter.

"No, Brandon from the mailroom got the same answer when he offered Jonathan a blowy. Maybe he doesn't like oral sex."

"Right, he's not gay then. No one in their right mind would turn Brandon down."

Was she really that much older? Alice wondered. At forty-nine, if they were thirty, she was probably old enough to be their mother. What they'd said about Jonathan was ridiculous, wasn't it? Okay, maybe he did have a sort of hero worship, or an unrealistic crush on her, but nothing more than that, no genuine feelings.

Alice waited until they had been gone for several minutes before leaving. She wouldn't hold it against the girls. When you listened in on private conversation, you can't complain if you don't like what you hear. She would apologize to Jonathan tomorrow for her abrupt departure. She couldn't tell him the reason. She couldn't tell him the effect of the alcohol on her brain had given her the urge to push her stool closer to his and feel his breath against her ear again. Safer to go home and see what the closet had to offer.

❧

Alice sighed with relief. On the hanger hung a tan trench coat, and beneath it a pair of blood-red stilettos. "Kind of a cliché, but why not?"

Alice slipped on the coat and the shoes. She decided to leave her hair clipped up and opened the sliding glass door.

The lights and noise hit her like a wall. She stood on the sidewalk in Times Square in Manhattan, her favorite city on the planet. The lights, the people, the energy drew her back again and again. This was Oz to her. She wouldn't have been surprised to see flying monkeys. It didn't matter that the Yellow Brick Road was sidewalk-gray. Surely inside one of these glass palaces lived a wizard.

In New York individuality is high style. There are the hipsters painfully in their twenties dressed alike, appropriate for their age. There were those in lovely business attire, no doubt their careers demanded. Then there were the real New Yorkers, those no conventional description could define. A woman walked toward her wearing an emerald green fascinator on her head, complete with veil of green fishnet, a bright purple velvet jacket and skirt, and neon orange running shoes. She looked at least seventy. To Alice, this completely unique creature was a true New Yorker.

Raised entirely in the Midwest, Alice had first come to New York as an intern, twenty years ago. Extremely high real estate prices and a crackdown on crime had transformed the once seedy Time Square into a glittering tourist attraction. She fell in love with the great lady of a city and came back as often as she could for fun or profit. This night, the air felt crisp and cold against her cheeks. Snowflakes spun and shimmered, highlighted by the huge moving screens advertising Apple and BMW. She put her hands into the pockets of the coat to keep them warm. In the right pocket, she felt a folded piece of paper. Alice stopped in the middle of the sidewalk and people streamed around her. Though night had fallen the lights of the animated billboards were more than enough to read by.

Walk three blocks east down 42nd Street to the Manhattan Hotel. Room 1499. NOW.

She hurried, shivering from anticipation as much as cold. Her red heels machine-gun-clicked on the pavement as she hurried along. The Manhattan Hotel was a small boutique hotel, quaint and lovely, nestled in the mid-town neighborhood. The bright hunter-green paint on the door trim matched the awning, where the hotel's name was written in gold script. No valet waited to take her luggage if she'd had any. She entered through a revolving door so tight she barely fit. Once inside, she didn't see a desk or any kind of lobby, merely a set of shiny brass elevator doors. She pushed the button for the fourteenth floor.

Walking off the elevator and following the arrow on the wall to 1499, Alice was surprised to see the door standing open about an inch. She knocked several times, then cautiously pushed it open. The small room held only a desk and a double bed covered in a gold paisley spread with fringe on the bottom. There was barely enough room to walk around the bed. Alice checked the bathroom, assuring herself she was alone before closing the door.

Though the room was tiny, two enormous windows formed its corner, overlooking the city. Oddly, there were no curtains, and the blinds were pulled all the way up. She stood spellbound for a minute, admiring the buildings sprinkled with the glitter of lights and scraping the night sky.

In the middle of the bed lay an envelope. It wasn't sealed and held a single sheet with the same printing as the note in her pocket.

I own you. You have no will but mine. You will undress and kneel naked with your head down near the door, which is to be left open. When I come in, you will not look up, but remain kneeling like the subservient slave girl you are.

She laughed out loud. No one owned Alice Hightower. But this was all just some kind of crazy dream, so—whatever. Instead of feeling afraid or offended, she was a little bit wet.

She hung the coat in the tiny closet and took a pillow off the bed to kneel on. Who knew how long she would have to wait for her owner to come and claim her?

A few minutes later, she heard the door open. She looked up.

"Wait!" said the man in a fierce voice. Alice had no intention of crossing him. She lowered her head. By tilting her head just a bit and opening her eyes ever so slightly, she could see him. Tall and powerfully built, his shaved head, neatly trimmed dark goatee and mustache gave him a distinctive and handsome presence. He wore a gray hoodie and black jeans. They were not the ridiculous "skinny jeans" some men wore, but they hugged the musculature of his legs anyway. She watched obliquely as he stripped off his clothes in fluid movements.

When finally he stood naked, she noticed he was completely hairless from the neck down. This accentuated his muscles and made Alice shiver with desire. He stood there looking at her with his truly marvelous erection inches from her face. It was certainly above average in size, but it was the man and not the cock that made Alice swallow hard.

"I am your master and will be addressed as such. You are a mere slave girl who exists only to please me. If you please your master, you will be rewarded with pleasure. If you do not, there will be punishment." His voice projected, as if he were on stage.

Alice had never been submissive to anyone. Maybe, just maybe, this would be fun. The contractions between her legs let her know at least one part of her thought so.

"You will not speak unless spoken to and will do only what I tell you. Now, slave, I will fuck your mouth." The naked man took a step forward and put his hands on the back of her head.

She opened her mouth to say something but quickly forgot as he slid his cock roughly past her lips. Alice wanted to properly taste and caress him with her tongue and lips. She reached up to hold on to his buttocks to steady herself. They were smooth and rock hard with muscle. The wild thrusting of his hips slammed her up against the bed. It wasn't easy to fully appreciate this lovely instrument of eminent pleasure or to work her tongue properly. None of this seemed to bother him at all. He thrust his hips without a word.

Alice gripped his muscular ass and did her best to hang on. She looked up at him. His eyes were closed, his face calm, as he continued to move his hips. She tried to protect his considerable endowment from her teeth, but the fierceness of his thrusts made it difficult.

He stopped abruptly, took a half step back, walked around behind her to kiss her neck and whispered in her ear, "Trust me, my favorite slave. Master will only give you what you deserve."

He took her hands and gently wrapped something soft and silky around them, binding them together. She stiffened, recalling the terrifying underground sacrifice fantasy. He kissed her neck again, slowly dragging his tongue down to her shoulder. His breath against the cool trail of his tongue made it hard to remember to breathe.

He reached around her while still caressing her shoulder with his tongue, to take her nipples between his fingers. With his knees, he spread her legs widely. *Oh, yes, I want that. If he wants to tie my hands, who cares.*

But just as suddenly as he'd tied her wrists, he pulled on the scarf and they were free.

"No! I want that pussy now!" With his hands on her waist, he half guided, half lifted her to the bed. Pinning her beneath his powerful body, he raised her hands over her head and again wrapped them in the scarf.

Why am I letting this man tie my hands? Because I trust him. Maybe he isn't real, but he owns me.

His dark brows remained furrowed in a fierce scowl. Even by the dim light of the room's desk lamp, Alice could see the color of his eyes, silver with the reflected lights from the windows. As she spread her legs, he leaned back and lifted them onto his shoulders. Plunging deep into her, he moaned softly without changing his expression at all. She reached up to touch those magnificent arms, strong shoulders, and spectacular chest that didn't look quite real. He certainly felt real. This must come from hours of heavy weights and maybe steroids. It didn't matter, he was gorgeous.

He slid in and out of her with an unexpected gentleness. Alice closed her eyes.

"No! Your eyes will remain open, insolent slave!" The man bellowed at her. "For this you will be punished." He pulled out of her. Removing the clip and grabbing a handful of her hair, he guided her by the waist and moved her to the window. The man held her hair but didn't pull hard or hurt her. When she could feel the cold of the window glass against her butt, he let go. He raised her still bound hands above her head and turned her to face the window.

"But how can I obey, if I don't know the rules?" Alice said.

"Silence!" The man now pressed her against the glass of the window. He spread her legs with his knee again and leaned his weight against her. Feeling the smooth power of him against the length of her body caused her to moan softly. As he pushed his erection into her, he said, "Now the whole city of New York will watch you get fucked."

Punishment? This is intensely hot. She pressed her cheek against the glass and arched her back. Her master pumped into her with force. He clutched one of her breasts in one hand and reached around to rub her clit. Now she understood this master-slave thing. *This is all a game. It has to be if punishment is merely more pleasure.*

"Thank you, Master," Alice said. "I am a very bad slave."

"Yes, you are, and you will pay dearly." His voice was low and husky with passion as he pounded Alice in full view of anyone who cared to look out their window. Two buildings were close enough to see people sitting at desks. A bolt of electric excitement shot through her.

She felt him stiffen and come silently. She was close but "no cigar," as her granddad used to say, under different circumstances, of course. He turned her around gently by the shoulders and smiled at her. His was a thousand-megawatt smile. Everything else in the room disappeared for an instant.

"Now, slave girl, I will punish you with my tongue."

Alice's knees nearly buckled as he pushed her down on the bed by her shoulders. His face grew serious, and he trained those fierce silver eyes on her. She opened her legs wide. He pressed his face into her crotch and rubbed his facial hair against her. He stopped that delicious motion and she felt his tongue against her clitoris.

"No, stop, please!" Alice smiled this game of incredible pleasure.

"No," came his muffled answer. He now stroked her with delicious accuracy, and she came long, hard, and loud.

He sat up, clearly proud of his accomplishment.

"Wow," Alice said.

"Thank you. And thank you so much for helping me prepare." His voice was different now, higher and softer than before. "I've been studying domination for a role but have never completely dommed a woman. You were the perfect submissive." He kissed the inside of her thigh and moved up beside her on the bed.

"Submissive is not something I've ever been called before." Alice propped herself up on her elbows.

"That's why you were so perfect. This was exactly what you needed." He mirrored the astonishment on her face with his own expression and they both laughed. His smile again made her wet.

He told her he was an actor and had landed a big role requiring him to be masterful. Alice found him so magnetic that she lay there just watching his lips as he spoke, spellbound, seeing nothing else. He was handsome, but there was another magic about him. Charisma, Alice knew.

"Now, I need to thank you properly. How about some dinner? I need to eat." They dressed and walked to a little diner a few blocks away. He held her hand. Alice picked at a Caesar salad and just watched, soaking him in as he spoke. He told her he was going to be the lead in some movie or another. She just smiled.

When he finished his huge Cobb salad, he paid the bill and led her back to room 1499, where they rehearsed until he felt more than confident he could pull off the role. Alice agreed.

᪥

Clinical Notes on Client Hightower, Alice B.

Client again spent the entire appointment relating one vivid sexual fantasy after another in an animated manner suggesting she believes them to be real occurrences. The suggestion of hypnotic regression to examine her sexual past, once agreed to by the client, was vehemently rejected.

Chapter Twelve

LOVE IN AN ELEVATOR

Alice smiled at nothing as she walked to the Excellcardia building. It was January, but the air held a little breath of warmth, as often happened during St. Louis winters. Winter's hold on the city lessened a little for a day or two. The wind stopped blowing from the north, the sun shone brightly in the deep blue sky, and people were happy. It was still winter, but the little thaw made the harsh season so much more bearable. The best thing about St. Louis weather was how suddenly it changed. No matter how awful a day or even a week's weather could be, there was hope for better, tomorrow or even later that afternoon.

Still smiling, Alice was surprised to see Jonathan already at his desk. She checked her watch: seven-twenty-two. She knew the time, of course, but it seemed so odd to see him here, she had to double-check.

"Are you trying to make me look bad?" she said. He looked stricken. Her smile faded. "What is it?"

"Your cell phone must have been off or out of charge, so they called me. The Mary Center—about your mother." Alice didn't take another step but dropped her red leather purse with a thud. Her face went blank.

Jonathan got up from behind the desk, picked up her purse, and with his arm around her, walked her into her office. He led her to her chair. She sat down her face still blank. Jonathan knelt in front of her.

"She's dead, isn't she?" It came out flat and cold.

"Yes, I am afraid so," Jonathan said. "She suffered a massive stroke, evidently, as she didn't respond when they tried to wake her for breakfast."

"When?"

"They called me at home an hour ago after trying to reach you. I knew your phone must be dead so I decided to come here and wait. I'll make sure your phone is fully charged before I leave for the day from now on."

"I need to go. I…"

"I'll drive you. No arguments." He grabbed his coat off the hook in her office. At the elevator, his arm still tight around her, he pushed the button.

"Thank you, Jonathan. There's no hurry. The traffic will be a terrible this time of day on 170. It doesn't matter when we get there. Whenever we get there, she'll still be dead." Alice's words were barely a whisper.

§

Alice's traffic prediction came true. It took over an hour to get to the Mary Center. She sat beside Jonathan and watched the cars out the window as they crept along the highway and finally the city streets through heavy traffic. Jonathan parked and Alice opened the door and got out of the car. She stood beside the car, looking down at the piles of dirty melting snow in the parking lot of the Mary Center. "I must be a monster, Jonathan. My mother is dead and all I can feel is relief."

"Of course you're not a monster. You're in shock."

"Yeah, I'm shocked, but mostly I'm relieved." Her voice was flat and her eyes dry.

He took her arm tenderly and led her up the stone stair-case. *I will never have to climb these horrible stairs again. When they bring me here, I'm sure they'll use some secret entrance for the crazy.* This thought made her laugh.

Jonathan stopped and turned to her. "It'll be all right, Alice. She's at peace." The look on his face was so sad, she almost laughed again. Didn't he know this was the best thing that could have possibly happened? Didn't he know she'd hoped with all her heart for something exactly like this every day for a very long time?

"Yes, she is." They were the only words she could manage without sending a completely insane-sounding message to this lovely man with so much pain in his eyes.

Jonathan held her arm tightly now as they approached Beverly's room. Dr. Langer stood by the door as if expecting them. The slightly annoyed look on the doctor's face struck Alice as inappropriate. She should look devastated. This place just lost a good paying customer, but no doubt there was another soul waiting to take Beverly Hightower's room.

"She went peacefully, in her sleep," Dr. Langer said.

"Yeah, that's the best way to go." Alice looked anywhere but at the doctor who opened the door to her mother's room.

Beverly Hightower, or what had once been her, lay on her back. The spread had been pulled up and tucked under her arms. Someone had folded her hands, smoothed the bed, and even combed her hair. She really did look as if she were merely sleeping. Her lips had lost some of their pink, but her skin still had a faint trace of color. She didn't yet look like a corpse; she still looked like Mother. Alice let out a breath she hadn't real-ized she'd been holding. She looked more like Mother than she had in a long while. Gone were the wild terrified looks and the dull empty stares. A tear escaped down Alice's cheek before she caught it, wiped it, and turned back toward the door.

Jonathan had waited outside the door while she went in. His eyes now searched her face for some sign of what she needed from him. Alice felt calm. "Mother made her wishes clear to me years ago. There will be no maudlin ceremony."

"Memorials are for the living, Ms. Hightower," the doctor said. "They can help achieve closure."

"No. It's what she wanted, and I respect that." Beverly's friends had stopped coming to visit years ago. Even her last boyfriend—a ridiculous thing to call a man in his early seventies—hadn't visited in over a year. Alice's brother Sean would have loved to come to a funeral. He would have thrown himself on the casket, had there been one. His probable drama was one superb reason to have Beverly quietly cremated and interred in the mausoleum she'd chosen years ago.

Alice couldn't even call her brother. She had no idea where he was. He was always running. Sean ran to things and from things, sometimes simultaneously. He was always chasing the perfect job that was, of course, in the very next town.

Sean had tested as a genius on IQ tests as a child and was good at nearly everything he ever tried. He could play any sport with a little practice and was always put in the honors classes. But sometime during high school, he stopped going to class. Mother said it was because he wasn't being properly challenged, but Alice knew the truth. Sean would much rather smoke weed than go to school. Frank, Beverly's boyfriend du jour at that time, was a police detective and would not have illegal narcotics under his roof. There were endless fights. Beverly threw the detective over soon after, but by then, Sean was far away. No nuisance of an odd little sister could make him stay. Alice told herself she was glad Sean quit school and left. Now she was the smarter of the Hightower siblings, to the teachers, anyway, but never to Mother. Alice didn't need her brother's sick jokes or late night peanut butter sandwiches, and she certainly no longer needed him to beat people up who teased her.

She heard from him occasionally when he worked whichever step of a twelve-step program required reconnecting with family. She also heard from him when he was in deep and heavy trouble and needed money. She'd paid for at least three stints in rehab. It always broke her heart when he relapsed and disappeared. She hadn't seen him for any reason in two years.

Sean hadn't been there for Mother during her final struggle. As soon as her behavior became too disturbing, he bailed. He cried a big, messy, self-indulgent river of tears, said goodbye to Mother like he would be back tomorrow, and left Alice to explain. Beverly accused Alice of keeping him away.

His last humiliating act had been to write letters and hit up their mother for her measly monthly Social Security. He was investing it for her, he told their mother. The truth was, if Alice could have made him leave sooner, as Mother suggested, she would have. She couldn't take the heartbreak of another of his failures to get his life together. He had "invested" quite a lot of money for Alice too. Although she knew well there would be no return on her investment, she always hoped the money would somehow help. Sean had moved quickly from weed to more expensive pursuits. Cocaine would probably kill him.

Alice would call the last number she had for him and leave a message. She could never have been so angry at him if she didn't still love him, no matter how futile her feelings.

Arrangements were made. It seemed to Alice as if someone else made them. Was it really her voice arranging the cremation and the internment? Jonathan drove her back toward her apartment. When he stopped the car, she didn't get out but looked at the floor mat, unmoving. Several minutes passed.

"Alice, is there anywhere else I can take you?"

"I don't know. Back to the office? I don't really care. I just don't want to be alone." She raised her eyes to his, and he gave her the kindest of looks.

"It's almost lunchtime. Have you never wondered where all the wonderful Chinese food I bring in comes from? Maybe it's time you learn something you don't know."

Again Alice stared out the window while Jonathan drove somewhere. It didn't matter where. Darkness seeped deep into her bones, and she was weary to the bottom of her soul. Invisible fibers of a deep dark down mood gathered. With each passing second, they collected, wrapping her brain tightly in a cloud made of steel wool. The fibers wove into strands; the strands became ropes and then cables, tying her up in sadness.

By the time Jonathan stopped the car, Alice could barely move. The effort of sitting upright was all she could manage.

"Here we are, Alice. Woo's Dim Sum World, a ridiculous name, to be assured." He spoke to her in a chirpy tone, not expecting or even waiting for any response. Somewhere deep in her down state, Alice felt grateful.

Jonathan got out of the car, opened the door on her side, and extended his hand to her. She looked up slowly, but it was just too much effort to stand. She stared straight ahead.

"Alice, stand up." Jonathan's voice sounded oddly both gentle and commanding. She obeyed. He reached over and took her hand like a high school boyfriend. Jonathan's reassuring smile remained firmly fixed as he led her to a storefront in a suburban strip mall.

Woo's Dim Sum World, proclaimed the huge bright red letters on the glass of the front window. *Chinese and American Food*, smaller gold letters promised. Jonathan let go of her hand just long enough to open the door and pulled her gently inside.

As the warm and pungent air of the restaurant rushed around her, she felt her cloud of darkness disperse a little. Alice inhaled the scents of spices, fish, and cooking oil, and she felt hungry. She sat down at the table Jonathan pointed to and forced the corner of her mouth up a little, as he sat across from her.

"This is my family's business. I worked here until I went away to school in London. My aunt came here at twenty-five from Canton, found the money from somewhere, and opened it. She and my mother were half-sisters, with different fathers. I regret I am only one quarter Chinese."

"It smells incredible," Alice felt the cloud melt a little more. She felt lighter with every scented inhalation. The cheerful red tablecloths and painted golden lions on the walls lifted her mood. Dr. Elliot had warned her about this: rapid cycling, common in bipolar II individuals. She didn't think it possible, yet it seemed to be going on in her head. The cold down retreated and the warm inappropriately happy high replaced it within her.

"Yes, it's pretty good. My Auntie June would die rather than sell anything less than the best in quality." A tiny Asian woman rolled a heavy stainless steel cart up to their table. On the cart were segmented stainless cylinders a foot tall and seven inches in diameter. The woman removed a lid from the top of one of the cylinders. Through the fragrant steam, Alice saw fat juicy dumplings. Jonathan nodded. The woman lifted the top section off the cylinder, placed it on the table, and replaced the lid.

"This your girl, Jonny?" The woman smiled at her with the same gentle smile Alice often saw on Jonathan's face. Her tiny frame looked almost too frail to hold up the heavy coil of jet-black hair on her head. "She pretty, but she maybe too old for babies."

"She's definitely too old for babies." Alice said, now smiling at Jonathan.

"Auntie June, this is my boss, Alice Hightower." He looked at Alice with pride on his face.

"Okay. The pork dumplings very good," Auntie June said.

Alice picked up her chopsticks and plopped a steaming dumpling on her plate and then into her mouth. Her eyes opened wide. "Wonderful." She took two more from the container.

Auntie June rolled away, smiling, and a younger woman rolled up pushing another cart. This cylinder held shrimp glistening in a spicy orange sauce. Alice put several on her plate. Two more carts rolled up, leaving behind fragrant and delicious goodies, before Jonathan said something in what must be Chinese, and the parade of carts stopped. Alice knew two of the languages Jonathan spoke were Mandarin and Cantonese, but she'd never put it together. His thick dark hair was rich red-brown rather than blue-black. His eyes were round and coffee-colored, rather than the almond-shaped black of Auntie June's. But they had the same smile.

Jonathan had filled his own plate from the stainless containers. Alice ate as if she hadn't eaten in days. As she ate, Jonathan talked.

He told Alice of his childhood and working at the restaurant until he was twelve. Evidently Auntie June had never heard of child labor laws. His mother was a prima ballerina and Auntie June, and his mother shared a mother. His mother's father was English. She traveled with a London company all over the world, so it was decided that her son should live with Auntie June in a more stable home. His father brought him to London to go to school at Eton after his mother died of breast cancer. She was thirty.

"I never knew either of them well, really. My mother was a beautiful fairy who visited holidays and always smelled like roses. My father, Charles Cosgrove Salter, terrified me. He showed up only on my birthday. My Auntie June was much more of a parent than either of them. I was born in the United States quite by accident. I came a month early. Auntie June took care of me since shortly thereafter.

"When Mother died, my father decided I needed a proper English education, and sent me off at twelve. He was so disappointed when I didn't follow him into the banking business."

"Why didn't you?" Alice said between bites.

"Because the piano owned my heart. Unfortunately, though my heart was in it, my hands fell woefully short. I didn't have the brilliance or the passion necessary to succeed on the concert stage."

"Why did you choose to be an administrative assistant? Wouldn't your father have taken you into his business after you gave up on a concert career?"

"Oh, I'm sure he would have, but I'm an American. London never felt like my home. I'm no quitter by my nature. I didn't realize I wasted my time attempting a concert career until too late. My typing is tolerable. I have some organizational skills and have always loved exploring new software, so I took the first position I qualified for. That led me to Excellcardia and you. I never intended to make it a career, but I've found a home assisting you."

"Well, the concert stage's loss is certainly our gain." Alice said smiling at him.

The delicious meal stoked the hyper furnace inside of Alice. She insisted on returning to work and could barely sit still in the car on the way. Once in her office, Alice paced and dictated letter after letter. When she managed to sit at her desk, it took her no time at all to answer the afternoon's hundred emails.

Late in the day, Alice felt the need to visit the production units to check on some details for an important international delivery. She'd always loved these times she'd formerly called high-energy. So much got done. She now knew they were actually called hyper-manic episodes. The psychiatric label didn't really matter; she could still enjoy them if she was careful. She didn't have to exercise bad judgment just because she was hyper.

❧

The elevator doors closed leaving her alone with Brad James. "Sorry to hear about your mother," he said.

"Thank you. To tell the truth, I'm relieved. She would never get any better, and now she is at peace."

"It's still never easy to lose a parent." He moved closer to her. Her cheeks got hot, and she found it hard to breathe. Why did this man, of all men, have this effect on her? And why was he so close to her with no one else in the elevator? Worst of all, why did she want him closer still?

The lights flickered in the elevator. It stalled, and then dropped a few inches. Brad pushed the button, and the door didn't open. He leaned into the door and forced it open. Through the crack, Alice saw only the concrete and metalwork of the building. They were stuck between floors. He immediately opened the little box, took out the phone, and spoke into it, while Alice stood by and watched. He alone did that to her.

Alice heard the response. "Sorry about this, Mr. James. The elevator company has been called, but you might be in there a while."

Brad hung up the receiver and turned to Alice. Standing in front of her, his eyes were mere inches from hers. She saw concern in his eyes. He said nothing but took her in his arms, holding her tight. "I'm so sorry about your Mother. Bad news travels fast, I'm afraid." Holding her for a moment, suddenly his lips were on hers.

His fingers deftly unbuttoned the little mother-of-pearl buttons of her jacket; and then they were inside her blouse caressing her breast exactly the way he knew she loved. There was that look. The look that told her exactly how much he wanted and needed her. His blue eyes so close to hers made her as wet as his touch.

"Brad, please. You know we can't—I won't do this again," she pleaded, but still she made no move to stop him. Her knees felt like jelly and she kissed him back. Wrapping her arms around him, she pulled him closer. She wanted to lose herself in this man, no matter the cost.

With a violent jerk, the elevator moved upward. The doors

opened with a harsh metallic screech. Three sets of eyes outside the elevator went wide. Security Chuck cleared his throat, Louise gasped, and Henry Petrus merely scowled and pushed past them onto the elevator.

Brad had turned around with his hands outstretched. Alice hoped he turned quickly enough that his incredulous pose hid her as she pulled her blouse together and buttoned her jacket.

"Well, thank you, Chuck, for your prompt service. I trust this matter is permanently addressed." Brad walked out of the elevator, his brows knitted in a look that said, "You must have imagined that you caught me with my hands all over the boss's boobs."

"Alice," Louise said. "I need to speak to you,"

"Sure. I'm going back to my office. I think I'll take the stairs, though."

Louise took the elevator and was sitting in the white leather chair in front of Alice's desk when Alice arrived. Her arms were crossed, she didn't look happy.

Alice sat in her own high-backed white leather executive chair and crossed her arms.

"What in the world were you thinking, Alice Hightower? Fooling around with anyone in this company would not have been wise, but Brad James? He is married, for God's sake. How long do you think it will take for tape from the elevator's surveillance camera to get out?"

Alice's mouth fell open. How bad was her judgment now? How could she have forgotten there were cameras in the elevator? Dr. Elliot had warned her. She picked up the phone and dialed Chuck's extension before she took her next breath.

"Make sure the tape is destroyed and no copies are possible," she said into the phone.

She hung up and let out a long slow breath. "Louise, it just happened. I won't make an excuse for it. My mother died this morning, my defenses were down, and he is—"

Louise uncrossed her arms and leaned toward Alice. "Oh, I

am so sorry. You, understandably, weren't thinking straight. I blame James. He took advantage of your vulnerable state."

"I am hardly vulnerable. Maybe I should be, but I just feel numb. You have to remember Brad is responsible for our huge expansion into the European market."

"Yeah, well. He has his uses, I guess."

"Oh, yes, he does." Alice smiled slightly.

"I guess it's not all on him. That was you in the elevator, furiously buttoning your blazer. Good thing Chuck is so loyal. I'm not sure Henry even noticed. You may get lucky, but what a risk. Don't you realize there's twice as much scrutiny of your leadership because you're an attractive single woman."

"Thanks for the 'attractive.' I admit it wasn't the smartest thing I've ever done, but I think I can trust Chuck."

"You'd better hope so. There might be evil forces in this world, hell, in this building, who would love to see a female CEO laid low." With a shake of her head, Louise left the office.

Alice's heart still beat a mile a minute. She could still taste Brad's lips and feel his tongue—*What is wrong with me?* She could ruin a professional reputation it took decades to build by resuming her affair with Brad. Alice called Dr. Elliot and begged to be seen ASAP.

The rest of the afternoon passed at the unbelievably slow pace Alice had learned was part of her manic state. The minutes crept by like hours. Late in the day, Jonathan stuck his head in her door as she paced the perimeter of her office once again.

"I've finished, but I can stay if you need me."

"No, you go. I got a week's worth of work done today, thanks to the old manic-state thing. We might need new carpet, though. I seem to be wearing a path in this one. But you go home."

Alice wolfed down some Chef Boyardee before the sun set. No matter what Dr. Elliot said, there was no way she was taking a sleeping pill and missing out on the action tonight. *How much fun will manic sex be?* She slid open the closet door.

On the golden hanger tonight were only a ragged brown skirt and a dirty white blouse.

"Well, little Alice, you are moving down in the world." Maybe this was some kind of Cinderella garb. Alice wasn't a huge fan of fairy tales, but she slipped on the skirt and blouse. It had a faint rank odor she couldn't place. The blouse was an off-the-shoulder number and the skirt turned out to be rather well made, if dirty and worn; neither had labels. There were no shoes or undergarments.

"Oh, goody," Alice said to Otis. "An historical romp and possibly some fantastic man from yesteryear; what more could a manic girl want?" She rubbed her cat's furry black head, flipped the lock, and stepped through the balcony door.

Alice stepped onto a rough wooden surface that pitched so violently she was knocked off her feet. On her hands and knees she smelled salt air, damp wood, and fish. She could hear waves crashing against the walls, which were evidently the hull of a ship. No building moved like that.

An arm grabbed her around the waist and lifted her as easily as if she were a rag doll. The man carried her across the deck, dropped her next to a wooden door and knocked softly.

"The captain wants you in his cabin," he said. "Take care, wench. You do him a good turn, or I'll be throwin' ye overboard meself. The nerve of some gal stowing away on this ship!" The big man wore brown pants with leather boots to the knee and no shirt over his muscled chest. His long gray hair was tied back with a blue scarf. His face bore a fresh pink scar. The injury that caused the scar must have been the reason he wore a black patch over his right eye.

"Are you a pirate, sir?" Alice worked hard to keep from giggling.

"I be the Queen's own privateer. Ain't no pirates aboard this ship. First mate, Robert Tuttle, at your service. Below decks in a storm ain't no place for a woman. The captain would have the skin whipped off me back if anything happened to a woman on his ship. Protects them like his bloody sisters, he does. You musta been on board the *Esperanza*, I reckon. Good thing you speak English. There were surely some younger and prettier, all weeping in the Spanish king's gibberish. I'd say for what most men have on their minds, talkin' don't matter much. Lucky for you, he don't agree."

Mr. Tuttle opened the door with a squeaking of rusty hinges. The cabin looked much larger than Alice would have imagined. A bay of windows made up the entire back wall of the cabin. Light shone through diamond shaped panes and flooded the cabin with the eerie gray-green of a stormy sky. At a desk beneath the window a man sat facing the sea view. Alice could see only his wide back, a brown velvet jacket, and blond curls tied with a brown ribbon. Yo ho, she thought.

"I brought her, Captain Bradford. She ain't none too clean, which ain't exactly her fault, as below decks in a storm ain't no clean place at'all. There's a lull in the storm. Should be smooth sailing for a patch. I expect you'll be wantin' water for a tub?" asked Mr. Tuttle.

"Yes, Robert." The voice that answered was as low and rich as a foghorn that protects ships in a harbor. That voice sent a shiver through all of Alice's timbers. She noticed a large copper tub in a corner of the room. The weight of all that copper must have kept it from sliding in rough seas. Next to it stood a screen covered in deep blue brocade.

Captain Bradford pushed back his chair, stood up and turned to face them. He was well over six feet tall. The blond curls were obviously a wig, as the man who towered over her was easily sixty years old. Weathered by sun and sea over many a long voyage, Alice guessed. He surveyed his catch with large, expressive dark blue eyes and smiled at her warmly. His face was wide and his jaw strong. She wondered why he bothered with the wig but supposed it must have been the style of the day, which judging by his attire might have been somewhere in the early eighteen-hundreds. He wore long buff-colored pants, a ruffled white shirt, and a green silk waistcoat with a striped silk ascot in shades of blue and green. His tall brown leather boots were all that really marked him as a pirate, or privateer, as the first mate had corrected her. Jonny Depp and The Pirates of The Caribbean movies had shown her how pirates dressed.

The captain took a step forward and reached out his hand to her. "Welcome, Miss?"

"Hightower, sir. My name is Alice Hightower." As he took her hand and kissed it, Alice felt a little shudder start at the base of her spine and work its way up to her neck.

"How fortuitous. This vessel is the *Lady Alice*. I am so delighted to have you as my guest." The lines at the corner of his eyes as he smiled gave him a sunbaked Sam Eliot look, a look that only got better with age. The lines gave his face warmth and interest. This was a handsome and elegant man; his age was immaterial.

Again that deep voice boomed at her. "You may remove your clothes behind the screen, my dear Alice. There you will find a bathing gown to preserve your modesty." Alice had read that back in the day when servants bathed their mistresses, it was not deemed proper for a servant to see their mistress completely naked. Over the side of the tub hung a thin gauze and lace garment that, when wet, would be completely transparent. It tied with two pink satin ribbons. *My modesty indeed.* Alice chuckled. Though she had hardly any modesty to preserve, she was happy to follow the captain's instructions.

She wasn't really all that dirty but removed the filthy blouse and skirt. This outfit was by far her least favorite of all the clothing she had ever found in her closet. *If this man wants me clean, I'll get to scrubbing.* Alice donned the filmy white gown and stepped into the long copper tub. The perfect curve of the tub cradled her neck, and her arms rested into hollows fashioned into the sides. Thin as it was, the little dressing gown did protect her butt from the cold copper of the tub.

As soon as she made herself comfortable, Robert appeared carrying two huge buckets of steaming water. He poured them carefully into the foot of the tub, eyes respectfully averted, and dropped a fragrant little bag into the water. Imagine, thought Alice, a pirate who keeps scented sachet aboard his ship. The temperature of the water perfect, the lavender-and-lemon-scented steam caressed her inside and out. Tiny waves of pleasure washed over her with the gentle rocking of the boat.

Alice loved baths, but her schedule rarely allowed her the luxury of taking them. Showers were so much more efficient. As she soaked in her island of liquid pleasure, she became aware of the captain standing over her and let out a little moan.

"I am so glad you are enjoying your bath." His voice was nearly as warm and soothing as the water itself. He knelt beside the tub.

"Won't you join me, sir?"

"Oh no, dear. This is for your pleasure alone." He picked up a sea sponge and asked, "May I?"

"Certainly, Captain. Whatever you desire," Alice said.

He unbuttoned the bath gown slowly and slipped it off her. With a gentle touch, he slid the sponge along the length of her body. Starting at her toes, he slid ever so slowly up the long length of her legs. His eyes caressed her body as he sponged her, and she could only lean back and enjoy his touch. He slid up each arm. When he reached her breasts, he took particular care to circle each nipple softly with the rough sponge. Alice moaned, and the captain laughed as he watched each nipple grow hard.

Captain Bradford stood up, and taking Alice's hand,

helped her to her feet. He led her across the room to a bed, a huge affair suspended by ropes, understandably.

The captain picked up a piece of soft cloth, knelt beside her, and tenderly dried every inch of her. He wiped the space between each toe and lifted a foot to spread her legs. Alice moaned a soft lover's cry. The captain responded by reaching up to dry the wet between her legs that had nothing to do with the bath, and everything to do with his touch.

"You have pleased me, he said, "from the moment Robert opened the door and there you stood proud, even in a dress fouled from below decks. I'm surprised I never noticed you on the deck of the *Esperanza*. Most of the women aboard cowered in fear. What a treat that you speak English."

"Please, take me now." *Did I just recite a line of a romance novel?* But what else could one say when about to be ravished by a scrumptious pirate captain? This evening was exactly what her ragged, hyper nerves required.

"Everything in its time." The captain walked to a chest near the head of the bed, took out something white, and brought it to her. Alice stepped into a high-waisted gown of white damask, and the captain buttoned every one of the tiny cloth-covered buttons up the back. From the style of it, Alice knew her guess about the time period was right. The gown looked like something Josephine Bonaparte might have worn.

When all the buttons were done, he stopped to kiss her neck.

"Ummm. Captain Bradford, would you mind terribly unbuttoning those twenty buttons you so carefully just buttoned?" Alice concentrated on looking as fetching as possible, back arched, demure smile attempted.

"I would indeed." His breath was warm against her ear. "Dinner first, Miss Hightower, and my Christian name is Peter." There was that voice once again. The rich timbre of it wrapped her in velvet calm.

A knock on the door broke the spell. Alice sighed as those

lips left her neck. Robert carried in a covered tray, folded a table out of a nook in the wall of the cabin, and set the tray down. Pulling off a cloth, he revealed two plates of food that smelled delicious, then he turned and left without a word. Peter brought wine glasses and a bottle to set beside the plates. He pulled the chair from the desk and gestured for her to sit. After tucking in her chair, he produced a stool for himself.

"This is the finest Amontillado. You were not the only treasure to be found aboard the *Esperanza.*" Peter filled Alice's glass with the lovely amber-red liquid.

"I thought only pirates steal treasure from the boats they seize?"

Peter's laugh was as rich as his speaking voice. "Touché, Alice. We are privateers, not pirates, and in truth are commissioned by the queen to seize certain ships for political reasons. The rest is a business transaction. Goods will change hands; prisoners will be exchanged for ransom and go home unharmed with stories of marvelous adventures to tell. We are businessmen who provide a highly profitable service for the crown. We are well rewarded by Her Majesty. Pirates are hanged."

"I stand corrected, sir." Alice sipped the sherry. Now she knew why Edgar Allan Poe wrote about it. Would write about it, she corrected her thought. The rich warmth of it caressed her mouth from the tip of her tongue until it disappeared down her throat to warm her belly. They toasted each other and ate a meal of flaky white fish, boiled potatoes, and hearty brown bread. Except for a little too much salt on everything, the meal was delicious.

Alice grew eager as their plates emptied. "What now, my captain?"

"Now for tonight's entertainment. Lie down on the bed, my dear."

"With pleasure." She did as he said and was surprised when he didn't follow to the bed.

He removed a book from the shelf above his desk, pulled his stool close to the bed, and opened the book. He smiled at Alice's apparent surprise. "I want to please you first with words. 'She is beautiful, and therefore to be wooed; She is woman, and therefore to be won.' Alas, they are not my own, but of a far higher quality."

The words of William Shakespeare flowed over her as Peter read sonnet after sonnet.

Shall I compare thee to a summer's day?
Thou art more lovely and more temperate.

By the time he closed the book after reading several of Shakespeare's finest sonnets. Alice could not have been more wet if he had caressed her with his hands and lips rather than his words. His deep, rich voice and Shakespeare's lovely words had her more than ready.

Peter rose from the chair, his eyes locked on hers. She moaned from the tension and the need of him. He slipped off his wig. Beneath it, his hair was a lovely thick silver, cut short. He slowly removed his clothes and Alice moaned again. The captain proved well equipped to please, with a nice-sized and quite youthful erection.

Across his chest were the scars of battles, but he stood as strong and lean as any man half his age. Alice moved toward him, and he turned her and began to slowly and meticulously unbutton every button. When he finished, he put his hands on her shoulders, pushed her gently back down on the bed, and knelt with his legs on either side of her. He kissed her looking deep into her soul with his fathoms-deep blue eyes. He held still and waited for something. She listened to his breathing now as ragged with desire as her own. In a moment, the *Lady Alice* rose and fell more violently. The captain plunged deep into her.

He lifted her legs onto his shoulders to get deeper inside her, then held perfectly still, waiting. The sound of the wind grew louder, and the ship's movement raised and lowered the bed in a perfect rhythm as old as the sea. Peter gripped a plank on the wall and held himself taut and motionless. Alice moved with the bed sliding up and down on his now stationary cock. The motion of the pounding waves their rhythm. With one hand, his rough fingers sent waves of pleasure through her. He bent to kiss her neck, but never attempted to impose his own movement.

Peter continued this way until Alice could take not one more excruciatingly slow thrust. "Oh, God, Peter, please, please, please," Whimpered the normally loud and salty Alice.

Holding her gaze, Peter let go of the plank and thrust hard against her. The sudden contrast to the slow strokes made Alice come like gangbusters. She sometimes felt like she lost consciousness briefly when she came, but this felt like she left her body completely. She made no sound, but lay beneath him, shivering slightly in the wake of smaller dying waves of ecstasy still lapping at the shores of her flesh.

Peter opened his eyes, and she realized he must have come just as she did. She felt his semen run out and pool beneath her.

"I'm afraid, Alice, at my present age and state, this is all I have to offer you in the way of cocksmanship. Only ten years ago, I could have risen to the occasion thrice. I would love to pour you some more sherry and read to you a bit, if you like?" He searched her face for an answer.

Finding his answer in her smile, he pulled the coverlet up over her and kissed her on her forehead. Now, the waves of calm started at her toes and swept over her body.

"Yes," she whispered and closed her eyes.

Clinical Notes on Client Hightower, Alice B.

First observable manic behavior. Client's speech noticeably pressured as she related the death of her mother with wholly inappropriate affect. Client also related an incident of sexual activity she herself deemed to have been an example of extremely poor judgment. This statement was followed by tears and pleas for help. Client again refused suggestion of medication. It was suggested she might consider another therapist if she did not wish to participate in recommended therapeutic modalities.

Chapter Thirteen

HE AIN'T HEAVY HE'S MY BROTHER

Her day proceeded swimmingly. That was a funny and oddly appropriate term Jonathan used often. Today she felt calm. The memories of last night's pleasure, though amazing, were only part of what made her feel happy, though she had little reason to be. Her mother was still dead. She'd been caught in an embarrassing position with her VP of sales in full view of surveillance cameras. Her psychiatrist wanted to fire her. Today, however, she felt completely equipped to handle all of that, and to Alice, few things felt better than dealing with her challenges well.

Meetings went smoothly, and though she didn't have the superhuman energy of the previous day, it was a good day.

Jonathan poked in his head as he prepared to leave for the day at five-thirty. "Brad James is here. If you need me to stay?"

"No, send him in and you can go."

He looked disapproving but took his coat off the hook and turned to leave.

Brad pushed past him, brow furrowed and lips tight. "Alice, I..." He stood in front of her desk with his hands spread wide and a guilty expression on his handsome face.

"Stop." She stood up behind her desk and waited to see the

elevator doors close on Jonathan before she answered further. "This is not up for discussion. That can never happen again. It was completely irresponsible for me to have let this go that far."

"It certainly didn't feel irresponsible. Don't you miss it—us?" He flashed her that dangerous look. The one that first turned her knees to jelly, and her panties to a puddle; the one that made her break her cardinal rule—no married men.

"There are cameras in that elevator, you're my direct report, and you are married. There is no longer any 'us'. Aren't those enough reasons?" Brad's expression softened and he took a step back.

"Olivia and I have been growing apart for months, hell, years. Say the word, tell me you want me as much as I want you, and I will hand in my resignation." He was using those incredible eyes against her as a weapon. Her mouth went dry.

"That is exactly what I don't want. Nothing that happened between us can jeopardize our working relationship. You are far too important to this company's success. And I told you, I'm not the kind of woman who breaks up marriages."

"But how about you, Alice? Am I important to you?"

Alice closed her eyes, took in a long deep breath, and dropped into her chair. "We are grownups. We can't always have what we want just because we want it. Besides, I'm poison. Ask either of my husbands."

"If you are poison, Alice, that might be as good a way to die as any."

When she opened her eyes, he stood looking at her. *Will I ever become immune to that?* She looked down and concentrated. "You are too vital to Excellcardia, and my self-respect is too important to me. I hope I can salvage it. I'm sorry." Alice spoke the words without ever looking up.

She could feel him standing there for a long minute. Then he was gone.

Alice squeezed her eyes tightly together. *This man will not make me cry. I can handle this.*

In the elevator, she hit 10 on a whim. Nothing like a dose of wagging doggy tails to make a person feel better.

There was light coming from under the door of Henry's office. She walked past the dog kennels and, after knocking softly, turned the handle and stuck in her head.

"Hello, Henry."

He sat at his desk, staring at nothing, and didn't look up as she came in. Henry's face had a strange melancholy look she'd never seen before. A bottle of some brown liquor sat on his desk. He took a sip from a paper cup, poured some of the liquor into a second cup, and held it out to Alice.

She took it and sat in the chair beside his desk. "What are we celebrating?"

"Oh, it's not a celebration. More like a wake. I'm drinking to the death of my career. I'm drinking to the death of my Nobel Prize dreams. I've worked my entire goddamn life toward this. All my research for thirty-four years has led to this. All for nothing." He put down his cup and ran his hands through his shaggy hair.

"What is it, Henry? What are you talking about?" Fear bubbled up inside her gripping her tight in the middle of her chest.

"With this measly budget, it'll take another year to get enough dog trials to proceed to human ones. By then some other company could bring it to market and make us obsolete."

"Henry, you don't know that." She reached over to put her hand on his shoulder. "No one could come up with anything as revolutionary as your work. I will go back to the board as soon as the patents and clearances come through. Stop worrying." She hoped her words reassured him. It did push her fear back down just a little. Alice sipped the brown liquid and made a face. "What is this?"

"Oh, some rotgut I keep on hand to drown my sorrows.

The bottle says whiskey." His scowl lifted. Her work was done. No time for wagging tails now.

🐾

Alice hurried to her car. The winter clouds were thick and though the sun hadn't set, it was nearly dark. A figure leaned against her car on the driver's side. She stopped. Her parking spot was too far from the light. *Should I run? Scream?* She did neither, but stood, frozen.

"Oh, come on, Alice, I won't hurt your precious rich-bitch car," said the figure shrouded in the shadow.

Alice let out a breath when she recognized the voice.

"Sean?" She felt, first of all, relief. He was alive. Part of her wanted to run to him and wrap her arms around the sweet big brother he used to be. The rest of her was afraid.

"None the fuck other. Ain't you glad to see your favorite and only brother?" He ran to her and put his arms around her. She lifted her arms briefly to return the hug. He stepped back, laughing. Even in the dim light, she could see her brother looked thin and his face held twice the lines as the last time she saw him. He must be back using crack, she thought. The fear, this time felt far too familiar. *Will this be the last time I see him?* Why couldn't he be the brother she had loved so deeply as a little girl? she wondered standing in the gathering dark of the parking lot. Couldn't she just wrap her arms around him and shake the stupid out of him?

He had been such a handsome young man, with their father's jet-black hair and their mother's large gray eyes. Sean had been to rehab more times than Alice could remember. She hoped each time would be his last. She'd paid for three visits to rehab with that hope. From the way he looked and the sick old-sweat smell as he hugged her, she guessed it had not.

"Who would have thought weird little Alice would grow up to be such a success? I guess you thought you could bury

184

Mom quick, and quiet, and no damn nevermind about Sean. I called the Mary Center. Did you think I'd never find out?" His eyes looked glassy even in the low light.

"I had no idea where you were. She wanted to be cremated and didn't want any sort of service. I just did what she wanted." Alice took a step back. He closed the distance, intruding too far into her zone of personal space for comfort in his present angry state.

"What about the will?" Sean said.

"She didn't have a will, and all she left was a lot of debts. I'll be happy to share those with you. I donated her clothes and bedroom furniture to Goodwill." She shook her head and took another step back.

"Fucking liar. I know she got a decent Social Security check every month. Did you squirrel those away in some fancy-ass offshore account?"

Now it was Alice's turn to laugh. "Right. Her checks wouldn't cover a week at the Mary Center. I had her power of attorney and applied what money she had toward her considerable expenses. You are welcome to talk to my accountant." It hurt to have to explain her actions to him. This was her only brother. He hadn't been there to help or comfort, but still he made demands.

Sean moved with amazing speed, grabbing Alice and yanking her purse off her arm. As she stood rubbing her wrist, he turned the purse upside down, spilling the contents onto the concrete beside the car. Dropping to his knees, he picked up her wallet, removed the bills and searched through the credit cards. Suddenly, out of the dark, a figure hit Sean from behind knocking him flat on his face. The tall man in a long dark coat put his foot on Sean's back when he tried to get up.

It was Brad James she realized. "Don't hurt him."

"You know this punk?" Brad said. He removed his foot from Sean's back and stepped on his hand. Sean groaned and let go of her money and credit cards.

"He's my brother." She picked up her purse and bent to retrieve the spilt items. There were only a few; Alice didn't carry more than absolutely necessary.

Brad dug in his heel even after he had dropped her valuables. "That's for the trouble you've caused your sister. If you don't want your ass kicked more completely, you'd better take your lowlife self as far away as possible. If you ever show up here and give your sister one ounce of grief, I'll do much more than stand on your hand."

Alice had never seen Brad angry. She was impressed and turned her focus from Brad standing entirely too near. She resisted the urge to order the contents of her purse, which was usually as orderly as the rest of her belongings. That would have to wait; time was growing short.

With everything back in her bag, Brad removed his foot from Sean and backed away. As soon as he did, Sean got to his feet and ran across the parking lot as if being chased by something extremely large and terrifying. Alice blinked back tears as she watched her brother disappear across the dark parking lot.

"He really isn't a bad person," she said. "It's the drugs that made him like that. Kind of funny to see he can still run so fast. He used to be a star soccer player. Cocaine took all that away from him."

"Drug use is a choice, Alice." Brad moved toward her and put his hands on her shoulders. "You all right?"

"Sure. He wouldn't have hurt me. I really am grateful for your help, though." She tried to back away, but he tightened his grip and pulled her closer.

"Brad, please. I need to get home and I don't want to rehash this again." Alice saw a brief flash of what looked like pain in his eyes before he smiled and stepped back, spreading his arms.

"Sure, Boss Lady, anytime. Enjoy your evening."

He watched until she got safely into her car. She could see

him standing in the small circle of light watching her as she drove away.

🙰

On the drive home, Alice forced herself to concentrate on reviewing the business matters of the day. She had a half-hour until sunset. The traffic on 270 was heavier than usual, and by the time she got home she had barely ten minutes left.

As she finished the last bite of her mini-ravioli, the doorbell rang. Alice looked through the peephole of her door and let out a breath of relief to see Jonathan. She was afraid it would be Brad. She didn't have the strength to refuse him one more time. Alice couldn't imagine what brought Jonathan here tonight. He beamed at her and put his eye up to the hole. Alice opened the door and gave him a look, both eyebrows raised.

"I had to check to make sure you were all right. I agree with Ms. O'Neil, that James is not to be trusted."

No, he certainly is not. "Well, you can see I'm fine. Thank you for checking," She started to close the door.

"I also thought you might need a bit of cheer." He held up a bottle of wine. "It's a tradition in my family to toast the passing of a family member, and, well…."

She couldn't just slam the door in his face. He'd come to her rescue many times in the past. How could he know that in six minutes she was expected somewhere for an undoubtedly delicious adventure? Not tonight, she thought. *Tonight, Jonathan is here to cheer me, and cheer me he will.*

Alice was glad she hadn't yet changed and still wore her pale pink work suit. She wouldn't have felt comfortable drinking his wine in the bathrobe she usually wore when she opened the door to the magical closet. Especially since it seemed plausible he harbored some not-so-professional feelings for her.

Jonathan hadn't changed either and wore his lovely charcoal suit, lavender shirt, and lavender tie with matching pocket square, of course. It must have been a windy evening, because his usually perfectly behaved dark hair had broken free of its product and several stray strands fell over his left eye in curls. He looked even more boyish than usual. It was hard to believe he was only four years younger.

Alice got two wine glasses and an opener from her kitchen. Jonathan sat down on the far side of her white leather couch. Alice opened the wine, poured, and handed him a glass. Very properly, she sat down at the opposite end. What harm could come of two colleagues enjoying some wine and conversation? At least she wouldn't have to worry about losing this valued employee to an ill-advised romantic encounter. He was always the perfect gentleman. She was the one who slept with coworkers.

"The man at the wine store assured me this Chardonnay is an exceptional vintage." Jonathan took a small sip and gave her a questioning look.

Alice took a large sip and sighed. "It's lovely, Jonathan. Thank you. It has a nice full body without being overly sweet. It is buttery with just a tiny touch of oak to keep it crisp."

"I should have known, among your other talents, you were a wine connoisseur. I am not, however, surprised." He raised his glass to her.

"I'm no connoisseur." She felt a little guilty about making him think she knew more than she actually did. "I know what I like, and I took one evening course at the community college. I don't drink wine very often, but I admit it relaxes me." Alice kicked off her shoes and folded her legs under her. Taking another sip of golden liquid, she smiled at Jonathan.

"I usually drink wine only in social situations," he said. "For relaxation I have my music. Nothing relaxes me like playing a lovely long session of soft sweet Chopin or a few stormy Beethoven concerti." He set his glass down and reached up to loosen his tie.

"Do you play every day?"

"Of course. One of the few presents my father gave me was a Steinway grand piano for my twenty-first birthday. It's like a plant that needs to be watered. It needs to be played as much as I need to play; and I could no more stop playing than I could stop breathing." His lovely dark eyes looked at her, so full of passion.

"How could you give up the concert stage? I really doubt you ever lacked talent or passion." Alice had noticed his hands before when he handed her a contract, lunch, or a cup of coffee. Long tapering finger certainly belonged more to a concert pianist than an administrative assistant.

"Well, truth be told, I couldn't handle the business end of it. Most concert pianists have agents and sometimes a relative to arrange things. I couldn't seem to attract the former, and the latter would never have done. My mother died long before, and I hardly think my father would have made arrangements for 'an entertainer,' as he always called me with great disdain. I found myself hating the thing I loved most because of all the myriad annoying details that kept me from playing. I moved from one dreadful hotel to another with nothing of my own to show for it. I booked dates, but I couldn't seem to get ahead. As I passed forty, I realized I needed to build some kind of a stable life. So I set out to find a real job. Thus Excellcardia, and you, Alice." His voice was softer now, and the look in them difficult to read.

"I'd love to hear you play sometime," she said over her glass. The wine sent crazy messages to her brain. *What would those hands feel like caressing her?* Was she smiling at him like any number of girls at the holiday party? Did she want to loosen that tie further and—*Stop, stop, stop!*

"Well, that can certainly be arranged. You're more than welcome anytime." This time the look in his eyes was unmistakable. She had seen the same look on Brad's face earlier in the day. He wanted her.

Her cheeks went hot, and the blood roared in her ears. She slugged the rest of the wine in her glass and stood up. "Thank you, Jonathan, for the lovely wine and the cheer. Part of me misses my mother, but most of me feels lucky not to have to watch her deteriorate further, as selfish as that sounds. This has been a long day, and I'm really tired. Forgive me?" She hoped she didn't sound rude. When her eyes met his, the look was gone. Could she have imagined it? She wasn't that irresistible.

"Certainly. I'm so glad you enjoyed it. My offer of a private concert is genuine. I play much better to an audience. I also would like to go with you when you take your mother's ashes to the mausoleum."

"Already done. I had them delivered there directly. That little brass urn is not my mother. My mother's gone. I do appreciate your offer, but I'm not overly sentimental about that sort of thing. I loved her with all her faults, and I followed her wishes, that's all."

"As you wish, Alice. He smiled at her. She returned his smile and closed the door behind him.

"Meow," Otis said.

"Well, aren't you the lucky boy tonight? You get me all to yourself. The sun has been down for nearly an hour and I'm just too tired to deal with another man anytime and anywhere tonight." She reached down to rub the kitty's head.

Alice yawned. A good night's sleep in her own bed might be the perfect thing, for a change.

❧

Client has DNAed last three appointments and has not rescheduled. It was strongly suggested in a phone conversation the client would be better served by another therapist. A name and information release form was faxed to client.

Chapter Fourteen

CENTERFOLD

H er first order of business, after three meetings and two conference calls, was to find a new therapist. Dr. Elliot's receptionist had said she would fax over a list when she gave Alice the news that she would be better served by another therapist. Jonathan handed her the fax. On the paper was one name, Dr. Cynthia Lester.

Alice called the number. A gruff voice answered. "Dr. Lester's office." No "May I help you?" or any of the usual receptionist's happy patter.

"Dr. Elliot referred me. I would like an appointment, please."

"Tonight at six p.m.," said the voice. Alice knew the sun would set at five-fifty-eight today. She'd missed last night's adventure, and her palms were a tiny bit itchy at the thought of missing another. *What the hell.* Some things, like her sanity, are more important than great sex. Aren't they?

"Thank you. I'll be there." The rest of her work day passed without incident. At least she hadn't compromised her virtue or professional reputation by banging any more of her employees today. There were hopefully no pictures of her boobs burning up the internet from the elevator surveillance camera. Work got done. Devices were made and sold. At the end of the day, she felt clearheaded and strong.

As Alice climbed the steps of the two-story yellow brick building to her potential new shrink's office, hope crept up from somewhere deep. *Maybe this doctor could help sort out the crazy.*

The walls of Dr. Lester's outer office almost glowed with bright salmon color. A cozy peach and mint-green paisley loveseat and two rust colored leather chairs made the room look welcoming and homey. On the walls, hung abstract prints in pastel colors. Soft light came from a single lamp sitting on a tiny round table in the corner. The room felt decidedly feminine; so very different from the beige-on-beige of Dr. Elliot's office. On his walls hung pictures of dogs with dead ducks in their mouths and fish about to bite hooks and die. This felt better.

On the ledge below the wavy-glassed reception window sat a sign. "Dr. Cindy will be right with you," it read. Dr. Cindy sounded like a sweet little grandmother who might offer milk and cookies along with the head-shrinking.

Before Alice could test out the comfy looking loveseat, the door opened.

"Ms. Hightower?" said a slender woman dressed in black. Her pants hugged her lean form in a way that made Alice, who would never be described as lean, a little jealous. She wore a silver and black striped vest over a black tunic-style blouse. Short silver and blonde hair was moussed up and brushed back stylishly. She peered at Alice with intense black eyes. The black framed reading glasses perched on her nose appeared to be part of her outfit and not the result of any deficiency in her eyesight. This chic woman would certainly not be offering any milk or cookies.

Alice followed her down a short hall to a room she immediately called the blue room, though not out loud. She knew from Industrial Psych 101 that blue produced a serene and soothing effect, but she would not be easily soothed. These walls were a rich aqua, and the couch a deep royal and teal flowered print, a far cry from the usual stark black leather shrink's couch, like Dr. Elliot's. It looked like something Scarlett O'Hara would have reclined on after Mammy tightened her corset too tight. Sitting on it, Alice could not help but run her hand over the buttoned tufts in the silky velvet.

"So tell me, Alice, what brings you here?" Dr. Cindy spoke in a low Lauren Bacall voice. No introduction, no pleasantries, straight to the point.

"Well, I guess the fact that I'm bipolar." Alice looked at the floor.

"Oh, are you? I don't see it written on your forehead."

Alice looked up at Dr. Cindy. "Well, Dr. Elliot said—"

"Yes, I consulted with Barry, after you made your appointment and faxed me your HIPAA form giving me your permission. We work differently, Dr. Elliot and I." Dr. Lester grew quiet, and Alice took this as her cue to elaborate.

"I come from a long line of crazies. My mother, who recently died, was institutionalized with bipolar depression. I think I'm heading down the family road."

"Alice, you are headed down the road you choose for yourself. I feel using diagnoses to label people is pointless. Bipolar II is a mood disorder, not a mental illness. Your mother died from a stroke, Barry told me, not from mental illness. I don't really like that term, either. It presumes there is such a thing as mental wellness. I don't believe there are hierarchies of mental states; some being well and others sick. Some of us have struggles not conducive to living happy or fulfilled lives. But none of us should be judged for our individuality. We are all individuals, Alice. Labels and generalized treatments are not the answer for everyone." Dr. Cindy removed her glasses and smiled for the first time. It was a warm and reassuring smile, worth the wait.

Alice liked Dr. Cindy already. Referring her to this office

might have been the best thing Dr. Elliot had ever done for her.

"I'm here to suggest ways to handle the bumps in your road. That's all. I have a doctorate in psychology, not a medical degree, so I can't prescribe drugs. The latest research demonstrates great success focusing on cognitive talk therapy and lifestyle changes rather than medications as the first course of treatment for many. The drugs used for bipolar disorder can have devastating side effects when used long-term. Together, we can help you handle your challenges. It's your road. Your family genetics only suggest the path others took. You choose your own way."

Dr. Cindy's confident manner and calm words relaxed Alice and she took in a slow cleansing breath. This woman sounded a little new-agey, but her words were strangely comforting. Alice answered questions about her past experiences with treatment. The hour flew by; all too soon Dr. Cindy looked at her watch. "I suggest you come in as often as you can at first. I really want us to get a grasp of exactly what you need and make a plan. Same time tomorrow?"

Alice didn't want to miss another evening's frivolities. Her adventures served as a kind of therapy, too.

"No. I have plans. The next afternoon would be fine if you have an opening," Alice said. Maybe she could cancel a couple of meetings and leave a little early.

❦

Another night of sleeping in her own bed gave Alice an unusual lightness in her step; the first step towards implementing Dr. Cindy's suggestion of a healthier lifestyle. The closet would be there tomorrow. She noticed the surprise on the faces of her co-workers that her usual morning nod of acknowledgement included a smile.

Already halfway through her first cup of coffee, Alice

noticed Jonathan standing in the doorway to her office. He hadn't come in and helped himself to coffee as usual but stood in the doorway with his hands at his sides balled into fists. The expression on his face was strange. It looked like he had been punched in the stomach after someone killed his dog.

She was on her feet in an instant. "Oh, God, Jonathan. What is it?"

He walked toward her, took his cell phone out of his pocket, swiped his finger across the screen, and handed the phone to her. "I received this first thing this morning. From an unknown source, of course."

Alice couldn't imagine what could upset a cool character like her assistant—until she looked at the screen. There was a still frame from a video that could only have come from the elevator surveillance camera. Alice's blouse was open to her waist revealing her breasts above her bra that Brad had conveniently pulled down for better access. Brad's hand clutched one breast and the other was obscured by his head. The sight of her own face, head thrown back in obvious ecstasy, made her want to throw up.

"Oh." Her voice was barely a whisper.

"Is this real? Is that Brad James and—you?" Jonathan's outrage seemed to only intensify as Alice's lack of any denial gave him the answers to those questions. He dropped into the chair in front of her desk and looked at the floor. "When—Alice? When did this happen?"

"It was the afternoon right after my mom died. I realize what poor judgment I used, but I just…"

"Do you, Alice? Do you really realize what you've done? This picture wasn't sent only to me. It's part of a message blast. God knows how many people received this. Did you not realize there are cameras in those elevators?"

"No—I mean—Yes. I called Chuck immediately. He assured me he would take care of it, that the tape would be destroyed." Alice dropped back into her chair.

Jonathan put his head in his hands. For a second she thought he was sobbing. After a very long moment, he stood up. The look in his eyes was fierce and angry. "What if someone sent this to the board members? What then? Your reputation is seriously jeopardized by this, and right now you're the face of Excellcardia. For what, Alice? For Brad James?"

"I know it was reckless. I just couldn't..."

"Reckless?" Jonathan shouted. "Being alone with that bastard is reckless. Fucking him in full view of surveillance cameras was catastrophically irresponsible!"

Alice had never heard Jonathan raise his voice, let alone curse. She couldn't look him in the eye. It was a relief when she heard him slam the office door. She looked up to see him on the phone at his desk, talking animatedly to someone.

❦

Alice looked up from her laptop to see Security Chuck standing outside her office nervously shuffling his feet. She motioned for him to come in.

"How could this have happened? You assured me the tape would be destroyed. Why weren't they?" Alice tried to remain calm. Incompetence was not something she could ever tolerate, certainly not when it came to the possibility of the board firing her for moral turpitude.

Her phone made the little bell sound of a text three times. She was almost afraid to pick it up.

OMG, ALICE, I AM SO SORRY, from Brad.

ALICE THIS IS BAD, from Louise.

NICE TIT BOSS, from "restricted."

She pushed the button to turn off the phone.

She looked up when Chuck cleared his throat.

"I told you to destroy the tapes. If you destroyed them, can you tell me how and who could've made a copy?"

"Dr. P said—"

"What does Henry Petrus have to do with security? Exactly what did he say?"

"He said he would take the tapes and make double sure no one could restore them. He said he had some sort of process."

"You disobeyed my direct order."

"I figured he was acting on your orders to—" Chuck stood shaking.

It was clear she would get no more from him. She needed to go right to the source. "From this second forward, you discuss security matters with no one but me. Understood?"

"Yes, Ms. Hightower." Chuck left her office without ever looking up.

Alice phoned Henry. No one picked up his office phone. She tried the lab's central number.

"Research," a young woman's voice said.

"This is Alice Hightower. Where is Henry? I need him now. I don't care if you have to go into surgery and drag him to the phone, but I need to talk to him now!"

"Dr. Petrus left two hours ago."

"What! He never leaves before seven. Check again."

"I saw him go," the voice said. Alice slammed down the receiver. A huge dark coil of fear and worry was born and settled deep in her chest. She checked her electronic rolodex for Henry's home number and dialed. He didn't answer. The coil squeezed tighter.

Alice looked up to see the elevator doors close on Jonathan. His face had a hard look she couldn't remembered seeing before.

It was nearly six. Most of her staff had gone home. There remained only one thing to do.

She reached into her purse for Dr. Cindy's card.

❧

"Thank you so much for seeing me," Alice said. "This may not seem like an emergency to you, but I assure you, it's a disaster." The gentle scent of the lavender candle flickering on a table next to the velvet couch did little to alleviate the fear growing deep inside her, but it smelled nice.

"The nature and severity of an issue depends upon your perception of it, Alice," Dr. Cindy said calmly. "If it feels like a disaster to you, it's a disaster."

"I'm not sure where to start. I feel like my world may be coming apart. I always enjoyed sex before. It was fun, but I could usually do without it during dry spells, until— I made a really bad choice and had an affair with a co-worker. He's extremely hot and seemed just what I needed until…"

"Until what, Alice—? Please continue."

"He's married. He didn't mention it at first, or maybe I didn't ask, but even when he told me it was all I could do to keep away from him. It was like he lit a fire deep inside me. I couldn't seem to do without him or at least the sex. I had sex with him several times even after I knew he was married. Yesterday, it nearly happened again, in an elevator, in full view of security cameras." She covered her face with her hands. A tear dripped on her black suede skirt, forming a little diamond. She moved her leg and watched it as it rolled off through her fingers.

"You said nearly. What stopped you?"

"The elevator doors opened and, well, there were people standing there. It had to be obvious to them what we were doing. The elevator had a surveillance camera. My mother had just died, but I was fooling around with my old lover in front of cameras." Alice rubbed her palms against her knees.

"It is fairly common for woman to experience changes in sex drive as they approach menopause. The estrogen wanes and the natural testosterone can have a greater influence increasing a woman's sexual urges. Most women enjoy this change. The activity in the elevator was most likely an attempt at self-soothing. Unwise, but understandable."

"Yeah, well. I am extremely bad at men. I just tend to meet someone I'm attracted to and either jump their bones or marry them. Neither has ever worked out."

"Many women find satisfaction in self-pleasure. You may—"

"It is not just the orgasms. It's the touching, the kissing, the complete loss of—of—of—

"Control?" Dr. Cindy suggested. Then she stopped talking as if waiting for Alice to absorb what she'd said.

Astonishment replaced her previous feelings of anguish. *How could I want to give up control? Control is my life.* She considered but decided against sharing the heightened fear caused by Henry Petrus's disappearance. Giving voice to the Fear Monster might make it more real, more threatening. As long as it stayed deep in her chest, she could handle it.

"Now that's a topic we will explore next time," Dr. Cindy said. "I'm afraid our time is over for today."

Alice sighed. She felt relieved and sensed she'd learned something significant about herself this session. She wasn't a sex addict. Part of her pleasure came from giving up the control she'd always thought was so essential to who she was.

She hadn't yet mentioned the fantasies, either. Of course, she would have to, eventually, though it wouldn't be easy. She didn't look forward to seeing in the expression on Dr. Cindy's face, that half-pitying, half-fearful look of someone who's just concluded you really are crazy.

"I'll call you as soon as I can. I have to handle a proverbial shitstorm at work, mostly of my own causing. Thank you."

❦

As she unlocked the door to her apartment, she realized she couldn't remember driving home. She felt too exhausted to turn her cell phone back on. Who knows who has seen those pictures by now and where was Henry? The board would certainly fire her if those tapes were circulated. Worst of all what if Henry—? That thought was too terrible to voice even in her head.

As the CEO of Excellcardia, Alice could not run from any issue. She couldn't avoid her company's challenges, even one involving a salacious picture of with her vice president of sales' hands all over her. She took her phone out of her purse and pushed the on button. The screen came to life and she looked at the little message icon. Only three messages? Nothing new since this afternoon. Maybe it wouldn't be so bad. Henry was entitled to go home early once in a while. He was loyal. He wouldn't forget that she'd hired him from a dead-end job and tripled his salary. The idea for Biocardia was Henry's, but without the funding she had secured for him, he would never get the recognition he deserved. The fear monster crawled into a corner deep in her chest and waited.

Chapter Fifteen

PARADISE BY THE DASHBOARD LIGHT

The next morning, Alice learned that Henry Petrus had called in sick for the first time in the three years he had worked at Excellcardia. Alice had a terrible feeling about this sudden illness but shoved it down deep. Jonathan arrived. He hung up his coat on the rack in her office without his usual cheery morning greeting.

"I am so sorry, Jonathan." She offered her brightest and most apologetic smile along with a cup of coffee, black with two lumps of sugar.

He did not return her smile, but neither did he look as angry as he'd been yesterday. "The text blast was evidently more limited than we'd first feared as far as I can determine. I cannot locate the sender, but you, Louise, James, and I are the only recipients I can verify. That doesn't mean there aren't others." He took a sip of coffee, and as he looked at her over the coffee cup, his face softened. "May I ask a personal question?"

"Sure. I'm not sure what I have to hide from you at this point." They both laughed, which seemed to warm the temperature in the room ten degrees.

"Are you in love with James?"

"Oh, God, no. It just kind of happened. I felt sad and vulnerable, and the elevator got stuck and he was just—there. I admit he is an attractive man, but under normal circumstances, nothing would have happened. I warned you, Jonathan. I told you, you might not want to work for a crazy person. Or at least a person with such terrible judgment." She couldn't tell him the truth about her and Brad. She couldn't say anything to bring more sadness to those eyes the exact color of Dove chocolate.

The expression on Jonathan's face revealed more than simple relief. He actually seemed pleased with her answer. "So he took advantage of your vulnerable state. Not surprising."

"He didn't force me, if that's what you mean. But that momentary insanity will certainly not be repeated, I assure you. Where is Brad?"

"In Cincinnati at Central Ohio Health meeting with their CEO. He'd heard rumors they might want to change vendors and he was off. I took the liberty of calling to check on Dr. Petrus on my way in this morning. He sounded quite ill but assured me he would be back in a day or two."

"I really need to talk to him about the elevator tapes. He had no business taking it upon himself to do anything with them. Even if he didn't care about my reputation, he wouldn't bite the hand that feeds him and his work." Still she thought, Henry was up to something, but that was a conversation they would have to have in person. Her nagging suspicion didn't go away, but business had to get done. Alice turned to her computer screen and began to wade through emails while Jonathan briefed her on the day's meetings.

❦

Too many hours later, Alice sighed as she opened the door to her apartment. There wasn't much time until sundown.

Bolting down some Spaghetti-Os, she ran to the closet. Just at sunset, she opened the door.

A wave of relief washed over her. There on the golden hanger hung a knee-length red fringed dress. On the floor, a pair of red pumps with lovely low heels, something with red feathers on it, and a pile of undergarments. Alice picked up the champagne satin panties and matching satin bandeau-style bra —not a great deal of support, but beautiful. Both the bra and the panties were trimmed with luxurious matching lace. The pumps looked like modern Mary Janes, but with a chunkier heel than currently fashionable. Alice slipped on the dress and smoothed her hair back behind her ears, slipping on the shiny gold circlet with a little red feather. Normally she wore little or no makeup on these adventures, but she couldn't resist applying a dab of red lipstick. "What self-respecting flapper would have been seen without lipstick?"

Music blared as she opened the balcony door. She stepped into a large windowless room. Stone pillars curved into a ceiling covered with pale green and gold ceramic tiles that looked faintly iridescent. Figures of pelicans carved out of the stone decorated each pillar and a huge chandelier hung from the tiled ceiling. No frilly crystal number, this chandelier had the strong clean lines of art deco design and was made of dark metal and green glass. The bar in the corner was topped with copper, far too extravagant to be modern. The lack of windows and curved ceiling gave the impression of being underground.

A four-piece band in the opposite corner played smoky jazz, and the scent of cigars hung in the air. Two dapper couples danced on a small dance floor, holding each other close. Small tables covered with white linen cloths surrounded the dance floor. Men in cut away coats sat with ladies in sequined, beaded or satin dresses at the tables. As Alice stood there, drinking it all in, the loveliest couple in the room walked toward her.

"Say, kiddo, we haven't seen you here before." The speaker,

a tall elegant blond man seemed to belong in a black and white movie about the roaring twenties in his white-tailed tux and bow tie.

"No," said his companion, handing Alice a glass of something bubbly. "We would surely have noticed you." Her curly platinum blonde hair was cut in the short bob of the 1920s flapper, and she looked at Alice with eyes large, blue, and expectant. Her silver dress looked a lot like Alice's own, but without the fringe. She appeared a little younger than Alice and was perhaps the most stunning woman in any time period Alice had ever seen.

The man put his arm around Alice's shoulder and said to her, "Okay if you sit at our table? We have a swell view, not too close to the band. They're not very good tonight, but at midnight there's a wickedly good pianist."

He led Alice to a table on the far side of the band near a grand piano and pulled out her chair. "I'm John. Isn't that it tonight, Mary?"

The lovely woman laughed, turned and confided to Alice. "No one uses their real names. This place isn't legal, you know."

"My name is Alice."

"Oh, what an excellent choice." John said. He pulled out Mary's chair, and after tucking it in, pulled his chair closer to Alice's. He put his hand on her knee. John was nearly as pretty as his companion. His pale hair, slicked back with some heavy product, managed to lie in perfect waves. "I too am a fan of Mr. Dodgson's. Did you know he greatly regretted writing *Alice's Adventures in Wonderland?* Simply loathed the fame it brought him." John never took his dark green eyes off Alice.

"Have you tried the champagne, dear? It isn't the horrid stuff they usually serve here." The gorgeous woman took a sip from her own glass.

Alice smiled and took a sip. "Delicious."

"Yes, it's real French champagne. The owner gets it special

for me." Mary took another sip and giggled as the bubbles tickled her nose. She gave Alice a coquettish look.

I'd swear, thought Alice, they're both flirting with me.

As the bubbles in the champagne caressed her brain cells, she wasn't sure which one of this gorgeous couple she was more interested in. She'd never previously been attracted to women at all, but this Mary wasn't just any woman.

"The owner thinks Mary is the bee's knees. He would get her anything she wants, and rightly so. Don't you agree, lovely Alice?" Alice felt his hand on her leg slowly sliding northward. Alice turned to John and looked deeply into his eyes. Yep, sure enough, she was still heterosexual. She wanted him. She had to admit, Mary was gorgeous, but it was John's touch that made her wet with desire.

"Yes, she is lovely," Alice said. His hand slid higher, hesitated just a moment, and then slid beneath the silk panties to dip into the pool between Alice's legs. His eyes went wide with his discovery.

Alice spread her legs slightly, and his fingers slid deep into her. The tablecloth hid his movements, but it wouldn't have mattered to Alice at that moment. Pleasure removed all reason, and Alice wanted only this pretty man and his talented fingers. He rubbed her clit with a delicious rhythm while looking into her eyes. It took every bit of control she had to hold still, her champagne glass still poised near her lips. She concentrated fiercely on the bright red lipstick print her lips left on the crystal flute.

John's talented fingers made her come in less than a minute. The effort not to move or cry out sent a single bead of sweat running down her neck between her breasts. She looked sheepishly at Mary. The blonde woman followed the track of that sweat bead with hungry eyes.

"I will need a big spoon to attend to that properly." John licked his fingers. His velvet words held a slight southern drawl.

"Oh, my." Mary's eyes were wide but hardly innocent.

"Our driver is right outside," John said to Alice. Unless you might prefer to wait to hear the piano player?"

"He is lovely," said Mary. "But there is a woman who's never more than three feet from him. She's quite a dish herself, all large, luscious bosoms and big derriere. Isn't that what you like, my love?" She looked at John over her champagne glass.

"Among other delights. You know me too well, my love." John's eyes were half closed and his voice husky.

"I can hear the pianist another time," Alice said. John's little playing of her own slippery keys made her hungry for the full concert.

He stood up and put his hands on his hips. Mary hooked her arm through his on his right. What was Alice to do but take her place on his left?

The trio climbed a steep set of stairs and stepped outside into a light mist. The tiny droplets coated their hair and sparkled on their lashes beneath a streetlamp. The rich heavy air that caressed them was warm, but still Alice shivered.

"Here comes our driver now," said Mary. A long gold car stopped at the curb. Alice had never seen anything like it. The limousine's long luxurious lines put modern cars to shame, and the interior looked large enough to live in. The driver got out and opened the door.

"Let's hurry before we get all wet." Mary said.

Too late, thought Alice.

"Damn this infernal N'awlins weather." Mary continued. "If it isn't raining, the air alone is thick enough to soak you to the bone." She climbed in and slid across the long seat to the far door. John motioned for Alice to get in next, which put Alice in the middle.

John and Mary's driver was dressed nearly as well as the couple he served. A gray morning coat and pants were topped off with immaculate white gloves. He produced a bottle of champagne, pushed a button, and a silver ice bucket popped out of the back of the front seat. The driver popped the cork, passed out three glasses, and filled them with a disinterested air. After placing the bottle in the bucket, he closed the door and took his place in the driver's seat, never once looking at any of the three in the back seat—the complete picture of a discreet employee.

John leaned across Alice to kiss Mary. "Don't get all excited, little girl. I won't be sharing this big ole scrumptious drink of water. I'm betting you taste even better than this champagne, Alice."

"Oh, pooh." Mary kissed her husband on the forehead. "You can be a selfish son-of-a-bitch. But I guess this is your turn. I absolutely wore out those two last night and left you nothing but snoring lumps, so I suppose you are entirely entitled." She sat up, pushing John away. "Philippe, take the long way home," John instructed the driver.

"Yes, sir." The driver slid the frosted glass partition closed.

Mary reached over to pull a blue velvet curtain across the glass.

"There now, Alice, John whispered against her ear. "You needn't be the least trifle bit shy. We have complete privacy." He leaned in to kiss her. Alice parted her lips, and his tongue took possession of her mouth as she felt her dress being unzipped. He tasted like champagne and caviar, tart and salty. Still he explored and caressed as her silk bra and dress were artfully removed.

"Oh, my God. These are some spectacular bonbons, my dear." He took Alice's breasts in his hands.

"Well, John dear, you don't seem to mind breasts of any size, as I seem to recall." Alice closed her eyes and felt lips brush her left nipple and then gently suck it. A deft tongue circled the nipple at the same time, sending an electric current to her crotch.

"See, Alice," John murmured, how it feels to have someone treat those luscious sugar lumps like they were her own."

When the lips left her breast, Alice whimpered at the loss. As John continued to kiss her lips, she closed her eyes and felt her dress and panties being tugged off past her hips and down her legs. She could hear clothes rustling and zippers unzipping.

"Now, where is my big spoon?" John got down on his knees in front of Alice. Mary's lips returned. His tongue fluttered against her clit like a hummingbird's wings. Assisted by Mary's lips on her nipple, she came in her usual loud fashion.

"Thank you for the ovation," John said, "but that was merely the warm-up. Get down on your hands and knees, please. Mary, you know what to do."

On the floor of the limo, Alice found a soft blanket perfect for the position John suggested. She hadn't long to wait, and she felt him slide into her. His was not an earth-shatteringly large cock by the way it felt, but it certainly filled the bill. He slid in and out of Alice slowly and precisely as he gently pulled on her nipples with his smooth fingers. As she enjoyed the climb up pleasure hill toward a climax, Alice felt curls tickling the inside of her thighs. A warm wet tongue slid along her belly and came to rest on her clit, stroking. At the divine combination of sensations, Alice tried to slow her ascent. *If this stops, I swear, I will die.* It was hopeless. Mary's tongue and John's cock were too much for Alice, and she came hard.

John continued his strokes, and Alice realized Mary's tongue was stroking John's cock as well as Alice's clit. He pulled out of Alice and slid into Mary for the grand finale. Alice caught her breath and watched.

John came inside Mary quietly and collapsed against her. When he recovered and sat up, he said. "I am sorry, Alice. I'll do you the honor next time. But I am a tad old-fashioned, and I like to plant my seeds in my own garden first, so to speak. More champagne?" Somehow he was still sporting an erection.

"Sure," Alice said. After a second glass of champagne, the night's erotic activities continued in the back seat of the limo.

She certainly didn't mind the long way home. *Where do they live anyway, Arizona?*

Finally, Alice couldn't hold her eyes open one more minute. She fell asleep cuddled between the gorgeous and energetic couple.

Chapter Sixteen

UN-BREAK MY HEART

The cold rain reminded Alice it was still January in St. Louis as she walked out the doors of the Excellcardia building. The rain last night in New Orleans had been anything but cold. Both memories of last night and anticipation for tonight's possibilities made her shiver as she opened her car door to head home.

This would've been an ordinary work day except Henry Petrus had called in sick again. It scared her but she had to let that go for at least one more day. Ignoring her feelings was something Alice was very good at. The dark dread that Henry was seriously ill or worse accomplished nothing. There were no more messages with pictures of her in flagrante dilecto and business had gotten done. She'd ignored the growing fear during the numerous meetings, conference calls, and correspondence that made up her days at Excellcardia. One hour with Dr. Cindy, a quick bite, and where, when and who would be on tonight's menu, wondered Alice.

Alice stood still smiling when Dr. Cindy opened the door to the outer office.

"It is good to see a positive expression on your face." Today the doctor wore a burgundy skirt and a matching blouse. Black over-the-knee boots finished the outfit perfectly.

Alice got comfortable on the couch, opened the water offered her and leaned back.

"So last time, Dr. Cindy said, "We dealt with an incident you felt was disastrous and we discussed your changes in libido. A good start, I'd say." Dr. Cindy picked up her pen waiting for Alice to say something significant enough to record.

"Yes, and you said part of my increased desire for sex might be a need to give up control."

"How does that make you feel, Alice?"

"It seems unbelievable, but it feels true." Alice paused. She felt she'd reached an important conclusion and savored the discovery for a bit. "I spend my days maintaining control. For some reason I enjoy giving it up, in the form of sex." Alice looked off in the distance rubbing the velvet buttons beneath her hands.

"You mentioned Dr. Elliot and hypnotic regression before. Is there a reason you didn't want to try it?"

"No. I just don't think there is any big secret to reveal. It seemed like a waste of time. My parents wouldn't have won any parenting awards, but I think they did the best they could. I was an odd little kid. I'd go days without saying a word to anyone but myself. Everyone called me 'that weird girl' and I didn't have any friends. Characters in the books I read kept me company. By college I grew out of it, or made myself grow out of it, but I never made friends easily." Alice looked up, meeting the doctor's eyes. "Maybe I don't want to revisit that weird girl again, after trying so hard to be normal."

"Why do you think you found it hard to make friends?"

"I don't know. I just couldn't believe they would really like me." Alice rubbed the velvet tufts a little faster.

"I have time this evening. Regression can be helpful to

recall childhood memories that may explain our actions as adults. If you really would prefer not to, I can accept that."

Alice found herself feeling more curious about her early childhood than she'd ever been before. Unlike Dr. Elliot who seemed to insist on her doing the regression, Dr. Cindy simply suggested it might help. Alice agreed.

"I'm willing to try," she said.

The doctor instructed Alice to get more comfortable. Alice kicked off her shoes, black stilettos with large silk bows, and reclined. The doctor reached into a drawer in the small lamp table and produced a metronome. Hypnosis, she told Alice, was nothing more than a concentrating of one's focus. There would be no surrendering of her will. The repetitive sound of the metronome supplied a point of focus. Alice took a deep breath and listened to the doctor's voice, soft and relaxing. She drifted along on it for a while.

"I want you to think back," said Dr. Cindy, "to a time when you were much younger. Let yourself remember a time when you felt the need for control."

"I tried so hard to control it."

"What, Alice? What did you try to control? How old were you?" asked Dr. Cindy.

"I'm twelve. I'm trying hard to keep weird things from happening to my body. I hardly eat a bite. My clothes are loose, and Mama is so proud."

"Did it work? Did you keep your body from changing, Alice?"

"No." Alice's voice was soft and breathy. "They happened anyway. My mama said I should be proud to have a woman's bosom, but I am so embarrassed. Boys stare at me."

"Thank you for sharing that with me," Dr. Cindy continued in her soothing tone. "Can you go back farther. Can you remember way back when you were even younger? Can you remember a time when you felt you didn't have control?"

"Yes." Alice's voice was childlike. Her arms were stiff at her side with her hands in tight fists. Her breath came in shallow pants.

"How old are you Alice?"

"Six. I'm scared."

"Why are you scared?"

"Because they left me and I'm scared they won't come back."

"Who won't come back?"

"Mama, Daddy and Sean."

"Why wouldn't they come back?"

"Because I'm a very bad girl. I just wanted to make my hair smooth like Mama's and when I came outside, they were all gone." A child's tears streamed down her cheeks. "They didn't come back for ever and ever. The nice lady told me she'd take good care of me, but I want my Mama." The tears became sobs. "I'm sorry, Mama, I'll be good, promise. Please come back. Please, please, please!"

Dr. Cindy, voice still soft, told Alice to remember where she was now and leave her past scene behind as nothing to fear but something to learn from. She urged Alice to let go of the feelings but remember. Alice sat up. She was forty-nine once again.

"How do you feel?" Dr. Cindy leaned forward in her chair.

"Okay, I guess. Hypnotism isn't magic. I'd always remembered those things. There are not the kind of things you forget, even if you're six." Alice wiped her eyes on the tissue Dr. Cindy handed her. "I just didn't remember how scared I was as a little girl, or how certain I was the whole thing was my fault." Alice sat up straight, crossed her legs, and continued. "My mother always told the story of the family leaving me behind as if I enjoyed the attention. She said when they came to pick me up I was eating a candy bar and drinking a bottle of pop. Mother claimed she'd thought I was on the floor of the car—for seven hours? But her version became my version. I never realized it hurt me so much."

"I think that's where the magic lies. Remembering those early feelings can help explain a lot of things, Alice. People abandoned in childhood often feel unworthy of love. It is not easy to un-break a child's heart, once broken." Dr. Cindy looked at her watch and gave a satisfied sigh. "Well, we have had quite an hour, but I'm afraid—"

"My time is up." Alice stood up and headed for the door without a word. She felt lighter. She hadn't had time to tell Dr. Cindy about the fantasies, but maybe that was for the best. Dr. Cindy still thought her just a woman troubled by things in her past instead of the raving lunatic she really was. Alice wondered, then, what tonight's closet lunacy would offer.

There would've been plenty of time to get home before sunset if it hadn't been raining. In St. Louis, when anything fell from the sky, people felt compelled to look up while driving and thus crashed into each other at an alarming rate. By the time Alice pulled into the garage of her building, she had barely fifteen minutes to spare. She pushed the elevator button furiously, though she hated it when other people did that. One push was enough, but this evening she couldn't help herself. She couldn't wait for the evening's adventure to begin.

She reached her apartment with only seven minutes to go until sunset. Alice tossed her tan Burberry raincoat on to a chair. Her neatness compulsion would not make her late for a very important date. As she headed to the bedroom, someone knocked on the door.

Alice didn't intend to answer it but had to peek through the peephole to at least see who she planned to ignore. It was Susan, and the look on her face made Alice forget about going anywhere. Her friend's bright green eyes were wide and blank at the same time. Her hands hung at her sides, and her shoulders were bent.

Alice opened the door and wrapped her arms around Susan without a word. Susan didn't move a muscle until Alice took her hand, walked her into her apartment and sat her on the couch. This had to be bad. Susan is never without her armor, the sense of humor that protects her heart. She'd made jokes at her own mother's funeral—but not tonight.

"Susan, please tell me, what could be this bad? Are your kids okay? Is it—?"

"There's a tumor in my left breast." Susan stared straight ahead, and no emotion registered on her normally animated face.

"How large is the lesion?"

"Six millimeters."

Alice exhaled with relief. "That's really pretty small, thank God. Worst case, a lumpectomy, maybe a little chemo and you're fine. Even you can spare that much boob." Alice's pitiful attempt at humor did nothing to change Susan's expression. "Where's David?"

"He's on his way home. He told me to come over here and wait for him."

"Smart man. And to think I tried to talk you out of marrying him." Alice searched Susan's face—nothing. This called for desperate measures.

"I have wine. We need to celebrate finding the tumor so early." Alice walked to the kitchen, reached up into her white-washed maple cabinets, and took down the only bottle of wine in her apartment. Someone had given it to her for a gift, eight —no, ten years ago. She poured two glasses and handed one to Susan.

"You have wine?" Susan's voice held a tiny bit of sarcasm.

Alice felt a spark of hope. "Sure. I can be a good hostess, and it's aged and everything." There was pride in her voice.

They both took a sip simultaneously. Susan spit hers back into the glass, while Alice swallowed hers and made a face.

"It tastes like an outhouse floor. I can't believe you swallowed it," Susan said. They both laughed. "Martha Stewart you are not. Is this even red wine? It looks more like coffee than wine."

Alice examined the bottle. "It says chardonnay." She vaguely remembered something from wine class.

"Oh, God, Alice. White wines don't keep like reds." Susan sat her glass down on the black acrylic coffee table. "Oh well, I'm so sorry about your mom. I got the text just as I was about to have my biopsy. Did I miss the memorial?"

"No. She didn't want one, and I just couldn't."

"Memorials can help with closure, you know."

"Yeah. Only she's dead and a memorial she didn't want won't change that." Alice shrugged and smiled at her friend. Susan made a brave effort at a smile, too.

By the time David showed up, Susan's wit was showing through the fear a little and Alice felt she could breathe again. But as soon as they left, a heaviness settled on her shoulders and she couldn't leave the couch.

Susan's mother had died at fifty from an aggressive form of breast cancer. Alice's own mother was dead. She just couldn't lose her best friend. Thick fibers of deep darkness gathered inside her. Her breathing seemed to slow, and her heart rate too. She couldn't move. Her legs and arms were too heavy. If she just lay down on the couch, maybe later she could...

Chapter Seventeen

RESCUE ME

Twelve hours later, Otis's black paw roused her. He batted at her face and meowed loudly. She sat up. She should be at work but that didn't matter. Nothing mattered. Alice fed the cat, stopped to pee and then lay down on her bed. She didn't even change into her pajamas. That didn't matter either, although she'd been in her favorite hot-pink suit for twelve hours already. The leaden fibers thickened in her head, wrapping her and insulating her, shutting out the world. She rolled onto her right side and tucked into a ball. In the other room, her cell phone made the little sound it made for messages. She closed her eyes.

Time passed. Time had no meaning to her, wrapped deep in the dark in her head. Somewhere far away, she heard her front door open. Otis, who lay curled up behind her knees, jumped down at the sound of someone entering the room.

"Alice! What are you doing? You couldn't bother to make a simple call? I made excuses for a day, but—oh, Alice." Jonathan's voice grew soft.

She heard his voice, but it sounded so far away. He pulled back the covers, sat on the edge of her bed, and just looked at her. Alice opened her eyes just wide enough to see pity on his handsome face. *Oh, God, please, not pity.* Something stirred deep inside her.

"How did you get in here? I—"

"You gave me a key some time ago to feed your cat when you went out of town, remember? I took the liberty when you didn't come in to work and didn't answer your phone."

"Go away," Alice said into her pillow.

"Hell no! I will do no such bloody thing." He reached over and lifted her to a sitting position like she were a rag doll. "You will get up now and shower, or I will carry you and scrub you myself."

Alice didn't even squirm as Jonathan carried her to the bathroom. He sat her down tenderly and began to peel off her clothes. His movements were not at all sensual but were those of a caregiver helping a patient.

She felt nothing. She was not even embarrassed as he unhooked her bra and slid her panties to her ankles. She simply stared ahead, unable to move or say much of anything, the weight of her darkness still too great.

"If you do not walk into that shower on your own, right now, I swear I will carry you." Alice said nothing and didn't move a muscle. Jonathan made good on his promise, throwing her over his shoulder again and depositing her in the shower. He turned on the water, testing it with his hands before he moved her into the stream.

"If you refuse to scrub yourself—that I am afraid I cannot do. I'll leave you in there until the stink is washed away." He shut the glass door to her shower and left her alone.

Alice felt the warm water flow over her. It ran down from the top of her head and over her body. She didn't lift her arms or move at all. It would have been too difficult. Her eyes fixed on the white ceramic tiles, seeing nothing but hard cold white.

Deep down in the dark inside her, something stirred again. The lovely warm water seeped through, and she could feel the heavy metal fibers of darkness that locked her mind begin to dissolve.

She heard Jonathan open the bathroom door. Moving would still have taken incredible effort, but thinking was becoming possible again. Alice couldn't resist just letting the situation unfold.

"Alice Hightower, walk out of the shower this instant." Jonathan's voice sounded so commanding she could do nothing but obey. With every breath, her head cleared, but she wasn't ready reveal that yet.

She moved slowly and walked with her eyes straight ahead. It still took a far greater effort than normal to move. Her whole body felt stiff and heavy as she took step after step. Sitting on the edge of the bed, she suddenly felt acutely aware of her nakedness. As if he read her mind, Jonathan looked away and laid a pair of black nylon pants and a red St. Louis Cardinals sweatshirt across her lap. *What, no underwear?*

She slowly pulled on the sweatshirt and pants. She was still wet, so it took some effort to pull on the pants. Then she sat staring ahead, waiting for instructions, capable now of thinking and moving, but not wanting to, she remained a spectator for a while longer.

Jonathan knelt in front of her and looked at her. She raised her eyes to his and saw only tenderness. He gently picked up each of her feet and slipped on shoes. "Will you come with me, Alice?"

She nodded slowly and stood up. Jonathan took her hand and led her into the kitchen, where he opened a can of food and dumped it into Otis's bowl.

He picked up the raincoat she'd dropped on the chair what seemed like weeks ago and helped her into it. He led her to the garage and into his car, which smelled like wood and exotic spices. She kept her eyes lowered. It was too much to ask where they were going, although she was alert enough now to wonder.

Ten minutes later he pulled into the garage of a building that was once a grand old hotel. Was it possible he'd lived so close to her all this time? She'd heard the Chase Park Plaza was developing luxury residences in an effort to revitalize the surrounding area. The lavish lady's top floors had been turned into posh condominiums. Jonathan slid his key card into the slot and the elevator took them to the top floor. Wide hallway, plush carpets, and stained glass skylights—this was no ordinary apartment building.

He stopped at a set of dark wooden double doors. A brass plaque read *J. S. Salter*.

"This is me." Jonathan turned and looked at Alice. Her green eyes met his brown ones and she smiled.

"I think, maybe, I'm paying you too much, said Alice."

"I knew you were still in there. "Who knew all it took was a conspicuous display of wealth to bring you back to me?" Jonathan turned from her and slipped the plastic key into the slot next to the door. "My father settled a good deal of money on me for my fortieth birthday. I suppose he did it out of some feelings of guilt. He has left me out of his will apparently. He remarried rather quickly after my mother's death and has three younger sons. I suppose it suited him to be rid of me." Jonathan opened the door and pulled Alice in by the hand. The man-scent of leather and wood greeted her once inside the door.

"Having no idea what to do with the money and with the stock market in a snit at the time, I bought this little place." He dropped Alice's hand, spreading his arms wide.

Alice inhaled sharply. "Wow," she said. Her voice cracked. She hadn't used her voice much in so long, it had evidently gotten rusty. The place was magnificent. It looked like Jay Gatsby's place if he lived in the Central West End of St. Louis instead of in West Egg on Long Island.

On the floor inside the door was a circular medallion of four different colors of marble, fifteen feet in diameter. Intri-

RABBITHOLE

cate diamond patterns surrounded the letters *J.S.S.* at its center, cut out of onyx marble. Dark wood panels lined the walls up to the fifteen-foot ceilings. Colored light fell in a hexagonal pattern from the intricate stained-glass skylight depicting a tiger and a dragon in battle.

"It's a Chinese thing. The tiger represents the physical, the dragon the spiritual. They are in battle within each of us don't you think? The window came from the townhouse of the Chinese ambassador in London. During the great collapse of 2010 in Europe, such treasures could be had for a song."

"Thousands and thousands of songs, I'll bet." Alice still looked up in awe. When she looked at him, Jonathan gave her the wide warm smile he shared with his Auntie June. Why hadn't she noticed before that Jonathan didn't merely look good in a pretty suit, but an incredibly handsome man? Probably because she'd never let herself notice.

Looking around the large room, Alice thought the furniture looked like a museum display from several centuries and at least three continents. There were two ebony wood tables with zebra skins tops she doubted were imitation. An exotic orchid with lacy lavender blooms sat on one table. Carved wooden tables sat on either side of a dark wood and rose brocade couch that would have made Queen Victoria's royal butt feel regal. The three chairs in the room had an Asian flair, carved with more dragons and tigers. Near the back of the room sat the true focal point, a genuine Steinway grand piano.

"I've never seen a grand piano up close," she said. My aunt Sharon owned an upright that no one ever played." She walked to the piano and ran her hand reverently over the smooth dark wood. "Is this the one your father gave you for your twenty-first birthday?"

"I'm pleased you remembered. Yes, it was in storage for years. I designed this room around it." He stopped talking for a moment and looked down at Alice. She found it hard to breathe or looked away, rubbing her palms on the thighs of her

221

sweatpants. She suddenly thought of chocolate and felt hungry.

"There were times when I was traveling that I could barely afford the storage fees. She couldn't exactly be stuck in a storage shed."

"Of course not. Play something for me, please."

"Certainly, but I want to get some food into you first. Decide if you prefer Mozart, Beethoven, or Chopin."

"Oh, I want all three," Alice said. She stood, smiling widely, with her hands on her hips. Her brain was working again, and she felt almost light.

"We'll see. Here, in my home, you're not my boss."

She followed him into a galley-style kitchen, much smaller than her own. The countertops were green-flecked granite and the floor black and white marble in a checkered pattern. Tall plain maple cabinets lined both sides. The black appliances reminded Alice of her own kitchen—nice, but hardly fitting the rest of this magnificent apartment.

"I'm not much of a cook. I can make you an omelet, if you'd like," Jonathan said.

"Anything will be fine. I'm really starving. I honestly can't remember the last time I ate." Alice sat on a clear Lucite bar stool she pulled out from under a small wooden table painted apple green. She turned the stool so she could watch while he cooked. Had she ever noticed how wonderfully wide his shoulders were? She had noticed his nice round ass, though at work it was usually not so prominently displayed as it was in the jeans he wore today.

He didn't ask her what she would like in her omelet; he knew, having brought her lunch every weekday for three years. "It's delicious," Alice said, her mouth full of ham and gouda omelet. Jonathan set his plate down and merely watched her shovel in the cheesy goodness.

When she set down her fork, he reached up and wiped a

dab of cheese off her cheek. He looked at her as if she were magic. "You know, Alice, don't you, I have feelings for you?"

She just looked at him. "You can't. I'm a disaster. You're one of the few people who actually knows what a total and complete disaster I can be."

"A beautiful disaster. You are a semi-truck full of long-stemmed red roses, spilled on the highway, some scattered but most still tied tight in lovely bundles." The picture and the aptness of the description made them both laugh. When she finally stopped laughing, his arms were around her and he kissed her. *Why didn't I—oh, Alice, just enjoy it, for God's sake,* she told herself as she felt his tongue against hers.

He took her hand and led her down a long hall to his bedroom. At least she assumed it was his bedroom; the man-smell was strongest there. Alice could always tell who slept in a room by the smell. She loved the musky leather tang that marked a room as a man's. This man's room contained a king-sized bed, but no other furniture. It was a stark white bed with tight hospital corners, no headboard, just a double wall of snow-white pillows. The walls were bare, and it resembled a monk's cell more than a room that belonged in this gorgeous man.

There was no door to the bedroom. A curved wall of glass blocks must have hidden the bathroom fixtures. As a matter of fact, none of the rooms in his home appeared to have doors. There were archways and short walls, but no actual doors except the front one. *What is his aversion to doors?* Alice nearly chuckled, but quickly lost the thread of that odd thought in the more engaging one at hand.

She felt strange and shy to be in his bedroom. She'd known Jonathan for three years and never let herself entertain any thoughts other than professional. Admiration of how good he looked in his suits didn't really count; she often admired Louise's chic style too.

Alice looked down at the bare wood floor until he raised

her chin and kissed her again. His black pants were off, and he tugged down her sweatpants with a gentle urgency.

"Stop, Jonathan. We can't." But she made no effort at all to stop him.

"Really, Alice? I think we already are."

Incredibly, this no longer felt wrong to Alice. She might get fired for fraternizing with an employee, but not this one. Surely there were no security cameras in Jonathan's bedroom. She lay back and anticipated the delicious weight of him. He was on her and in her in an instant, his tongue exploring hers, his hands caressing her, and his cock pleasing her.

The skin between them seemed to dissolve. Alice felt each of his thrusts as if her own muscles produced them. She couldn't tell where she ended, and he began. When he exhaled, her lungs filled. With each beat of his heart, her blood flowed. He moved more quickly now, and their hearts beat faster. It could have been hours or days because nothing else existed for Alice. She squeezed him with her deep secret muscles, and they breathed deeply. He stopped his movement and she quickened hers. He squeezed his eyes tight. Their shared pleasure peaked hard. She breathed in sharply, and the oneness shattered.

For several long minutes, Alice and Jonathan lay locked together, saying nothing, his head on her shoulder and her arms still locked around him. Her fingers caressed the muscles of his back. Finally, Jonathan reached under her and rolled over on his side, taking her with him. They lay together silent, as if no words were quite sufficient.

"Are you still hungry, Alice? This place has a four-star restaurant downstairs."

"I don't think my commando sweatpants would be appropriate."

"I might have had ulterior motives in leaving undergarments out of your ensemble." Jonathan laughed a devilish little-boy laugh. "The penthouse suites have room service privileges."

"Fantastic. I'm still pretty hungry and you didn't eat more than a couple of bites. You'll need your strength for my private concert."

Jonathan kissed her on the nose and stood up. *Oh my God. He looks better naked than in his suits.* Jonathan's lean hard muscles weren't obscured by hair. His abs were clearly visible as he bent to pick up his black jeans. Alice enjoyed the unobstructed view of his lovely cock. He was certainly a man of many gifts.

"I'm glad you approve, Alice," he said taking note of where her eyes were. She pulled the covers up, tucked them under her breasts, and simply watched him dress. The sight of him pulling a pair of royal blue boxers over his nice tight derriere almost made her gasp.

They ordered an extravagant dinner of steak and ate by candlelight in the dining room. It was less opulent than the "concert hall," as Jonathan told her he called the largest room. He had furnished his dining room richly with a dark wood oval table and six chairs. With no china hutch or sideboard, it was obviously a man's idea of a dining room. On the long wall hung a portrait of a young blonde woman. The sadness in her large blue eyes marred her beauty a little. She looked no older than twenty-five.

"Who is the gorgeous blonde?" Alice couldn't help but ask when she couldn't hold one more bite.

"My late wife."

Alice searched his face and found she could not read his expression. "Oh." Her voice grew soft.

"She's been dead for more than a decade now. It is a lovely portrait, though, and I like the frame. As you can see, I've always had a fondness for blondes. But only natural ones." There was Aunty June's smile once again.

"I've always thought that red would suit me. Did you suspect the carpet didn't match the drapes in my case, sir?"

"Oh, no. I've seen you augment your natural color from

time to time, but I felt certain the cuffs would indeed match the collar, and you did not disappoint."

Alice noticed when Jonathan was happy, his Chinese heritage shone in his beautiful dark eyes that took on an almond shape when he smiled.

They retired to the concert hall, after placing the dishes in the hall. Jonathan thrilled her with two hours of piano pieces she'd never heard played better. His passion and talent were overwhelming. While his fingers produced the lovely notes, Alice watched his face and saw on it what could only be called ecstasy. She'd seen that same look as they had sex. She sat spellbound during the entire performance, far too content to think of anything but the magic of this performance.

The concert ended and Jonathan sat beside her on the brocade couch, catching his breath. A strange thought crossed her mind and she felt compelled to ask. "Will you tell me about your wife, or is it too painful?"

Jonathan put his arm around Alice and inhaled deeply.

"Her name was Caroline. She was an exceptionally talented violinist. We met at a competition in Manhattan where she lived. She won and I lost. I moved there to be near her, and not long after fell in love, and a year later, we married. She was not strong. The rigors of the concert stage were too much for her. She took her own life two years later."

"Oh, I'm so sorry." Alice felt the blood rushing in her ears. *He falls for the crazy ones.* He's repeating some kind of tragic pattern. Her head felt light, and she wanted to throw up. She had to get out of there.

"I've had a wonderful time, but I really need to go home and get some things done. Will you drive me home, please?"

Jonathan looked disappointed but smiled. "Of course. I just hoped—well—if you want to go home, I'll be happy to take you."

Otis meowed his loud approval of her return and jumped on her lap.

"My big sweetie, we have a problem." Alice sat on her bed, petting the cat and gently rubbing the little scar where his left ear should have been. "There is a very lovely man who thinks he has feelings for me. He's wonderful and talented and totally wrong for me. He's also my assistant. How's about that for inappropriate? Just like you, he doesn't seem to notice that my ass is too big for the rest of me. He knows about most of my crazy and doesn't seem to deter him. But he just imagines it's me he cares about. He's just attracted to the crazy ones. He'll get over it. He has to."

Chapter Eighteen

LYIN EYES

Alice decided ignoring Jonathan's declaration of feelings would be the best way to handle the situation. She wouldn't satisfy his need to take care of another woman with mental issues. She would plead a dead phone battery as the reason she'd ignored his texts.

Sitting straight up in her chair behind her desk, she waited for Jonathan to get to the office. At seven-forty-eight, as usual, he pushed the door open to the same point where he left it every morning, and smiled at her—a gorgeous, wide, warm smile that should have made her feel wonderful. "Shall I make the coffee this morning? I believe you're neglecting your most important duty as CEO. The day cannot begin without proper caffeinating."

"Sure, but first we need to talk," she said. "Will you close the door, please?"

"In my experience, that's never a good thing for a woman to say." He pushed the door closed a little more but left it ajar a few inches and walked to the coffee maker.

"I'm very grateful for your help, Jonathan. I might still be curled up in bed if you hadn't come. The sex was fun; but you know this can't happen. Our working relationship is too important." *Doesn't this sound familiar?* She'd meant these words when she said them to Brad, and she meant them now, too. Her job was her life, and for sexual release, she had the balcony boys. They would never have "feelings."

"I will always be grateful for your help and concern, but ours is strictly a business relationship. I'm sorry if I led you to believe otherwise. Really sorry." She hoped she looked caring and not the cold-hearted bitch she felt like at the moment.

Jonathan stood frozen with his hands on the coffee pot, for a surprisingly long moment.

"What is it with you and the door, anyway?"

He walked to the door and slammed it shut. "There. Your door is closed." He turned back toward her. "Very well, a business relationship it is. I will go through your mail as usual. You received an invitation to the Open Door's formal gala needing an immediate response. I had intended to escort you, but it hardly seems a business-like thing to do. I will leave it to you to return the RSVP." He finished making the coffee and handed her a cup. When his eyes met hers, his expression looked as cold as the feeling inside her. His coldness hurt. *Very good reason never to fall in love: too much pain potential.*

She moved through this day as she had many others. Concentrating on work was her solace. Alice and Jonathan worked together like cogs in a beautifully efficient machine. She couldn't do anything to stop a machine as important to her life and happiness as her company.

With each passing hour, she felt more relieved at her decision. Alice had always expended great effort to avoid emotions, which only made it more difficult when they reared up and bit her in the ass. Why was it so hard to forget yesterday? And why, if she'd made such a wise decision, was there a knot of pain in the middle of her chest? Dr. Cindy could help, she felt certain.

At her appointment, the doctor discussed new research focusing on cognitive talk therapy and lifestyle changes to deal with mood swings in Bipolar II individuals. She suggested Alice try to get more sleep. More than a few hours of sleep a night might be a good thing. The doctor spent a good deal of time outlining a regimen to handle Alice's ups and downs.

"These aren't just my suggestions. The latest research in several respected professional journals backs me up. The new findings seem to indicate the long-term side effects of drug therapy are much more serious than originally thought," the doctor said. "The effects of too little sleep have long been documented. New research suggests that it is during sleep that our brain clears the amyloid. Amyloid, you may know, it thought to be the major culprit in Alzheimer's."

"I'm not surprised about the effect of pscyhe meds. A simple sleeping pill made me feel like the walking dead. I can't imagine what anti-psychotics would do." Alice leaned against the back of Dr. Cindy's antebellum couch, gently rubbing the tufted button cushion with her right hand.

"I think the things I suggested may help you better handle your stress. The symptoms of Bipolar II do sometimes worsen with age, but not always. Now, do you want to talk more about this man who says he cares about you?"

"There's nothing else to say. His wife committed suicide, so she had to be clinically depressed. I won't let him fall into an old pattern. He takes care of me wonderfully well as my assistant at the office. I won't have him feeling he needs to take care of me twenty-four-seven." Alice sat up straight, put her hands on her knees, and looked at the floor.

"Don't you think he might really love you? Don't you think you deserve to be loved?" Dr. Cindy peered at Alice over her reading glasses.

"You know, Doctor, I don't know if I really believe there is such a thing as romantic love," Alice said.

Dr. Cindy raised her eyebrows. "That is something that

will have to be left for another time. Unfortunately, time's up. Let's see how those suggestions I gave you work out and talk about love more next session."

§.

The knot of pain in her gut when she thought of Jonathan touching her, lessened with each day that week. When Friday finally came, Alice couldn't believe how ready she was for the weekend. She'd felt no compulsion at all to do anything but get a good night's sleep all week. She'd wondered occasionally about what might be behind the closet door, but several nights of truly restful sleep seemed to be exactly what she needed.

Just as she got up to head home, Brad James opened the door to her office wide. "Hey, Boss Lady, ask me how much money I made for Excellcardia in two little days."

Behind him, Alice saw Jonathan heading to the elevator. There was no look of concern or even a good-bye. His day was over, and he left, like any other employee.

She wanted to be on her way, but Brad's success deserved attention. "I got your report. I'm impressed." Alice concentrated on keeping her voice cool, but appreciative. She moved toward the desk.

He grabbed her wrist, turning her to him. "That's not really why I'm here, Alice. We have unfinished business between us. I know you want me as much as I want you."

"You're wrong. We had some fun. But it can't happen again."

"You forget who you're talking to. I've been inside that hot little volcano you call your pussy. You need me too." He pressed her against the wall, and his expression made her shiver involuntarily. He looked at her as if he needed her like he needed his next breath. That look had gotten her into plenty of trouble in the past, but no more.

Alice pushed him back forcefully and glared at him. "What I need is my business, not yours."

"Please don't tell me you're fucking that little lap-dog with the fake English accent."

"He went to school in England for years. His accent is—"

"You are, goddammit! You are fucking him!" Brad stepped back. "He's not what he seems, Alice. They charged him with murdering his wife, you know. He lawyered up big-time and eventually got off, but that doesn't make him innocent."

"How do you know that? That can't be true. It would have shown up in the background check we do for employees."

"I lived in Manhattan at the time, fifteen years ago. The local tabloids were all over the story. His father is Winston Churchill's great nephew or some such shit. I think because women think he's so pretty, the story got a lot of coverage. That kind of money can have history rewritten."

The sound of blood rushing in her ears nearly deafened her.

"I am smart enough not to jeopardize this company's welfare."

"Oh, horseshit, Alice! We've had this conversation before. There's something real between us. Hell, I left my wife because I thought we might have a chance. I can talk to a headhunter if working for you is the problem. Believe me, they'll be interested. As soon as I can find the right fit—"

"No, you can't!" She'd beg if she had to.

He pressed her against the wall again, far too close. "Yes, I can. I think we should at least see if this thing between us goes anywhere. It'd sure be fun to try, wouldn't it?" His eyes seemed to bore into her soul. He was handsome, and there certainly were sparks between them—hot enough to burn her to a crisp. She wouldn't let them.

"Not going to happen, Brad. I just don't feel that way about you, or any employee, for that matter."

He leaned into her, kissing her in the way he knew she

loved. His hands reached under her coat to her breasts. She could feel her vagina contract. *Traitorous little whore;* part of her wanted him badly. But she couldn't let any feelings she might have for him affect the job she did as CEO. She pushed him away again. "It was a nice diversion. Hardly something to leave a spouse or a job for." She watched his eyes turn flinty. "I need to go."

"Sure." Brad turned and walked out the door. Did she imagine it, or did she see genuine sadness in his eyes?

Alice walked back to her desk and sat in her chair, not bothering to take off her coat. She stared into space and trying hard not to feel anything. Louise's voice startled her.

"What the hell, Al? You look pale. Got some freeze-dried kale and tomato chips in my purse somewhere." Louise rummaged through her brown leather Coach purse. "They're the nacho-cheese-flavored ones. Really only a little cumin on them, but they'll pink up those cheeks." Louise held out a rumpled package. Alice curled her lip. Louise sighed and put the bag back in her purse.

"I saw Brad James in the elevator. He didn't look happy at all. Looked right through me and didn't say a word. So rude. What is it? Tell Auntie Lou." Louise slipped off her camel cashmere coat, threw it over her arm, and sat in the chair in front of Alice's desk.

"It's nothing I can't handle." Alice couldn't meet her eyes.

"Oh, yeah, you can handle anything, except men, alright. Don't forget who you're talking to. I saw the two of you in the elevator. You and the king of smarm aren't getting serious?"

"He left his wife for—for me." She stared intently at the objects on her desk. Too bad she really wasn't the little blonde girl in the pinafore on the cover of *Alice's Adventures in Wonderland.* She could forget all this and disappear down a rabbit hole just like opening her closet door.

"Oh, did he now?" Louise looked down at her coat, and when she looked up, her expression no longer concerned, but angry. "I saw them at the diabetes fundraiser last weekend. She had on the most amazing little Vera Wang. Far too frilly for me, but it looked lovely on her tiny figure. They sure didn't look estranged to me. The two of them burned up the dance floor. Not a bad little dancer for a white guy. He had his arm around her the whole night." She crossed her arms and leaned back in her chair.

Again Alice felt the blood rush to her ears. She wasn't stupid. She couldn't let herself fall for the lies any man told her —tonight, anyway. She wondered if men were capable of understanding the concept of truth.

"I've gotta go, Lou." Alice ran to the elevator and then to her car as if being chased.

Chapter Nineteen

FLESH FOR FANTASY

D r. Cindy would help her organize the chaos she felt. If the traffic gods were on her side, she might even get home in time for a bit of closet action, as well. What she really needed would be hanging in her closet soon. Maybe it was time Dr. Cindy learned just how deep the crazy ran.

❧

"You are safe here, Alice. Nothing you say can change what I think of you. I'm here to listen and to help, never to judge. Tell me about these fantasies." Dr. Cindy put on her black-framed readers and picked up a yellow legal pad. *Was there some kind of law that shrinks had to use yellow legal pads? Why weren't they called "shrink pads?"* Looking at Alice over her glasses, she said, "Let me decide what's crazy. It's what I do."

Alice told her all of it. She explained how she had first discovered the clothes hanging in her closet and put them on, how it happened every night at sunset. She described some of the fantasies in detail. After a while, the doctor stopped writing and just listened. Alice talked nonstop for a half an hour.

When she finally stopped, Dr. Cindy was silent.

"What do you think these fantasies mean? Alice asked. "Why do I have them?"

"It doesn't matter what I think, Alice. They're your fantasies. What do they mean to you? Do you enjoy them?"

"Well, yeah. Who wouldn't? It's like they're making up for the fact that for most of my life sex wasn't really that important to me. Doctor, maybe that's it. Maybe I'm somehow trying to give myself the sex life I need now." Alice squeezed her eyes as tight as she could, but still the tears ran down her cheeks. Dr. Cindy handed her a tissue and waited patiently. Some minutes passed, and Alice took a deep breath.

"Suddenly the two men at work I have slept with both think they care about me. That's messy and ridiculous. Fantasy men are always gone in the morning. Real men hang around to complicate things. Why haven't the fantasies disappeared since I have a couple of real opportunities?"

"Do you want them to disappear?"

"Well, no. I just assumed they would, now that I don't really need them." She looked sideways at Dr. Cindy. "The most insane thing is they don't seem like fantasies."

"Insane is a legal designation and has no value here. Tell me what you mean, Alice." Dr. Cindy leaned forward in her chair.

"The adventures feel completely real to me." Alice leaned forward on the couch and waited. Would Dr. Cindy to laugh or scoff or something?

"Many people experience dream states that seem very real. What makes them feel more than a dream to you?"

"Evidence the next morning. Like marks on my body, bite marks, and chafing. And when I look up details from the fantasies on the Internet, they're real places, or people who actually lived. Sometimes there are things I couldn't have known about."

The doctor's face was expressionless, as if she heard crazier stuff every day. "How does that make you feel?"

"Completely nuts. They couldn't be real."

"Is it possible that the research precedes the fantasy? Perhaps the fantasy is based on the internet research you did?"

"I do the research after, not before the fantasies. Given that I've had amazing sex since the events began, I can't imagine that my mind still needs to make these things up. Besides, I really don't think I'm that creative." Alice laughed a little at her words.

"You have had satisfying sexual relations since the fantasies began?" Dr. Cindy was scribbled furiously on her pad.

"Well. Yes. That completely irresponsible thing with the married co-worker who says now he wants to leave his wife—or actually, he says he did leave his wife, but that's probably a lie. And now my assistant tells me he cares for me—and that experience was far beyond sex. It was a practically religious experience."

Dr. Cindy took off her glasses, put down her pad and was silent for a moment. "There's been some ground-breaking research on people whose patterns of brain activity differ from most. This research suggests that among people who are labeled as having mental pathology, there are some who display incredible talents, including the manipulation of time, space, or forms of energy. You might want to contact an organization called the Higher Minds Society. They're located here in St. Louis and their research could be helpful to you. Some people's impossible may be other people's reality.

"Huh." Alice had no earthy idea how to respond to this. Maybe her first impression of Dr. Cindy was right, and she was new age kooky after all.

"I know it sounds hard to believe. These individuals are always extremely high functioning, like you. Some are exceptionally talented musicians, brilliant scientists, or maybe even very successful CEOs. It is as if the cerebral irregularity that generates unusual brain wave patterns conveys unusual gifts...at the price of some psychiatric pathology, however." The doctor looked at her watch and smiled her benevolent doctor smile. "Well, that's something we'll need to explore further, but I'm afraid we're out of time."

Alice knocked on Susan's door. Susan looked tired as she answered the door. Maybe Susan would be able to watch her sleep and help end this mystery. Had she started chemo already? Watching her best friend suffer would not be easy, Alice thought, and then reproached herself. Could she be more of a cold-hearted bitch? This was her best friend in the world.

Alice hugged her friend tight "How are you, Suz?"

"Not bad, considering. What can I do for you?"

"Do you remember when you said you would help me with my sleep walking problem, stay over and see what I do?"

"Sure."

"I'm not sure if you're feeling up to it, but I would appreciate it. Whenever you feel like it and have time."

"David's flying out tonight right after dinner, and I'm reading the new Stephen King, and I haven't been sleeping much anyway, so sure. How about tonight? I'll sit my nasty butt right on your white couch and read. What if you don't do anything?"

"Perfect. Just tell me whatever. I really appreciate it. You still have your key, don't you?" Alice said. Susan nodded, and smiled at her friend as the elevator doors closed.

Otis fed, her own food wolfed down, Alice took a shower, mostly to wash off all the emotions of the day. All the dangerous and life-complicating emotions washed down the drain with the lovely hot water. She experienced the gentle joy of feeling like a whole responsible human being in complete control of her tidy emotions. One who maybe needed a little harmless fun.

Alice slid open the door. A long blue gown adorned the golden hanger. The sleeves were long, and the neck cut low. It laced in the front below the scant cloth that would barely cover her breasts. Touching the dress, Alice was surprised at how coarse and stiff the wool fabric felt. No label. Thank you once again, messed-up brain. A naughty romp in the past felt like what she needed once again.

The long, braided cord had to be a belt. The shoes were soft brown leather with funny pointed toes and no real sole or heel. Hmmm, really old.

"Twelfth or thirteenth century, maybe, Otis?" She should have paid more attention to ancient history in college.

Alice was grateful for the silk under shift that lay folded beneath the shoes. The wool was way too scratchy for her twenty-first-century skin. The gown smelled like rosemary and evergreens. With her hands at her sides, the large, belled sleeves were long enough to touch the floor. The wool didn't stretch at all, but the garment fit as if she'd lain down on the cloth and had it cut around her. The gown had just enough extra fabric in the chest and ass, so hard to find in modern clothing. It always amazed her how these outfits fit her so perfectly. Could she have produced all this like Dr. Cindy suggested? Could she really be taking these trips to other times and places? Maybe Susan could help her answer this impossible question, tonight.

Alice slid open the balcony door. Her eyes strained at the gloom. Something hit the back of her knees. She fell forward onto damp moving wood that from previous experience she guessed to be a boat.

"Pa dina knae kvinna," someone growled.

"What?" Alice said.

"I speaka da Anglish. Better you to stay when put." The voice sounded even deeper and more stern this time. Alice felt a warm figure next to her and heard whimpering. In the air, the choking scent of salt air, smoke, and man—make that, men. The man-scent of leather mixed with sweat and the sick sweet smell of blood. She seemed to be surrounded by tall figures. She heard coughing and more of the same lilting foreign language all around her. *Swedish, or Norwegian maybe?* It did remind her of her lab partner in Quantitative Analysis who was from Sweden.

The rolling below her feet stopped with a thump and she heard the boat's hull scraping on rocks. The boat must have run up on dry land. Someone picked her up and threw her over his shoulder. These were big men. *Yum.* A cheer went up from the crowd around her. A woman screamed, and the entire crowd surged forward in a mass.

As Alice's eyes adjusted to the darkness, she could see a fire burning ahead. The man carrying her set her down with surprising gentleness on soft grass.

"Do not move." The man now facing her stood six and a half feet tall and had shoulders nearly three feet wide. Just as she found herself wanting to do what he said, he disappeared into the dark. She could see other giants around her. Some carried bales or boxes, and one carried another woman who was not as keen to be carried as Alice. The woman struggled and screamed; the man carrying her laughed.

As Alice looked around her, a hand touched her gently on the shoulder. "Come." The giant who had carried her ashore turned and she followed.

"I certainly hope to," Alice said. He was gorgeous. Long, light brown hair hung below a leather helmet almost to his waist. The fire was reflected in his light eyes. It was too dim to tell if they were blue or gray. His leather pants fit him like a second skin, perfectly displaying impressive muscles. His short animal skin vest couldn't hide the powerful arms that would have made a bodybuilder proud. One hand held a huge wooden hammer. *Vikings! Oh, goody.*

She followed him to a pile of furs near the fire. The Viking sat down on a pile of furs and motioned for her to sit beside him. Alice sat.

"You are my prize. I will not hurt you." The beautiful giant looked tired. There was blood running down his arm. Dried blood from a slash wound caked the stubble on his strong jaw, and his cheeks bore scratches and darkening bruises.

Alice reached over and opened his vest. The fur lining, soft as mink, was soaked in warm blood. Part of her wanted to close the vest and move on to another Viking, maybe less handsome but also less wounded, whom she might find seated around the fire.

He smiled at her. "I am Erik. My mother was an Anglish and my father's greatest prize. Please to know your name?"

"I am Alice." She peeled back the vest further to reveal a wound across his chest, ten inches long and deep. No bubbles came from the wound and his breathing wasn't labored; evidently it had missed his lung. Those muscles were good for more than making Alice breathe heavy—they had protected his vital organs. It had been more than twenty years since medical school, but Alice knew that if the bleeding wasn't stopped, Erik would never swing that hammer again. "That is a very serious wound. If that bleeding isn't—"

"A scratch. The blood will stop." Erik closed his eyes. "I will rest and soon to make you to howl with pleasure. Come." He opened his arms and motioned to her. Erik certainly knew what she was after, but she needed to stop the bleeding first.

"It might stop by morning because you will have bled out. Do you carry anything like a needle and thread on these boats?"

"We have no need for sewing. What know women of battle?"

"The best I can do is cauterize. I am afraid it'll hurt. You'll have to try and keep the wound clean, or the infected burn will kill you as sure as the blood loss but not as fast." He said nothing and showed no emotion. She pulled up her skirt and he smiled.

"No. That's not—you don't have to—I mean." She stopped trying to explain and started tearing off silk from the bottom of the shift. The unhemmed silk tore easily. She made enough strips to wrap around him several times and tie tightly. Her skirt had hiked up nearly to her chest, giving Erik an unob-structed view of a good deal of Alice. Even with his wound, his eyes assured her he would indeed make her howl with pleasure to his last breath.

"Now, that look is certainly a compliment in your present state, Erik." Alice said. "Do you have a knife?"

Without a word he reached into a pocket in his vest and handed her the biggest knife she had ever seen. She took the knife to the fire, passing knots of people involved in various activities. There were sounds of talking, shouts and moans of all types all around her in the dark. She ignored it all, stuck the huge knife it into the flames until it glowed red, and hurried back to Erik. She quickly drew the knife along the wound. The smell of the hot blood and burning flesh made her gag. He didn't flinch but looked at her with lust.

She tied the pieces of torn silk into one long strip and began wrapping it around him. When she pulled him close to wrap the cloth around his back he kissed her. She continued to wrap, intent on making a bandage to at least outlast the next battle.

She finished and leaned back on her heels, proud of her work. The wound merely oozed a little now. Erik's eyes were closed.

"Come and lay with me," he said without opening his eyes. Alice obeyed settling next to him on the mossy ground. He wrapped her in arms still caked with someone else's dried blood and kissed the top of her head. His fingers slid beneath the rough wool to find her nipples hard. She gasped.

He moaned his breath warm against her face. "You will ride me now, yes?"

Alice breathed deeply the scent of Erik and wanted to do just that. Salt air and blood couldn't cover the smell of man, hot, gorgeous and wanting her. She moved to kneel in front of him and untied the leather lacing that held his pants closed. Unbelievably she found a vigorous and exceptionally large erection beneath the leather. *He must have gallons of blood to have lost so much and still have such an erection!* She gasped again and again Erik laughed. His eyes were open now. She could see the fire reflected in those light eyes half closed with desire.

She pulled up the heavy wool skirt as he reached down the front of her dress kneading and caressing her. Though Alice was no virgin, taking Erik inside her would take some doing. She had never before encountered quite this generous a male endowment. She lowered herself slowly and moaned as he filled her completely.

He leaned forward and kissed her softly. He did not move his hips but let her lead. His kissing and caressing her breasts had paved the way and Alice slid slowly up and down the generous length of him. She was careful not to put any weight on his wound but increased her pace until she climaxed hard and loud.

Her cries brought cheers from several men in the direction of the fire. Alice determined to feel Erik come hard inside her, kept up her rhythm. He reached up to touch her breasts again, closed his eyes and let out a long, loud, warrior's cry—or what Alice thought was a warrior's cry. She had never seen a Viking battle, and by the look of his wounds, was glad of it.

He opened his eyes. Inside her, he was still hard enough to cut glass. She checked his wound. It had stopped oozing.

"Battle heats the blood," said Erik.

"And stiffens the cock," said Alice.

"Yes, the first time, but now tis Alice puts lightening in my rod. Please to make my brothers cheer again. Alice, my prize, you are as soft as my mother's eider geese." He caressed the cheeks of her ass.

She rode him to a loud climax two more times until Erik finally closed his eyes and pulled her to his chest. He held her tight. She closed her eyes, kissed his bare chest above the bandage and fell asleep.

Chapter Twenty

YOU GOTTA FRIEND

Otis gave her his usual morning greeting and she headed to the shower. Watching the water run down the drain from her hair, she saw a flash of red. Alice reached up and felt dried blood caked in her hair. It wasn't her blood. She wasn't wounded. Had some of Erik's blood gotten in her hair as she lay next to him? How?

Alice thought about it as she dried herself and dressed. The experiences always felt perfectly real, but how could they be? Maybe Dr. Cindy was right, and Alice actually travelled someplace where she rode a huge horny Viking half to death? Or maybe Dr. Elliot had been right, and psychosis was inevitable without medication. Maybe Alice had just imagined Dr. Cindy's explanation, which would prove Dr. Elliot was right.

A loud knock on the door saved Alice from more disturbing thoughts.

"Well, you owe me, it was a little strange," Susan said. She took a sip from a hug purple ceramic mug. "Got any cream? Of course you don't. You always get coffee at the office. You gotta have something for weekends." Susan opened the pantry and took out a jar. "Powdered crap. Better than nothing, I guess. I think you look so young because you take in so many preservatives."

"Well? Spill," Alice said.

"It was weird." Susan pulled out a stool and sat on it. "Not as weird as the time we went on that haunted house tour and the ghost tapped on the wall behind us."

"Okay, okay. Just tell me."

"I let myself in quietly about eleven, like you said. I thought Stephen King would keep me awake, but at a really scary part of my book, I closed my eyes for a bit and managed to fall asleep. I woke up because I thought I heard the balcony door open. My watch said 4 A.M. So I got up to look in your bedroom and there you were asleep."

"Did you look for me out on the balcony earlier? Or check when you came in that I was in bed."

"Right. Where else would you be? I told you I fell asleep. It's twenty degrees out there and if you had gone out there before I arrived, you'd have been out there for six hours."

"Maybe I had a coat or a blanket. Did you look at all?"

"No. If you know what's going on, why did you want me to watch?" Susan sipped her coffee looking slightly annoyed.

"So I could have been out there and come back in while you slept?" Alice said.

"If it was anybody else, I'd say no way. But, honestly, Alice, I have no idea. The one really odd thing was—like I said, I thought I heard—like the balcony door open. And then I heard noises. Strange noises that couldn't really have come from your balcony. Or I thought I heard noises."

"Like what?"

"I thought I heard men yelling and the sound of waves. I know it's nuts."

"You sure you were awake? That Stephen King book might have messed with your mind?" Alice's heart was beating wildly. Was Dr. Cindy right? *Alice get a grip.*

"Totally. Those books always mess with my mind. No, I'm

not sure at all. Even an uber-wench like you couldn't have been out there in the cold. No one could have opened that door. Sorry. I guess I let you down. If you want, I could drink a lot of coffee and try again."

"That's okay. I appreciate your efforts." Alice didn't know whether to be shocked or elated. For now she just had to stuff that down too.

Alice realized it at that moment this Saturday she had no place awful to be. As much as she loved her mother, she was grateful not to have to go to the Mary Center. She was also extremely grateful her lovely, brilliant mother was no longer disintegrating in front of her. Wherever she was, she was herself again.

"I think I owe you breakfast for your effort," she told Susan.

They walked to the Benton Park Cafe around the corner and ordered breakfast. When it came, Susan put down her fork and just looked at the beautiful plate of Eggs Benedict. "My surgery is next week, Tuesday. Then chemo, three rounds."

Alice felt the blood rush in her ears. How could she be so immersed in herself she hadn't even asked about Susan's treatment?

"I'm opting for a complete mastectomy," Susan continued. "Bailey is coming home from school. College has really helped her grow up and she's even thinking about going to nursing school. She'll be great."

"Susan, I just don't think I..." Alice couldn't look her friend in the eye and pushed her eggs around the plate with her fork.

"I know how you are about blood and stuff, don't worry. It's okay. I'll keep you advised by text without too many gory details."

Alice was grateful for her friend's strength. *She deserves a much better friend than me.*

❧

As sunset approached, Alice was tempted to peek into the closet, but she'd promised Susan to watch old episodes of *Star Trek: The Next Generation* with her; they'd been addicted to the series in college. The least she could do for her friend is relive some old college times. The closet wasn't going anywhere. For tonight, the adventures of Jean-Luc Picard would have to suffice.

❧

The next morning, Alice began taking Dr. Cindy's advice seriously and was trying diligently to live healthy. She remembered the Hans Selye "fight or flight" stuff from Psych 101 and knew what constant adrenaline overload could do to a person. It made sense that as one aged, the stress became cumulative. After all, Alice handled things pretty well most of her life. A regimen of more sleep, healthy variety in exercise, and an improved diet was worth a try.

The doctor had assured Alice that she should continue the talk therapy sessions to reinforce appropriate coping methods and keep tabs on her progress. It sounded so much better than the certain zombiedom of psychiatric medications. Dr. Cindy had said she couldn't guarantee they would never be needed, if they were, meds would be used in judiciously low doses and for the shortest duration possible. The other stuff she'd talked about, differing patterns of brain waves producing some sort of effect on time and matter, sounded entirely too nuts to be real.

Alice had to admit the regression had given her a new perspective on her love of control and lack of trust. Maybe she would try a little less control and a little more trust.

This weekend marked the beginning of Alice's "Operation Smooth Pavement," implementing the doctor's advice to help even out the bumps in her emotional road. She actually bought things from the produce department at the grocery store. It was a little complicated shopping for fresh food, but she was learning.

She wasn't completely sure what to do with all of the food she bought, but she brought them home and put them in the refrigerator. *So that's what those drawers are for.* She didn't intend to never open that closet door. After all, a girl had needs. It didn't matter how exactly her mind did what it did to create the fantasies; they were amazing fun, always. She would take a few nights off to get over these pangs of emotion anytime she remembered her amazing encounter with Jonathan or had unclean thoughts of Brad.

Sunday morning breakfast included a half a grapefruit, after which Alice went to yoga with Susan. She wasn't good at it—standing on one leg was not going to happen and she couldn't hold the poses long, but Alice had to admit it made her feel good. She still did her time on her elliptical, but what could it hurt to change it up?

Chapter Twenty-One

NO MORE MR. NICE GUY

M onday morning and Alice felt wonderful. The sky looked bluer, and she stumbled only once in her tallest shiny black pumps. The little patent bows on the toes made her happy today. Today felt like that kind of day. No ordinary shoes would do.

Her emails half done, Alice got up from her desk and glanced toward Jonathan. He sat at his desk as usual, but the look on his face could only be called stricken. Alice pushed the door the rest of the way open quickly. "What is it? Please tell me."

Jonathan looked up at her and said only, "The patents."

"What?" From its hiding place deep inside her, the fear monster stood up on its hind legs.

"The patent department emailed me about the patents. They have all been denied on the grounds of similar patents recently pending. They suggested in the report our patents were copied from those filed a few weeks before by another company. The communication actually suggested the other company might consider charges of industrial espionage." Jonathan spoke in a monotone and didn't look up.

"That's impossible. All of the patents?" Alice's voice had climbed an octave.

"Every single one. I can see where perhaps one or two could be similar in nature, but how could they all be denied. There are twenty-seven extremely original concepts in those patents. Our attorneys did thorough searches, and Dr. Petrus—"

"Henry. Did he know about this? Is that why he hasn't been here in days?" Alice clenched her fits at her sides. "Henry Petrus has some serious questions to answer, now."

Alice looked into Jonathan's eyes. "Will you go with me?" she asked. She'd seen compassion in his eyes before, but not at work, and not lately.

"Of course," he answered. As they rode the elevator to the tenth floor, Jonathan grabbed her hand and squeezed it tightly. They both stared straight ahead and said nothing. This is no minor setback. This was fifty million dollars and three years completely and absolutely wasted. *How can I possibly justify this kind of loss to the board?* She would be lucky if she merely lost her job. The board would have to make someone pay for the huge loss and she could be charged with seven kinds of negligence. She might never be able to work in any field. The knot in Alice's chest grew tighter as the elevator numbers flashed. Finally it stopped at 10.

Jonathan dropped her hand and followed her. They stopped briefly for the retinal scan and then walked through the doors toward the offices in the research lab. The only sound was the tap-tap-tap of Alice's pretty black happy-pumps down the hall to Dr. Petrus's office.

Alice knocked on his door and opened it. Henry Petrus was not inside. Something looked wrong. There were no folders on his desk. Where were the assistants that usually met them at the door? The Wall of Blondes was gone.

"He's gone!" Alice stood staring at the blank wall. "Why

didn't I suspect him sooner? He was the only one that could have sent those texts of Brad and I in the elevator."

"You see the good in everyone. You couldn't have known he was capable of such treachery," said Jonathan.

Alice heard footsteps behind them. As she turned to see who it was she felt something hard against the small of her back.

"I am a little surprised, Alice," Henry said. "I thought you were much smarter than you have shown yourself to be."

Alice tried to turn around to face him, but Henry pressed the hard object into her back. The fear monster sprang, bit deep and her heart pounded wildly.

"Don't turn around Alice, and don't even think about it, Mr. Salter. I will absofuckinglutely shoot her in the back. Believe me I can stop her heart in seconds."

Alice stood still as a stone statue. "Henry, what—"

"What? Why, money, of course. It would take years to human trials on the measly budget you got me. Keep looking straight ahead and I'll explain it to you if you insist. I did all my brilliant research here using Excellcardia's funds and then sold the brilliance of my work to the highest bidder. I was so happy when you asked me to work here for you. I knew you could be fooled. That big old heart that makes you care so much about the dogs makes you vulnerable, you know. You didn't think this miraculous advancement in medicine was only worth the few measly hundred thousand a year you pay me, do you?"

"Let her go," Jonathan said. "There is no need to hurt anyone, he stretched out his arms in a plea. Alice stood between the two men, facing Jonathan. Any attempt to get the gun from Henry would result in a bullet for her.

"What are you going to do? You'll take her place? Well, I intend to get rid of both of you, so don't bother offering yourself up. I heard through the grapevine you were infatu-ated with our illustrious leader. Who knew it was really true?

So sweet, Alice. He's ready to die for you. Aren't you touched?"

Alice felt the hard barrel of the gun dig into the flesh of her back. She found it hard to breathe. "Henry, I found you at Medcap and gave you more money than you had ever made before. Excellcardia was making sure your life's work could become reality. All the money in the world won't make up for the recognition you would gotten when Biocardia came online."

"Oh, you really don't understand, do you, Alice?" He laughed, obviously taking extreme pleasure in her distress. "My patents were approved. They were simply approved under another entity. I used you like a tired old whore."

Alice's heart pounded and her cheeks burned. How could she have been so stupid? How could she have trusted Henry Petrus?

Jonathan pleaded. "There must be some way, Dr. Petrus, we can work this out in the interest of—"

"Fuck no. I'm holding all the cards. Can't you hear Alice Cooper singing "No More Mr. Nice Guy?" Start walking down the corridor. And you, Salter, walk on ahead. No hero-ics." Henry laughed.

Alice did as she was told. Jonathan walked along a little ahead of them. They moved down the long hall toward the wall of stainless steel doors. There were two sterilizers, three refrigerators, and a walk-in freezer that stored all the specimens and any casualties from among the subjects to be studied.

"This is us." Henry opened the door to the freezer unit and motioned for them to enter, keeping the muzzle of the gun tight against Alice's back. "Yeah, I don't want to shoot you. Not really my style. If you could have waited one more hour, I would've been gone. Walk into the unit and in about five hours you'll be frozen stiff. No one will look in here for much longer than that."

Alice followed Jonathan into the freezer and turned around

to face Henry. Jonathan took a step forward to stand between Alice and the man with the gun. "Let Alice go. I'll take the blame and you can disappear. No one need be the wiser."

"Right, nice try, Salter. You really were my favorite blonde, Alice, for a long time. You supported my research and believed in me when nobody else did. You're right, that little rat hole of a lab I was working for before Excellcardia never would have given me the funding I needed. You made sure I was funded, but that's all. You were as cold as the rest of the blondes on my wall. Genius like mine is worth a lot more than the cheap-ass Excellcardia board was willing to fork over."

"What will everyone say when they find the two of you dead. Everyone knows she loves to fuck her underlings in confined spaces like elevators. What a great shot that was. I think I'll print that out for my new improved Wall of Blondes.

Chuck is a good man with a few nasty little vices I happen to know about, and, of course, exploit. Good thing dog pain meds work as well on humans? In higher doses, of course. How about the fake security breach? Brilliant, if I do say so, and I do. It made you think Chuck was doing such a good job and trust him completely." Henry stopped talking, breaking up with laughter, but he didn't lower the gun for a second. "That elevator tape would have made a good release on the amateur porn sites. Really hot, Alice. Who knew those are real?"

Over Henry's shoulder, Alice saw Brad James. Brad walked slowly and put his index finger to his lips, but something on Alice's face alerted Henry, and he turned dropping his gun hand to his side. Brad grabbed Henry by the shoulders and the two men struggled. With the sudden crack of gunfire all struggling stopped. Henry took a step back. Brad's face registered nothing but anger. *The bullet couldn't have hit either of them.* Alice breathed again.

"Well, quite a nice little ménage they'll find whenever they open those doors. You get in there too, James. Henry motioned for Brad to follow Jonathan and Alice into the freezer. "Whose arms will they find you in, my dear Alice?"

"What about your work? What about your Nobel Prize?" Alice now pleaded.

"Oh, the money I'll be getting will buy all the blondes I could ever want. That will assuage my damaged pride. Blondes don't seem to be able to resist the super-rich. Donald Trump has no trouble getting broads, and I have way better hair. Besides, the new owner of Biocardia has promised to give me credit under a pseudonym. I'll know when my work is recognized. Now get down on your knees, all three of you. By the way cellphones won't work in there in case you were wondering."

The three of them got to their knees.

"There's no reason to kill anyone," Alice said struggling to keep her voice calm and hide her growing terror. "Let us go or lock us in a supply closet. We'll give you our cell phones that'll give you all the time you need. If you kill us, the police won't stop until they track you down."

"Right. They can try. Do you really think anyone with the kind of brain that came up with Biocardia would be easy to find? Besides, I love the thought of them finding you all frozen together in some kind of threesome popsicle."

He waved the gun, smiled and closed the door.

"There has to be a way to open this door from the inside." Jonathan got up and ran his hand around the perimeter of the shiny steel door.

"Because these specimens might want to get out?" Alice sat back and crossed her legs and Brad James collapsed onto her. She reached out to him and her hand slid beneath his suit coat. Brad's warm blood covered her hand. "Oh my God, Brad. He shot you!"

"Yeah. Feels pretty bad." Alice tore open his suit coat. A red circle six inches in diameter marred the snowy white front of his shirt, right in the middle of his chest. His tie was now more red than blue, and his face nearly as white as the shirt. "I'm sorry, Alice. I should have gone—to call the police. I thought I—could stop him and I didn't want to leave you."

"Jonathan, get some of that ice. If we put some pressure on it—" Alice leaned in close to Brad. His voice was softer now and his breathing labored.

"Really, Alice? You—do—care. You know I—could have given up—everything for you." Brad's face was taut with pain, but he managed to smile slightly at Alice.

"Did you really leave your wife, Brad?" Alice reached down to smooth the rumpled silver of his hair.

"No." He laughed, and it sounded more like a cough. "But I would have. Alice I…" Brad stopped talking and his blue eyes closed. The sound of his labored breathing stopped. Alice knew that with a chest wound very likely near his heart, CPR would have been unwise.

Alice reached over and held him close to her for a long moment. Did a little bit of her die with Brad? She let him go gently, though there was nothing she could do to hurt him now. Then she slowly backed away.

"Idiot," Jonathan said. "His ego has killed us all. If he'd just gone for help."

Tears streamed down Alice's face. Jonathan knelt beside her and wrapped his arm tight around her.

"That's who he was, Jonathan. I'm sure he thought he could handle it. He always seemed able to handle everything. Who'd have thought Henry would…" Alice broke down into sobs, collapsing against Jonathan.

"Did you truly care for him?" Jonathan's voice felt warm against her ear.

"Of course I—cared—for him. He's dead and—it's my fault. I should have known Henry was…"

"Alice, blaming yourself won't help at all." As Jonathan held her tightly, she shivered. "We need to do everything we can to keep warm." He took off his silver-gray suit coat and put it around Alice's shoulders.

Standing up, Jonathan searched the shelves. "Let's see what there is to wrap around us." His voice had the same stiff-upper-lip tone he used every day to say things like "Shall I answer that call for you?" or "I can take care of that." The sound of it soothed her.

"It won't matter. Dr. Petrus insisted this freezer be super-high-efficiency." Alice searched the lower shelves from her knees. "It cost an extra ten thousand dollars to freeze the specimens faster. It does minimize the tissue damage of the specimens. Too bad for us." She pulled something from the corner of the freezer. "These plastic sheets. They might buy us some time."

Jonathan took from her the roll of clear plastic sheeting three feet wide and unwrapped several feet. Kneeling beside Alice, he wrapped it around the two of them.

"Right, like someone will miss us and come looking for us in the specimen freezer." Jonathan's actions gave her a tiny glimmer of hope.

"It will be better to wrap our bodies together, to hold in the heat. I hope you don't think I would take advantage of the situation," said Jonathan.

Jonathan dropped the plastic and kissed her, fiercely. "I really do care for you, you know. I have for a quite a long while."

"I just don't know if it's possible for me even if we had time. I'm a messed-up piece of work and I can't be sure—"

"Shut up for one single minute, Alice, and let me kiss you." He reached up to take her face in his hands.

"But I—" The pressure of his lips on hers, his tongue on hers, silenced her. Still the tears continued. She broke free of his kiss and shook her head. "I need to tell you about Brad. We had an affair. It was brief and has been over for a while, but if we are going to die in here, I want you to know the truth."

"I know, Alice. But when you reassured me you were not in love with him, it was enough."

"How could you—"

"Brad told me something that day in the cafeteria, something he could not have known otherwise. Right before I broke his nose, he told me you were a screamer." Jonathan touched his lips to her cheek and caught a single tear.

Chapter Twenty-Two

COLD AS ICE

The freezer door opened. Louise stood in the entrance, looking astonished as she took in the scene.

"What in the name of God!" Louise cried.

"Oh, Louise, thank God," Alice said. Jonathan helped her to her feet, and they stumbled out of the cold to huddle beside Louise.

How...why are you...? Then Louise caught sight of Brad James's body through the open freezer door. The pool of blood around him had begun to freeze at the edges. A look of horror spread across Louise's face. "He looks—"

"Dead?" Jonathan said. "Henry shot him and locked us in here to freeze to death."

"How could you have known we were here?" Alice sniffed back tears.

"I didn't know." Louise reached into the freezer and her Louboutin pump slipped in Brad's blood. She grabbed the metal shelf to stay upright and pulled something from behind a row of frozen vials.

"Oh my God. How horrible." She tore herself away from the grisly sight of Brad's body and held up a bag. "I keep my emergency supplies here. Salems and Dove chocolates in a heavy-duty Ziploc for my moments of weakness. Figured they'd be safe behind the tubes of dog puree and frozen beagle corpses."

"Thank God you have at least a couple of vices or we would all have been corpses. She hugged Louise leaving hand-prints of blood on Louise's winter-white wool jacket. Alice gave a small gasp when she saw the prints. The blood on the white jacket…Brad's blood.

Louise, always efficient, took off the jacket and folded it neatly with the lining out.

Alice turned to Brad lying on the floor of the freezer and the awful reality hit her again. Tears ran down Alice's cheeks. Brad had been far from perfect, but he was handsome and charming, and his brilliant instincts had made Excellcardia millions. And although he had belonged to someone else, he lost his life trying to save her. Why did it hurt so much? Maybe it had been more than just an unwise affair? She couldn't just leave him there alone in the freezer as awful as it was. She stepped back through the door and couldn't look away.

Brad's eyelashes fluttered.

Alice dropped to her knees and felt for a pulse. Nothing, but he still felt warm.

"I can't get a pulse, but he's still warm and I swear I saw his eyelid move. Call 911 Louise. I don't think we should move him or risk CPR since we don't know exactly how close to his heart the bullet is. I'll wait here for the paramedics. Jonathan, go to security and see if Henry has left the building yet. Look at every camera yourself we can't trust Chuck. It hasn't really been that long." Alice looked up at Jonathan, "I have to—"

"I know." He turned and hurried down the hall and Louise punched three numbers into her cell phone.

"Lou, you are a lifesaver, literally. I need you to go to my office and try to head off the chaos of the rumor mill. Send out reassuring emails, whatever. Improvise, please."

Alice reached over and took Brad's hand in hers. *He's still so warm. Maybe there's a chance.*

"I'm here, Brad. I won't leave you." Alice held tight to his hand.

The paramedics were taking so long. All she could do was hold his hand and pray.

At last, two capable looking men with appropriately serious expressions quickly wheeled a gurney up to the freezer. Leaving the gurney, they stepped into the freezer. The tall one with the handle-bar mustache and shaved head shot her a reassuring look. She scrambled out of their way and looked over their shoulders as they exposed his chest and hooked up leads.

"I couldn't get a pulse, but—A little flutter of hope stirred inside Alice.

"Hey, this guy's alive! Couldn't feel a pulse either, but the twelve lead shows me he's still kicking. Shocky pattern though. Get the AED and that bag of O neg, Josh." Alice could hear the blood rushing in her ears.

The AED's mechanical voice said, "Stand clear, Shocking." Alice winced as she saw Brad stiffen with the electrical surge of the AED.

"He converted," said the tall EMT whose name tag read Justin C. He smiled a smile worthy of his 6'6" frame at Alice. "This guy is tough or lucky or both. This freezer is cold as hell and that didn't hurt either."

She took Brad's hand again after they cut off his jacket and shirt and quickly and efficiently started an IV. Justin squeezed the bag to get the lifesaving blood into Brad as fast as possible. As Alice held Brad's hand tightly, she felt him squeeze back.

"Oh my God, he squeezed my hand!"

"Yep, we're just that good and he's one lucky dude." Justin high-fived his partner.

In the ICU surgical waiting room of Barnes Hospital, Alice paced. She paced between the orange upholstered chairs and stared at the brown tile floor. The television blared some news, but Alice heard nothing but the blood rushing in her ears. The door opened and the other three people waiting looked up with hope in their eyes. Alice recognized Dr. Saville, Brad's surgeon who looked tired but triumphant as he walked toward her still in his ceil-blue surgical scrubs.

"The bullet missed his heart and most of the larger vessels. His prognosis is pretty good for someone shot in the chest." He seemed to assume she was Brad's wife and she let him. If she had told them she was his boss and ex-lover they wouldn't have let her anywhere near him. HIPAA laws would have kept them from telling her a thing. Alice was sure Jonathan or Louise had called Olivia James.

After seven hours the real Mrs. James was still not there. Why had she not called Olivia herself? Alice knew very well why. What if Olivia James could tell from her voice she had been more than just Brad's boss?

The nurse at the ICU desk told her he might not regain consciousness for a while, but Alice couldn't leave him to wake up in the hospital alone. So she paced in the hall outside the ICU suite, and no one stopped her.

"Are you Olivia?" Brad's nurse asked. The woman beamed at her and flashed two dimples from her round pleasant face. "He's asking for you."

Alice hadn't actually said she was Olivia James. The nurse assumed by the concerned look she wore and the fact that she had paced the hall by Brads room for hours.

She looked past the drain tubes and bags of fluid. His eyes were open and as blue as ever.

"I'm sorry," she said. "Olivia isn't here yet. I didn't want you to wake up alone."

"Thank you." He closed his eyes and reached out his hand

to her. She took it. His strong hand in her's reminded her just how much she'd loved those hands all over her.

"Thank you so much, Ms. Hightower," said a voice from behind her. She dropped Brad's hand and turned. Olivia James stood behind her, dark eyes appraising. She felt like an ugly duckling, standing in the blood-stained and rumpled gray stripped suit she'd worn for fourteen hours now. Mrs. James wore a perfectly crisp pale pink pleated dress and matching jacket. The matching shoes were Pradas. Alice didn't own any, but she knew what they looked like.

"I'm so sorry, I couldn't get here any sooner. I was visiting my mother and there was an ice storm and my flights kept getting canceled. I tried calling the hospital, but my phone was dead." Olivia walked to her husband's bedside leaned over and brushed her husband's lips with her own. "The doctor said you're going to be fine in no time."

Alice wrinkled her brow and sent a beam of negative thoughts Olivia James's way. How could she have taken this long to get here and never even call? Olivia turned to Alice. She gave Alice a dazzling smile and said sweetly, "I cannot thank you enough for taking good care of Bradley for me."

Crap, thought Alice. *Did she have to be nice?* That sweetness made her resentment and jealousy feel a lot more like guilt.

"It was the very least I could do. Be good to yourself, Brad." Alice didn't wait for a reply but headed out the door.

Chapter Twenty-Three

TAKIN' CARE OF BUSINESS

"I'm fine, Jonathan. Don't hover, please." Alice sat at her desk, sipping her morning coffee and staring at her computer monitor. "I made a list of priorities. I see you've done the first three. I appreciate your handling the police. I'll answer their questions this afternoon. I'm not sure what I have to tell them that can help, but if Henry thinks he will get away with this, he is sadly mistaken. I want a top-notch detective agency on this too. We can't count on any slow wheels of justice. We need to draft a statement for the press and one for the board. I want legal to get a cease-and-desist order against Patterson. We have proof that we did all the research and I damn sure they do not." Alice typed furiously on her laptop as she spoke.

"We also need some kind of plan to replace the revenue lost because of the Biocardia theft." She looked up from her laptop and waited for his reply.

"I have a press release here for your approval, Jonathan said. "I agree we need to go on the offense with the board. Here's a list of headhunters suitable to find replacements for Chuck Johnson of Security, Dr. Petrus and Mr. James." His eyes searched hers as she reached out to take the pages. "You look tired, I can handle most of this if you want to take—"

"First, never tell any woman she looks tired. That's a polite way to say she's showing her age. Second, I'm not going to wait for the board to call a meeting to fire me. My only hope to keep my job is to come up with a plan and call a meeting myself. We may be able to recoup some of the losses with legal action but that will take time."

Alice stopped typing and looked up. "Last but not least, I'm hoping Brad will be back. The surgeon said the damage was actually relatively minor by some miracle."

"Yes a miracle indeed." Jonathan filled his cup with coffee, dropped in two sugar cubes and headed to his desk. He stopped in the doorway and turned back. "Are we going to ignore what happened between us in the freezer." He walked across the office to stand right in front of her desk and now stood with eyebrows raised.

"That's what I'd like, but I'm guessing you have a different idea." Alice stood up and walked around the desk to stand beside him with her arms crossed. "Jonathan, that was—I don't know. Maybe the cold comfort of a near death thing, don't you think?"

"Cold comfort?" He glared at her. "You kissed me because you thought the man you loved was dead and I was available? The last man on earth scenario? It that it? I can accept our previous encounter as comfort sex, but that kiss felt genuine."

His anger surprised her. She walked back to her chair and sank into it with a sigh. "The truth is, I'm probably incapable of feeling anything real for either of you right now, or maybe ever. I need you to help handle the biggest crisis of my career. When Brad recovers, I'll need him too. Please, can't you just give me a little breathing room?"

Jonathan walked out of her office without so much and a "Very well." Alice felt nothing but relief. At least she didn't have to deal with a bunch of messy emotions while she fought a life-or-death battle to save Excelcardia and her position as CEO.

She could not do this alone. She picked up her phone and dialed a familiar number.

❦

Dr. Cindy Lester looked up from her yellow shrink pad and said to Alice, "You seem to be responding well to this situation most would consider catastrophic."

"You know, it feels like I am, if I do say so myself. Before, when work got really tough, I just called a headhunter and moved on." Alice sat on the edge of the couch with her hands in her lap, looking at the doctor.

"What do you think is different this time?"

Alice thought a moment. "Me. I feel different. I feel more, I don't know, like I can handle anything? More…"

"Capable, perhaps?" The doctor wrote a few lines. "What do you think brought about this change? You've accomplished enough in the past to indicate you have always been quite capable."

"I'm not sure. Maybe facing that thing from my childhood made me feel somehow less— weighed down?"

Alice's answer seemed to please the doctor. She sat up straight and set her yellow pad down on the table.

"That is often the effect of facing a traumatic past event. The discovery can help the discoverer move on in their life."

"I was six. I hope I have moved on since then."

"In most ways, certainly. Do you feel your emotional attachments are all they could be?"

Alice had felt so good about the previous revelation that the doctor's question felt like a punch in the gut. "If you mean men, well then, no. I suck at relationships with the opposite sex."

"Would you like to talk more about your fantasies?" Dr. Cindy picked up her pad and began to write again.

"Sure. That's the one place I can certainly handle men."

"Do these adventures always consist of sexual interactions?"

"Yeah. But there are other good things about them. They take place in amazing places and in different time periods, as wild as that sounds. I enjoy visiting the historic places."

"Do you feel compelled to have sex with the men you encounter?"

"If by compelled you mean I really want to, then yes. The situation just seems to be…." Alice stopped talking and looked at the floor searching for the right words. "It just seems like it's natural to the time and place and I go with it. It's just great, satisfying fun. I guess I set it up in my head that way. I never know where or when or with whom they'll be. Like a scene you'd imagine while you masturbate, except in more detail."

"Have you had casual anonymous sex often in the past?" Dr. Cindy kept her eyes on the pad.

"Never. Too risky."

"There certainly could be physical risk involved. Why do you feel that there is no risk in these fantasies?"

"It feels like there is sometimes. There was this one time in some kind of dungeon." Alice shivered at the memory.

"Did you feel you could be hurt?"

"Yes. But for some reason I'm not afraid." The doctor waited for an answer and Alice tried to explain. "Real things scare me. Real men and real emotions. I'll take a dungeon any day."

When she left, Alice felt drained. This day seemed to have lasted forty-eight hours. Alice wanted nothing more than to crawl into bed and sleep for two days. She didn't feel the lead in her brain that signaled a depressive episode. This had been one hell of a day and she desperately needed sleep.

Pajamas on, everybody fed, she was going to sleep even if it was only eight o'clock. Tomorrow was Susan's surgery, and she would text a best friend's encouragement before her head hit the pillow. *Good luck tomorrow. I'm sure everything will go well.*

Did that really sound like something one texts to her best friend? What could you say to a woman about to lose a breast?

Susan answered immediately.

Bailey has finals she can't miss but will be here by the weekend. Don't worry. It will be fine. David's stuck in "Right this way, Boss *but should be back in town by the time I am in recovery.*

Alice sat up. She pulled on her jeans, hooked her bra back up and yanked a sweater over her head.

In three minutes she was knocking on Susan's door.

Chapter Twenty-Four

MISSING YOU

Four people sat around the shiny granite conference table that morning. The two empty chairs reminded Alice to call the hospital later to check on Brad and touch base with the police and the private detectives about Henry. She didn't see how the second batch of questions the police detective had asked earlier this morning would help at all. They could ask her every day if it would help. The private detectives had turned up nothing so far. Henry would not get away with this no matter how many detectives she had to hire. She sat up straight in her chair, took a deep breath and tried hard to exude confidence and competence.

"I want to thank you all covering for me yesterday and for being here this morning on such short notice. I think we'll have morning meetings every day until this crisis is over. This company is strong enough to survive this, but I need all of you to help to make our recovery as quick and painless as possible."

"First, Louise, until we hire a new head of research, I need you to wear that hat, too. What miracle life-saving devices does your staff have that are even close to production?"

"Sure. I'm already on that. We've been working to miniaturize all the implantable defibrillators and the entire line of pacemakers. Smaller, easier to place and of course that life-saving leap in technology comes with a decent price increase. They could be ready to go into production fairly soon."

"I'll need a schedule as soon as possible. I can't give the board approximations." Alice looked up from her laptop. "Clearances, Arthur? How long will that take."

"If it is merely miniaturizing existing cleared devices, it should proceed rather quickly." Today Alice welcomed his rat-like, yellow-toothed smile without a single shudder.

"What about legal action against Patterson? Has the cease-and-desist order been filed? Has a hearing been scheduled? There is plenty of proof we did the research first. I want extensive pictures of our research facilities to document our work. Patterson can't fake that. See if our patents could be approved if we proved Patterson engaged in industrial espionage?

"The cease and desist has been filed but Patterson countered immediately. We are working on scheduling a hearing. Patterson's legal is twice the size of ours. You know it could take years to recover our losses if at all." Arthur squinted and waited for further instructions.

"Do everything you can, Arthur and write me up a report with some positive spin. That possibility may help soothe the board's jitters. Jonathan we need someone from sales here tomorrow. None of this works unless we can give the board sales projections that show us recovering as much of the loss as soon as possible. We need to have a presentation ready for the board by Friday. Thank you all."

For a nanosecond, as her very capable staff filed out of the conference room, Alice felt that maybe she could pull this off. An email alert caught her eye on her laptop screen, she clicked the icon. Her brief confidence evaporated as her she read the email.

She didn't notice Jonathan hadn't left with the others until he put his hand on her shoulder. "You saw it?" she asked.

He nodded.

It's fine," she said. If the board wants to see me this afternoon, I can handle it."

"I have no doubt." His smile would have melted any woman's icy heart. She had to admit, not out loud of course, that hers melted a little.

Alice forced herself to concentrate on business. "Let's get today's meeting notes together into some kind of handout. Put in some pictures of the devices we could shrink, imply some numbers by doubling the current sales figures. Use nice paper and shiny folders like this has been our plan for ages. Just don't let me go in there naked." *Now that was a scary thought.*

§

The old tracks she had worn in the office carpet would no longer serve. The gravity of this episode of pacing demanded a whole new pathway. She would see the board in fifteen minutes. Jonathan walked in her office laid a stack of folders on her desk and handed one to her. She read as she paced.

"There's a typo on page 4, and I'm not crazy about the font for the page headings, but otherwise, it'll work. Well done." He answered her compliment with a business-like nod and went back to his desk.

Alice had eleven minutes to run over what she planned to say and paced. The plain black pumps she wore didn't seem right. They went with the somber black suit she had chosen this morning. This board meeting called for something different. She opened the bottom drawer in her credenza and took out the red peep-toe stiletto shoes she'd stashed for broken heel emergencies. She hadn't worn them since her last board appearance. At six foot two inches in these shoes, she felt powerful and confident, exactly what she needed.

She stopped at Jonathan's desk on her way to the elevator nine minutes later.

"Off to face the firing squad." Did her voice actually crack?"

"I believe Missouri uses lethal injection," Jonathan replied.

"That makes me feel so much better." And somehow it did.

&

An hour later, Alice walked off the elevator to stand in front of Jonathan's desk. She didn't wait for him to look up from his keyboard.

"It is no guarantee, but the board is giving me sixty days to give them a more complete report. I'm still CEO." She walked into her office on those red shoes as if she wore them every day. Jonathan followed her.

"There's far too much blue-sky and empty promises in that document, but the reasoning is sound. I convinced them Excellcardia doesn't need the bad publicity and chaos of a search for a new CEO, on top of the wasted funds."

Alice again paced as she gave him orders. "I want to see the list of research candidates as soon as possible. I want a full report on the miniaturization Louise mentioned. It sounds good, but how far out realistically is production and can that be sped up any? Now to sales, I need the heads of each sales team to meet with me tomorrow, morning." Jonathan nodded in response to each command and Alice had no doubt they would be carried out flawlessly.

&

That evening, Dr. Cindy wore a lavender tunic with matching leggings. Alice always thought that look too casual for her, but Dr. Lester's long slender legs made it look entirely professional.

"Your fantasy encounters, real or not, do they make you happy?" Dr. Cindy pushed her readers up on her nose.

"I enjoy them, sure. The men in them don't seem to notice the little tricks time had played on my body, which wasn't that great to begin with. They all seem to find me completely doable."

"And you don't think you are attractive enough in real life?" Dr. Cindy looked intently at Alice.

"Time has taken its toll. My ass is as big as a barn, and my thighs are all kinds of wiggly skin and spider veins."

"Dr. Elliot mentioned that you may have an unrealistic body image. Does that sound possible?"

"I see me naked every day. I'm no Gigi Hadid." She thought for a moment. "I did have a little case of anorexia at twelve."

"Do you think the two real men who, from what you say are quite attractive, would be interested in someone unattractive?" The doctor wore a wry smile.

"No, but..."

"Alice, have you ever considered that perhaps there might be some benefit to relating to real men? You told me previously, that in the past when relating to men, you..." the doctor searched her notes. She seemed to find what she was looking for and said: 'I either jump their bones or marry them.' The doctor was silent for a moment. Alice had learned this meant something important was coming after that silence. "There are advantages to getting to know a person before forming a physical attachment. If dating someone you work with is a real barrier, there are a lot of online dating options."

"You know, Doc, it did seem that the sex with Jonathan and even with Brad felt better, richer, than any of the random fantasy hook-ups. The fantasy sex was like an incredible cartoon. The real sex felt more like a full-length feature film." She looked down at her black tights covering her knees just visible below the herringbone skirt she wore today. Several minutes passed in silence. "I'm not sure I can do it, manage feelings and all. Maybe I should at least try." Alice felt a deep need to change the subject. "Can you tell me more about that research concerning people's brain waves manipulating space?" Alice hoped this question would take the doctor's mind off her man troubles.

Dr. Cindy took the bait. "I'd suggest you talk to a researcher I know. We're lucky to have a very important research center for alternative psychological science in St. Louis." She crossed the room to a large wooden file cabinet, flipped through the hanging folders in the top drawer and pulled out a slip of paper. "Here it is."

Carl Hoffman
Hillhouse Institute.
7241 Laclede Place, 63124
314-960-1956

Alice couldn't imagine having any free time for the next sixty days. If she did, would she really want to spend free time at any place "alternative?"

Dr. Cindy must have read the doubt in Alice's face. "I respect your skepticism. I once thought it one step from voodoo myself, until I visited. There are reputably published articles on the subject but visiting the Hillhouse Institute in person can answer a lot of questions."

"Thanks, not sure when I can find the time for a while. It's an interesting concept."

Dr. Cindy returned to her chair and picked up her note pad. "Do you ever engage in any other activities besides sex in your fantasies?"

"There are sometimes lots of things going on in these places. Once I used some of my medical school stuff to dress a wound and stop some bleeding. We don't usually converse much, though." Alice tilted her head and considered that possibility.

"Do you ever explore the historic places you find behind your balcony door?"

"I could, it just that there's always some opportunity for sex and I…"

"It might be interesting to see what other experiences that might be gained from such a fascinating journey." The doctor took off her reading glasses, stood up and opened to door to the hall. "Next time, Alice."

ॐ

Driving on the Highway to Hell during rush hour was an exercise in patience as an extreme sport. In her present hyper state, Alice found it difficult to keep from lapsing into blatant road rage. She kept wondering what it might be like to explore the environment behind her balcony door for its historic value.

Arriving at home and wolfing down some canned ravioli and a small salad, she texted Susan to see how she was faring before she set off on any exploration. She'd been home from the hospital for two days. Susan's husband David was a wonderful guy but far too dedicated to his job. As if Doctors Without Borders was more important than her best friend's recovery. He could save some anonymous kid's life after Susan was all better.

Hey there. How are you holding up? How's the pain 1-10? Susan must have had the phone nearby as her answer arrived in seconds.

Not bad. Something was wrong. Susan never gave two word answers to anything. Alice changed her clothes and took the elevator to check on her friend.

She found Susan alone and in need of a dressing change. There were several colors of bodily fluids to be dealt with, but however she felt about that, Susan needed her. She needed company too. The task accomplished, she stayed and kept her friend company since neither of them was going to get much sleep. Susan because of pain and meds, and Alice because she her work worries, and brain chemistry had her far too hyper to sleep. Who knew she could be so good at changing a surgical dressing? Two games of scrabble and three streamed episodes of *Orange is the New Black* later, Susan finally nodded of and Alice headed home to her kitty and a few hours of sleep.

Chapter Twenty-Five

MY FAVORITE MISTAKE

Maybe delivering files to Brad James personally wasn't the wisest of decisions. Alice wondered who she would be if she'd made only wise choices in her life? Someone who wouldn't have been standing on the porch of the James's Tudor manse in a tony part of Clayton. She looked up at the windows and wondered which room was their bedroom. She was certain Olivia James woke up fresh as a basket of spring flowers. Alice woke up smelling like a herd of water buffalo running to the spring waterhole. Thank God Brad had never experienced the joy of morning Alice. Their rendezvous had always been short and sweet, afternoon or evening affairs conducted on spotless white hotel sheets.

The files she held in her hand could've been sent electronically. True, she missed him. But she was there in her official capacity to see for herself how Brad was recovering, or so she told herself as she rang the doorbell.

He'd sounded fine, even eager, on the phone two days ago. Would lovely little Olivia James ice-pick her with those gorgeous eyes when she caught Alice lusting after her husband? The door opened.

Barely four weeks after being shot in the chest, Bradley

James looked better than ever. He may have gained a couple of lines around his eyes, but they didn't mar his looks one little bit. He smiled his magnificent genuine smile at her. Alice had to suppress a gasp.

"Thanks for coming, Alice. Come on in."

As she stepped through the door, a grey muzzled old friend ran up to her and put his paws on her brown suede skirt.

"Barney!" She bent down, and the dog rolled over on his side for a tummy rub.

Brad stood over them as the tummy rub came to an end. "I've always loved bassets. We had one when I was a kid. He's good company too." Bending down he took Barney's collar, pulled him into what looked like the kitchen and threw him a treat from his pocket. He closed the door and turned back to Alice.

"He's a good little buddy, but it's time for his nap and if thinks you'll rub his belly, he won't leave you alone." He winced slightly as he straightened up. "Right this way, Boss Lady." Brad motioned for her to follow.

She followed him across a marble foyer down a long hall. Alice noticed that his jeans fit that muscular behind as well as his black sweater hugged his arms and chest. She took off her coat as she walked and threw it over her arm.

The room at the end of the hall was all mahogany furniture and burgundy button-tufted leather, obviously a man's office. With a sweep of his arm he motioned for Alice to sit at a massive table where two of the chairs had been pushed close together. She laid the folders on the table and sat down. Brad pulled his chair near and sat with his knee touching hers.

As he examined each page, Alice remembered how those hands felt caressing her. She was grateful she had gone over the sales projections a hundred times and didn't have to pay much attention.

"These projections are low. If we add a few of techs making phone calls all day long, I think we could double this." Brad looked up from the pages spread across the table and gave Alice a confident smile.

"Wonderful." The word came out all dreamy and Alice felt flushed and embarrassed to hear herself. Brad's smile vanished as he looked into her eyes.

"Olivia left me," he said.

"When—why?" Alice looked away and took in a deep breath. "I'm sorry, I have no business prying into your personal affairs."

Brad leaned a little closer.

"She waited until I was out of the hospital to tell me. She was kind enough to look after me for a few days after I got home. That's the when. As for the why; she left me for a woman she says she's in love with. No way I can compete with that." His smile returned, but Alice saw pain in his eyes. She put her hand on his arm. "I'm sorry."

"Yeah." He leaned closer and kissed her. Just a soft brush of his lips, nothing like the deep passionate ones she so vividly remembered. She couldn't say a word. She wanted very badly to brush all the files off on the floor and let nature take its course. That nature, of course, being Brad inside of her making her come harder than she had ever come in her life. *Was he healed enough? Did he still even want her?* The kiss was almost brotherly.

"I'm sorry," he said. "I know you and Jonathan are—I shouldn't assume."

"Jonathan is my assistant," she said—and at this point, nothing more." Brad smiled broadly and this smile reached those gorgeous eyes. He leaned in again taking her face in his hands, he brushed her cheeks with his thumbs as he kissed her. This kiss was tender but not in the least bit brotherly.

He pulled away from her and said, "I know Excellcardia is in deep trouble and you are occupied putting out fires. I've had too much time to think lately. You know I care about you, Alice. I'm still pretty sore and I've recently failed at one relationship, so I'm sure as hell not much of a catch. You probably deserve better. But I wondered if maybe when things cool down some, we could…"

"Have dinner?" She laughed. In the past, their meetings almost always consisted of a quick drink and hours of amazing sex. Satisfying in one way but they had never really spent much time getting to know one another. Maybe she could date Bradley James now that he was single. It sounded funny to think of going on an actual date with a man she had known so intimately in the past and she laughed. Brad laughed too. He stood and backed up a step as if he needed to get away from her.

"I'm really doing great or so says my doctor, but I still get pretty tired." He sat on the edge of the table.

"You can work half days as long as you need. I can't fix this without you." She hoped he couldn't see the genuine fear she felt by the look in her eyes. Alice stood up and headed toward the door. Brad followed.

"I'll be in tomorrow at eight. If I get too tired, there's a couch in my office, remember?" There was the Bradley James she thought she knew so well. Alice blushed and he grinned the wide silly grin he always gave her after he said something naughty.

"See you tomorrow," she said. It's going to be one hell of a fight, but with you on board, I feel better about our chances." She certainly couldn't betray her want for him with another kiss, but a handshake seemed ridiculous. She wrapped her arms around him. He hugged her back tightly and kissed her cheek.

She was too tired after work for the next two weeks to do anything but stop by Susan's to see if her friend needed anything, give Susan a little best friend encouragement that her scar didn't look that bad, and fall into bed. She told Dr. Cindy as much at their next session.

"Does that bother you?" the doctor asked,

"I don't know. I work until nine p.m. even on weekends. We do seem to be making some progress. Our sales of our current devices are way up. Some new stuff will be in production in less than a month."

"Do you miss the physical release?"

"I wonder if I still have it in me—to go these places and have sex with strangers? Especially since, what if I actually go to those places somehow?"

"Do you think this is a bad thing or a good thing?"

"It might be more normal to be afraid. I have been thinking about what you said. Maybe I could date men I'm interested in, instead of just hooking up. I think the sex might be better with an emotional connection. I did have some amazing times in my fantasies with men from who knows where and when. The next night, I was more than ready to go again. Those guys were kind of like junk food; hot and filling, but not really satisfying." Dr. Cindy stopped writing and looked at Alice with a tiny smile turning up the corners of her lips.

Alice raised her eyebrows. "Am I cured?"

"Do you still have episodes of hyper-manic energy? Have you had any crippling dark depressive states lately?"

"Yes and no." Alice looked at the floor and was silent for a minute. "Hyper pretty often, but not much dark. I think I am handling it better now and it's fairly convenient to be hyper for my work situation, actually." She was a bit proud of this realization and looked up at Dr. Cindy. "I haven't had time to check out the Hillhouse Institute. Things at work are settling down a little and I need to make the time. I'd like some answers before I open that door again."

"That does sound like a very healthy idea."

ও

It was nearly seven p.m. when Alice returned to Excellcardia to finish up a few things. She knew most of her team would still be working. As she looked up at the building lit against the dark night sky, she closed her eyes and said a tiny silent prayer the board would let her stay on as CEO. She had her flaws that could probably be catalogued in a small library, but she did a good job running this company. *Please let them see that.*

Chapter Twenty-Six

FIRE DOWN BELOW

Alice sat typing on her laptop. Jonathan poured himself his first cup of morning coffee and sat down in the chair in front of her desk. She looked up at the sound and swallowed hard.

"I am entirely certain next week's meeting will turn out well for Excellcardia and for you, Alice."

"Thank you." She wished she had any degree of certainty. As hard as she and her teams had worked, the predicted income loss was still tens of millions of dollars. It was not a real loss, but a projected loss based on the revenue that would have been before Henry had stolen Biocardia. That might make no difference at all to the board, to them a loss was a loss. Still, in the past two weeks, overall sales had gone up a remarkable twenty percent from the previous month. She hoped desperately that would make a difference.

"I want you to know how proud I am of you." Jonathan took a sip of his coffee and looked at her over his mug. His lovely chocolate eyes shone with Aunty June's light.

Alice shifted in her chair. "I really appreciate all the extra time and effort everyone has put in, but especially you." She set down her coffee and just looked at him. "We wouldn't be anywhere near this close to our goal without you." She had to admit, if only to herself, that her respect and affection for this lovely and multi-talented man could be more than just appreciation for a valued employee. "Do you think, maybe, we could share a celebratory dinner soon? Even if they fire me, we could celebrate a job well done, if you'd like."

Jonathan's face showed no emotion.

She had spent months keeping him at bay, she couldn't blame him for doubting her now. "I would like to have dinner with you for more personal reasons," she said. Her cheeks felt hot.

The smile on his face let her know he understood this would not be just a business dinner and was happy about the prospect.

"Please fix the typo on the heading on page ten of that report and run off one more proof with the updated sales figures. I'm taking the afternoon off."

❧

According to Alice's GPS, the Hillhouse Institute, the current headquarters of the Higher Minds Society, was in the Central West End area of St. Louis. Most of the graceful old brick and stone mansions had been lovingly and meticulously restored. Though not as ornate as the Mary Center two blocks away, 4927 Laclede Place was no exception. Huge stone lions flanked the sandstone stairway. The small brass plaque on the corner of the three-story building that read Hillhouse Institute, the only hint of what lay within. The brass door knocker gleamed with a high polish that shone against the dark wood of a door at least ten feet tall. She felt like Dorothy standing at the Door to the Emerald City. She wondered if there just might be wizards in alternative psychology?

It was a bright day in late winter, and she was playing hooky from work, so how could this be anything but interesting? In thirty seconds the door opened and a pretty young woman in a white lab coat stood smiling at Alice. The girl's blue-black hair reached nearly to her waist. She appraised Alice with dark, almond-shaped eyes.

"You are Ms. Hightower, I expect. I'm Patty Mckeown head of data storage. Won't you come in?"

"Please call me Alice." Alice followed Patty across the gray marble floor of the institute's foyer to a set of modern stainless steel doors. The doors opened, apparently motion activated, to reveal a large elevator.

Patty led the way in and pushed a button marked eight. Alice wondered how a building that appeared to have three floors could have an eighth one? When the elevator moved it became clear they were dropping rather than ascending. Very odd, she thought, for a house built 150 years ago. She giggled. *Down the rabbit hole you go again, Alice.*

The elevator stopped and the doors opened. A slender man in black stood so close to the elevator door that Alice took an involuntary step back. His black hair matched his goatee and black framed glasses. His well-tailored suit was of a modern skinny cut. He reminded Alice of a photographic negative of Colonel Sanders before he discovered the deep fryer.

"Welcome, Ms. Hightower. I'm so glad you decided to stop by. The man extended his hand to shake hers. Alice hated it when a man shook her hand like they would another man's. She didn't need to trade iron grips with men to demonstrate virility as they loved to do to each other. She believed in equality with every fiber of her being, but a woman deserved a gentle squeeze and release. There were after all anatomical differences, thank goodness. Carl Hoffman looked Alice directly in the eyes while executing the perfect squeeze-and-release hand-shake.

Patty handed her off to the anti-Colonel and headed down a long hall. Alice no longer felt like she was in a Victorian mansion. The stark white walls and institutionally appropriate black and white speckled vinyl floor could have suited any institution from a school gym to a prison lunchroom. She could see identical doors stretching down both sides of a long hall in two directions. Alice could hear the faint hum of machinery somewhere far down the corridor.

"I'm Carl Hoffman, Alice. Cindy Lester is a friend. You might find some answers to some fascinating questions here."

"Who knew there was such a thing as alternative psychology?" said Alice.

"This institute is alternative like Galileo was alternative before he was proven correct. Follow me?" Carl set off down the corridor to the right, Alice struggled to keep up with him.

"We need our facilities far below ground to shield our measurements from the radiation given off by nearly everything in our modern world. The radiation of a cell phone a mile away can register as unwanted data on extremely sensitive instruments." Alice wondered just exactly what he needed to measure.

He stopped at door and opened it. It looked like all the others except for the small black plastic plaque that read "Interview, Carl Hoffman." Alice felt a little uneasy. She came here to get information, not give it.

Inside the room was a metal desk with a black cloth covered office chair behind it and a straight-backed wooden chair in front of it. On the desk sat a PC monitor, keyboard, and a small stack of papers. A row of three black metal file cabinets lined one wall. There were no pictures on the walls or decorations of any kind anywhere in Dr. Hoffman's office.

"You will forgive the bare appearance of my office. I don't spend much time here."

Does this guy read minds? she wondered.

"You'll find many of us at the Hillhouse Institute have various talents. Reading the thoughts of others is a quite rudimentary skill. Dr. Lester suggested your skills may be quite remarkable." Alice's mouth fell open.

"Tell me about these experiences you have, please." He sat behind the desk, opened a drawer, took out a pen and a lined note pad, and smiled at her for the first time. It didn't look like his face was quite familiar with smiling, but Alice began her tale.

She sat own and told him about the clothes and the places she found behind the balcony door, leaving out only the juiciest details of the amazing sex she'd experienced. She tried not to even think about the sex as she figured he could pick that out of her brain. It was embarrassing to share those details with a man who looked little more than half her age.

When she finished, he lay down his pen and stared at her.

"I understand, Alice, you originally thought these experiences were hallucinations?"

"Sure. It seems impossible I could actually have manufactured clothes with my mind and transported myself to another time and place. Besides, my mother suffered from severe Bipolar depression and often had hallucinations. But you already know that don't you?" Again he gave her the creepy smile.

"I wonder if you would let us take some measurements of your brain waves. It is painless and will take only a few minutes. Dr. Lester may have told you, we of the Higher Minds Society are investigating the theory that some people have brain waves so different from others they can affect matter. Like sound waves can affect the surface of a pond, or microwaves can heat food. Energy produced by some individual's brains can have unexpected effects. We have found a few who can affect the fabric of time. From what you have told me, you may be able to affect both time and space."

"Right." If her tone didn't sound skeptical enough, he could read the doubt in her head anyway.

"I don't expect you to accept this without proof. You wouldn't be here wasting your valuable time if you didn't think there was something to this theory."

"So you want to do an electroencephalogram?"

"It is basically the same procedure, electrodes on your scalp and the whole nine yards. The main difference is the sensitivity of our equipment, which produces a three-dimensional model of brain activity rather than a set of squiggly valleys and peaks on a piece of paper."

"That model might be pretty messed up, I have a mood disorder too, though not as severe as my mother's, apparently."

"It won't hurt, won't take long, and you will be under no obligation at all to have any further contact with us unless you should so choose. It may give you answers to some interesting questions."

"All righty then. Where do I go?" Carl led her back down the hall to a room marked "Initial Measurements." The room's soft blue walls held abstract art that looked like photomicrographs of brain cells. The only furniture was a white leather recliner with what looked like an old-fashioned beauty parlor hair dryer next to it. The "hair dryer" was hooked to a lighted panel in the wall with several thick cables.

"Please be seated." The chair looked comfy and there appeared to be nothing to cause her pain. It might smash her do a little, she thought as she pulled out her hair clip and lay back in the chair. Mr. Hoffman lowered the glass dome to touch her head. She felt numerous pointed electrodes touch her scalp and heard the click as Carl closed the door on his way out. The probes weren't sharp so there was no pain. There was a soft humming and felt a slight tingling in her scalp. Soft classical music played through the head piece and she relaxed into it, shedding some tension, briefly.

"All done," Carl said. It couldn't have been more than five minutes. He raised the glass dome from her head and they returned to his office to await the data.

How he found it Alice couldn't guess. There seemed to be no landmarks other than the small black labels at eye level on each door. Carl opened what seemed to Alice to be a random door, and there was the white room once again. She sat in the chair in front of the desk and watched as he typed on the keyboard. Alice couldn't see the screen but watched his face intently as if this was an examination she really wanted to pass. And wasn't it? Far better to be some kind of superior-brained human than a raving lunatic.

He stopped typing and stared at the screen for what seemed like a long time to Alice.

"Well?" she said, leaning forward in her chair.

"This is merely a preliminary test." His face was unreadable.

"So I am just some run of the mill, bipolar chick?"

"No, you certainly are not. Of all the preliminary scans I have seen, yours is one of the most remarkable. Scans of this caliber often come with unwanted side effects which might be interpreted as pathology." A look of wonder spread slowly across his face, followed by the appearance of another awkward smile.

Alice didn't know what to say. She didn't entirely buy this magical brain wave stuff; yet her adventures seemed so real and left real traces.

"I understand your concern," Carl said. "Imagine how I felt when I learned that I wasn't just a really good guesser but could actually read people's thoughts?"

"Like a lunatic."

"Exactly. Please come back when you have the time for a complete work up and some tests of your abilities. I have a feeling this could be a fascinating journey. It will take several hours so please let me know when you are available."

"I'm pretty busy right now." She hoped that would continue to be true; the alternative was that she'd have a good deal of free time on her hands. If worst came to worst, she thought, there might be some fascinating discoveries to be made here.

"You may have a great deal of free time soon and there

may indeed be some fascinating discoveries to be made here." This time he gave her a broad genuine smile as if he just couldn't help himself.

"Yes. Could you not do that?"

"Unfortunately, no. But I can pretend I don't know if it makes you more comfortable." He really was kind of cute for a millennial, she thought. His smile grew broader.

"Please." He handed her a card from his pocket. Let's s schedule a session as soon as convenient."

"Oh, my God. He knew," said Alice out loud as she drove home. *I didn't tell him about the men or the sex, but he knew.*

Chapter Twenty-Seven

TORN BETWEEN TWO LOVERS

With the preparations complete for Monday's board meeting, Alice headed home at the unusually early hour of seven p.m. The elevator stopped on the ninth floor. When the doors opened, Brad James got on.

"So, Boss Lady, you're leaving early too." She moved to the back of the elevator. Brad walked in and stood next to her at a respectable distance. He looked straight ahead as the elevator moved on.

"Anywhere else, eleven hours would hardly be considered a short day. I hope you're continuing to recover." Alice looked straight ahead too, remembering the last time the two of them were alone in this elevator. She swallowed hard.

"Right as rain. I really think the board will be impressed with our projections and the recent uptick in sales."

The elevator doors opened. Alice and Brad walked across the empty lobby in silence. When they reached the brass and glass sliding doors they turned toward each other.

"I was about to grab a drink and some crab cakes at McCormick and Schmick. Would you like to join me?" Those weapon's grade blue eyes, that smile; No woman in her right mind could refuse that combination.

He was just asking her to share a drink and a little dinner, after all, not to have hot and naughty sex. How long had it been since she had time or energy for even balcony sex with historical strangers? He was single now and she had to eat. She loved Otis dearly, but his dinner conversation was abysmal.

She smiled at him. "I'd love to."

Alice wondered if his car could fly, or maybe he knew a short cut. There he sat at the long cherry wood and brass bar sipping a dark beer. She sat down next to him, and as if by magic, the bartender sat a martini glass in front of her.

"Tanqueray, up, three olives," the bartender said.

"Thank you." Dating might be more complicated than the quick drink and hit the sheets she'd shared with Mr. James previously. She picked up the glass and took a quick sip for courage.

"I ordered some crab cakes and tuna sashimi. It's excellent here. I hope you like it." His knee brushed her thigh as he turned toward her. It wasn't inappropriate. The barstools, comfortably backed and padded were close together. Still she could feel the blood rush to her cheeks.

"I appreciate it, actually. I don't like small choices like food. So thank you." She turned her stool a little to face him and took another sip. The conversation continued about food and work and anything but the past the two of them had shared. They ate two orders of crab cakes and enjoyed each other's company. Food consumed, Brad asked for the check and she made no attempt to ask to split it. This wasn't a just a drink with a co-worker. He'd asked her to dinner, and she had accepted his invitation. *That's how dates work, isn't it?*

Brad walked her to her car across the large dark West County Center parking lot. When she reached her car, she turned to thank him. He leaned in and caressing her cheeks with his thumbs, kissed her. He didn't raise her hands over her head and pin her to the car with the hard length of him as he'd done before. He kissed her gently, almost reverently, but just before she closed her eyes, she saw that look in his. Alice couldn't help herself, she let out a little sound that sounded an awfully lot like a moan of pleasure.

Brad backed away. This was no longer an adulterous affair. They were both single, so the rules of the game were different and the stakes higher.

"The doctor has cleared me for any and all activity I feel up to," Brad said.

Alice knew exactly what he was implying. Part of her wanted to lay down right on the cold asphalt of the parking lot and have him inside of her. *This was a first date, wasn't it?* Was the three date rule from her college days still the norm? She was tired, it was late, and he was charming in assuming nothing. So different from all their previous passionate fuck or die encounters.

Alice reached up and stroked his cheek. "Rain check, please?" She could see the disappointment cross his face, but he agreed it had been a long day and there would be another time.

Alice smiled like a high school girl kissed by the popular boy at the dance, all the way home. Was she actually Katie Scarlet O'Hara with two handsome beaux vying for her affections? *Maybe this dating thing would be unbelievably fun.* Who said a lady ever had to choose?

❧

It had been a long and draining day. However, her dinner with Brad had added just enough spring in her step to make her curious about what if anything, might be behind her closet door. It had been weeks since she looked, and the closet seemed to call to her.

"Wow!" Alice said to her reflected image. There hung the loveliest gown she had ever found in her closet. The velvet was stiff and heavy and the most gorgeous deep purple. Pearls and gold beads embellished the entire high-waisted bodice and a two-inch-wide band at the hem. The sleeves were decorated with gold and silver threads in a diamond pattern from shoulder to cuff. She couldn't believe how heavy the gown was with the weight of the precious metal threads and pearls. Alice couldn't understand why the sleeves needed to be tied on separately which didn't look easy. The brown suede slippers must have been made for a princess. It looked like something Lucretia Borgia would have worn, according to the HBO series anyway. Alice doubted any Renaissance princess would have to tie on her own sleeves. Could she resist seeing where this gown would take her? Any hot guys encountered didn't necessarily need to be enjoyed. The prospect of anonymous sex had mostly lost its allure. Considering that these adventures might be real, changed things considerably. She managed to wrangle on the lovely gown, tie on the sleeves and open her balcony door.

Alice stepped onto a stone floor and stood looking at a window. She could tell it was daylight outside in this place, though she couldn't see clearly through the thick colored glass. Brocade curtains of a deep blue hung on a heavy metal rod set into the stone of the wall. The small panes of stained glass set in lead reminded her of a church window.

She could smell linseed oil and turpentine and she thought of her mother's paintings. Beverly Hightower's considerable talent had not, unfortunately, been passed down to her daughter. Alice remembered helping her mother clean her brushes and watching her create.

This window was beautiful, *but how's a Princess to see out of it?* Alice heard a noise behind her and turned to see a man dressed in claret-red velvet. His back to her, he sat at an easel. The noise she heard was the sound of a paint brush scratching on canvas. A black hat like a beret, only larger, sat on the man's head at a jaunty angle. Shoulder-length brown hair hung below his hat. The subject of his painting took her breath away.

A girl stood in a pool of light from a small, round window high up on the stone wall. She posed on a wooden platform, wrapped in a piece of pale blue silk that left a shoulder and one perfect breast bare. Her white-blonde hair hung in soft waves down her shoulders and spilled over the silk. The girl looked up briefly and Alice inhaled gasped again. There was something so familiar about her.

Then the painter turned to Alice. "*Benveuto, saro finito presto,*" he said.

"Sorry, I don't speak, Italian I'm guessing?"

"Of, course not. English, I should have known." The man spoke without a trace of an accent.

"But…."

"I didn't expect you so soon, Alice."

"How?" These adventures had always been fun, and it often seemed she was expected. If this guy was from the four or five centuries ago, why how could he speak perfectly unaccented English? The painter was pretty hot with large brown eyes and a strong Italian nose, and the half-finished painting was magnificent. Too bad she had sworn off boffing strangers, no matter how talented. He stared at her, unblinking, clearly he had no intention of answering her question. Then he turned back to his painting. The model didn't seem to notice Alice at all. She seemed drugged.

"You can stay and watch if you wish," the painter said, "but do not interrupt, this must be finished soon. Tomorrow my dear sister will retreat from the world."

"Where is she—"

"Silence, woman. I have work to finish." The man returned to his painting. Alice sat on a small wooden stool and watched. The skill of the man was spellbinding. With each stroke the woman's form emerged out of the blank white canvas. Alice leaned her head against the stone wall and shut her eyes for just a minute.

&.

The next day, Alice couldn't get last night's travels out of her head. Why did the model look so familiar? Who was the strange man from some long distant century who knew her name and spoke perfect English? But the closer she got to the Excellcardia building, the more the concerns of the real world took over, leaving the memories of her night behind. Tomorrow she would make her presentation to the board. She had to convince them she should remain on as CEO or she would be on her own.

Earlier that morning she'd helped Susan pack for a short, well-deserved vacation to Jamaica with her husband. How better to celebrate the completion of a successful round of chemo? Now she had to go over the presentation binders one more time. The lot was empty on Sunday morning, except for Jonathan's red Miata in its usual space.

"I knew you couldn't resist." Jonathan handed Alice a binder as she walked off the elevator. She sat down at her desk and he returned to his own, leaving her in peace to read.

"Perfect," Alice said an hour and a half later. At the sound of her voice Jonathan stood in front of her desk.

"Yes, I was tempted to leave in a single typo for you to discover, but the waste of trees seemed too much to bear. I knew you would insist on reprinting them all." The look on his face held just a touch of mischief, she thought.

"Thank you." Alice couldn't think of anything more appropriate to say. She and every member of her staff had done an incredible job over the last few weeks. There was nothing left to be done. "What do you say to that celebratory dinner I promised you? We should celebrate our accomplishments no matter the outcome."

Jonathan stood without moving as if he couldn't believe what she just said and moving would break the spell. "I'd love it. We shouldn't stay out late with such an important meeting tomorrow."

"Where should I meet you?" Alice put on her coat and turned to him for his answer.

"No, a gentleman picks a lady up at her home." Alice stopped in her tracks and turned back to him.

"Yes he does. Does six work for you?"

§

As Alice watched the sun set through her living room window, she thought again about the odd experience last night. Should she just take a little peek inside the closet? She couldn't go anywhere, Jonathan was coming for a very important date with a—for the first time in a while she had no idea how to describe herself. Previously, she might have said crazy chick, mad woman or lunatic. After the Hillhouse Institute visit, and last night's bewildering journey, she really didn't know.

Alice heard the doorbell and walked out of the guestroom to the door and opened it. Jonathan wore a lovely black suit and held a stunning bouquet of yellow roses and pink lilies.

"How gorgeous, thank you." She stepped back to let him in.

"We can go anywhere you like, Alice. Shall I call Tony's or Top of the Met? A night like tonight requires the most special venue, don't you think?"

"Yes, it does." Could she trust this hot man with a mysterious death in his past? He was great in bed, but could she invest any real feelings in him? He followed her into the kitchen and watched as she put the blooms in a vase.

"I hope you don't mind if I ask you a very personal question," she said keeping her eyes fixed on the flowers.

"The more personal the better." He moved close enough to her to affect her heartbeat.

"Were you charged with murdering your wife?"

He took a step back and leaned against her kitchen counter. "Yes. When my wife took sleeping pills, I was the one who found her. We had argued loudly; loud enough for the neighbors to hear. I'd gone out for the evening alone and returned quite late. CPR would have been useless. I could tell by her color and—she was—she was so cold. I sat on the bed next to her for a long time, searching my head for what I could have done to prevent her death. The prosecutor used the fact that I did not perform CPR to claim I wanted her dead." Jonathan's voice was soft now and the sorrow of it cut scalpel deep. "I knew she was troubled, but I had no idea how troubled."

"I was in jail, for fourteen months awaiting trial. They held me without bail because my father's wealth made them judge me a flight risk. In the end the charges were dropped and there was no trial. Can you imagine how the 'poor little rich boy' was treated in jail? Great care was taken to make sure I received no special treatment and fully appreciated the whole of my incarceration."

Alice saw deep penetrating pain in his eyes when she screwed up the courage to meet them. "Why didn't our pre-employment investigation reveal this?"

"My father spent a great deal of money making sure no evidence remained of what he called, 'my mistake.' I did intend to tell you when the time was right."

That explains his issues with doors, Alice thought. She had no idea where either of her experiments in dating would lead, but she liked and respected this man with eyes like Dove chocolate.

Alice looked into his eyes again and she believed him. He didn't look like he would rip her heart out and stomp on with his shiny Italian leather shoes.

"I think Tony's. I love their pate."

"Tony's it is then." He pulled his phone out of his jacket and tapped in a number.

"You'll excuse me for a minute, I need to change." A girl can't go on a first date with an incredible man in the same clothes she had worked in all day. On the way to her closet Alice could not resist taking that peek and turned into the guest room. She slid open the door. There on the hanger was a diaphanous bit cloth as pink and fluffy as an ice cream float. A pair of silver sandals lay on the floor below the hanger.

"What in the hell…?" She so longed to examine the outfit more closely, but Jonathan waited. He was a delicious and very real man that waited to take her to an amazing dinner. She closed the closet door and headed to the closet in her bedroom.

Alice chose a pair of velvet jeans and a champagne-colored blouse that was just a little too sheer to have ever been worn to work. She cut the tag off and tried to remember when exactly she had bought such frivolous top. It must have been a gift. Susan always left the tags on any gift she gave, thoughtful enough to not mind an exchange.

Slipping into her very favorite silver spangled platform shoes, she smiled at her reflection. She was dressed appropriately for a first date. Jonathan was so hot and wonderful company, why did Alice find herself thinking of Brad?

It might take courage to face the challenges of dating, rather than just step out her balcony door. Maybe at this point in her life it was time to take on this new challenge.

She was going somewhere wonderful to celebrate a job well done with a fascinating man. Tonight she would celebrate all she had done for her company. She felt certain Excellcardia could survive the damage done by Henry Petrus. She would make sure Henry answered for his treachery no matter how long it took, no matter what happened. The company might have to go on without her, if the board so decided, but all her efforts of the past few weeks would insure its survival.

Her best friend was recovering nicely. There were, two real and delicious men interested in actually getting to know her. Who said a girl ever had to choose? She would need to deal with feelings good, bad and probably ugly, but Dr. Cindy would help her handle her emotional ups and downs. Who knows, maybe the check she wrote this morning for one more rehab would be Sean's last, and she could have her big brother back in her life.

Alice now knew what only a moment before seemed impossible. If she were no longer CEO of Excellcardia, she would survive too. Alice took Jonathan's hand and stepped out her apartment's front door to this night's Wonderland.

❧

Turn the page for a preview of…

Pool of Tears
Nights of Alice Book II

Available in 2022

❧

**Don't miss out on your next favorite book!
Join the Melange Books mailing list at**
www.melange-books.com/mail.html

POOL OF TEARS

Chapter 1
Born To Be Wild

I t was suicide prevention week and Alice Hightower was doing all she could not to consider that option. Few would blame her for the brief thought that ending it all might be the easiest way to deal with her life shattering into tiny painful pieces. Suicide might have seemed the easy way out of her troubles. No matter the difficulty, easy wasn't Alice.

There were probably worse things in the world than discovering you are pregnant at forty-nine, but Alice couldn't think of many. She had never been exactly thin. Eating judiciously her entire life, she managed voluptuous. Her work power suits had fit her well for several years. Soon the entire person growing inside of her would change that and nearly everything else about her life.

Were there such things as maternity business suits and if there were, would they be appropriate for her job? Alice doubted anyone at her company, Excellcardia, would say a word if she wore a black trash bag to work, but it wouldn't feel CEO-like to her.

All these trivial notions about what she could or couldn't wear did little to deflect her thoughts from another very real issue in her life. The man she had grown fond of and who'd said he loved her, had disappeared from her life. If she closed her eyes, here in her apartment, she could still see that look on his face.

Had that doctor's appointment been only a week ago? She could play the scene like some horrible heartbreaking movie on the inside of her eyelids with them closed. For some masochistic reason, she just had to do it one more time.

Alice remembered how she and Jonathan had held hands like excited young parents in the Doctor's consultation room. She had felt the need to tell Jonathan she was pregnant and didn't expect him to be excited about the news. Children had never fit into Alice's busy career life. Bringing a baby you never dreamed of wanting into this wicked world hardly seemed a good thing. But when Jonathan looked at her with his chocolate-colored eyes that held only love and joy at that prospect, Alice thought it might be okay.

The doctor had looked up from his laptop and smiled a perfect, bleached-white-enough-to-pass-the-tissue-test-white smile at them. Alice found his Justin Bieber haircut more than annoying. How old do you have to be to graduate Medical school now, Alice wondered? She had been twenty-six and though she had forsaken medicine for business immediately after graduation, she had had more bedside manner than this kid could manage.

"Great news, Mrs. Hightower, the blood tests indicate that your hormone levels are really high for a woman of your advanced age. How cool, right?"

Alice's mouth dropped open. She closed it and said, "How is that possible?"

"Oh it's possible. You've still got eggs, add sperm and kablam—pregnant."

He leaned back in his chair. "Most of the time late-life pregnancies are not sustainable for lots of reasons. Your eggs are wicked old. So of course you'll want an amnio. The rate of genetic abnormalities is off the charts. But it seems possible to carry this baby to term, if that's what you want." The doctor had looked quite pleased to share his news.

Alice's mouth fell open again and Jonathan beamed. "I… I…" said Alice.

"We just need to know what to do to ensure the health of our child," said Jonathan. He gripped her hand tightly and leaned over to kiss her on the cheek.

"I was getting those Depo-Provera shots and…. I thought I had six months before another one," said Alice.

"The efficacy of that type of birth control is less dependable in the last few months. My best guess based on the size of your uterus…" He looked up in the air like he was working some imaginary calculator "…At least eight weeks," said Dr. Bieber.

Jonathan's face went blank. Alice knew what the doctor's guess meant and so did Jonathan. They had only been together for a little over a month. Several minutes passed before Alice could bear to look at this man who had held her hand until the calculations in his head caused him to drop it like it was hot. She stared at the Betsy Johnson silver spangled pumps she had worn because this was a momentous occasion. Jonathan's Clark Kent good looks were not marred at all by his stricken expression when he realized there was no way this baby was his. Alice had always had a hard time believing anyone that beautiful could ever have loved her.

Without a word, Jonathan had stood up and walked out the door without closing it.

Alice opened her eyes and took in a deep breath. She had to keep breathing. Now she was breathing for two.

Eight weeks! thought Alice as she sat on the immaculate white couch in her apartment. The doctor's calculation meant not only could Jonathan not be her baby's father, but it might be difficult to discern just exactly who was. How could one tell a child that its father could have been a Roman soldier dead for two thousand years, an eighteenth-century pirate captain, or one of several members of a seventies rock group? As crazy as those suggestions were, there was one other person who believed that her nightly fantasy adventures could be real. Dr. Cindy, her therapist, had suggested that she actually did travel in time and could do so each night at sunset. Could this person in her belly be absolute proof that Alice's aberrant brain gave her some sort of power over time and space as Dr. Cindy suggested? You can't get pregnant all by yourself, fantasizing. Or she could be stark raving bonkers like several members of her family. There was one other option for paternity that made the impossible nature of the fantasy men as fathers almost preferable.

This day at Excellcardia, hadn't been any tougher than many others, she thought as she kicked off her black patent peep-toe pumps. No one ever said the job of CEO was an easy one. Alice always preferred a challenge, but the industrial espionage that had nearly taken her company down, had stretched her love of a challenge to the breaking point. She could still see Bradley James, her vice president of sales, in the high efficiency freezer surrounded by a pool of blood that had turned to ice around the edges. She had been so certain that Brad, Jonathan and she would die in that freezer just as Dr. Pertus had planned. The three teams of detectives she'd hired, had so far failed to locate the "not so good doctor," but Alice would never give up looking for him. No one steals her company's ground-breaking process, sells it to a competitor, and gets away with it.

"Come on up sweetest boy," said Alice to a chubby black

cat who balanced perfectly on his three legs, looking up at her from the floor. She patted the cushion next to her. The cat did not move but stared at her with round emerald eyes.

"Oh what the hell? How much of that fur can actually get on the couch in just a few minutes?" The cat did not jump up but rubbed against her legs. "Smart boy, I'll get your food." No matter what she said, Otis obviously knew she would not have been happy with even one of his black hairs on her white couch.

Alice walked past the solid block of black granite that served as her bar/dining table into the kitchen. She got a can of Fancy Feast out of the pantry, pulled the pull top and dumped it into a bowl on the floor. She did not feel the slightest bit hungry and headed across the large, high-ceilinged room that served as her living room, dining room and kitchen. The exposed wooden beams in the twenty-foot ceilings of the classic building, made her feel as if she were the Red Queen in her castle. She walked down the hall feeling sorry for herself and exhausted. She had planned to turn left into her bedroom and turn in early. *Get over yourself, Alice.* She should have known the risks of dating real men instead of fantasy ones. No man from another time could break her heart. She turned to her right into the guest room. Whatever she found in there would take a girl's mind off of all of her troubles. Thirty quick minutes on her elliptical and she might open that closet door.

She remembered finding a lime green mini dress in that closet that once donned, had taken her to a place where she had enjoyed Tweedle Don and Tweedle Dan, twin doctors from the late nineteen sixties who shared absolutely everything. She felt the corners of her lips turn up just a bit at the memory. She hadn't peeked into the closet since she had embarked on her experiment to date real men.

Alice had hoped the fact that Brad was her vice president of sales and Jonathan was her administrative assistant would not complicate matters. There was no official company policy against it. Why couldn't dating two men have stayed fun and causal? She stood in front of the closet wondering. Why had she believed Jonathan when he said he loved her in such a short time? Why had Brad given up so easily? The mirrored door reflected here deep, tired blue-green eyes. Real men aren't as good at sharing as fantasy doctors Dan and Don, unfortunately.

She knew it was a minute after sunset, she always knew, and reached over to slide open the closet door. There on the gold hanger she knew she had never purchased was something pink and fluffy. Some sort of outfit made of silk and netting in several soft shades of pink. On the floor below the hanger was a pair of silver sandals. They would be just her size, they always were.

The something pink turned out to be a short midriff bearing top and a long flowing skirt, kind of "I dream of Jeannie" style. Alice remembered watching reruns with her mother when she was little. The outfit didn't look half bad on her, being pregnant somehow made her abs look tighter, for now anyway. She removed the clip from her dark blonde hair that fell to her shoulders. Taking a deep breath, she slid open the door to her balcony where instead of the street below, she would find this night's Wonderland.

Alice squinted against the bright sunlight and stepped out of the door to a completely different place and time. In front of her she saw a huge archway covered in tiny cobalt blue tiles. It must have been fifty feet at the top. Perhaps the door to a palace, she thought? Alice felt very small in the doorway, heard running water and smelled jasmine.

"Curiouser and curiouser." Alice giggled and walked through the arch into a garden. Flowering trees grew in pots surrounding a sunken pool. The water bubbled as a little stream splashed from a smaller bowl into the pool. She walked over and looked into the water. The bottom must have been covered in the same deep blue tiles as the path that led to the pool because the water had the same blue. "At least this pool isn't filled with my tears." Alice was happy right now not to actually be the little Victorian Girl in a pinafore of whom Lewis Carroll wrote. Her nocturnal adventures were certainly not for seven-year-old girls.

Soft footsteps to her left caused her to turn to see a slender man. He looked like the Genie in Aladdin except he was tanned instead of blue. His neat mustache and closely trimmed beard would have looked appropriate on any self-respecting resident of a wishing lamp. The man wore only white wide legged pants gathered at the ankle. Of course his head was shaved. She expected Will Smith's voice to come out of him, but he said nothing, bowed and motioned to her to follow him.

On either side of the doorway were smaller versions of the grand entry arch. There were four on each side and Alice followed the genie through one of the arches on the right. He led her into a large courtyard. Sunlight bathed the low chairs and large cushions covering a good deal of the floor. The pillows in many shades of peach, pink and lavender and were arranged around low tables. Sitting on most of the chairs and pillows were young women dressed exactly like Alice.

"A harem?" said Alice to the genie. "I guess I'm dressed for it." He looked bewildered at her words. Bowing once more, the genie vanished through an archway. *He must have other wishes to grant.*

The young women who had fallen silent when she walked into the room, now all talked at once in a language she could not understand. Each one's dark hair in various shades hung down their backs. One stood up and the others fell silent.

"The Emir wishes me to welcome you to our home," said the girl. She wore palest baby-pink and had hair and eyes as dark as midnight.

"Great, you speak English," said Alice.

"The Emir enjoys languages and there are many of us who speak several.

I am Yasmina and your name please?"

"Alice. So what exactly is going on here?" Alice was used to finding pleasure in her nightly travels. She was not attracted to women and certainly wasn't interested in sex with any of these "Harem Girl Barbies."

"My master has arranged a pleasure ceremony." She clapped her hands and through an arched doorway six men strode into the room.

"Now that's more like it," said Alice. The men all looked similar, tall, muscular and due to their naked state, she could see they were well endowed and uncircumcised. All six had short dark hair, dark eyes and light brown skin as if they had just come off a day at the beach, without bothering with swim-suits—no tan lines at all. Every hair had been removed from their beautiful bodies.

The young ladies on the pillows smiled and clapped at their entrance. The men's serious expressions did not change as they stood in a line looking straight ahead.

Yasmina walked in front of the line of men speaking first in a foreign language and then repeating in English for Alice's benefit, "Which of you will be chosen to prepare the Emir's newest wife?" She clapped her hands and two girls led in a figure swathed in gauzy white fabric with only dark, heavily lined eyes visible. *I'll be happy with any of the leftovers.*

"This is Sulia, the Emir's newest wife. She is a virgin, and the Emir wishes that situation to be remedied." The girls leading Sulia unwrapped their gauzy package. She stood naked. Her flesh shone pink and plump against the line of light brown men who responded with cocks quickly at full attention. The naked girl's black eyes scanned the men. She smiled shyly, looked each man up and down and stopped in front the very last one. She wisely chose the man with the smallest endowment, more suited to one's defecwering.

The girls raised their voices in a cheer. The man hoisted Sulia onto his shoulders and carried her a few feet laying her down gently on a large lavender pillow. Two girls knelt beside the couple and each took turns kissing Sulia's lips and sucking her erect pink nipples. The girl moaned and the man laughed. He knelt, parted her legs with his knees and began to stroke between the dark hair surrounding her virgin sex with his fingers and she moaned louder. Just when she sounded very near a climax, he reached under her lifting her hips and inserting his cock. She let out a cry that rang with both pleasure and pain. Immediately the man withdrew his tool and stood up, evidently the Emir wanted to plant the seeds himself and must have merely wanted the way paved. A girl in a peach outfit knelt in front of the man licking him clean as he put his hands on her head and stood, legs locked, and eyes closed.

All around, pretty lips sucked dark nipples as little wisps of tops came off. Dainty hands slipped between soft legs as skirts were raised. Alice felt someone reach around to caress her own nipples through her thin pink top. They now stood at full attention in response to the deflowering spectacle. The man caressing her breasts, turned her around and led her to three pillows. He smiled at her. Jasmina stood beside the man. "The Emir would appreciate the honor of watching the golden haired one couple with anyone she wishes."

"Fine by me. Where is he?" asked Alice. The girl motioned toward a window covered by a wooden screen carved of leaves and flowers. Alice waved at the screen and smiled back at the man who now lay below her with a cock hard enough to cut glass. She pulled up her skirt straddled the man slowly lowering herself onto his magnificent appendage.

"I am Hassan, golden one," said the man deep inside her. He took her nipples between his fingers and rolled and pulled on them as she slid up and down on his erection until she came with a long loud exclamation. She bent down to kiss his lips.

"Thank you, Hassan. But now it is your turn to come," said Alice as Hassan tried to wiggle out from under her.

Hassan smiled at her and said, "Please to honor my brother, Husane, with your golden glory.

"Sure, whatever you want." Alice rolled off of Hassan and another of the handsome left-overs straddled her. He stroked her clit with long, smooth fingers and reached up to caress her breasts, kneading them and softly brushing her nipples with his palms. She felt herself climbing up pleasure hill as his fingers stroked. She needed to be full of him and sat up and taking his muscular ass in her hands, she drove him deep into her. He began a delicious rhythm and soon she came loud enough to scare a dozing cat who ran off among the pillows.

"Wow. Are there any more at home like you?" Alice held his shoulders and stroked his arms that seemed carved from brown stone.

"Well…yes, there is my little brother Omar," said Husane.

"Oh my," said Alice when a pair of muscular brown legs appeared next to her sporting another delicious hard on.

"I'm sorry, he does not speak English." Husane shook his head.

"Ask him if he minds if I suck that gorgeous cock of his, please."

"No man would mind such an honor," he said. Alice got to her knees and wrapped her lips around little brother Omar's cock. She encircled the delicious appendage with her lips wetting with her saliva every erect inch of him.

"There is nothing little about your brother Omar," said Alice and she slid her mouth over each vein and along the steel encased in silk cylinder that she enjoyed so much. Omar was young, probably not much more than twenty and in no time, he gave a long moan and filled her mouth with his pleasure.

She felt strong arms reach around her and she spread her knees as something hard, lovely and masculine filled her from behind.

"Please to serve you once more." Alice couldn't tell if it was Hassan or Husane but he felt perfect. She moaned with each stroke and felt him come inside her just a few strokes before she climaxed. He laid his head on her shoulder and tenderly caressed her back, her arms and her thighs. Leaning back on a stack of pillows, Hassan/Husane pulled her with him.

Alice relished a little time to rest, leaned back and watched the dark-haired beauties at play. The pretty lips, lovely breasts and perky asses enjoyed each other's company immensely. Touching anything soft not her own was not to her taste, but she had to admit it was fun to watch the girls moan and writhe.

"To each her own," said Alice, safe in the knowledge she would wake up tomorrow morning in her own bed. She closed her eyes for just a minute, her head resting on a strong shoulder while a pair of smooth hands caressed the curve of her hip.

THANK YOU FOR READING

❧

Did you enjoy this book?

We invite you to leave a review at your favorite book site, such as Goodreads, Amazon, Barnes & Noble, etc.

DID YOU KNOW THAT LEAVING A REVIEW...

- Helps other readers find books they may enjoy.
- Gives you a chance to let your voice be heard.
- Gives authors recognition for their hard work.
- Doesn't have to be long. A sentence or two about why you liked the book will do.

ABOUT THE AUTHOR

As a little girl, Melissa Rea would fall asleep whispering stories to herself in the dark. She got in to trouble in elementary school for embellishing when the truth just seemed too mundane. She grew up and the stories became just daydreams and she pursued a sensible career. Melissa filled her spare time with the wondrous worlds of Bram Stoker, Mary Shelly, Robert Heinlein, Philippa Gregory, Stephen King, Dean Coontz, Jackie Collins, Jennifer Weiner, Sarah Dunant and any and all authors who caught her fancy. And still, the stories in her head were there, now influenced by the delicious words of others. One day, the stories could no longer be contained, and she began to write novels. *Conjuring Casanova* was published in 2016 and was a Recommended Idie Book by Kirkus Review. It won first place in the Beverly Hills International Book Awards for Romantic Comedy, a first place in ReadersViews Reviewers Choice Awards for Romance and was a finalist in Forward Reviews Book of the Year in the Romance category. She lives in St. Louis where she has a solo dental practice and lives with her husband and rescue cats.

https://www.facebook.com/melissareaauthor/?ref=bookmarks
https://www.facebook.com/melissareaauthor/?
ref=bookmarksmelissareaauthor.com/